Public Face Private Vice

Public Face
Private Vice

Keith Wainman

Matador
9 Priory Business Park,
Wistow Road, Kibworth Beauchamp,
Leicestershire. LE8 0RX
Tel: 0116 279 2299
Email: books@troubador.co.uk
Web: www.troubador.co.uk/matador
Twitter: @matadorbooks

ISBN 978 1784623 548

British Library Cataloguing in Publication Data.
A catalogue record for this book is available from the British Library.

Printed and bound in the UK by TJ International, Padstow, Cornwall
Typeset in 11pt Aldine401 BT Roman by Troubador Publishing Ltd, Leicester, UK

Matador is an imprint of Troubador Publishing Ltd

For Chelsea, my superstar, and Charlie.

For Carol, for reading and encouraging.

CHAPTER ONE

'Well, we just have time to look at what tomorrow morning's papers are saying, and they all lead with the same story.' Gerald Parkin held up the front page of the Times. 'Health Service job cuts, the Telegraph, minister says no nurses to be sacked, and the Independent, doctors could lose jobs.' He laid down the papers. 'We will be back same time tomorrow, hopefully still with a functioning health service.' The closing music began and the credits started to run on the screen.

'Good show, Gerald,' he heard his director say through his earpiece.

'You think so. I don't want that idiot politician on again, the man is incapable of stringing a sentence together,' Gerald replied.

As Gerald stood, a floor assistant came up to him and started to unplug his microphone. He looked at his watch: eleven fifteen. 'Hurry up, I have a late dinner engagement to get to.' The assistant struggled to pull the wire from under Gerald's jacket. 'Leave it, I will do it.' He pushed the assistant's hands away. 'Will you get some people working on this show who know what they are supposed to do,' he said to the floor manager. He pulled the wire from under his jacket and passed it and the microphone to the assistant.

'There, that was simple wasn't it? If you ask nicely someone will show you how to do it.' He turned away and walked past the three cameras and to the back of the studio, stopping to speak to the floor manager, and said, 'I think that floor assistant should be

1

kept to making coffee or I will be putting in a claim for a new suit.'

'I will make sure they know what they're doing, don't worry, Mr Parkin,' the floor manager assured him.

'I thought that was your job already,' Gerald said. 'See it doesn't happen again.' He carried on walking to the back of the studio and pushed open the door to the director's booth. 'I hope tomorrow's programme will be more interesting, I nearly fell asleep in part of that interview,' he said, standing next to the director and the programme editor. 'I bet our viewers were all dozing off.'

'I think you're being a bit hard,' the director said.

'You do, do you?' Gerald said. 'I had to try and think of something interesting to ask him and then listen to the same answer to every question. I wonder how that man was ever elected. Oh I remember, his father was a cabinet minister years ago'.

'Tomorrow's show should be good, we have the foreign secretary coming on,' the editor said. 'I have scheduled a programme meeting for three o'clock tomorrow afternoon.'

'Make sure the researchers have done their homework and dug up some facts to press him on. See if we can get something on the rumoured closure of some of our embassies,' Gerald said. 'I can press him on that and on the United Nations situation.'

Gerald turned away without saying goodbye and went out of the door. He made his way to the corner of the studio went through another door and walked along a corridor passing a number of people who congratulated him on a good show. He made no response and did not even acknowledge them. He came to a door with his name on and pushed it open. Inside he went to a chair in front of a large mirror and sat down.

A young woman who was from the make-up department

had been waiting for him to return to the dressing room for some time. She stepped forward.

'Hurry up, I don't have a lot of time,' Gerald said. The woman started to take off the make-up. 'Don't get any powder on my shirt or jacket, I don't have time to change,' he said.

After a few minutes she stood back. Gerald tilted his head back and forward. 'That will do, you can go now.' The woman put her things into her make-up case and left without saying a word. Gerald picked up the phone on the table and dialled the number for security.

'This is Mr Parkin. Make sure my car is out front in five minutes.' He put the phone down not waiting for a reply. Standing he looked in the mirror to check his hair was neat and his suit and tie were not looking too worn out. He had wanted to go home and change but would not have time, and he did not wish to miss this dinner engagement.

He left his changing room and made his way to the lifts at the end of the corridor. The studio and changing room were on the second floor of the new BBC building. He knew it would make a good show if he ever got one of the BBC managing directors on to justify the cost of this building, he smiled to himself. It would never happen though. He got to the lifts and pressed the call button. He had worked for the BBC for over twenty years, first as a reporter on news programmes, then ten, years ago, getting his own show. He was now considered to be one of the best political interviewers on television. His thoughts were interrupted by someone coming and standing beside him. 'Hello Gerald, saw the show, very boring, are you losing your touch?'

He turned to see Jim Hendricks grinning at him. 'Oh, it's you,' Gerald replied. 'What are you doing here so late, I thought you would be home in bed'.

Jim Hendricks smiled back. He was the lead interviewer

on Radio Four's morning news programme. 'If all your programmes are as bad as that, I'm glad that I am,' he said.

'How is that dying radio show you do?' Gerald said. 'Do you still get much of an audience?'

Jim Hendricks laughed. 'If it wasn't for the interviews we did in the morning, you wouldn't have anything to talk about on your show in the evening.'

'I am sure when you have retired you can look back on your mediocre career with fondness,' Gerald said. The door of the lift opened. Gerald stepped in followed by Jim. Gerald pressed the ground floor button and the doors closed.

'Are you off home now?' Jim asked.

Gerald turned to look at him. 'Some of us have a social life outside of the BBC,' Gerald said. 'I know that's not something you would know anything about.'

Jim laughed as the doors of the lift opened into the lobby. Gerald stepped out without saying goodbye and walked over to the security. 'Is my car outside?' he said.

'Yes, sir. It's waiting for you,' the security man said.

Gerald turned away, went through the new entrance and out into the court and made his way to the road where he saw the Mercedes car that the BBC supplied for him. The driver held the door open. As he got in he saw Jim Hendricks walk past.

'Hendricks,' Gerald called. 'I hope the trains are still running.'

The driver shut the door, walked around and climbed in. 'Where to, sir?' he said.

Gerald made himself comfortable in the seat. 'Eaton Square, and hurry.'

The car pulled up outside one of the imposing houses in Eaton Square, and the driver came round and opened the door. Gerald climbed out. 'Pick me up at two am,' he said and walked up the two stairs that led to a large blue-painted door.

He pressed the bell and the door was opened within a few seconds by a tall thin man dressed all in black, wearing white gloves. 'Good evening, sir. Very nice to see you again,' he said.

Gerald entered the brightly lit hall with a high ceiling that went at least two floors up. Two large chandeliers lit the hall and a staircase stretched up in front of him, dividing into two as it reached the first floor. 'Good evening, Cameron,' Gerald said.

Cameron nodded as he closed the door. 'Would you follow me please, sir?' he said and turned and led Gerald past the bottom of the stairway to a set of double doors which he pushed open and entered. 'Mr Parkin is here,' he announced, and stood to one side. Gerald walked past him into a large room with a dining table in the centre. Five people were seated round it. They all looked over towards him, waved and welcomed him.

A woman who had been standing at a table by the wall came across. 'Gerald, I thought you weren't going to get here. That will be all, Cameron, I will call if I need you,' she said. Cameron went out, closing the door behind him.

'You know I would never miss one of your little parties,' Gerald said.

Lady Natalie Dorres took him by the arm and led him to the table. 'Well come on and sit down, we can get dinner started, you know everyone.' She waved her arm, pointing to those seated.

A man at the end of the table said, 'Parkin, you have kept us waiting for dinner, so sit down so we can eat.'

Gerald took his seat. 'I do apologise, Your Lordship, had one of those terrible politicians on this evening.'

'Well, you're here now, get the food in.' Lord David Dorres was from old English aristocracy. They had this house in London, but had a large estate in Dorset and thousands of acres in Scotland with a castle. They held shooting parties there which anyone who was anyone had to be seen at.

'David, let Gerald get a drink first,' Lady Dorres said to her husband. Lord Dorres sighed, sat back and took a drink from his own glass. Lady Dorres poured a large glass of red wine for Gerald.

He held it to his nose, took a long sniff, then a small sip. 'Delightful,' he said.

'It's from our vineyard in France,' the man sitting opposite Gerald said. 'We are going into full production later this year. The previous owners of the place let it run down. I brought a couple of cases with me tonight for David and Natalie.' The man was Sir Mark Coale. He was chairman of the third largest oil company in the Britain, owned a large estate in Gloucester, houses in the Caribbean and America, and now a vineyard in France.

'I would say you have a winner,' Gerald said.

'You must come out over the summer and stay for a week and have a look round the place,' Sir Mark said.

'Let's get the food in,' Lord Dorres interrupted.

Lady Dorres pressed a small bell. The doors opened and Cameron appeared. 'You can begin to serve dinner now,' she said.

Cameron left the room. Gerald took another drink of the wine and said hello to the other three people at the table. Sir Martin Olivier, who was on the Arts Council and a director at the opera house. His family had a number of auction houses around the world as well as art galleries; he had one of the finest collections of British modern art. Gerald had dined at his house in Chelsea and been given a tour of the collection.

The other two people were Stanley and Amanda Moore. Stanley was a banker, his family had been in banking since the nineteenth century, had profited from the banking troubles and were now one of the most powerful private banks the general public had never heard of, but held huge influence and power in the banking world. Amanda Moore was American, from a banking family out there. She had worked for some of the biggest financial institutions in America, and was now head of American and Far Eastern investments for the Moores' bank. She also had a weekly column in the Financial Times and was considered one of the world's most influential woman. Gerald felt comfortable amongst all the guests. The door opened and Cameron led two other servants in with dinner.

When dinner had been finished and all the plates cleaned away, Lord Dorres lit a large Havana cigar, and passed the box of cigars around. 'So Parkin, what's going on in the world. Do you have any news of some juicy scandals amongst those crooks in parliament?'

'Oh yes, Gerald, what have you heard?' Amanda Moore asked.

Gerald loved her soft American accent. She was a beautiful woman, he knew things about her husband that he had picked up at other dinner parties he had been to which she would love to know. He took a cigar from the box as it was passed to him.

'I have heard that the Home Secretary is getting very close to one of his assistants. Apparently they shared a room when on a visit to Rome for a three-day European crime summit.'

'I think his wife has brought a few paintings from me,' Sir Martin Olivier said. 'And if I remember one was for his birthday. She's one of the horsey set, comes from a racing family in Newmarket.'

'Another politician chasing after a young female assistant, don't they ever learn?' Lady Dorres said.

'Who said anything about it being a female?' Gerald said.

Everyone started to laugh around the table. 'What are the chances of it getting out,' Amanda Moore asked

'I dare say in a couple of months' time, the home secretary will step down to spend more time with his family,' Gerald replied. 'I heard from an editor of one of the tabloids at a press lunch last week that they have been watching him.'

Gerald lit his cigar. The only person not smoking at the table was Lady Dorres. It had fascinated him the first time he had seen Amanda Moore light up a large Havana. He blew the smoke out. 'Sir Mark, I had an interesting conversation with one of the advisors to the energy minister last week. He tells me that they are talking to the French about a joint oil pipeline from the new oil find in the Irish Sea.'

Sir Mark looked across the table. 'That would be a bit strange,' he said. 'We have been negotiating with the government for that deal, and have been getting indications that it would be ours. In fact we have started to invest in a new plant, ready to use.'

'Apparently the French want it to prop up their state oil company,' Gerald said. 'They can't afford all the job cuts. The French president thinks his government would have to resign and fight an election if it doesn't go through. He's promised to support the prime minister on his new proposals to streamline the European Parliament.'

'I don't care about a load of French workers', Sir Mark replied. 'We have sunk over £50 million into that project already.'

They carried on chatting and exchanging gossip. It was two fifteen when Gerald finally left. His car was outside and as he sat in the back being driven home, he was in a nice relaxed mood. He enjoyed the late-evening dinner parties Lady Dorres invited him to; she always had a nice mix of guests and he knew he was there to provide the gossip. He picked up some good titbits himself that always came in useful. He had met Lady Dorres when he worked for the Sunday Times. A story had come his way about cocaine use at a Buckingham Palace garden party. He came to a mutually beneficial arrangement which suited both parties, so the story never saw the light of day, but he got entrée into the high society and powerful of the country. He also knew Lady Dorres' cocaine habit was still going strong, and she had strange people who called at odd hours to her house to drop off supplies. He got to his house in Docklands at just before three. He told his driver to pick him up at one o'clock to take him to the BBC.

CHAPTER TWO

Superintendent Charlie Smith had just walked into the squad's office at Scotland Yard. 'Afternoon, boss,' Detective Constable Danny Kane said, looking up from his desk, ' How was your evening out?'.

'Had a good time thanks, Danny, anything come through for us?' he replied.

'No, just clearing up some paperwork and running a few checks on outstanding cases,' Danny replied.

Charlie carried on walking through to the back of the office. 'Morning, Harry,' he said.

Chief inspector Harry Davis, Charlie's number two, looked up. 'Afternoon, boss, did you have a good time last night?' he said with a smile.

'Why is everyone I speak to so interested in my social life?' Charlie said.

'It's because you have such a caring team around you,' Harry said, 'and it's not often two Chief Superintendents go out on a date together.'

'Harry, you know me. It's on a need to know basis, and the squad don't need to know,' Charlie said. 'Now what have we got on today.'

Harry laughed. 'Well, I have been doing the most important job of all, the time sheets and overtime.'

'Well, don't let me spoil your enjoyment, where are Manjitt and Jordan?' Charlie asked.

'They're off collecting all the files from the last job we had.' Harry looked at his watch. 'They should be back in an hour.'

Charlie sat down at his desk. 'Is there any tea on the go?' he asked. Harry looked over. 'I will get some. Hippie. Get the boss some tea,' he called across the office.

Danny waved his hand, stood and went over to the corner of the office where the squad's tea things were kept. Charlie watched him.

'Harry, do you think I should tell him to get his hair cut?' Charlie said.

Harry looked at Danny making the tea. 'He wouldn't be Hippie if he had his hair cut, now if you are talking about his dress sense then I might go along with you.'

Danny came walking towards them with a cup in his hand. He was wearing purple bell-bottom trousers and a lilac shirt with a pair of trainers, the colour of which was not discernible. His hair hung halfway down his back. 'There you go, boss,' he said as he put down the cup on Charlie's desk.

'Danny, I have been looking at your hair,' Charlie said. 'I know I am not a boss who tells his team how they should dress but I have to say, when are you going to get it cut?'

'Boss, I only had it trimmed last week,' Danny said.

Charlie looked at Harry, who was laughing. 'Ok, Danny, thank you for keeping it so neat and tidy.'

'That's okay boss, thank you for noticing,' Danny said. He turned and went back to his desk.

The phone on Harry's desk rang. He picked it up. 'Serious Crime Office?' He listened for a minute. 'Give me the address.' He wrote on the pad then put the phone down. 'One for us, boss, an address in Docklands.'

Harry and Charlie stood up and walked through the office. 'Come on, Hippie,' Harry said. 'We have work to do.'

Danny stood and joined them as they left the office.

Charlie parked his Bentley outside the address in

Docklands. He pressed the button on the console and the roof came up and locked. All three climbed out.

'Boss, I don't think its a good idea having the top down when Hippie's in the back,' Harry said.

Charlie looked at Danny, whose hair was all over the place. 'I am going to buy him some hair bands,' Charlie said as they walked towards the address.

Two uniformed officers were standing in front of some blue and white police tape that had been placed to form a square, from the fence that ran along the street to a lamppost along from that to another lamppost and back to the fence. As they approached, one of the officers stepped forward. 'Sorry, you can't come this way.'

Harry held up his warrant card. 'Who's in charge here?' Harry said.

'Oh sorry, sir, Sergeant Daniels, he's inside,' the constable replied. He lifted the tape and Charlie, Harry and Danny ducked under and went up the two steps and into the house. The two constables looked at each other. 'Can you believe they just turned up in that Bentley? How much do senior officers get paid?'

Charlie pulled on some gloves as he entered the house. He saw a uniformed sergeant standing at the doorway that looked like the kitchen. 'Hello sergeant, I'm Chief Superintendent Smith, what have we got?'

'Hello, sir, the body of a man. He's in the kitchen, looks like someone has smashed his head in,' the sergeant said.

Harry and Danny went into the kitchen pulling on their gloves. 'Who found the body?' Charlie asked.

'We had a call to the station about 1.45,' the sergeant said. 'I came over with a constable, the door was locked but we could hear music. His work had said they had been trying to reach him on his home phone and mobile. His driver was outside, he had come at one o'clock to take him to work. I got the driver to ring his mobile. I listened through the letterbox and heard it ring, I shouted a bit but got no answer, so had to force entry. I found the body where it is. The victim's name is Gerald Parkin.'

'Thank you sergeant, you did a good job, has anyone touched anything?' Charlie asked.

'No, sir, but it looks like he's has been burgled. The front room is a mess and I had a quick check around the rest of the house just in case anyone was still here. The other rooms have been turned over. I have his driver sitting in his car outside.'

'I will have some more officers coming over. Can you get some of your officers to do a quick check of the neighbours, see if anyone saw anything?' Charlie said.

'Yes sir,' the sergeant said and left.

Charlie walked into the kitchen. Harry was kneeling by the body.

'What have we got?' Charlie said.

'It looks like someone really gave him a good beating. I checked his pockets; someone has been through them, they were turned inside out. He has no wallet or money,' Harry said.

'You get forensics over here, Harry, and go and speak to the sergeant, he said he has the victim's driver outside. Have a word with him, find out a bit about our man and give Jordan and Manjitt a call, tell them to get over here. Danny, you start upstairs, have a quick look around.'

Harry and Danny left the kitchen. Charlie had a look around the kitchen. It did not look like there had been a fight and he couldn't see anything that looked like it had been used to hit the victim. He switched the radio off that was on the kitchen table.

He left the kitchen and went into the front room. Drawers had been pulled out and papers were spread all over the floor.

Apart from that, it didn't look like a fight had taken place in there either. A table was beside the sofa with a cup of half-drunk tea or coffee in it, and a plate with one piece of toast was beside it. He looked at a number of photographs that were standing undisturbed on a table against one wall. He recognised a few of the people in them, standing next to the victim.

Harry came back in. 'I spoke to the driver, boss. Our victim, Gerald Parkin, works at the BBC,' Harry said. According to the driver, he's one of their top television interviewers.'

Charlie held up a picture. 'Well, he certainly had some important friends. He's in lots of pictures with some well known faces.'

Harry came over. 'I must watch the wrong television, I didn't recognise him.'

'You and me both, Harry,' Charlie said. 'What else did the driver say?'

'He dropped him home early this morning, just before three, and came back here at one to drive him to the BBC,' Harry said.

'Was he working late?' Charlie asked.

'No, the driver said he dropped him off at a house before midnight yesterday for a dinner engagement,' Harry replied. 'Then he went back and picked him up after two and brought him home.'

Danny came into the room. 'All the rooms upstairs have been rifled. The drawers and the cupboards are all open, with things all over the floors.'

'Danny, the victim is called Gerald Parkin, he works for the BBC.'

'I thought I recognised him,' Danny said. 'He interviews politicians, bankers and industrialists on his show. He was merciless when he questioned them; he could ruin someone's reputation.'

'Well, I think you might have added a hundred potential suspects to our case,' Harry said.

'Danny, his driver's outside,' Charlie said. 'Harry has had a quick word with him but you go and see him. Get the address for the dinner he was at last night and see what the driver can tell us about Mr Parkin. What was he like, where else had he taken him over the last few weeks, anything out of the ordinary.' Danny left the room. 'Let's have a quick walk round the house, Harry.'

They had been in and out of every room in the house and came back downstairs, just as forensics arrived. 'The body is in the kitchen,' Harry said. The forensic team passed them and went into the kitchen.

Charlie went back into the front room. Harry followed him. They heard someone call from the front door, turned and saw Detective Sergeant Jordan Rhodes and Detective Constable Manjitt Virdee coming through the door. 'Afternoon boss, Harry,' they both said.

'Hello, you two,' Charlie said. 'Our victim is Gerald Parkin. He worked for the BBC.'

'I have seen him on the television a few times,' Manjitt said. 'Quite a celebrity.'

'Never heard of him,' Jordan said.

'He would be on the front pages, not the back of any paper you read,' Manjitt said.

'Well, he will be on the front pages tomorrow,' Harry said.

'Jordan, you and Manjitt can go over to the BBC,' Charlie said. 'Find out what he did yesterday, speak to the people he worked with, did he have a wife, ex-wife, girlfriend or boyfriend, what was he like? You know the stuff we need.'

'The BBC. I better get an autograph book,' Jordan said. They left Charlie and Harry, passing Danny as he was coming back into the house.

'Hippie,' Jordan said. 'You look like you some old rag doll.'

'Less of the old,' Danny said. Danny came into the front room. 'The driver says he has not taken him anywhere out of the ordinary in the last few months. I have the address of the house he had dinner at last night, it's in Eaton Square,' he said. Our Mr Parkin was a horrible sod, the driver's words, not mine.'

'Eaton Square, very nice,' Harry said.

'Well, you get to go visit, Harry,' Charlie said. 'Take Danny with you, see who else was at the dinner, find out what you can. I am going back to the Yard to see Assistant Commissioner Crick. Seeing as he is from the BBC, the press will be all over this, and I want him to worry about that so we can get on with the case. I will drop you at the Yard to pick up a squad car. Oh and tell Mr Parkin's driver he can go, but get his home address and phone number in case we need to speak to him again.'

As they left, Charlie went to the kitchen and asked forensics to call his office when they had finished and send their report over as soon as it was complete. He would be back with his team later to give the house a search. He saw Sergeant Daniels outside, and told him to contact him at the Yard with anything he got from the house to house, then climbed into the Bentley and pulled away.

When Charlie got back to the Yard, he left Harry and Danny to pick up their car to go to the address the driver had given them in Eaton Square. Charlie took the lift up to the seventh floor to see Assistant Commissioner Crick. He knocked on the door, heard 'come in', opened the door and entered. ' Charlie, good to see you,' Crick said. 'Come and sit down.'

'Hello, sir,' Charlie said as he took a seat across the desk from Crick.

'I see from this afternoon's reports you have a murder case in Docklands,' Crick said.

'Yes, sir, that's why I came to see you,', Charlie replied. 'The murdered man was Gerald Parkin. He works for the BBC.'

'Not the Gerald Parkin who has the evening interview programme'? Crick asked.

'It would appear to be him, had his head caved in,' Charlie said.

'You have a lovely way of putting things, Charlie,' Crick replied. 'I would expect there will be a lot of press interest in this case, seeing as he's one of the BBC's big names.'

'That's what I wanted to see you about sir. Can I leave the press side to you. That will leave me free to concentrate on the case, and as you say, my flowery language might not be what the press wants to hear,' Charlie said.

' Okay, Charlie, leave that side to me,' Crick said, 'but make sure I am kept up to date on any leads you get – I don't want any questions that I can't answer coming up in a press conference.'

'Will have a report on your desk each morning,' Charlie said as he stood up.

'Each morning, Charlie,' Crick said.

'Yes, sir, each morning.' Charlie turned and walked to the door. As he pulled it open he heard Crick call him.

'Charlie, I don't want one of those reports on the case that your Chief Inspector Davis writes.'

Charlie turned. 'No sir, I will do it for you.' He left the office and made his way to the squad room. He was going to do some background checks on Mr Parkin and watch some of his old television programmes if he could find some.

CHAPTER THREE

Harry and Danny had arrived at the house at Eaton Square. 'Nice area to live,' Danny said as they left the car. 'Bet they don't get too many drunken fights around here.'

Harry rang the bell on the door. It was opened by a man who looked at them, looking Danny up and down twice. 'Can I help you,' he said.

'Hello, sir, we are the police.' Harry showed his warrant card. 'Are you the owner of the house?'

'No,' the man replied.

'Well, is it possible we can see the owner?' Harry asked.

'I will see if they are available,' the man said and closed the door. Danny started to laugh. Harry looked at him. 'Sorry, Harry, but your face was a picture when he shut the door,' Danny said.

'We will see whose face is a picture when he comes back,' Harry said.

They waited a couple of minutes until the door was open again by the man. 'I am sorry, sir, but it's not convenient at the moment,' he said. 'If you would like to make an appointment to call, I will give you the telephone number.' Harry looked at Danny, who was smiling and stifling a laugh.

'Well I am sorry about that, but I always work on the principle of when it suits me,' Harry said, and stepped in the door pushing the man backwards. Danny followed him in. Harry had the man by the arm. 'I'm not sure who you think you're dealing with, sir, but we are investigating a murder, and

I always like to think I can rely on the public's help. That includes you. Now if you would kindly take us to see the owners of the house? By the way, sir, what's your name?'

'Cameron,' the man replied as they walked through the hallway.

'And what do you do here?' Harry asked.

'I am His Lordship's butler,' Cameron said.

Harry looked at Danny. ' Lord who?' he asked.

'Lord Dorres,' Cameron said.

'Never heard of him,' Harry replied as they reached a set of double doors.

Cameron knocked and opened them. 'Your Lordship, the police are here to speak to you.' Harry and Danny followed him in.

'I thought I said I was not available,' Lord Dorres said, looking up. He was seated in an armchair reading a newspaper.

'That's my fault,' Harry said. 'Now is the only time that suits me.'

Lord Dorres stood up. 'And who might you be?' he asked.

'I am Chief Inspector Davis, and this is Detective Constable Kane,' Harry said, pointing to Danny.

'Cameron, you can go, but bring me a cup of coffee,' Lord Dorres said. Cameron went out closing the door behind him. 'Inspector, I don't like my house being invaded by the police.'

'That's Chief Inspector, sir, and this is not an invasion. I would just like to ask you a few questions about a Mr Gerald Parkin,' Harry said.

'Gerald, what has he been up to? And do they let police officers walk about dressed like that?' Lord Dorres said, looking at Danny.

'He put his Sunday best on when he knew we were coming here,' Harry said. 'Now if I could ask you a few questions about Mr Parkin.'

Lord Dorres sat back down. 'What has he done?'

'He was found dead at his house earlier this afternoon,' Harry replied.

Lord Dorres looked at Harry and said, 'That's terrible, I'm sorry to hear that, what happened?'

'He was found with head injuries at his home. We are just trying to trace his movements, and how he seemed to the people who last saw him,' Harry replied. 'Now if I could just ask you a few questions, Danny, take notes.'

They heard a knock. The doors opened and Cameron came in, carrying a cup of coffee. He placed it on the table beside the chair Lord Dorres was sitting in. 'Will there be anything else, Your Lordship?' he asked.

Dorres shook his head, and Cameron turned and left the room.

'I understand Mr Parkin was here last night,' Harry said.

Lord Dorres picked up the coffee cup and took a small sip. 'Yes, we had a small dinner party.' He opened a drawer in the table took out a box, opened that and took out a cigar.

'How was he? Did he seem to have anything on his mind? Did he seem worried?' Harry asked.

Lord Dorres reached into the drawer, took out a lighter and lit his cigar. He puffed a few times and blew out a long stream of smoke. 'Parkin, no. He was in fine form, his usual chatty self.'

'So he didn't say anything that you thought was strange, or mention something that he was worried about,' Harry asked.

Lord Dorres rolled the cigar between his fingers. 'I thought I answered that question, Inspector,' he said

'I must have misheard you, sir. Did he mention anything that he was worried about?' Harry said.

'That's Lord Dorres to you, Inspector, and no, he did not mention anything.' Out of the corner of his eye Harry saw Danny with his hand over his mouth trying to stifle a laugh.

'Could you tell us who else was at the dinner party, please, sir?' Harry put a lot of emphasis on the 'sir'.

Lord Dorres took another puff on his cigar, then put it down in the ashtray. He slowly blew the smoke out, picked his coffee cup up and took a drink.

'I don't want to rush your answers, sir,' Harry said. 'I can see you're a busy man, but we are investigating a suspicious death that could be murder, so if you could just give us your undivided attention it would be appreciated.'

Lord Dorres put his coffee cup down on the table and looked at Harry. 'Inspector, I had lunch with the Home Secretary and the Commissioner last week, I'm sure they would not appreciate your line of questioning.'

'Sir, I am not interested in the Home Secretary or the Commissioner, unless they were here at your dinner party last night, so if we can get back to you just answering a few simple questions I can be on my way,' Harry said.

'Ask away, Inspector,' Lord Dorres said.

'I will make it as simple for you as I can, sir, as I can tell you're having difficulty with long questions,' Harry said.

Lord Dorres picked his cigar up from the ashtray, put it between his lips and took a smoke, looked at Harry but said nothing.

'Did Mr Parkin seem worried?' Harry asked.

'No,' Lord Dorres replied, blowing out the cigar smoke.

'Did he mention anything that was bothering him?'

'No.'

'Did he say anything about anyone he was worried about or had argued with,' Harry continued.

'No, unless you include the man he interviewed on his programme last night,' Lord Dorres replied.

'Who was that? Did he say he had argued with him?' Harry asked.

'I don't know the man's name, some politician. He just said the man was stupid and it was a terrible interview,' Lord Dorres said.

'Was Mr Parkin married, or involved with anyone?'

'Not as far as I know.'

'Who else was at the dinner last night?'

'My wife and myself, Parkin and a few other friends.'

'Is your wife at home, sir, could we speak to her please?' Harry asked.

'She is at home, but I don't think she can tell you anymore than I already have,' Lord Dorres said.

'If it's possible, I would just like to ask her a few questions,' Harry said.

Lord Dorres took another smoke of his cigar, leaned over and pressed a button on the wall. Nothing was said for a minute, then with a knock on the door Cameron appeared. 'Yes, Your Lordship,' he said.

'Cameron, ask Lady Dorres to join us.' Cameron went out.

Lord Dorres picked up his coffee. 'Does the thing with you ever say anything, Inspector?' He pointed his cigar at Danny. Harry looked at Danny, who had a big smile on his face.

'Only when I tell him to, sir. He was brought up by his parents to have manners,' Harry said.

The door opened and Lady Dorres came in. 'What is it, David,' she asked.

'These two are from the police,' Lord Dorres said, waving the cigar vaguely in Harry and Danny's direction. 'Apparently Parkin was found dead. They want to ask you a few questions. I have already told them all I can remember about last night's dinner, but this one…' he pointed at Harry, '…insisted he had to speak to you.'

'Parkin dead, that's terrible, he was in fine health and his usual self last night,' Lady Dorres said.

22

'Did he speak to you about any problems he had?' Harry asked.

'No, he never said anything about problems. How did he die?' she asked.

'He was found with head wounds. We are still open-minded, but suspect he was murdered,' Harry replied.

Lady Dorres paced the room, passing behind Lord Dorres' chair and back around to stand in front of Harry.

'Murdered. I can't believe it,' Lady Dorres said. 'He was as talkative as always last night, it was a very good evening.' Lady Dorres turned and went to stand behind Lord Dorres' chair.

'If you could give me the names of the other people who were at the dinner so I can contact them and ask them some questions?' Harry said.

'I don't know if I should give you their names. They are very important people. I will contact them for you, let them know you want to speak to them,' Lord Dorres said.

'I am afraid it doesn't work like that sir. I ask you for their names and address, you give them to me. I then speak to them,' Harry said.

'He seems a rather uppity policeman,' Lady Dorres said to her husband.

'I know, I've been trying to humour him since he and the thing with him turned up,' Lord Dorres said.

'Sorry to interrupt your conversation,' Harry butted in, 'but we are investigating a potential murder, and unless you give me the names of the other people who were at the dinner last night, I will arrest you both and take you to the police station and charge you with obstruction.'

'He's joking,' Lady Dorres said to her husband.

'Of course he is. I will phone our solicitor, you can leave the house now, Inspector,' Lord Dorres said. 'You will be hearing from my solicitor about your attitude and I will give him the addresses to pass on to you.'

'You will be able to make a phone call from the police station once you're there.' Harry took a pair of handcuffs from his pocket. Danny took his out too. 'Are you going to come along quietly, sir, or are we going to handcuff you and your wife?'

Lord Dorres stood up. 'You do know what you're doing, don't you inspector? Do you know who I am, and the friends I have?'

'I can assure you, sir, I do know the law and I know what I'm doing. I will ask you one more time for the names and address of the other people at the dinner,' Harry replied.

Lord Dorres stood glaring at Harry. 'Give him the names, David,' Lady Dorres said, 'but we will be making a few phone calls about you, Inspector.'

Lord Dorres took a book from the drawer in the table. 'You come over here.' He pointed to Danny, who walked over to the table. Lord Dorres opened the book, pointed at a name and Danny wrote it down along with the address. Lord Dorres turned the pages and pointed to two other names which Danny copied down. Danny turned away and walked back to Harry.

'Have you got everything you need now?' Lord Dorres said.

'Yes, thank you, sir,' Harry replied. 'You and your wife have been most helpful.'

'Well get out now,' Lady Dorres said. She pressed the bell on the wall and Cameron opened the door. 'These two are leaving, show them out.' Harry and Danny turned to leave.

'I will be making a complaint about you, Inspector,' Lord Dorres said.

'I have no doubt you will,' Harry said as he went out of the door. As Cameron showed them to the front door, Harry turned to him. 'You were here last night when they had the dinner party?'

'Yes, sir,' Cameron said.

'We will want to get a statement from you in the near future, so we'll call back and take it,' Harry said.

When they were seated in the car, Danny said, 'Harry that's what I love about coming out to question people with you. It's a real education in making friends for the police.' He started to laugh.

'Do you know any of the people whose names he gave you?' Harry said. 'And please tell me there are no more lords amongst them'.

'No you're safe there, no lords, and I don't recognise any of them,' Danny replied.

Harry started the car. 'He called you thingy.'

Danny laughed again. 'As a policeman, I have to say that's one of the nicer things I've been called. And did you notice Her Ladyship seemed a bit hyper?'

'Yes, I did,' Harry said, 'and I noticed the residue of white powder under her nose. And we have an excuse to come back at short notice to take a statement off the butler. They drove off, heading back to Scotland Yard.

CHAPTER FOUR

Manjitt and Jordan had arrived at the BBC. They'd spoken to security, were given passes and they were taken up to the fifth floor and the office of Mr Kenny Williams, the programme editor of Gerald Parkin's show. They were seated in a bright, sparsely decorated room.

'Thank you for seeing us so quickly. I am Detective Sergeant Rhodes, and this is Detective Constable Virdee. We want to ask a few questions of anyone who saw or spoke to Mr Parkin last night.'

'Yes, of course. This is tragic. I heard from his driver when he could not rouse him, so I had the police called,' Williams said. 'Anything I can do to help I will. What happened to him?'

'We're keeping an open mind, but his death is suspicious. Can you tell us how he was yesterday?' Jordan asked.

'He was his normal self. I have worked with him for many years, he wasn't the easiest person to get on with,' Williams said, 'and I can't say he had many friends among the people he worked with, but he was the best at his job.'

'Did you spend much time with him yesterday?' Manjitt asked.

'He came in for a programme meeting yesterday about three, he seemed fine.'

'Who else was at the meeting?' Jordan asked.

'Apart from me, John Page the programme director, and two of the programme researchers. We went over the schedule for that evening's programme, discussed what the line of questioning should be and what we had found out on the subject, and how we would play the interview.'

'And Mr Parkin seemed fine, didn't seem to be worried about anything?' Manjitt said.

'No, he seemed his normal self,' Williams said.

'Do you know if he was romantically involved with anyone?' Jordan said.

'Not that I know of, I didn't mix socially with him so he might have been, but I wouldn't know,' Williams replied.

'Did he upset anyone or have arguments?' Manjitt said.

'Gerald was top of his profession. He upset lots of people, but it didn't bother him. He treated everyone the same, with complete disdain. He could not abide people working on his programme who didn't get things right first time. I think we have the highest turnover of staff at the BBC.'

'So he wasn't a well liked person?' Manjitt asked.

'Respected by the people who worked with him, but not liked,' Williams replied.

'Do you think he could have upset anyone enough for someone to want to kill him?' Jordan said.

'What, here at the BBC?' Williams said with a surprised look on his face. 'I don't think so. You will probably find it hard to get anyone to say something nice about him, but he was very good at his job and that's the bottom line, how many viewers tune in, that's how success is measured.'

'His programme is broadcast in the evening, so can you tell us what he did between the broadcast and your meeting in the afternoon?' Manjitt asked.

'No, sorry, it was always the same. We had our meeting about the programme in the afternoon. Gerald would be back here about an hour before the programme started just to check everything was ready,' Williams replied.

'You have been very helpful,' Jordan said. 'Could you take

us to see the other people who worked with him yesterday?'

'Of course.' Williams stood up. 'They should all be down in the studio.'

They followed Williams along the corridor to the lifts. 'The studio is on the third floor,' Williams said as they waited. Jordan nudged Manjitt in the ribs as a well-known pop star walked past talking to someone. As they got into the lifts, Manjitt asked 'Did Mr Parkin work on any other programmes?'

'He did special one-offs on a particular subject, and he was always the lead presenter on the general election coverage,' Williams said as they got in the lift and Williams pressed the button. The doors slid silently closed. 'He used to write the odd article for newspapers, that's where he started his career before he came to television.' It took only a few seconds and the lift doors opened at the third floor. They got out. Williams led them along the corridor. 'That was Gerald's dressing room.' He pointed to a door.

'Is it alright if we have a quick look inside?' Jordan asked.

'Yes, of course.' Williams opened the door for them.

'It's not kept locked,' Manjitt said, as she opened the door.

'No, none of the doors have locks on,' Williams replied.

Manjitt and Jordan had a look round the room. 'Not much in here.'

'Gerald didn't spend much time here,' Williams said. 'After the show was finished he would be out of the building within half an hour. Most people would stop and chat, grab a coffee, but Gerald would be gone.'

They left the room, walked along the corridor, through a door and into the studio. Jordan looked around. 'It's much bigger than I imagined,' he said.

'That's because on the television you only see that small part in front of the camera.' Williams replied. He led them to the back of the studio and opened a door. 'This is the director's booth.'

A man was seated with a folder open on a desk, reading some papers in it. 'And this is John Page.' The man looked up. 'John, these are police officers. They are investigating Gerald's death.' John Page stood; he was a tall, thin man.

'Hello, Mr Page. I am Detective Sergeant Rhodes. We just want to ask a few questions about Mr Parkin,' Jordan said.

'Yes, of course. Take a seat, it has come as quite a shock to all the people who worked on the programme.' He sat back down.

'Thank you, Mr Williams, if we could just speak to Mr Page in private?' Manjitt said.

'Oh yes, of course.' Williams went out of the door, leaving the three of them alone. Manjitt and Jordan sat down.

'What happened to Gerald?' Page asked.

'We can't really say yet,' Manjitt replied, 'but we would like to know how he seemed to you yesterday.'

'His usual cantankerous self, upsetting people, having a general moan about things,' Page said.

'Did you speak to him much yesterday?' Jordan asked.

'At the programme meeting in the afternoon, and just before we went on air. And he came into the booth for a moan after the programme finished.'

'Did he speak about anything that was troubling him?' Manjitt asked.

'What, Gerald? No, he never spoke about anything but the programme and the people on it, and the ones he didn't want on it again.'

'So he upset lots of people,' Jordan asked.

'Yes,' Page said. 'He would upset the pope if he met him. I don't think you will find many people he worked with who would say he was a friend, but you could not fault his work. That's why he was the number one interviewer at the BBC. The other presenters got the castoff interviews he couldn't be bothered with.'

'So other presenters worked on the show with him?' Manjitt asked.

'No, not directly,' Williams said. 'Gerald worked Tuesday, Wednesday and Thursday. Monday and Friday were shared between two other presenters, but Gerald always made sure the meaty interviews were his and the others got the more lightweight stuff.'

'You will have to give us the names of the other presenters. We will need to have a chat with them too,' Jordan said.

Page took out a pen and wrote two names onto a piece of paper and handed it to Jordan. He looked at the two names, Daphne Waite and Grant East. 'How did Gerald get on with those two?'

'As he got on with everyone else he worked with. He didn't have much time for them. I don't think he thought they were any good at interviewing. I remember him saying at a Tuesday meeting once that he had watched Monday's programme. He said the only way Daphne would have got a job was by sleeping with the director. I had to remind him I was the director, and I had not slept with her.'

'Did he argue with everyone?' Manjitt asked.

'Gerald didn't argue, he just made his opinion clear and left without waiting to hear what anyone else had to say,' Williams replied.

'He didn't sound a very nice person,' Manjitt said.

'I have worked with him for five years. I have to admit I didn't like him, but he could do his job. When a programme was going out, I would be sitting in here watching the way he destroyed some of the politicians and others with his questions and probing. There was no one better.'

'Can you think of anyone who would want to see him dead?' Jordan asked.

'Half of the people in parliament. Lots of people didn't like him, but to do him harm, I don't know.'

'Do you know if he was seeing anyone romantically?' Manjitt asked.

'Not to my knowledge. But as I said, he didn't stay around to socialise.'

'Mr Williams said there were two researchers in the programme meeting yesterday. Are they around?' Manjitt said.

'No, I think they're off doing some background on a future programme,' Page said.

Jordan took out his card and gave it to Page. 'When they come back, could you get them to ring me? I just need to have a word with them, and if you think of anything else you think might help us, you can call me at any time.' Manjitt and Jordan stood up. 'You have been very helpful.'

They left the booth and walked back into the studio. They saw Williams talking to someone. He noticed them and came over. 'We are finished here, thank you, Mr Williams,' Jordan said.

'I will walk you to the lifts.' They followed Williams across the studio and out of the door into the corridor that led to the lifts. As they did, they saw a young girl coming out of Parkin's dressing room. 'Excuse me, miss,' Jordan said. 'What were you doing in there?'

The girl turned and looked at them. 'I just put my make-up bag in there for later.'

'She's from the make-up department,' Williams said.

'Did you do Mr Parkin's make-up yesterday?' Jordan asked the girl.

'No, I was on the morning news yesterday,' she said.

'Thank you. Sorry we stopped you,' Jordan said. The girl turned and walked off. 'If you could find out who did Mr Parkin's make-up yesterday and let me know.' He handed Williams one of his cards.

'Yes, of course,' Williams said. They got to the lifts

and Williams said goodbye and left them, the lift arrived and Manjitt and Jordan got in. Manjitt pressed for the ground floor. 'He doesn't seem the nicest of people, our Mr Parkin,' she said.

'It won't make things easy. We could have potential suspects in everybody we speak to.' The doors opened and they went across the lobby to the security desk. There were three security men seated there. One stood up as they approached. Jordan and Manjitt unclipped their passes and handed them to him.

'Were you on yesterday evening?' Jordan asked him.

'No, not me,' he replied.

'Could you tell us at what time Mr Gerald Parkin left last night?'

'Yes, we have the log. All staff carry their BBC ID cards, and they register automatically when someone enters or leaves the building.' He tapped in the name. 'He left at 11.28, but I can do better than that, I can show you,' he said. He invited them to come round to his side of the security desk, where there were a number of television screens. He tapped on a keyboard in front of him. 'This is the CCTV from last night,' he said, as pictures appeared on the television. They saw Parkin and another man leave the lift. Parkin spoke to the security man for a moment, then left the building. 'Who was the man with Mr Parkin?' Manjitt asked.

'That's Mr Hendricks. He works on the morning show on the radio,' the guard said.

'Is he still in the building?' Jordan asked. The guard tapped at his keyboard again.

'No, he left at 10.30 this morning. His programme goes out from six o'clock in the morning and finishes at nine.'

'Thanks for your help,' Jordan said. They left the security desk and walked to the main doors. 'We can come back and have a chat with Mr Hendricks later. He might have spoken with Parkin before he left last night, and Hendricks was here late if his programme starts at six in the morning,' Jordan said as they passed through the main doors. 'Let's go back to the Yard.

CHAPTER FIVE

Charlie had just finished watching some old interviews done by Gerald Parkin which he had found on the internet, when Harry and Danny came into the office. Harry sat down. 'What a fun time that was,' he said.

'Who was it who lives at the house?' Charlie asked.

'A Lord and Lady Dorres, and a butler called Cameron,' Danny said, standing behind Harry. 'I learned an awful lot from Harry's skilful and engaging way with the public.'

'Go and make me a cup of tea, Hippie, or you will skilfully find yourself directing traffic somewhere nasty.' Danny went away, laughing.

'It was a good interview then?' Charlie asked.

'That Lord Dorres lives in a different century to the rest of the world, but I think I got through to him in the end. We got the names and addresses of the other people at the dinner so we can check them out. And I left the butler out of the questioning, which gives us a reason to call back there when we want.'

'What did we find out about Parkin,' Charlie asked.

'Not a lot really. They seem to think he's a great one to have at a party, always good for being chatty.'

Danny returned with the tea. 'He threatened to arrest him if he didn't give the names to us. You should have seen the lord's face. I don't think anyone has ever spoken to him like that in his life,' Danny said. 'Oh, and boss, he said he was great friends with the Home Secretary and the Commissioner.' Danny went away to his desk, still laughing.

Charlie lent back in his chair stretching his arms. He looked at Harry. 'I take it that I might be getting a few phone calls.'

Harry smiled and shrugged. 'I treated him as I would anyone else, no more no less.'

'Do you think anything went on at the dinner. Harry?' Charlie asked.

'It's hard to say after speaking to those two, but you might want to ask if our man Parkin had any drugs in his system.'

'Why's that, Harry?'

Harry put one finger against his nose and made a sniffing sound. 'Her Ladyship certainly uses them.'

'I will send a message over to forensics to check that,' Charlie said. 'You and Danny start running some checks on the other people's names you have before we see them. Once Jordan and Manjitt are back, we will all go back to the house to give it a proper search.'

The phone on Charlie's desk rang as Harry stood up. Charlie put his hand up and Harry waited. After a couple of minutes, he put the phone down. 'That was the Commissioner's office. They have had a complaint about one of my officers, an Inspector Davis. He was rude and threatening to Lord Dorres, which was uncalled for, and I should look into it and get back to them.'

'I don't think we have an Inspector Davis on the team,' Harry said.

Charlie smiled. 'I will give it a day, and send them a memo saying that. It will buy us a few days of peace before they realise it's Chief Inspector Davis. And Harry, I want a report each evening that I can put on Crick's desk for his press conference the next day. Try and make it interesting.'

'When have my reports not been interesting?' He picked his cup up and went over to Danny to start doing checks on the names they had got.

Jordan and Manjitt got back to the squad room about an hour later. Charlie called Harry and Danny over to listen to Jordan's briefing on what they had gathered.

After listening, Charlie said, 'So, we have a man who according to those he worked with was obnoxious, and did not socialise with work colleagues, and someone who was great fun to have at dinner parties according to others. Let's leave everything as it is now and go back to the house for a proper search. When we get back we can assess what we will do then.'

They arrived at the house and Charlie was able to park the Bentley right outside. The police tape was still up and a uniformed officer was standing outside the door. They walked up the stairs, Jordan showing his warrant card to the constable. Once inside, Charlie said he and Harry would search downstairs, and the others take the upper floor.

'Let's start in the kitchen, Harry,' Charlie said. They pulled on gloves and began the search. Apart from where the body had been lying, the kitchen was mostly undisturbed. They looked through the cupboards and drawers but found nothing. They walked through the hall towards the front room. Harry stopped by a door that was tucked under the staircase. He opened it, and there were jackets hanging up and shoes on the floor. Harry patted the coats down one at a time and rifled the pockets. He found two keys on a key ring, and some old bills that seemed to be from restaurants. He checked nothing was tucked into the shoes. He put the bills in an evidence bag and wrote where he had found them on the front. He walked to the front door and tried the keys. Neither fitted. He dropped them in another evidence bag, walked back and found Charlie in the front room picking up some of the papers from the floor. 'Found some keys in a jacket pocket in the cupboard under the stairs. They're not the front door keys,' Harry said.

'A lot of these papers appear to be bills and private letters,'

Charlie said. Harry joined Charlie picking up the papers from the floor, making a stack on the table. Once they had all the papers, Charlie held open an evidence bag and Harry slid all the papers in and laid it down on the table. 'Right, let's see if we can find something that might help us,' Charlie said.

Harry started on the right-side of the room and Charlie on the left. They began to search, going through the drawers then pulling them out and checking inside and underneath the frame.

'Bingo,' Harry cried.

Charlie turned around to see Harry holding up one of the cushions from the sofa. In his other hand was a mobile phone. 'It was tucked down the side, he must have been sitting on the sofa having his toast.'

On a table next to the sofa, a piece of toast sat on a plate next to a cup. Harry picked up the cup and smelt it. 'Coffee. The phone must have slipped between the cushions when he was sitting down, so he was in here when whoever killed him came to visit.'

'No forced entry, so he must have known who it was, or at least had a reason to let them in,' Charlie said. 'Is the phone switched on?'

'No.' Harry tried pushing the on key but got no response. 'Must be out of charge.'

'Bag it. We will take it back to the station and charge it up. Hopefully it might give us something to run with.'

Harry dropped it into another bag, and carried on the search. Nothing else was found.

They stood in the middle of the room looking around for anything they may have missed. 'For someone who worked in the media,' Charlie said, 'he doesn't have a computer and I have not seen a laptop or tablet lying around.'

'Maybe whoever visited took it with them,' Harry said.

'Harry, do you still have a video player at your place?' Charlie asked.

'No, boss, I'm in the twenty-first century now. I have Sky Plus and an old DVD player,' Harry said.

'Me too, Harry, but our media man has a DVD player and a video player, and I have not found any old video tapes laying around.' Charlie walked to the television and knelt down. Harry followed him. The DVD player was on top of the video, and Charlie checked behind for leads. Only the DVD was connected. Charlie lifted it up. 'Pull the video player out, Harry,' he said.

Harry pulled the video player from underneath and laid it on the table. Charlie put the DVD player back.

'I remember when I was in the drugs squad,' Charlie said, 'and we raided a dealer's house. We had searched everywhere and found nothing, and the dealer was looking really smug. But we brought a sniffer dog in and no one had noticed the dealer had two video players. The sniffer dog went mad by one of them – when we pulled it apart, it had two kilos of heroin in it.'

Charlie looked at the video player and turned it over. It looked like a plain old video player. 'That's what I want to see,' Charlie said. He pushed a button that was at the back beside the cable connecters and the whole back of the video player came away. Charlie laid the video player flat, putting the back of it to one side. He put his hand in and pulled out a book, laid that on the table, looked inside again and put his hand back inside and pulled out a small polyethylene bag. Inside were two data traveller flash drives. He held up the bag and Harry placed an evidence bag below it and Charlie dropped it in.

'Manjitt can have a go at those when we get back to the station.' Harry wrote on the bag and placed it with the others he had.

Charlie picked up the small book they had found and opened it. 'Seems to be full of names, dates and numbers.' He passed it to Harry. 'Stick it in a bag, Harry, we can have a read later.' Harry bagged it and they stood up.

'Well at least we know our man had something he didn't want people to find,' Harry said. They turned around when they heard the rest of the team coming down the stairs. Manjitt came in, followed by Jordan and Danny. 'Well, did you find anything?' Harry asked.

'We know he never used his attic, just dust up there, as you can see from looking at Hippie.' Jordan said, pointing at Danny.

Charlie and Harry looked at Danny, whose hair and clothes were covered in a grey dust. 'I don't see anything different,' Harry said.

'Harry, I will report you for taking liberties with junior officers,' Danny said, shaking his hair and patting himself down. Clouds of dust came off him.

'Don't think you're getting in the Bentley covered in that,' Charlie said.

'The rooms were pretty much clean. It looks like he lived alone; only one set of clothes and the second bedroom was unused,' Jordan said.

'So you found nothing?' Harry asked.

'We had a good search of all the rooms, nothing,' Manjitt said.

'Hopefully our finds might give us a clue,' Charlie said. 'Now let's head off and go through what we have, then we can start having a few thoughts about where this investigation is going.'

They picked up all the evidence bags and walked outside. It was beginning to get dark. Charlie spoke to the constable. 'No one is to go in the house unless whoever's on duty has spoken to me.'

'Yes, sir,' the constable said.

'And make sure that instruction is passed on to whoever takes over from you.'

The constable nodded. They walked to the Bentley. 'Danny, where do you think you're going?' Charlie said.

'Come on, boss, I've got most of the dust off,' Danny said.

The rest of the team stood smiling, looking at Danny. 'I wouldn't let him get in if it were my car, boss,' Jordan said.

Charlie pressed the key fob and the boot opened. 'Get a blanket out of there and lay it on the back seat, and if I find any dust I will charge you for the valeting,' Charlie said.

They arrived back at the Yard and laid all the evidence they had gathered on to a table. Harry pushed a large whiteboard over from the wall and set it beside the table. Charlie looked at his watch. 'I think we have done well today, but we have a lot to get through tomorrow, so let's call it a night. You three get off home but in at seven in the morning.'

Manjitt, Danny and Jordan left Harry and Charlie alone in the office. 'You want tea Harry?' Charlie asked.

'Yes please, boss, what do you think we have?' Harry asked.

'Harry, I have no idea, but once we have sorted through that lot,' he pointed at the evidence, 'tomorrow we might have a better clue,' Charlie said.

Harry sat down in his chair. 'Your desk-phone-message light is flashing, boss.'

Charlie walked back with a cup of tea for Harry. He put the cup down on the table, pressed the hands-free button on the phone, then pressed message button. The phone told them there were three messages, the first was the voice of Assistant Commissioner Crick, saying he had a solicitor from a top London firm phoning up demanding an apology about the behaviour of an Inspector Davis, who had interviewed Lord and Lady Dorres, could Charlie get back to him. 'That inspector Davis gets everywhere,' Harry said, smiling.

'You will get me killed,' Charlie said. The second call was from the Commissioner's office, along the same lines as the first.

'I think we will have to launch an investigation to track this inspector down,' Harry said.

Charlie smiled. The third message was from forensics. It told them Parkin had been killed by four blows to his head. The blows had been from behind. They had found three different sets of fingerprints in the house and he had no drugs in his system. A full report would be sent up tomorrow.

'Well, that's something, but I don't hold much hope of any of the prints being our killer,' Harry said. 'It seems they came prepared to kill, so I don't think whoever it was would be silly enough to leave their prints.'

'You're probably right, Harry,' Charlie said. 'I want the local force to do a complete search of the area tomorrow, the drains, bins, see if we can find what was used to kill our man, we might get lucky. And have a look and find a charger for Parkin's phone, if you find one put it on charge before you go tonight.'

'I will get on to the local station tonight and speak to someone to get the search sorted,' Harry said.

Charlie stood up. 'I will see you in the morning Harry. Don't forget the daily report for Crick and put something interesting in it for him.'

'You know my reports, boss, filled with nuggets,' Harry said.

Charlie smiled as he turned away, heading for the door.

CHAPTER SIX

It was six forty and all the team were standing round the table. 'It's nice that you all got in early,' Charlie said. 'Manjitt, what's with the eye?' Manjitt's eye had a large bruise under it and a thin band covering some stitches on her eyebrow.

'I took a karate class last night,' Manjitt said, 'and ended up having a session with one of Britain's gold medallists from the last Olympics. He doesn't look too good this morning either.'

'You could just go and have dinner like normal people,' Jordan said.

'I think it improves your looks,' Danny said, and he felt a hard kick to the back of his legs that had him sinking to his knees.

'Danny, get up,' Charlie said. 'Now let's discuss what we have. Harry, you go first.'

'I stayed a bit late last night and sorted out all the bills and letters we picked up from the floor in the front room. Those…' he pointed to one stack, '…are all his household bills. They are all up to date, paid on time through standing orders. Those ones are all ones of purchases, nothing unusual, a new television, some furniture and bits and pieces for the house, now these ones…' he lifted up a small pile '…are a bit suspect, we have five receipts for jewellery, holidays and two cars.' Harry passed the receipts around. 'Now he didn't own a car and unless whoever killed him took all the jewellery, we never found it. As for the holidays, he might have gone on them alone, but it's a lot to pay for a holiday just for one. We have two keys that don't fit his front door that were in a jacket pocket and a couple of bills from restaurants.'

'I wish someone would buy me some jewellery that cost this much,' Manjitt said.

'Jordan you can check them out. Get in touch with the shops and travel agents, see if we can find out who they were for,' Charlie said. Jordan took the receipts. 'And get Mr Parkin's bank details, let's see what else he spent his money on. Danny, what have you got?'

'I have been checking out the names we got from Harry's good friend, Lord Dorres,' Danny said. 'I went on the internet last night when I got home.'

'Are you after promotion?' Manjitt said.

'I could do with the extra money, Manjitt might have a good idea there, boss,' Danny said, looking at Charlie.

'If you would promise to buy some new clothes and dress like a normal person I would put a good word in for you,' Harry said.

'Harry, how can you say that, when all your suits are from the eighties?' Jordan said.

'Leave the promotion and clothes to one side,' Charlie said. 'What did you find out?'

'All the names on the list are important and powerful people in the businesses they are involved in. I got some pictures of them.' Danny passed round pictures he found and had printed off the internet, 'Now I did a quick check into their businesses, nothing detailed but these people are serious players in international business.'

'Well done, Danny,' Charlie said. 'Now Manjitt, I want you to take these.' Charlie handed over the two data sticks they had got from the house. 'You're the tech wizard amongst us, see what you can get off them. Danny, I want you to go to the BBC and finish up speaking to the people who Manjitt and Jordan didn't get to see. Jordan, give Danny the names.'

Jordan handed over a list to Danny, pointing out the

names. 'Those two are fellow presenters, those are researchers and the last one is a make-up girl. The director got her name for me.'

'Make some phone calls to check they are going to be there, I want the BBC-end tied up today,' Charlie said. Danny nodded. 'Okay, get on with it.' The team went off, leaving Harry and Charlie.

'Let's get some tea, Harry,' Charlie said. 'We can sit down and go through Mr Parkin's book and switch his phone on. Let's see who he has been in touch with.' Harry picked up the book and phone and walked over to his desk at the back of the office.

'Did you send the daily report to Crick?' Charlie asked.

'Of course, boss, put all we knew in it,' Harry said.

Charlie walked over with two cups of tea, and put one down for Harry. 'Give me a copy of the report, Harry, in case Crick phones down to ask about it.' Harry passed over a sheet of paper, Charlie looked at it. 'Short and to the point, Harry, as usual.'

'I can't put in what we don't know, can I, boss?' Harry said.

Charlie put the paper down beside the telephone. 'Now, what's in the book?'

Danny had phoned the BBC personnel department and had found all the people bar Gerald Parkin's two fellow presenters who would be at work. He asked that they be informed he would be calling to question them that morning and to make themselves available, and could personnel get the presenters to call him so he could arrange to interview them.

He had taken the underground to Oxford Circus and walked up Regent Street into Langham Place and into the BBC. He went and picked up a pass from security, where he was asked to wait till someone from personnel came down to meet him. He had waited five minutes when a young woman in her early twenties came over to him. She said she would take him up to the make-up department first. Danny followed her to the lifts. They rode up to the fourth floor. She didn't speak to him. He followed her out of the lift and along the corridor, then she pushed open a door which led into a large room filled with boxes and tables. Five people were in there, they walked over to a young woman. 'This is Sharon,' the woman from personnel said.

'Hello, Sharon, I am Detective Constable Kane. I just want to ask you a couple of questions about Gerald Parkin,' Danny said. He turned to the woman from personnel. 'If you could give us a couple of minutes' privacy.' The woman walked away to the far side of the room.

'Sharon, this won't take long,' Danny said. 'Now you saw Mr Parkin last night when his programme finished.'

'Yes, but he didn't say much, just his usual grumpy self,' Sharon replied.

'So you did his make-up all the time?' Danny asked.

'No, thank God, it was the short straw. I am not being horrible, but no one liked him,' she said.

'Why was that, did he treat you bad or something?'

'He treated everyone bad, he was a pig,' Sharon said.

'Did he say anything to you about what he was doing last night, or where he was going?' Danny asked.

'He told me to hurry, he had a dinner date, don't know who with or where. Then when I finished he just told me to get out, no thank you. He was like that with us all, that's why none of us liked to go and do his make-up.'

'Thank you Sharon, I will give you my card so if anything else comes to mind or you hear anything you think might help, you can ring me,' Danny said. He walked over to the woman from personnel, said he was finished and followed her out of the door and along the corridor back to the lifts.

They went down to the second floor, along another corridor. 'I bet new people get lost in this place all the time,' Danny said. The woman glanced at him but said nothing, then she stopped at a door and opened it without knocking. Inside were about twenty people all at desks working on computers. He followed her over to a desk by the window, where he was introduced to the two researchers. It took him a couple of minutes to find out they had the same opinion of Parkin as Sharon, then he left the office.

'Now we are going to the studio of the main morning news programme to meet Mr Hendricks,' the personnel woman said. 'His programme will not have finished yet, so you will have to wait a little while.'

'It's nice of you to speak to me,' Danny said. The woman just looked at him, said no more and continued to lead Danny along the corridor.

Right at the end she opened a door and Danny followed her in. Three people were seated working buttons and switches on a console in front of them. They were looking through a large window that separated them from the studio. Danny could see two men with headphones on. 'You can sit at the back and please be quiet,' the personnel woman said. 'When you have finished with Mr Hendricks you can go back along the corridor to the lifts and down to the lobby to leave. I have to go and do some important work.'

'Thank you for help and I enjoyed our chat,' Danny said. The woman looked at him said nothing, turned and left. One of the men working the console turned and pointed to a chair at the back of the room. Danny went and sat down, put his feet up on the table and shut his eyes.

'His phone has about five missed calls on it from the morning he was killed,' Harry said. 'I would expect they might

46

be the driver and the BBC trying to find out what was wrong. He made a couple of calls, I will go through all his messages later.'

'His book has names, dates and numbers beside them. I think I recognise a couple of the names,' Charlie said. 'You'd better get a copy of *Who's Who* out, Harry.' Charlie pushed the book across the desk. 'We need to find out a bit more about our Mr Parkin. One of the people Jordan questioned at the BBC said Parkin worked in newspapers before the BBC. Give a couple of your old friends in Fleet Street a ring, see what they can tell you about him.'

Charlie's phone rang. He picked it up, spoke for a minute and put it down. 'That was Crick. He has a press conference at ten, checking if we had any new leads. He also thanked me for the report I did for him about the case so far, he said to tell you to put a bit more in the next one.'

Harry smiled. 'I will bear that in mind.'

Jordan came over. 'I have spoken to the jewellery shops. As far as they recall he was alone when he bought the items. The travel agent said one of the holidays was for him alone, but the other was for two. I have the address of the other person and the car dealers gave me the registrations for the two cars. I ran them through the system and have their addresses, and surprise, one of them belongs to our holiday partner.'

'And the names of the two?' Charlie said.

'The one who got the holiday and car is a Miss Angela Cook, aged twenty-five. I did a background check on the system. We have nothing on her. The other one was a Tim Green. We have a bit on him, he has an affray charge from three years ago and he was charged but not convicted of fraud.'

'What were the cars he bought them?' Harry asked.

'Miss Cook got a Mercedes and Mr Green got a Jaguar,' Jordan said.

'Nice work if you can get it,' Harry said, nodding his head.

'Well, no time like the present. Let's go and pay them a visit. Harry, you get on sorting through those names in the book, see if they match any in his phone and get his home phone records sent over to us. Come on, Jordan, let's go,' Charlie said.

As they left the office Charlie stopped at Manjitt's desk and asked, 'How are we going with Parkin's computer data sticks?'

'He has normal emails and letters on them, but there are two files that have passwords on them,' Manjitt said. 'I have a friend coming up from the fraud squad who has a bit of software that will open them up for us.'

'Okay, while you wait, see Harry and get the list of people who were at the dinner. Ring them up and make appointments for us to call and see them tomorrow, and it must be tomorrow.' Charlie and Jordan left the office.

'Excuse me.' Danny opened his eyes to see a man standing above him. 'I am Jim Hendricks, you wanted to speak to me.' Danny put his feet down and stood up.

'Yes, sorry, sir, it was a long day yesterday. My name's Kane, Detective Constable Kane.'

'Pleased to meet you,' Hendricks said. 'Are you under cover or something?'

'How do you mean, sir,' Danny asked.

'Well, you're not wearing what I would expect a policeman to be dressed in,' Jim Hendricks said, looking Danny up and down. Danny had on a pair of blue velvet trousers and a yellow shirt with large red flowers.

'You sound like my Chief Inspector, but I made a special effort today,' Danny said.

Hendricks smiled. 'Would you like a cup of coffee or something, officer?' he asked.

'That would be nice. Thank you, sir, coffee,' Danny said.

Hendricks walked off and a minute later brought back a coffee for Danny. 'Now what is it you want to ask me?'

'Is it okay to talk here?' Danny said.

'Could you give us a few minutes please, boys?' Hendricks said to the people in the room. They nodded and went out, he sat down and Danny sat down opposite him.

'We are trying to piece together the movements of Gerald Parkin, and from the CCTV footage of last night you left the building at the same time as him. Did he speak to you?' Danny asked.

'Yes, but only to be his usual sarcastic self. He had a big ego and didn't like it that I didn't treat him as some kind of superstar.'

'So you didn't like him.'

'No, never have from the day he came to work for the BBC. He seemed to think that everything had to revolve around him in news and current affairs.'

'Did you work with him?' Danny asked.

'No, I have worked for the BBC for over twenty years, mainly in radio, with the occasional bit of television, but never with him. I know people who have, good journalists who I respect, and they all have the same low opinion of him.'

'But his show was the top news programme.'

'That's true, but it's the only one the BBC pushes, and they spend more money on it, divert all the big interviews to it, so you would expect it to do well. He gets the best researchers to do his homework.'

'So you're saying he didn't have many friends at the BBC.'

'Not amongst the journalists and people who worked closely with him, but he had friends upstairs, the bosses.'

'Why was that?' Danny asked.

'I have no idea, but when he first arrived, he came from the newspaper industry. I heard from a few people he worked with there that he was a bit shifty.'

'What do you mean by shifty?' Danny asked.

'Well, they said he got stories that other journalists had been working on for months, you know investigations into frauds, politicians having affairs. He would suddenly come up with the answers and take all the credit for breaking the story. It was the same on the one-off programmes he did here. You would hear rumours for weeks or months and then he did a programme which exposed something or someone,' Jim Hendricks said.

'Maybe he was just very good at his job.'

'I have known some great journalists in my time, officer, and trust me he was not one of them.'

'Well thank you, sir, for being so helpful.' Danny stood up. 'If I give you my card, you can call me if you think of anything else that might help.'

Hendricks stood and took Danny's card. 'Of course, it's been nice meeting you and realising that the police are not always how you expect them to look.' Danny left and walked along the corridor to the lifts.

CHAPTER SEVEN

Charlie parked the Bentley outside a block of flats in Chelsea Harbour. He and Jordan walked to the front doors which opened automatically. They entered the lobby area, a porter sat behind a desk, he looked up as they came through the doors.

'Can I help you?' he said.

'No, thanks,' Jordan said. 'We are visiting one of the tenants in the block.'

'Who is that, sir? I have to put it in the log. Are you friends or delivering something?' the porter asked.

Charlie carried on towards the lifts and pressed the button. Jordan walked over to the porter, took out his warrant card and showed it to the porter. 'You don't need to put anything in your log.'

'Yes, okay, sir, sorry but we have to check everyone who comes into the building,' the porter said.

'That's good to know, I might have a couple of questions for you when we come back down,' Jordan said, as he turned and joined Charlie at the lift. They got in. 'What number is it, Jordan?' Charlie asked.

'She lives at 114,' Jordan said. Charlie pressed the button for the fourteenth floor.

'I don't think these places are cheap to rent or own,' Charlie said.

They got out on the fourteenth floor, looked at the sign opposite the lift that told them 114 was to their left. They turned and walked along a carpeted corridor till they came to

114. Jordan pressed the bell. After a moment the door was opened by a young woman with long blonde hair, wearing an expensive-looking red dress.

'Yes, can I help you?' she said.

'Hello, Miss, we are police officers. I am Detective Sergeant Rhodes and this is Chief Superintendent Smith. Are you Angela Cook?' Jordan said, holding his warrant card up.

'Yes, what is it you want?' Angela asked.

'We would like to ask you about your car, can we come in?' Jordan replied.

'What's wrong with my car?' she asked.

'Well if we can just come in and speak to you, it might be easier than standing on your doorstep,' Charlie said.

'Yes, okay.' She stood aside and Jordan and Charlie entered. It was a large flat; the front room had a floor-to-ceiling window running its whole length with a balcony. She closed the door and led them to the middle of the room, where two large sofas and a coffee table stood.

'That's a beautiful view of London from your window,' Charlie said.

'Yes, it's lovely in the evening with all the lights, now what's wrong with my car? It's not been stolen has it? I left it parked in the garage last night,' she said.

'No, it's not been stolen. We would like to know how you know Gerald Parkin?' Charlie asked.

She stood quiet for a moment. 'Gerald Parkin, oh the television man. I read about him being killed, but what's that got to do with me?'

'Do you know him, or have you met him?' Jordan asked.

The woman walked to the coffee table. 'I am not sure, I meet a lot of people.' She picked up a newspaper off the coffee table. 'I read about him in this.'

'Miss Cook,' Charlie said, 'I am not someone who likes

52

their time wasted, especially when I am investigating a murder. Now if we ask you a question, you give us a truthful answer, otherwise we can take you down to a police station and carry on this interview there. Now, we can start again, do you know Gerald Parkin?'

She hesitated, then said, 'Yes, I have met him a couple of times.'

'Why don't we sit down and talk?' Charlie said. He sat down on a sofa and Jordan sat down opposite, leaving Angela Cook standing. She sat down on the sofa next to Jordan.

'Now would you like to tell us about the couple of times you met Mr Parkin?' Charlie asked.

'I think I met him at a dinner party I was at, and I might have bumped into him at an art gallery where there was an exhibition,' she said.

Charlie sighed and sat back. 'So you think you bumped into him twice, did you speak to him?'

'I really can't remember. I go to lots of parties and meet lots of people,' she said, looking from Charlie to Jordan.

'What do you do for a living?' Charlie asked.

'I work in PR and have done some modelling,' Angela Cook said.

'PR pays well, or do you have rich parents?' Jordan said, waving his hand around.

'My parents are not rich,' she replied.

'So let me get this straight. You think you met Mr Parkin twice and you can't remember if you spoke to him,' Charlie said.

'Yes, if I could recall anything else I would say, but I really can't place him,' Angela said, shrugging her shoulders.

Jordan laughed, Angela looked at him. 'I do apologise for my junior officer,' Charlie said, 'but he can't stop himself laughing when he hears a good joke.'

Angela looked back at Charlie, he moved forward and leaned across the coffee table. 'Now, Miss Cook, stop messing me about, I will give you one more chance to start answering my questions honestly or we are all off to discuss it down the police station.'

'What make is your car?' Jordan asked.

'It's a Mercedes,' she said.

'Well done, Miss Cook, a truthful answer, now let's carry on like that,' Charlie said.

'And where did you get the car from?' Jordan asked.

Angela sat quiet for a minute. 'It was given to me.'

'Given to you. Now that's a nice gift. Was it a birthday or Christmas present from a boyfriend? It's not from your parents, they're not rich,' Charlie said. Angela again said nothing. 'Please, Angela, I have told you I don't have a lot of patience this morning, so when I ask you a question just answer it, and truthfully. We know more than you think we do.'

She looked across the coffee table at Charlie, who now sat back again.

'Who bought the car for you,' Jordan asked.

'Gerald,' she said.

'For someone you say you hardly knew, that was a bit of a gift,' Charlie said. 'Or were you not telling the truth when you said you hardly knew him. Was he your boyfriend?'

'No, he wasn't my boyfriend. I knew him socially, we met up occasionally for dinner or our paths crossed at parties,' she said.

'And why did he give you the Mercedes?' Jordan asked.

'I did some favours for him, you know, work,' she replied.

'Work, was that to do with the BBC?' Charlie asked.

'No, he would ask me to find out a few things about people, and I would pass on what I discovered,' Angela said.

'So you are a private detective now, as well as doing PR and modelling?' Jordan said.

'No, not like that,' she said.'I went to some dinner parties and weekend house-parties, you know, there would be important people there. Gerald would ask me to let him know who was there and with whom, and what was said.'

'And these parties, how did you get invited to them?' Charlie said.

'Through friends I had met,' she said.

'Please, let's not go back to the evasions and lies, Angela, you have been doing so well,' Charlie said. 'Who arranged for you to be at these parties? Was it Gerald Parkin, and what went on?'

'No, not Gerald, a friend, Martin Oliver, they were just, you know, parties where adults could let their hair down,' she said.

'So people slept with each other,' Jordan asked.

'Yes,' she said.

'Did Gerald ever go to these parties?' Jordan said, making a few notes in his book.

'No, I never saw Gerald at the parties.'

'Is that Sir Martin Oliver? Did you get paid to attend these parties?' Charlie asked.

'Yes, Sir Martin. No, I didn't get paid.'

'Now, Angela, I am not interested in how you earn a living. This flat must cost a bit, do you rent it?' Charlie said.

'Yes, I pay rent,' Angela said, shifting about on the sofa uneasily.

'So did you get paid to go to those parties? I don't want to have your house searched, what would the neighbours say?' Charlie said. 'And have your bank account looked into.'

'I was given expenses,' Angela replied.

'Gerald Parkin paid you?' Jordan said.

'No, Martin gave me expenses for going to the parties, Gerald just looked after me when I got some information for him.'

'Apart from the Mercedes, what else did he give you?' Charlie asked.

'He gave me money and he took me on holiday to Italy. We went to Florence and Rome, I studied Italian art at university and he knew I hadn't been, so he treated me.'

'Did he give you any jewellery?' Jordan asked.

'No,' Angela said.

'You must have got him some useful information,' Jordan said. 'How did you meet Gerald?'

'When I left university I went to work for Martin in one of his galleries in Brook Street. I met Gerald there at an exhibition.'

'So how did Gerald know you attended these parties, if he was never at them?' Charlie asked.

'I don't know, he just invited me out to dinner one evening and proposed that I find out things for him and he would make sure I got rewarded,' Angela said.

'How did you come to start going to these parties,' Jordan asked.

'I had been at the gallery a couple of months. Martin asked me if I would like to earn some extra money. He introduced me to another girl who worked there, she explained what good fun she had and how much money she was making. I wasn't earning very much money, I thought why not?'

'Did Gerald ever come to your flat?' Charlie asked.

'No, never.'

'Angela, you have been very helpful,' Charlie said. 'I want you to do me one last favour. DS Rhodes is going to give you a piece of paper. I want you to write down all the people you can remember Gerald asked you to find out things about, and what it was he wanted to know. You can also put down any of the addresses where the parties were held. Now make sure you don't leave anything out, because if you do and I find out you will be spending time in Holloway Prison. Do you understand?'

Angela nodded, took the piece of paper and the pen Jordan

passed to her and started to write. When she had finished she passed the paper and pen back to Jordan. 'Now Angela, I don't want you to speak to anyone about our chat, do you understand?' Charlie said. Angela nodded. 'I will be speaking to some of these people and if I think you have said anything to them, I will be back and it won't be good for you. I won't tell them that my information has come from you, so don't worry about them finding out you have spoken to us, okay.'

'Please make sure they don't know it was me, they are important people and have some powerful friends,' Angela said.

'Your secret's safe with us, Angela,' Charlie replied. He and Jordan stood up. 'Now I might need to speak to you again, so don't go disappearing.'

In the lift down to the lobby Jordan said, 'Now that's what I call a good interview.'

Charlie nodded. 'It certainly opens up what we have to look into.' The doors opened and they walked across the lobby. 'One minute boss,' Jordan said. Jordan walked over to the desk where the porter sat.

The porter said, 'Hello, sir, hope you saw who you wanted.'

'Yes, thank you, now can I have a look at your log?' Jordan said.

The porter pushed his log book over to Jordan, who scanned the page, turned it over, took his pen out and wrote a few things down. 'Thank you, sir, you have been most helpful.' He turned and joined Charlie, who waited by the doors to the building. They left and made their way to Charlie's Bentley.

'What did you find in the log?' Charlie asked. Jordan passed him the piece of paper. Charlie looked at it. 'That's good, now give me the list Angela made for us.' Jordan passed it over. 'Here, take the keys, you can drive. I want to call Harry and have a chat about this.'

'Can we have the top down, boss?' Jordan said. 'There's nothing better than all those snobby people seeing a black man driving round in a Bentley.'

Charlie laughed. 'Don't go speeding, I don't need to go through the paperwork to avoid the points.'

'Boss, I wouldn't have it any other way. Where are we off to?' Jordan said.

'I have suddenly got a big interest in art, perhaps we should call in on Sir Martin Oliver at his gallery in Brook Street.' They got into the Bentley, the top came down and they pulled away.

Harry had taken the call from Charlie, made a few notes and carried on going through the book they had recovered from the house, listing names and dates onto a large sheet of paper. He had Gerald Parkin's phone next to him, which he cross-checked for the same dates in the message box to see if there were any matches. When he found one he circled the name and date on the paper. He saw Manjitt was still working on the computer at her desk, a young man was sitting with her and he could see them occasionally point at something on the screen and Manjitt would make a note.

Danny arrived back at the Yard after his visit to the BBC. 'Hello, Harry, how's the book work going, and who's Manjitt's boyfriend?'

'Hippie, how did it go at the BBC and that's a detective up from the fraud squad helping to go through the data sticks we got, so don't get jealous,' Harry said.

Danny smiled. 'In my dreams, Harry. I spoke to all bar the two fellow presenters, but I am expecting to get calls from them later. Our Mr Parkin was not a well liked man, nobody had a good word for him. I did get something from Jim Hendricks, he works on the morning news programme on Radio Four.' Danny then related what Hendricks had told him about the favouritism that Parkin seemed to get from the bosses at the BBC and the rumours he had been told about when Parkin worked in the newspaper industry.

'Get it written up, and I will have a cup of tea while you're at it,' Harry said. 'Then you can come and help cross-reference these names.'

Jordan turned the Bentley into Brook Street. It was filled with boutique clothes shops, expensive jewellery stores and art galleries. They found a parking spot just past Claridge's Hotel and walked back towards Sir Martin Oliver's gallery. They stopped outside the shop and looked through the window. 'Don't know if any of that stuff would suit my flat,' Jordan said.

'It's all a bit too modern for me. I am more a good picture person,' Charlie replied. 'When I spoke to Harry on the phone, he said it had been arranged for us to call on Mr Oliver tomorrow, so it will be a double surprise for him when he sees us.'

'That's Sir Martin Oliver, boss,' Jordan said.

'Oh yes, I must remind Harry about titles,' Charlie said as they went to the entrance and pushed open the door and entered. A young woman was sitting at a table just to the left, she looked up and smiled.

'Hello, gentleman, can I give you a brochure? It will tell you all about the exhibits we have, and if you are interested in any, I can talk to you about price.' Jordan took the brochure she held out.

'Is Sir Martin Oliver about? I would like to talk to him,' Charlie said. He looked at Jordan. 'Did I get that right?' Jordan smiled and raised his eyebrows.

'Yes, he's in his office. Who should I say is calling?' She picked up the phone.

'It's the police,' Charlie said.

The girl looked at him for a moment, then tapped a number into the phone. She spoke for a few seconds then put the phone down. 'He's sorry, but he is busy with a client at the moment, and he said to tell you he has arranged a meeting to speak with you tomorrow.'

'Never mind,' Charlie said. 'I will speak to him anyway, which way is his office?'

'I am sorry, sir, but he said he is busy,' the girl said.

'Could you stand up a minute please,' Charlie said.

The girl stood up. 'Now, miss, I am a busy man too. You are going to take us to his office, I don't want to hear another word about busy.' He raised his voice and said, 'Now.' The girl jumped slightly.

'This way,' and she led them through the gallery.

Jordan, walking beside Charlie, whispered 'Do you think she is one of his party girls?'

'We might find out during our conversation,' Charlie said.

They followed the girl through a door and up a flight of steps. The girl knocked on the door and opened it. Charlie and Jordan followed her in. 'I am sorry, Sir Martin, but they insisted they see you,' the young girl said.

Sir Martin looked up from his desk. He was in his mid-fifties, his hair was jet-black. 'Okay, Beverley, you can go. I will deal with this.' The girl went out of the door shutting it. 'I said I was busy. I told one of your officers you could have five minutes of my time tomorrow.'

'I think you told your young lady you were with a client,' Charlie said. He walked forward and sat in the chair that was on the opposite side of the table. 'You were not being truthful were you, unless of course you have the client hiding somewhere in the office.'

Jordan came over and sat on the edge of the desk. 'You see, we are busy people too,' he said, picking up some papers on the desk.

'I don't know who you to think you are, and you can put those down.' He took the papers off Jordan.

'I am sorry we didn't introduce ourselves. I am Chief Superintendent Smith and this is Detective Sergeant Rhodes, we want to speak to you about Gerald Parkin.'

'Listen, you might get away with this behaviour with petty criminals, but I know some important people. You can leave my office right now and come back tomorrow as arranged, and I might consider not putting in a complaint about the pair of you,' Sir Martin Oliver said.

'Boss, have you noticed how everybody knows important people?' Jordan said.

'I don't understand it,' Charlie said. 'Noone considers us important, I don't know what the world's coming to, now where was I? Ah yes, Gerald Parkin. You were going to tell us about him, Mr Oliver.'

Sir Martin sat quietly looking at the two men, the large bald one in the seat and the even larger black man perched on his table. They were both smiling at him seeming not to have heard a word he said.

'I don't like being intimidated,' Sir Martin said, 'and I have had enough of your silly games.' He picked up his phone and began to dial.

'I hope that's your solicitor,' Charlie said. 'You are going to need him. You can talk in your office now or tell your solicitor he can come to Scotland Yard, because that's where I will be taking you. Do you like parties, Mr Oliver? Parties with lots of young girls, who don't mind sleeping with the odd man or two?'

Oliver's hand froze over the phone. He looked at Charlie.

'I think you have his attention, boss,' Jordan said. Sir Martin put down the phone.

'Now I feel we got off on the wrong foot,' Charlie

said, 'and I know you are going to answer every question I ask you truthfully, and I won't have to take you away and lock you in a cell when I leave here. But if I think you're lying to me just once, my officer here will have you in handcuffs and I shall have twenty officers arrive here with all their lights and sirens on and search this place. I bet that would be great publicity. Do I make myself clear?' Sir Martin nodded.

'Now about Mr Parkin, you were about to tell us about him. You were at the dinner party he attended at Lord Dorres' house. How was he? Did he say anything to you about being worried?' Charlie asked.

'No, he came in later than everyone else, but seemed his usual self' Sir Martin said.

'What did you talk about?' Jordan said.

'Just the usual chit-chat and gossip.'

'Was there anything in particular that Mr Parkin mentioned or was interested in?' Jordan asked.

'Not that I recall.'

'Yesterday morning, can you tell us where you were?' Charlie said.

'I was here, got in at nine and left here about three. I went to a meeting of the Arts Council, then on to Covent Garden to see the ballet, had dinner after with a few friends then went home,' Sir Martin answered.

'Did you ever go to Mr Parkin's house?'

'No, I have never been to his house.'

'Did he visit you at your house?' Jordan asked.

'Yes, he came to my house for dinner on a couple of occasions.'

'And when he came to your house, was there anything you discussed with him that you think we should know about?' Charlie said.

Sir Martin shifted in his seat. 'We talked about the arts,

politics, you know it was just two friends having dinner.'

Charlie stood up and walked around the office looking at the prints that were on the walls. 'You have a nice life, Mr Oliver. I expect, as you've informed us, you have important people who buy art from you and you mix socially with. I bet you could tell us some stories about them.' Charlie turned and came back to the table and sat back down. 'Now so far I get the feeling you don't really want to say too much. All your answers to my ears have been rather vague, what do you think Jordan?'

'Vague, that is a good choice of words, boss,' Jordan said.

'Now, Mr Oliver, in my police work I am always suspicious of people who are vague when I've asked them a question. So from now on you will expand your answers, so we get a little more detail. Because you see, I am investigating a murder,' Charlie raised his voice slightly and said, 'and I don't have time to mess around.'

Sir Martin looked at Charlie. 'I think I should ring my solicitor before I say any more.

'That's your choice, Mr Oliver, and I respect your bravery, but you go ahead,' Charlie said. Sir Martin picked up his phone and began dialling.

'Jordan, call a search team in,' Charlie said. 'Mr Oliver, when you speak to your solicitor you can inform him you are being arrested on procuring young women to act as prostitutes, what we know as pimping.'

Jordan stood up and took his mobile phone out. Sir Martin's hand stopped dialling. He slowly put the phone down. Jordan sat back down on the edge of the table, sliding his mobile back into his pocket. 'Pimping, not a nice word, bet that wouldn't go down well with all your important friends would it?' Charlie said. 'But if I think you are being cooperative with me, I can maybe forget about what I have learnt about you. I am interested in solving a murder, so do we have an understanding?' Sir Martin nodded.

'Now these parties you arranged, did you hold any of them at your house?' Charlie continued.

'Yes,' Sir Martin said.

'You can write down any other addresses you held them at, and don't leave any out, because if I find you haven't been truthful I will arrest you,' Charlie said. 'And I want the names of anyone who attended the parties. Now where did you get the girls from who attended the parties?'

'Some worked for me at the different galleries I have,' Sir Martin said, 'and they then occasionally brought a friend along to see me who I would interview.'

'So it was all very business-like. The girl downstairs, is she one of your party girls?' Jordan asked.

'Beverley, yes, she has attended a few.'

Jordan shook his head. 'I would not have thought it.'

'How did you come to start these little get-togethers?' Charlie asked.

'They started off as just parties for friends, where some of the men who were married would bring along girlfriends and not their wives. Then someone mentioned we needed to get some girls along who would be there for sex, but they didn't want just any girl, they had to be young and not from, shall we say, the seedier side of life.'

'You didn't want your normal run-of-the-mill prostitute, you wanted a little class and girls you had control over,' Jordan said.

'Yes, I knew from hearing shop-talk that a couple of girls who worked for me had reputations as enjoying a party and were not unhappy at ending up in bed with whoever they were with at the end of the night. So I took them out to dinner and put a proposal to them. It started from there.'

'And you paid them,' Charlie said.

'Yes, if they went to a party I added the money into their wages at the end of the month, if they did not work for me I gave them cash.'

'So you paid for everything, that must having be costing you a lot of money. What did you get out of it, apart from the sex?' Jordan asked.

'The people who came to the parties ran big companies or were very rich individuals. Their companies might buy a piece of art as an investment or just to decorate their offices. They would also bring friends along to exhibitions that were held at a gallery and encourage them to invest in an artwork or two.'

'That's a very nice operation you were running,' Jordan said, 'and profitable I would assume.' Sir Martin nodded.

'Did Mr Parkin attend your parties?' Charlie asked.

'No, he never came to one.'

'So how did he find out about your little get-togethers?'

'I had him over for dinner one evening and we had been drinking a bit too much and I let slip about the parties. He wanted to know all about them and we had a laugh about what went on.'

'Did you mention who went to the parties and where you got the girls from?'

'Yes, I was very indiscreet, but Gerald had an art of getting you to tell him things without you knowing what you said until it was too late.'

'Didn't you think it strange that Mr Parkin didn't want to come along to the parties?' Jordan asked.

'No, not really. Gerald was not, shall we say, in the inner circle of friends. He did not have the close connections. Yes, he knew people and got invited along to dinners and events, but he was there for who he was, a television star.'

'So he didn't have money, real power or a title, he was just someone who got invited along as a colourful character,' Charlie said.

'He was good for gossip about people, he made people laugh at a dinner with the stories he would tell. He always had something new about people to tell,' Sir Martin said.

'Did anyone ever tell you that they were upset with anything he had said?' Charlie asked.

'No, not that I can recall, he never said anything bad about people around the same table as him, but if they were not at another dinner and he was, he would tell stories about them.'

'Did he tell stories about you?' Jordan asked.

'I don't know, I would assume he did when I wasn't there.'

'So where did he get all his stories from do you think?' Jordan asked.

'I have no idea,' Sir Martin said.

'You have been very helpful, Mr Oliver,' Charlie said. ' I want you to write down where the parties were held, and who attended them and what they do for a living.'

Sir Martin began writing. After a couple of minutes he pushed the paper across to Charlie, who picked it up and looked at it. He passed it to Jordan.

'Now one last thing, you will not tell anyone about our little chat,' Charlie said. 'If you should be asked about the police visiting you, all anyone has to know is it was about Mr Parkin's murder. If I question someone and I think you have said anything I will be back with a search team and an arrest warrant, do we understand each other?'

Sir Martin nodded. Charlie and Jordan stood up, left the office, went down the stairs and into the gallery. The young woman was seated at her desk, she watched them as they came towards her. 'Sorry to bother you earlier,' Charlie said as he walked past and went to the door.

Jordan stopped at the desk, 'I want to apologise for the way my fellow officer was with you earlier, he can be a bit horrid sometimes, but if I could make it up to you...'

Charlie looked back at Jordan, smiled and called, 'Jordan come on, leave the girl alone.' Jordan shrugged and followed Charlie out of the door.

'I thought it might be a good idea if we tested Sir Martin's theory about the girls who worked for him and their reputations,' Jordan said.

Charlie laughed. 'Jordan, I have enough trouble with the reputation of my team at the moment without you adding to it, now let's get back to the office and see how everyone else has got on.'

'What are we going to do about Sir Martin and his pimping?' Jordan said as they walked back to the car.

'We will let him think he has got away with it. I don't want anyone panicking until we have solved this murder. But once we do we will nick him,' Charlie said.

'Boss you are a sneaky sod,' Jordan said as they got into the Bentley.

CHAPTER EIGHT

When they arrived back to the Yard, Charlie and Jordan walked into the office to find Harry at the big whiteboard writing on it. Danny was sitting at a table with lots of papers in front of him, calling names, times and dates to Harry.

'How's things looking, Harry?' Charlie asked.

Harry turned to see Charlie and Jordan. 'Our Mr Parkin knew lots of people, but for now I've weeded it down to people mentioned in the book who were also on his messages in his phone. The first ones I put up were the people at his last dinner. I have Mr Parkin here at the top.' Harry pointed to a picture of Parkin. 'We have arrows going from him to each of them, the pictures Danny got from the internet of the other dinner guests. Below that we are starting to put other names. If we get a connection with any of our dinner guests we can start to link it up.'

'Well I am glad you understand it Harry, you lost me when you started speaking,' Jordan said.

'We have a few more interesting names to add to your board,' Charlie said. 'Jordan give him the lists we got from Mr Oliver and Angela Cook, and the one from the security log from her flat.' Jordan handed the sheets of paper to Harry, who had a quick look through them.

'At a quick glance, apart from the names on the board I've seen some of these others in Mr Parkin's book,' Harry said.

'Danny, how did you get on at the BBC?' Charlie asked.

'I don't think there's a murderer among the people I spoke

to. None of them like him, but murder? I don't think so,' Danny said.

'Well leave the white board alone, Harry. I want to sit down with everyone and go over everything we know. Who's going to make the tea?' All eyes turned to Danny.

'The junior officer should always learn to do a bit of crawling,' Jordan said. Danny threw his hands up.

'Yours might have a funny taste,' Danny said to Jordan.

Charlie walked over to Manjitt and asked how she was doing. 'Hello, boss, going well, this is DS Cramer from the fraud squad. He came up to help me crack the passwords that were on a couple of the files. DS Cramer, this is Chief Superintendent Smith.'

The officer sitting beside her stood up and said to Charlie, 'Hello, sir, nice to meet you,' and held out his hand Charlie shook it.

'It's nice of you to come up and help.' Charlie lowered his voice, leaned in close and said slowly, 'I know you will not utter a word to anyone else living on this planet what you have seen or heard in this office. That includes senior officers. Otherwise your bright career might come to a shuddering halt.'

DS Cramer looked at Charlie, whose eyes stared back at him unblinking. 'No, sir, not a word.'

Charlie smiled. 'Okay, sit down, Cramer. So what have we got, Manjitt?'

'A lot of normal stuff,' Manjitt said, 'but it was the two files that DS Cramer cracked open for us that are a little gold mine.'

'Okay, we are having a little debrief on where we are with the case now, and how we are going to go on. So if you don't mind, Cramer, just carry on without Manjitt for a while. Do you want a tea or coffee?'

'A coffee would be nice, thank you, sir,' Cramer said.

'Danny, DS Cramer will have a coffee,' Charlie called out. Danny looked over and nodded.

'Don't forget me, Hippie, I want a tea,' Manjitt said. Charlie walked off to join Harry and Jordan.

'The boss is not as bad as you might think', Manjitt said to Cramer. 'But he does mean what he says.'

'I've heard some rumours about him,' Cramer said. 'He drives expensive cars, has a very big house in the country, always wears designer clothes. People ask where his money comes from.'

'Don't believe all you hear. You couldn't work for a better boss, he will back you to the hilt and is a good, honest copper,' Manjitt said. She walked over to join the others who were seated round Charlie's desk. Danny dropped a coffee off to Cramer, brought everyone their tea and sat down.

'Right. Harry, you give us a brief of what you got so far,' Charlie said.

'I had a word with an inspector who is leading the search for the murder weapon, nothing yet. I rang a few friends in Fleet Street, they told me our Mr Parkin was a bit of snide, nicked stories off others and seemed to have a lot of connections. Forensics gave me one lead: one of the set of fingerprints we got from the house belongs to our Tim Green, who Mr Parkin gave a Jaguar car to. I've started going through the book we recovered and his phone. He has dates and names, and with the names on the papers Jordan just gave me, I can see we have some connections, but where that takes us I don't know yet.'

'Danny, what you got?' Charlie said.

'Well, boss, as I told you earlier all the people I spoke to hated him, but not a murderer amongst them. I still have the presenters to speak to, but I don't think the BBC is hiding our killer,' Danny said.

'Okay, well done, Danny. Jordan, do you want to tell them what we found on our little journey this morning?'

'I had the pleasure of seeing the boss in action,' Jordan began.

'Just get on with the report,' Charlie said.

'I was trying to big you up, boss. Well, we questioned the girl, Angela Cook, she was getting information for Parkin from people she slept with and what she overheard at parties, which in turn, led us to Sir Martin Oliver. She worked for him at his gallery, but also got paid to attend parties where she was available to anyone who wanted to sleep with her. She was not the only one. Sir Martin was running lots of girls and organising the parties for his influential friends. In return they would make sure lots of expensive artwork was bought from his galleries. Parkin found out about these arrangements due to Sir Martin having too much to drink one night and spilling the beans. Parkin then got Angela Cook to work for him. Sir Martin didn't know that, but she was getting doubly paid. And the information she gave Parkin must have been good, her flat is luxurious'.

'So our Sir Martin is a pimp,' Harry said.

'That's what the boss called him,' Jordan said. 'I don't think he took too kindly to that, but he's worried about his reputation, so he came round to our way of thinking.'

'Manjitt, what have you got for us?' Charlie asked.

'Firstly I phoned all the people who attended the dinner party with Parkin the night before he was killed that we hadn't spoken to yet, and arranged to call and speak to them.' She pushed a paper over to Charlie. 'The times are on there, boss, and where they will be, although you can cross Sir Martin off now. The data sticks have been fun. Our Mr Parkin was quite a rich man and careful with it. He had a numbered Swiss bank account, and according to his last entry he has £28 million tucked away in it. But that's not all, he has a number of front companies operating through Jersey and the British Virgin Islands that were buying shares in various companies. That makes it really hard to trace it back to him as owner of the shares. Cramer is going to see if we can do a check on all the shares, and what companies he was buying into.'

'That's good work, Manjitt, complicates this case even more, but good work none the less,' Charlie said. 'I get a whiff of blackmail.'

'Me too, boss,' Harry said. 'The only trouble is we have potential suspects coming out of our ears.'

'Well, we covered the naughty-party end,' Charlie said. 'Sir Martin thinks if he doesn't tell anyone what we know, we will leave him alone, so the names he and Angela Cook gave us won't know what we have and as you see from the list, some of the names are familiar. Put a column on the whiteboard, Harry, of all names we know who went to the parties, also what companies and businesses they are involved in. Manjitt, when you get a name of any company Mr Parkin bought shares in give it to Harry. We can hopefully start to see how Mr Parkin was working his money-making scheme. Let's see if we can make some more progress today. Manjitt, you get back with Cramer and keep digging.' Manjitt stood up and left the group. 'Now, we didn't get to Mr Green this morning because we got sidetracked. So Jordan, you take Danny and go and see our Mr Green. Remember his prints were in Parkin's house, so he is a prime suspect at the moment. Okay, get on with it.' They got up and left Charlie and Harry at the table.

'Looks like we landed another simple case!' Harry said.

'Harry, you would be bored if it just turned out to be the husband what done it,' Charlie said. 'And before I forget, on that list we got from Sir Martin, he wrote down the addresses of where the parties were held. Cross-reference those with the names we have and put it on the board.'

'Will do, our Mr Parkin seems like a bit of a sneaky sod who was building up quite a nest egg,' Harry said.

'You're right, Harry. He never attended the parties himself, so I would imagine it was quite a shock for anyone when he approached them. I am going to pop along to see Crick, to see how the press conference went and keep him off our backs,' Charlie said.

Jordan and Danny parked the squad car outside the house of Tim Green. It was a normal semi-detached. 'I don't see a Jaguar parked anywhere,' Danny said.

They got out and walked up the garden path to the door and rang the bell. After a minute it was opened by a young woman. 'Yes?' she said.

'Hello, miss, we're police officers,' Jordan said, showing his warrant card. 'We would like to speak to a Mr Green. Is he in?'

'No, sorry, he's at work. Why, what's wrong?' she asked. 'I'm his fiancée.'

'Nothing to be worried about. Does he own a Jaguar car?' Jordan asked.

'Yes, he does.' The woman had a worried look on her face.

'We had a report it was involved in an accident last week and drove off,' Jordan said.

'That can't be right, the Jaguar is his pride and joy, it doesn't have a scratch on it,' she replied.

'Sounds like someone is using a copy of his number plate on their car. We will just need to speak to him so we can check and rule him out of our inquiries. Could you tell us where he works?' Jordan asked.

'Yes, of course. He works for Bailey and Crest, they're

theatrical agents.' She gave Jordan the address.

'Thank you, miss, we will be able to clear things up, sounds like there's nothing to be worried about,' Jordan said.

They went back to the car. 'I like your style,' Danny said. 'A dodgy number plate, quick thinking.'

Jordan started the car. 'That's why I am a detective sergeant and you're not,' he laughed as they pulled away.

Charlie was sitting in Assistant Commissioner Crick's office talking over the case. Crick's tan was more orange than normal. Charlie suspected he had topped it up because of his appearance at the press conference.

'The press conference went quite well today,' Crick said, 'but they will want to hear we are making more progress in the coming days. He was after all a top journalist himself, so they won't let this story rest. Look at these.' He held up a few of the morning papers which had the story on their front pages. 'And it's the same on the television, it's the main lead on the news bulletins. I will be looking for a bit more meat to give them in tomorrow's press conference, Charlie, so what progress are we making?'

'We have lots of people who might have a motive,' Charlie said, 'but I can't say we are any nearer knowing who did it or why. We have found out he was not the nicest man in the world, not what the public saw on the television. And I think he may have been blackmailing someone, or more than one person.'

Crick looked astonished at what Charlie said. 'Blackmail, what leads you to think that?' Crick asked.

'We've discovered a Swiss bank account with millions in it and front companies he had control of. Also just to warn you, sir, we have uncovered a high-class prostitution ring that he has connections to.'

'Well, I can't go in front of the press and tell them that. I want something about how we are chasing down the killer and hope to have an arrest soon,' Crick said. He had a worried look on his face.

'If I thought that, I would tell you,' Charlie said, 'but I think we have only scratched the surface. We still have a lot of people to speak to before we make some concrete conclusions.'

'Okay, Charlie, just put as much as you think we can give out in your report for tomorrow's press conference. And I do mean your report, don't get your Chief Inspector to write it up,' Crick said.

'Yes, sir. I will fill in as much information as I can for you. Is there anything else?' Charlie asked.

'One thing, I have had the Commissioner on again. He has had Lord Dorres' solicitors on about his treatment when he was questioned. Have you got to the bottom of that yet?' Crick asked.

'No, not yet, but I am sure it was just a misunderstanding,' Charlie said, standing up.

'Well, put it in your report for me so I can get back to the Commissioner. I don't want him on my back.' Crick waved his finger in Charlie's direction.

'Yes, sir.' Charlie left and made his way back to the squad's office.

Jordan and Danny pulled into a small car park next to the offices of Bailey and Crest theatrical agents.

'That looks like our Jaguar,' Jordan said. He parked next to it and checked the registration. 'Yes, that's it.' They got out, locked the car and entered the building, walking up to the reception desk in the lobby.

A receptionist smiled at them as they approached and asked, 'Can I help you, gentlemen?'

'We would like to speak to Tim Green,' Jordan said.

'Can I ask who wants him, please?' she said, still smiling.

Jordan took out his warrant card and held it up. 'We're the police. I'm Detective Sergeant Rhodes.'

'If you would just wait a minute I will get hold of him for you.' She pressed a number on the phone console in front of her and started to speak.

Danny and Jordan walked away from the reception desk to stand by the door. 'Have you noticed how lovely the teeth of all receptionists are?' Danny said.

'You know, I worry about you sometimes,' Jordan replied. 'I have no idea how your mind works.'

'No, it's true, you just see the next time we have to go into an office building and speak to a receptionist.'

They were interrupted by a man approaching them. 'Are you the police?' Jordan nodded. 'I'm Tim Green. You wanted to speak to me.'

'Yes, sir, I am DS Rhodes and this is DC Kane. We want to speak to you about your car.'

'Yes, my fiancée rang me and said you had called at the house. If you want to follow me we can speak in my office.' They followed him out of the reception area, along a passage and into a small office. 'Please take a seat,' he said. Jordan and Danny sat down. 'Do you want some coffee or tea?' Tim Green took a seat in the chair across the desk from them.

'No, thank you, sir.' Jordan said. 'What is it you do here?'

'We are agents for actors, writers, anyone who needs a contract negotiated in the film, television or associated industries,' Tim Green said.

'So you have lots of stars coming into the office, must be exciting,' Danny said.

'It can be, but there's a lot of contract work done before we would see them. It might be a new film or television programme that someone wants them to do, we would iron out all the details then have the meeting,' Tim Green said, smiling.

'So you do all that?' Jordan asked.

'I'm part of a team that run through the proposals that are sent to us and pass them on to the senior agents, who deal with the actors personally.'

'So you don't meet any of the stars,' Danny said.

'Yes, I might get called into a meeting when there are things the star might not be happy with or wants changed. I would try and redraft it to suit them. But that's enough of my work. I know how busy the police are. My fiancée said you had a query about my car being in an accident. I can assure you I haven't, its parked outside in the car park if you want to take a look.'

'Yes, sir we saw it,' Danny said. 'Don't worry, we don't think it's been in an accident. It must have cost a few bob. You agents must get well paid, you don't have any vacancies do you?'

'That's a relief, we don't get as well paid as you would imagine, but I always dreamed of owning a Jaguar so when the opportunity came to get it, I did.'

'Did you know the man from the television who was killed, Gerald Parkin?' Jordan asked. 'Did your agency act for him?'

'Gerald Parkin, yes, we did all his contract work, I was shocked to hear about his murder,' Tim Green said.

'Did he come to the offices much? Did you meet him?' Danny said.

'Yes, I met him twice when he came here, he was a very nice man.'

'You never met him socially for dinner or went to the BBC to see him?' Jordan asked.

Tim Green smiled and laughed. 'I'm not senior enough for that.'

'Have you worked here long?' Danny said.

'Since I was eighteen,' Tim Green said, still smiling.

'Tim, we have not been completely honest with you,' Jordan said. 'We did want to speak to you about your car, but we wanted to know where you got it from.'

Tim Green looked slightly confused. 'Where I got it from?'

'Yes, where did you buy it?' Danny asked.

'Oh, I got it from a Jaguar dealer in London,' Tim Green replied.

'Did you buy it for cash, or is it on finance?' Jordan said.

'I'm sorry I am a bit confused. Why should you want to know that?' Tim asked.

Jordan exchanged looks with Danny. 'Well you see, Tim,' Jordan said, 'w=e are part of the team who are investigating Gerald Parkin's murder, and your name came up in the investigation. We wondered if there is anything you can tell us that might help.'

'I don't think so, as I said I only ever met him a couple of times here,' Tim Green said. He moved in his chair uneasily.

'I get the impression you're not telling us the truth,' Danny said. 'You have a police record, don't you.'

'Yes, but that was a fight outside a pub years ago.' Tim Green had lost his smile and now had a worried look on his face.

'Now listen, Tim,' Jordan said. 'We are dealing with a murder, not some pub fight so you start telling the truth. I don't want any more lies.'

'I have no idea what you are talking about,' Tim Green said.

Jordan stood up, walked behind Tim and looked out the window. 'You've upset him now, Tim,' Danny said, pointing at Jordan. 'I will have to put up with him being in a bad mood for the rest of the day,' Danny leaned forward. 'Tim, I don't think you realise we would not have come all this way if we didn't have a reason to. Now think carefully before you answer any more questions because if he thinks…' Danny pointed at Jordan again, '…you're not telling the truth, he is going to tell me to arrest you for murder.'

Tim Green's face stiffened and he went pale. Danny and Jordan stayed silent, letting the last sentence hang in the air. Jordan turned around from the window, walked back around the desk and sat down. Tim Green looked at him but said nothing.

'Last chance, Tim,' Jordan said. 'Where did you get the car from?'

Tim Green ran his hand over his face. 'I think I should speak to a solicitor.'

'You are a silly boy,' Jordan said. He and Danny stood up. 'You can do the honours, Hippie.'

Danny walked round the desk. 'Stand up please, Tim,' he said. Tim Green stood up, his face showed confusion and worry. Danny took some handcuffs out. 'Turn around and put your hands behind your back.' Tim turned around. 'Tim Green, I am arresting you on suspicion of murder.' He then read him his rights.

'Murder? I have not murdered anyone,' Tim Green said, his voice cracking.

'We will question you later at the station. You had a chance to speak to us here, but now don't say anything else till then,' Danny told him.

'But I have not murdered anyone, you are making a mistake,' Tim Green said in desperation.

Danny pulled him to the office door, Jordan opened it. They walked him through the reception. The girl smiled, Danny waved to her. She stopped smiling when she saw the handcuffs on Tim Green. 'He will be out for the rest of the day,' Danny said to her.

Jordan stopped at the reception desk and had a conversation with the receptionist, who handed him a ledger. He turned a few pages and handed it back, walked over to Danny and the left the building with Tim Green between them.

Charlie walked back into the office. 'How are you two getting on?' he asked Manjitt and Cramer as he came to the desk where they were working.

Manjitt looked up. 'Hello, boss, it's going well. We have a list of share purchases and companies and the way he moved his money around. He was a smart man or had good advice. He has quite a few million pounds in shares as well as the money in the Swiss bank. I got his normal bank account details sent over, none of it appears in there, it's just wages from the BBC and a few other media organisations, nothing out of the ordinary.'

'Have you been giving Harry the details of what you have found out so far?' Charlie asked.

'Yes, but I don't know how he keeps track,' Manjitt said as she looked over towards Harry, whose desk and the one next to it where covered in paper. The whiteboard had different coloured lines snaking across it.

'As long as he knows what he's doing,' Charlie said. 'Cramer, how are you getting on? I hope you're not finding working with Manjitt too tough?'

'Boss, can you leave us alone?' Manjitt said. Charlie walked off smiling. He got over to where Harry was standing by the whiteboard and studied it. 'You know, Harry, I could swear when we visited Sir Martin Oliver's modern art gallery this morning he had something on show like this with a price tag of twenty thousand pounds.'

'It just shows what hidden talents I have,' Harry said. 'How was your meeting with Crick, what shade his tan at the moment?'

'It's a nice orange tone, and he wants a bit more in the report for tomorrow, and I shouldn't get anyone else to write it,' Charlie looked at Harry. 'Spice it up a bit.'

'Will do, boss,' Harry said.

'And I have to get to the bottom of the complaint Lord Dorres made about Inspector Davis.' Charlie smiled as he said it.

'I will put it in the report,' Harry said.

'Have you had any word from Jordan?' Charlie asked.

'No, nothing yet. I rang the search team, they have had no luck finding a weapon. I took a call from those two presenters Danny didn't see earlier at the BBC, I questioned them, don't think we have anything there.'

'How is your work of art coming on?' Charlie said, pointing at the whiteboard.

'I think I can start to see a few links, but we need a bit more background information on the companies.'

'Well I'm glad you can see some links, I defy anyone else seeing them,' Charlie said looking at the whiteboard. 'Tomorrow we are going to question the other people who were at the dinner with Parkin. We will have a briefing in the morning before we do. Tell everyone to be in for nine, I am off to see a builder.'

'What are you having done, boss?' Harry asked.

'I decided to have a swimming pool built next to the garage. Thought it would be nice in the summer.'

'Don't tell Jordan, he will want to use it all the time.' Harry laughed.

'See you in the morning, Harry, and don't stay too late.' Charlie turned and walked towards the door. He stopped halfway turned and came back, 'I just had a thought, those companies you said we needed more background on. I will make a phone call later, so make a list up for me and give it to me first thing in the morning, and bring a spare set of clothes in with you tomorrow, we will be having dinner out. You can crash at my place after.'

'Boss, what will people say?' Harry asked.

'That you're after promotion, see you in the morning.' Charlie walked off, stopping at Manjitt's desk. 'Cramer, this investigation is taking slightly longer and going off in directions we didn't expect,' Charlie said. 'If I spoke to your commanding officer and asked if I could keep you on the team till it's finished, would you mind?'

'No, sir, it's interesting,' Cramer said.

'That's good, I will sort it out.' Charlie turned and walked to the door, stopped, waved his hand towards Harry. Charlie pointed at Cramer and gave a thumbs up sign. Harry nodded.

Jordan and Danny came into the office after booking Tim Green into custody and having him put in a cell till they wanted to question him. 'Well you two, how did it go?' Harry asked as he sorted through the piles of paper on his desk.

'We have him in the cells downstairs,' Jordan said. 'He didn't want to talk to us without his solicitor, so we nicked him on suspicion of murder, just to shake him up a bit. We will let him stew for a while. The only problem is I checked his firm's signing-in book, he was at work on time and never left the building on the morning of the murder.'

'What do you make of him?' Harry asked.

'He knows something, and after sitting in the cells for a while, I think we should get him to talk to us,' Jordan said.

'Hippie, what do you think?' Harry asked.

'Jordan's right, he clammed up as soon as we started asking where he got the Jaguar from, and he said he only met Gerald Parkin at the office where he works, so we can hit him with the fingerprint evidence once we get him talking about the Jaguar,' Danny said.

'That's good, the boss wants everyone in the office for a briefing at nine tomorrow,' Harry said, 'but before you go home, see the custody sergeant and let him know we are keeping Mr Green in overnight while we make further enquires. You can break the news to him through the cell door. He can have all night to think things over.'

'Will do Harry, see you in the morning,' Jordan said.

'See you tomorrow, Harry,' Danny said. The two of them turned away and walked across the office towards the door. Halfway there Jordan nudged Danny and nodded his head towards Manjitt and Cramer. They both changed direction and headed towards Manjitt's desk.

'Manjitt, how are you two getting on with things?' Jordan asked.

Manjitt looked up. 'It's going well, we've found out some interesting things,' she replied, and she introduced Cramer to Jordan and Danny.

'How are you enjoying working so closely with Manjitt?' Jordan asked Cramer.

'Yes, it's been interesting,' Cramer said.

'Don't make to many sudden movements when you reach for something, you're likely to get your arm broken,' Danny said.

'You're right, Hippie.' Jordan laughed. 'Remember the last officer who came in to help out. When he tried to get hold of Manjitt's undercover secrets, he went flying across the office.'

'Will you two sod off and let us get on with some work?' Manjitt said. Harry had watched Jordan and Danny divert towards Manjitt.

'You two, get out,' Harry called. Jordan and Danny looked around.

'We're going, Harry, just wanted to make sure Manjitt was getting all the hands she needed,' Jordan said. He jumped quickly backwards just avoiding an elbow Manjitt shot out. He and Danny walked out of the office laughing.

'Manjitt you can call it a day now, briefing at nine in the morning,' Harry called across the office.

Manjitt and Cramer stood up. 'Okay Harry, see you in the morning.'

'Cramer, that includes you,' Harry said.

Cramer looked at Harry, 'Oh, yes, sir, nine o'clock. Have you got to rush off anywhere?' Cramer asked Manjitt. 'I was going to go and get a drink, wondered if you wanted to join me before you went home.'

'Yes, why not?' Manjitt said.

Harry watched them leave the office. He'd better get the report written up for AS Crick before he left, and put together all the company names that have come up from Gerald Parkin's data sticks. He would phone Charlie and let him know about Tim Green.

CHAPTER NINE

The team had all assembled in the office just before nine and Charlie spoke to them. 'Firstly DS Cramer will be staying with us while we are on this investigation, we've been short-handed since Oscar was killed, so welcome, Cramer.' Everyone nodded around the table. 'Today is going to be a busy day, there are a lot of things we need to clear up. Jordan, you have Tim Green in the cells downstairs, you can start with questioning him. While you do that, Danny, I want you to go to his house and search it. Call the local nick and get them to send a couple of officers along to help you. We might turn up something that ties him into Parkin, seize any computers and paperwork you find, we can sort through it when you get back. Manjitt, how much more is there on those data sticks you have been going through?'

'I think we are nearly at the end,' Manjitt said. 'Still some more figures we have to follow, but we should have it all sorted by lunchtime.'

'That's good,' Charlie said, 'the eye still looks a bit sore.'

'It's okay, boss, I get the stitches out next week and the swelling is going down,' Manjitt said, putting her hand to the swelling.

'Now, later today, Manjitt has arranged for us to go and interview the other people who were at the dinner with Parkin. If we believe Parkin was blackmailing people and from our chats with Sir Martin Oliver and Angela Cook it looks that way, we have to assume some of the people at the dinner were being blackmailed. So when we question them bear that in mind.

They're not going to come out and tell us he was, and blackmail is a good reason for murder. Harry, do you want to say anything?'

'We still have no murder weapon,' Harry said. 'I spoke to the inspector who's leading the search again. He's not hopeful. I've put it in Crick's daily report, he might ask the public in the area to have a look round when he does his press conference. You never know, we might get lucky and we still have one set of prints outstanding from Parkin's house. We know Tim Green, who's in the cells downstairs, was in the house, and Parkin himself, but one set of prints is unknown. So make sure one question you ask people is have they been to Parkin's house.'

'Right everyone, let's get moving,' Charlie said. 'We will get together again at lunchtime to sort out who's going to question the other dinner guests.' The team went off.

Harry passed over a sheet of paper to Charlie. 'That's Crick's daily report,' he said. Charlie read through it, looked up at Harry and was about to say something but continued reading. When he finished he put the paper on the table. 'I think I covered everything you wanted,' Harry said, 'And I got the bit in about the public helping looking for the weapon.'

'One of your better reports,' Charlie said. 'I think Crick will appreciate getting all his questions answered.' Charlie looked at the paper again and reread it. 'And this has already gone up to him?'

'You told me to make sure Crick had his daily report first thing,' Harry said.

Charlie smiled. 'Thank you, Harry. My meeting with him will be interesting. Did you make up the list of companies and share-buying that we have so far on Parkin?' Harry passed another sheet of paper over. Charlie looked through it. 'I want you to email it over to Julian. I spoke to him last night. He will get some of his friends from the city onto it for us. That way if anyone hears that people are asking questions it looks like just another city firm and not the police. He will be joining us for dinner tonight at my house, and going over anything he has found out.' Julian had been one of Charlie's most trusted friends for many years, and did all his financial investments and handled all his money. After speaking to Julian last night, he knew he was richer than he had ever been.

'I hope Maggie will be cooking something nice,' Harry said. Maggie was Charlie's housekeeper. Along with her husband Mike, they kept the house and land around it looking great.

'When I said you were coming over, Harry, she said roast lamb would be on the menu,' Charlie said.

'Lovely, if she wasn't married to Mike I would ask her to marry me,' Harry said, taking the list of company names and share purchases back from Charlie. He began typing an email to send over to Julian.

Charlie stood up. 'I am off to see Crick,' he said.

Jordan was sitting in the interview room when the door opened and Tim Green came in, followed by a constable.

'Sit down,' Jordan said, pointing to the chair across the table from him. The constable closed the door and stood inside. Tim Green look dishevelled and his clothes were all creased as he sat down and looked at Jordan, who pressed the button on the tape recorder. 'Good morning, Mr Green. I hope you slept well.' Tim Green looked at Jordan, but said nothing. 'Now I want to ask you about your relationship with Gerald Parkin.'

'I am not saying anything until my solicitor arrives,' Tim Green said.

Jordan sat for a moment. 'Would you like some tea or coffee?' he asked. He got no reply. 'Now, it's in your best interests to answer my questions. If you have nothing to hide there's no reason not to talk to me.' Tim Green still said nothing, just stared at Jordan, who waited a few minutes before saying, 'I am suspending this interview.' He looked at his watch and said the time out loud for the tape, stood, told the constable to take him back to his cell and left the room. He made his way to the custody area, and spoke to the sergeant there. He found out that they had got a phone call from a firm of solicitors who were representing Tim Green. He asked that they be phoned and told Tim Green would be questioned later that morning. Jordan went away to get himself some tea.

Danny arrived at Tim Green's house with two officers from the local station. He had gone there first after speaking to an inspector about the search, who had said he could have a couple of officers to help him. He had chatted to the officers who would be with him, explaining what he was looking for in the search. As he parked, he saw that the Jaguar was on the drive. He walked up the path, followed by the officers, and rang the door bell. It was opened by Tim Green's fiancée, who Danny recognised. 'Hello, miss, we are here to search the house. I have a warrant.'

She looked at him and said, 'You'd better come in.' Danny entered, followed by the two officers. She shut the door and led them to the front room.

'If I can ask you to remain in here, we will try and be as quick as we can,' Danny said.

'Tim has not killed anyone,' she said.

'I'm afraid he has not been very helpful to us in proving that,' Danny said. 'If he had just answered the questions we asked, it could have all been cleared up. I will leave one of these officers here with you while we have a look around.' Danny told one of the constables to stay in the room and he led the other one upstairs. They started in the main bedroom but found nothing of interest, and searched the rest of the upstairs. Danny got the constable to get up in the attic space, but after five minutes he came down, dirty but with no finds. They then went downstairs and had a good look in the kitchen but again found nothing. Danny and the constable went back into the front room.

'You found nothing, then?' Tim's fiancée said. 'That's because there's nothing to find.'

'We will just have a look round here,' Danny told the two constables to start searching the front room.

'Where's Tim's computer,' Danny asked.

'He doesn't have one,' she said. Danny looked at her for a moment.

'You are joking,' he said. 'I can see by the charger plugged in over there…' Danny pointed to the corner, '…that someone has a computer or laptop in this house.'

'He must have taken it to work,' she said.

'Well, from not having one, to taking it to work, which is it?' Danny asked. She looked at him but said nothing and shrugged her shoulders. The two officers were still searching, opening up drawers and cupboards and pulling out books and papers. 'If he hasn't done anything wrong and you want to help him, why are you being so evasive?' Danny asked. Again she made no reply. 'I see his car is parked outside. Can I have the keys to search it, please?' Danny said.

'I don't have them. Tim has the only set,' she said.

'Now we both know you're lying about that, don't we?' Danny said, 'because his car was parked at his work yesterday.' She said nothing and shrugged again. 'Do you really want to help him, because if you do you're not doing a good job. Do you have a car?'

'No, we only have Tim's,' she said.

'So where are the keys?' Danny asked. She said nothing

again. The two constables both signalled to Danny that they had found nothing. He told them to have a look in the back garden. 'You do know Tim is in very serious trouble, don't you? He is under suspicion of murder,' Danny said.

'Tim has not hurt anyone,' she said.

'Well if you really believe that, you would be doing all you can to prove it.' Danny looked at her but she made no reply. 'Now if you give me the car keys I will just have a look through it and we will be on our way.'

'I told you I don't have them,' she said.

'But you must have gone and got the car from Tim's work,' Danny said.

'I don't drive,' she replied.

'So who got the car for you?' Danny asked. She said nothing again. 'Look, I know you think we just want to blame Tim for the murder, but we want to catch the killer. If you know Tim didn't do it, why not help us to rule him out of the investigation?' Again she sat quiet. Danny walked to the window at the back of the house that overlooked the garden. He saw the two constables at the far end searching amongst the bushes. He turned and came back. 'Did Tim know Gerald Parkin well?' he asked.

'I don't know anything,' she said, her voice slightly cracking. Danny heard the two officers come back in from the garden. They told him they had found nothing. He told them to stay in the front room with Tim Green's fiancée. Danny left the front room, went outside the house and to the Jaguar. He walked around it trying the doors and boot. They were all locked. He took his phone out and called Harry. After two rings it was answered.

'Hippie, how have you got on at the house?' Harry asked.

'It's as clean as a whistle, Harry, nothing,' Danny said.

'Nothing, no paperwork, computer or anything?' Harry asked.

'That's it, Harry, nothing. There was a computer or laptop but that's gone, and any paperwork was just normal household stuff, bills and letters,' Danny replied.

'That's a bit strange, but maybe his fiancée has hidden them,' Harry said.

'I don't know, Harry. She seems really upset about Tim and is protesting his innocence,' Danny said, 'but I get the feeling she wants to say more but won't. And his car is parked outside the house; we left it at his work's car park yesterday. She let slip she doesn't drive, so how it got back here she's not saying. Also she says she has no keys for the car and we can't find any.'

'Okay, Hippie, you get back to the Yard,' Harry said. 'I will arrange for a tow truck to come over and bring the car back here for us to have a good look at. Tell the officers to stay with the car till the tow truck arrives.'

After speaking to Danny, Harry called Jordan over, who had been sitting reading the morning paper and having a cup of tea. He told him what had happened at the house search. 'Have a look through any of the things Tim Green had in his possession when you brought him in,' Harry said. 'Check his phone, get all his contacts and a list of all the phone calls he's made lately and messages.'

Charlie was sitting with AS Crick, who was reading the daily report. Charlie noticed Crick's eyebrows go up a few times in an expression of surprise as he read. Crick laid it down on the table in front of him. 'An interesting report, Charlie,' he said.

'I thought so too,' Charlie replied. 'I think everything you asked for is covered.'

'The man you have in custody,' Crick asked, 'is he our main suspect?'

'No, he didn't do it, but he knows something, he says he has not been to the house, yet his prints are there and we know

Gerald Parkin brought him a Jaguar. But we don't know why yet,' Charlie said.

'So if I am asked at the press conference about him, what should I say?' Crick asked.

'Just the usual, he's helping with inquires,' Charlie replied. Crick nodded.

'And the blackmail angle. You really think Gerald Parkin was a blackmailer? He was at the top of his career, why would he do it?' Crick said.

'I think it's a strong possibility, as to why I don't know yet, but we don't want that line of enquiry getting out yet,' Charlie said.

'And you also mention a prostitution racket and organised parties amongst the rich and famous,' Crick said. 'Charlie is this investigation going to cause me a lot of aggravation?'

'You know me sir, where the leads take us we go. Noone is beyond being questioned,' Charlie said. Crick nodded and picked the report up from the desk.

'Yes, Charlie, and that brings us to the Lord Dorres complaint and your report.' Crick emphasised the words, your report, looking directly at Charlie. Crick looked back at the report and carried on. 'Let me quote the piece about Lord Dorres, Charlie. It says there might have been a cultural misunderstanding due to the class divide and Lord Dorres thinking everyone should bow and scrape to him.' He looked up from reading.

'I think from questioning my team, that's the idea I got,' Charlie said.

Crick put the report down. 'And when I speak to the Commissioner's office, I should say that we think Lord Dorres is a snob.'

'I don't think that was the phrase in the report, sir, but if you want to put it that way it might sum it up better,' Charlie said.

'I will let you know how the Commissioner's office

appreciate our take on the class system, Charlie,' Crick said. 'If anything comes out of the press conference I will let you know.'

'Thank you, sir.' Charlie got up and left.

Jordan was sitting in a room off the custody area, writing the names and numbers down that were in Tim Green's phone and the last lot of calls he made. He noted Gerald Parkin's name was among his contacts. There was a knock at the door and a constable put his head round it and told him the custody sergeant said Tim Green's solicitor had arrived and was in the interview room waiting for him. Jordan said to tell the sergeant he would be there in a couple of minutes. He carried on writing the last few numbers down. When he was done he took the phone back to Tim Green's property bag.

When he entered the interview room and saw Tim Green's solicitor was sitting beside him, he introduced himself to Jordan as Mr Pannis from HDS Group Solicitors. Jordan sat, pressed the tape machine on, stated who was present in the room and began the interview.

'Now, Tim I want to ask you about your relationship with Gerald Parkin. You said you only met him a couple of times, is that correct?' Jordan asked.

Tim Green looked at his solicitor who nodded. 'Yes, that's right,' he said.

'And you only ever met him at your place of work,' Jordan asked.

Tim Green looked at his solicitor again. Mr Pannis leaned in and whispered into Tim's ear. Tim nodded and said 'No, not just at work.'

'So would you like to tell me where else you met him?' Jordan asked.

'I went to his house once to see him.'

'So why didn't you tell me this yesterday?' Jordan asked.

Tim again looked at Mr Pannis, who leaned in and whispered in his ear again. 'I was confused and frightened and didn't know what to say,' Tim said.

'When did you go to his house?' Jordan said.

'A couple of weeks ago.'

'Why did you go there?'

Tim Green again turned to Mr Pannis, who stopped making notes and leaned in and again whispered into Tim's ear. 'He gave me a car and after discussing it with my fiancée we thought we should give it back, as I hadn't done anything much for him to warrant him giving me a car.'

'And what did he say?' Jordan asked.

'He said he thought I did a good job on his contracts and it was just a thank you. I said I couldn't accept it but he was insistent that I did. He said he liked giving gifts, so I kept it.'

'Why didn't you just tell us that yesterday, it would have saved a lot of police time,' Jordan asked.

It was Mr Pannis who spoke. 'I think Mr Green has answered that question already and I believe there is no reason for his continued detention.'

Jordan looked at the solicitor. He was right. He had nothing to continue holding Tim Green. 'Just one more question,' Jordan said. 'Apart from the work on his contracts, did Gerald Parkin ever ask you to do anything else for him?'

It was Mr Pannis who spoke. 'I think Mr Green has answered all your questions. If you are not going to charge him, he would like to go now.'

Jordan knew that he was not going to get any more. 'Okay Tim, you are free to go. You can pick up your things from the custody sergeant. The constable will take you there.' He switched off the tape.

Jordan sat in the chair as Tim Green and his solicitor got up and followed the constable from the room.

Charlie was sitting with Harry relating Crick's thoughts on the daily report. 'I would say he thought it was interesting, but he sounded a bit reluctant about telling the Commissioner about our interpretation of the Lord Dorres' interview,' Charlie said.

'I think he will explain it in his way, for as long as I have known him he has a way with words,' Harry said.

Charlie laughed. 'He's a bit like you then, Harry.'

Danny walked into the office and came over to them. 'Boss, Harry,' he said, 'got nothing at all from the house.'

'You didn't find any paperwork?' Charlie asked.

'Nothing, no paperwork and there was not a computer in the house. How unusual is that in this day and age. It was like everything we might want to see had been cleared out,' Danny said. 'Hopefully the car should be dropped off here within the hour. We might find something in that.'

Jordan came into the office and walked over and joined them. No luck with Tim Green, I had to let him go,' he said. 'His solicitor pointed out we had no reason to hold him, but I got all the numbers from his phone. There is one strange thing, last person he phoned from the station on his mobile was his fiancée. The custody sergeant told me he didn't use the station phone at all, so it must have been his fiancée who contacted the solicitor for him.'

'She never mentioned anything about solicitors when I spoke to her,' Danny said.

'How did you get on at the house?' Jordan asked.

'Nothing at all there, but we have the car coming in,' Danny said.

'Jordan, run a check on his solicitors, see if they are local to him,' Charlie said. 'Danny, you get his bank details, and those of his fiancée, let's see if they had any strange money going through their accounts. If they have we can bring the two of them in for a chat. Do you think he is our killer, Jordan?'

'I don't think so, but he is hiding something,' Jordan replied.

'Boss, you better put a call through to Crick, let him know our suspect has been released before he announces we have a man in custody,' Harry said.

'Good thought, Harry, I will do that. But in the meantime you two get some more background on Tim Green, see where it takes us.' Charlie looked at his watch. 'Get on to that and in half an hour I want you back here.' Jordan and Danny left. Charlie looked at the whiteboard. 'You want to give me an update, Harry.'

Harry stood up and walked to the whiteboard. 'All these people here…' He pointed to a column of names on the left hand side of the board, '…were the last people to have seen him alive. I have put a line through the BBC staff that we have ruled out. These names here…' he pointed to a second smaller column on the right '…are people whose names appear in both his phone and the notebook we found. This column here…' Harry pointed to the bottom of the whiteboard, '…are the people whose names you got from Angela Cook and Sir Martin Oliver as attending the parties. As you can see, I have linked them up when they appear in more than one column. In the middle I have company names that Manjitt has given me and ones that were in his notebook. You can see I have lines going from the various names to companies. Beside the company names in red are the amount of shares and value Gerald Parkin had in them.'

'He had a lot of money invested in some of them,' Charlie said.

'Most of the share purchases were made through these two companies.' Harry pointed to two company names written below Gerald Parkin's name. 'So it would be hard for anyone to see if it was Parkin buying the shares.' Harry came and sat down. 'He had a bit of a secret life, our Mr Parkin. Noone liked him at the BBC and it didn't seem to bother him, but away from there he went to all the most exclusive dinner parties and moved in high society circles.'

Charlie nodded and said, 'He was probably blackmailing quite a few of them, and they are hardly going to shout about it, they have reputations to protect.'

Manjitt and Cramer came over. 'That's the last of the company names and figures.' She handed Harry a sheet of paper. 'We have totalled it all up,' she said. 'Apart from the £28 million he had in the Swiss bank, he owned shares to the value of £16 million when he was killed.'

'He was a very rich man and that's a lot of money to move around,' Charlie said. They were joined by Danny and Jordan coming back into the office. 'Manjitt was just filling us in on Gerald Parkin's total wealth.' Danny and Jordan looked at Manjitt.

'Well, how much?' Danny asked

'In total we can see he was worth about £44 million,' she said.

Danny whistled softly and said, 'I knew the BBC paid well, but that's a bit over the top.'

'Boss, he is nearly as rich as you,' Jordan said.

'No, the boss is premier league,' Danny said.

'My bank balance is not the issue, and if you two want a Christmas card you should remember that,' Charlie said. Once the team had stopped laughing, Charlie carried on. 'Now we are going to question the rest of the people from the dinner party. Harry has already questioned Lord Dorres, but I know he wants to get back and see the butler, so you take DS Cramer with you.' Harry nodded.

'There goes the career of an up and coming detective sergeant,' Jordan said as all the team looked at Cramer and laughed.

'Shut up, Jordan,' Charlie said. 'Your career path is in Harry's hands.'

'I can honestly say I have never worked with a better senior officer than Harry,' Jordan said.

'Well, now you have done your crawling,' Charlie carried on 'You and Manjitt are going to question Sir Mark Coale, he's in the oil business. Danny you're coming with me, we'll question Stanley and Amanda Moore. And remember one of them may be our killer and Gerald Parkin could have been blackmailing any of them. Grab yourselves a bite to eat and we will all be off. Harry, dig the list out that we got of people who had visited Angela Cook at her flat, I want to take it with me.' The team walked away, leaving Charlie and Harry sitting chatting.

Cramer turned to Manjitt and asked, 'Chief Inspector Davis, what's he like?'

'As sharp as a knife, he doesn't suffer fools and if you have a point to make say it, right or wrong, Harry will want to hear it,' Manjitt said.

'You will get an education in the art of subtle questioning when you're out with him today,' Jordan said as he picked up a cup and poured himself a coffee Danny laughed.

CHAPTER TEN

Harry and Cramer arrived at the London address of Lord Dorres. They couldn't find a parking space near the house so had to park a few streets away. They left the car and made their way back towards the house. As they turned the corner into the road Lord Dorres' house was in, Harry put his arm out and stopped Cramer, and said, 'That's a face I recognise from the past.' Cramer looked at where Harry was indicating. He saw a tall well-dressed black man leaving Lord Dorres' house. The man turned away from their direction and got into a car parked further along the road. 'Get the registration number,' Harry said. Cramer crossed the road and walked quickly to close the space between him and the car, which pulled out of the parking bay and drove away. Cramer crossed back over to join Harry. 'Did you get the number?' Harry asked.

'Yes, who was that?' Cramer said.

'He's a drug dealer,' Harry replied. 'I came across him a few times when I was in the drugs squad years ago. He went down for a few years, but I guess he's out and up to his bad habits again.' They carried on walking to Lord Dorres' house. Harry rang the bell and turned to Cramer and said, 'If you want to ask any questions, you just chime in. Don't wait for my invitation, and make notes.' Cramer nodded. The door was opened by Cameron the butler, he looked at Harry, recognition coming to his face.

'Hello, sir,' he said. 'I am afraid His Lordship is not at home at the moment, and in any case I have instructions that you should only be permitted to enter if you have made a prior appointment.' Harry turned to Cramer, a smile on his face. He turned back to Cameron and said, 'So when will he be back?'

'Not till later on this morning,' Cameron replied.

'It's just as well I don't want to see your boss then, it's you I have come to see, Cameron.' Harry stepped forward and eased his way inside, 'Come on, Cramer.' DS Cramer followed Harry in. 'Now, Cameron, is there somewhere we can talk?' Cameron was still holding the door open, but he slowly shut it.

'I don't know that there is anything I will be able to tell you,' Cameron said, 'but follow me, we can talk in the kitchen.' He led them through the house to the kitchen.

When they entered, Harry took a seat at a large wooden table that was in the centre of the room. 'Why don't you sit here, Cameron, and we can get started and I will be able to decide if you don't know anything.' Cameron sat down opposite Harry, DS Cramer stood by a giant fridge-freezer. 'You don't have a cold drink, do you?' Harry asked.

'There is some orange juice in the fridge,' Cameron said and went to stand.

'No, sit down, my officer can get me a glass. Do you want some?' Harry said. Cameron nodded. Cramer opened the fridge and removed a jug of orange juice.

'The glasses are in that cupboard,' Cameron pointed. Cramer got a glass out and poured and passed the orange juice to Harry, who took a drink.

'Very nice,' Harry said and put the glass down on the table. 'Have you worked for your boss long?'

'I have been in His Lordship's employ about eleven years,' Cameron replied.

'That's a long time, what did you do before?' Harry asked.

'I worked in a restaurant in the West End.'

'So how did you come to get this job, did you see an advert and apply for it?'

'No, His Lordship offered me the job personally.'

'Why was that?' Harry said.

'You would have to ask His Lordship that,' Cameron replied.

'But I am asking you, Cameron, why did you get the job?' Harry said.

'His Lordship must have seen something in the way I worked at the restaurant.'

'What was the name of the restaurant?' Cramer asked, his notebook and pen in his hands.

Cameron turned in his seat to answer. 'It was Classics in Mayfair, I was the maître-d'.' Cramer nodded and wrote it down.

'I always imagined that a maître-d' was a high-paid job,' Harry said, 'so why give it up?'

'His Lordship made me a very generous offer to join his staff.'

'Are there any other staff at this house apart from you?'

'No, I am the only one here.'

'So when you have a dinner party like the one Mr Parkin attended, what do you do for help? I can't imagine you would be able to cope what with drinks, cooking and serving,' Harry said.

'I call an agency that I have used for a number of years. They know the standard of staff I expect to be sent to cater for His Lordship.'

'And the name of the agency you use?' Cramer asked. Cameron turned his head and told him.

'Do you just stay here, or do you go to his other houses around the country?' Harry said.

'When His Lordship goes to one of his other properties, I will go too.'

'Are there permanent staff at the houses?' Harry asked.

'Yes, each house has its own permanent staff,' Cameron said. 'They are much larger properties than this.'

'And when you travel down to the other houses, do you become the head of all the staff?' Harry said.

'Yes, I will organise the staff to suit His Lordship's needs.'

'You seem to be trusted by Lord Dorres,' Cramer said.

'His Lordship has come to rely on me to make sure whichever of his houses he is at, everything runs smoothly,' Cameron said, turning to Cramer. He turned back to look at Harry, who picked up his glass of orange juice and took another drink. He put the glass down.

'That really does taste very nice. What about his wife?' Harry said.

Cameron looked a bit puzzled for a moment. 'You mean Her Ladyship?' Harry nodded. 'She travels with His Lordship whenever he goes to his other properties.'

'So she never stays at, say this house on her own, or any of the other properties?' Harry asked.

'There may be occasions when His Lordship is at this house or one of his others and Her Ladyship somewhere else,' Cameron said.

'So she doesn't travel all the time with him,' Harry said.

'Well no, but it's not often,' Cameron said.

'So when they are at different houses, who are you with?' Cramer asked.

'I will be wherever His Lordship is based.' They were interrupted by a bell ringing. 'You will have to excuse me.' Cameron stood up.

'Is that the front door?' Harry asked.

'No, it's Her Ladyship ringing. I will have to go and see what she needs,' Cameron said.

'I thought you said Lord Dorres was not at home,' Cramer said.

'He is not at home. You did not ask about Her Ladyship,' Cameron replied. 'If you will excuse me.' Cameron left the kitchen.

'There is a lesson for you, Cramer,' Harry said.

'What's that, sir?' Cramer asked.

'He told us at the door that Lord Dorres was out, and because we didn't ask about his wife Cameron never told us. So he only answers a question with the minimum of information, so make any question you ask precise.' Cramer nodded. Harry picked his orange juice up and took another drink. He stood and had a walk round the kitchen, opening a few drawers and cupboards to have a look inside. Cameron returned to the kitchen. 'Her Ladyship would like some coffee,' he said.

'You get on and make it, I will ask the questions as you do,' Harry said. Cameron went about making the coffee. Harry went and sat back at the table. 'So when His Lordship is at this house on his own and his wife is away, does he still have friends over for a dinner party?'

'He may have a few friends around,' Cameron said.

'And these parties, are they different from the normal dinner parties that would be held if his wife was present?' Harry said.

Cameron carried on making the coffee. He did not answer straight away. 'I don't understand the question.'

'I think you understand the question, Cameron.' Harry said, 'His Lordship has some friends around and they are joined by some young ladies.'

'Some of His Lordship's friends may bring a friends with them,' Cameron said.

'Cameron, I know more than you think. These dinners turn into orgies, don't they?' Harry said.

'I don't think I can say anything about what goes on at His Lordship's dinners.'

'Okay, I don't want details, Cameron, relax. Did Mr Parkin ever attend Lord Dorres dinners when his wife was not at home?'

'Mr Parkin is only, sorry, was only invited to parties when Her Ladyship was present.'

'And does his wife know about these parties when she is not at home?' Cramer asked.

Cameron finished making the coffee, placing everything on a tray. 'I think she may be aware but I don't really know.'

He lifted the tray. 'I have to take the coffee up to Her Ladyship.'

Harry stood up. 'We will walk out with you, thanks for answering our questions.' Harry and Cramer followed Cameron, who carried a tray with the coffee pot, milk and cup on it out of the kitchen. As they entered the hall Harry said, 'Just one last question, who was the man I saw leaving just before we arrived?'

Cameron stopped and turned. 'You must be mistaken, sir.'

'Cameron, that is the first blatant lie you have told me,' Harry said. 'Some of your other answers have been a bit hazy, but not lies, so who was the man who left before we arrived?'

'Oh yes, sorry sir, I forgot with all your questions. It was a friend of Her Ladyship,' Cameron said.

'And he goes by the name of?' Harry asked.

'I don't know his name, sir.'

'Cameron, you and I know that's not true,' Harry said. 'Shall I have a guess, as I said I know more than you think? So in future I ask a question, you answer it. The man's name was Micky Adams.'

'I recall now, yes, Mr Adams,' Cameron replied.

'What time did he get here?' Harry asked.

'A few hours ago. He came after His Lordship had gone out,' Cameron replied.

'Her Ladyship's coffee is getting cold,' Harry said, 'You'd better take it in.' Harry turned the handle on the door they were standing outside and pushed it open before Cameron could say anything. Cameron entered and Harry followed him in.

Lady Dorres was laying on a sofa wearing a nightdress, the television was on. She looked up. 'Cameron, you took your time with the coffee.' She saw Harry and Cramer follow Cameron into the room. 'What is he doing here?' She pointed at Harry as she sat up.

'It's okay, I just called in to ask Cameron a few questions,' Harry said, 'but now that I know you're here, I can ask you a few too.'

'I don't have to answer any questions, my husband told you to make an appointment. Cameron, put the coffee down and show him out.' She waved her hand in Harry's direction. Harry walked over to one of the chairs opposite the sofa.

'Do you mind if I sit here as we chat?' Harry said he sat down.

'You impertinent little man, get out of the house. I will make sure you are in trouble with your superiors. And take your friend with you.' She pointed at Cramer who was standing by the door. Cameron had put down the tray with the coffee on the small table by the sofa and was standing looking slightly confused.

'I didn't introduce you, this is Detective Sergeant Cramer.'

'I don't care who he is.' Lady Dorres stood up.

'Please calm down,' Harry said. He noticed a small mirror on the table with white powder on it. 'I just want to talk about your friend, Micky Adams.'

The room was silent for a minute. Lady Dorres sat down on the sofa. 'Cameron, leave us, but ring His Lordship and let him know the police are back here,' she said.

'Yes, Your Ladyship.' Cameron went out of the room closing the door behind him. Cramer walked over and stood at the end of the sofa.

'Now, Your Ladyship,' Harry said. 'I think that's being a bit too formal. May I call you Natalie, that's your name? You don't mind, I find titles a bit of a tongue-twister.' Lady Dorres looked at Harry and shrugged.

'Okay Natalie, let me tell you a few things, just to make sure you understand how this is going to work. I can ring the local police station and have twenty officers here in cars and vans with their lights flashing making lots of noise. I dare say someone will tip the press off about a drugs raid, and they will be outside with their cameras when you're taken out in handcuffs. Those pictures will be in the papers tomorrow. Or we can have a nice pleasant chat and I will leave at the end of it quietly.'

Lady Dorres sat back in the sofa, she looked at Harry. 'Ask your questions,' she said.

Harry smiled. 'Thank you, I am glad we understand each other, now I want to know about Gerald Parkin.'

'Gerald? I thought you wanted to know about Micky,' she said.

'We will get to him Natalie, don't worry, but Gerald first. Was Gerald Parkin blackmailing you?'

'Blackmailing? I don't understand.'

'Natalie, you are educated enough to understand blackmail,' Harry said. 'So please don't make me have to ask questions twice, or I will get on the phone.'

'Yes he was, he was a horrid man. I had to invite him to dinners and sit beside him and be civil and laugh at his jokes,' she said.

'How long had he been blackmailing you?' Cramer asked.

Lady Dorres looked up at Cramer. 'Over two years,' she said.

'What was he blackmailing you over?' Harry asked.

'Can't you guess?' she said.

'I need you to tell me,' Harry said.

'About my drugs.'

'Just the drugs, or was there something else?' Harry asked.

Lady Dorres was quiet for a minute. 'He had a video of me with someone.'

'A video, what was on it?' Cramer said.

'I was on it,' Lady Dorres said, her voice rising. 'I was in bed with someone.'

'It wasn't your husband, so who was it?' Harry said.

'It was Micky,' she said.

'So he was blackmailing you over the drugs and the tape. Did your husband know?' Harry asked.

'No, I never told him.'

'So he doesn't know Micky Adams is your lover,' Cramer said.

'No, he doesn't,' Lady Dorres said.

'We will not be telling him, Natalie,' Harry said. 'So don't worry. I'm glad you're being so honest with us. How did Gerald Parkin get hold of a tape of the two of you, and find out about your drug habit?'

'A friend of mine who knew Parkin used to borrow a flat off him to meet a friend. She knew I had a lover, and it wasn't always possible to meet Micky here because of my husband, so I would say I was going shopping and she would arrange to have the key. I would go there and spend a couple of hours. I didn't know but Parkin had a hidden camera in the bedroom.'

'What about your friend who got you the keys? Did you mention to her about the camera?' Harry asked.

'No, I thought she may be involved with Parkin, so I cut her out off my circle of friends,' she said.

'Where was the flat?' Harry asked.

'It was in Chelsea Harbour, it was a very nice place.'

'And you went there often?' Cramer said.

'We met there on a few occasions when I couldn't have Micky call in here,' she said.

'Does the name Angela Cook mean anything to you?'

'No, I don't know anyone called Angela Cook, why should I?' Lady Dorres said.

'It's just a name that's cropped up. How much did Parkin blackmail you for?' Harry asked.

'I paid him two hundred thousand pounds when he first approached me, and have given him ten thousand pounds each month since.'

'That's a lot of money. Hasn't your husband noticed the money going out?' Cramer said. Lady Dorres looked at Cramer.

'My father was extremely wealthy. He owned some mines in Australia and South Africa, sold them and made a fortune. I got most of his money, so I don't have to ask my husband for pocket money. Ten thousand pounds, I might spend that on a dress for a party. It was the arrogance of Parkin that made me angry, and having to be civil to him.'

'Didn't you tell Micky Adams about Parkin?' Harry said.

'When Parkin first approached me he gave me a copy of the video. He said I could have it as a memento. When I saw what was on it I phoned Micky and told him.'

'Do you still have the video?' Cramer asked.

'Do you think I am stupid enough to have it lying round? I burnt it,' she said.

'So when you spoke to Micky Adams about it, what did he say?' Harry asked.

'He said he would sort Parkin out and get the video and my money back.'

'So what happened? You were still being blackmailed, Micky Adams didn't seem to have been successful,' Harry said.

'Parkin was at an opening of a new gallery. I was not going but arranged for Micky to get an invitation. He got Parkin in a side room and threatened that he would give him a good beating if he didn't hand over the tape and stop the blackmail. Micky is a very big man, and intimidating. He said Parkin was very frightened and that he would meet him the next day and hand the tape over.

'He arranged to meet Micky at the London Zoo by the tiger enclosure. When Micky arrived, Parkin was sitting on a bench in front of the tiger pens. Micky sat down next to Parkin, who handed over the tape without a word. But Micky said as he got up to leave two men who were even taller and bigger than him came up, and before he knew it one of them punched him. He said he was knocked out for a few seconds, but when he regained his senses the two men were either side of him holding his arms and frog marched him to a room behind the tiger pens. When he was in there they beat him very badly. When they'd finished punching and kicking him, they lifted him up from the floor and one of the men opened a sliding door. Micky said they held him in the opening. There was a ten foot drop, and Micky said he was looking at two tigers looking up at him. One of the men told Micky he should never ever approach Parkin again, or he would be the tigers' lunch. They then closed the sliding door and carried on beating Micky till he lost consciousness. Some zoo staff found him later on that day. He woke up in hospital. He was in a terrible state, he was in there for four days.'

'Do you think Micky might have decided to kill Parkin for revenge, because of the beating?' Harry said.

'I have never seen Micky scared, he is a tough man, but believe me he was not going to go anywhere near Parkin again.

They did leave Micky with the tape Parkin had given him. You know what was on it? The film *Jungle Book*.'

'Did Parkin mention anything about it the next time you saw him?' Cramer asked.

'No, he was his usual smiles and jokes.'

'So how did you give the money to Parkin?' Harry asked.

'The two hundred thousand was a banker's draft. I used to slip an envelope into his jacket pocket with ten thousand pounds in at the end of each month, at whatever dinner we were at.'

'Did you ever go to Parkin's house.'

'No, I have never been to his house.'

'Thank you, Natalie for being so truthful. What you have told us we won't mention to anyone. But just one last question. Do you know anyone else who was being blackmailed by Parkin?' Harry said.

'No, I don't. Do you think he was blackmailing someone else?' she said.

'We have to keep an open mind, Natalie. Someone killed him, and blackmail might have been the reason. Now I will keep your secret, but if you hear anything that might help me find the killer, here's my card. Just phone me. And can you give me the address of the flat where you met Micky Adams, and the name and address of the friend who gave you the keys?' She took Harry's card and gave them the address of the flat and that of the friend, which Cramer wrote down.

Harry got up and he and Cramer left. As he pulled the front room door closed, he heard a loud sniffing and a sigh from Lady Dorres. Cameron was standing at the kitchen door, he walked towards them. 'Are you done now, sir?' Cameron asked.

'Yes, but we might have to come back and speak to you again,' Harry said, 'if I think you've not been honest in everything you told us. Did you phone Lord Dorres?'

Cameron opened the front door. 'No, I didn't, sir. I thought discretion was called for. I will let Her Ladyship know I could not contact him.'

Harry and Cramer stepped out of the house and walked along the road back towards where they had parked the car. 'How do you think that went?' Harry said.

'I think she was being honest,' Cramer said

Harry nodded. 'When we get back to the station, run Micky Adams' car through the system. Get his address. We can pay him a visit to ask after his health.'

Manjitt and Jordan had arrived at the offices of Sir Mark Coale, which were in a tall glass building in the centre of the city of London. They drove into the small entrance which led to a parking area in front of the building. There was a small roundabout which they drove around, pointing the car back towards the road and parked. As they stepped out of the car, a man dressed in black except for his white shirt approached them. He had an earpiece in with the lead disappearing under his jacket. A small microphone was attached to his jacket lapel. 'I'm sorry, you can't park your car there, it's for senior company staff,' he said.

Jordan pulled his warrant card out. 'This says I can park it anywhere, I am on police business.'

'This is private property, you will have to move it now, sir,' the man said.

Jordan looked at Manjitt. She shrugged her shoulders. Jordan said, 'I will try one more time. I am here on police business.'

'Sorry, sir, but this is private property, you will have to move it,' the man said.

'Give me the keys,' Manjitt said to Jordan. He threw her the keys and watched as she got in the car and drove it back the way they had come in. She turned onto the main road and stopped, reversed slightly so the car was blocking the entrance to the building. As she got out she took the emergency blue light and placed it on the top of the car and it started to flash. She locked the car and walked back towards Jordan and the man. Jordan was smiling.

As she approached, the man said to her, 'You can't leave that there, it's blocking the entrance to the building.'

'That's a public highway,' she said, she took her warrant card out, 'and this says I can park it where I like.'

'Thank you for being so helpful,' Jordan said, as he and Manjitt left the man talking into his radio and went through the thick glass doors and into the main reception area. They spoke to one of the receptionists about the scheduled meeting with Sir Mark Coale and were asked to wait. They stood by the doors and watched the man who had stopped them parking. He had now been joined by another man, and both were waving their arms and pointing at the squad car and talking into their microphones.

'Do you think they're annoyed?' Manjitt said.

'I don't think he is having a good day,' Jordan replied. They turned when they heard a voice behind them say, 'Excuse me,' and found themselves looking at two large men dressed similarly to the man outside. Both men were as tall as Jordan, maybe a bit taller than his six foot three. 'We are here to escort you up to the chairman's office,' one said.

'Lead on,' Jordan replied, and he and Manjitt followed them to the lifts. They arrived at Sir Mark Coale's secretary's office with not another word said. They stood for a moment beside his secretary's desk as a call was put through to announce they were here. After a few moments they were told they could go into Sir Mark's office. One of the large men opened the door for them and they entered. He closed it, but did not follow them in.

It was a modern-looking office. Sir Mark Coale sat behind

a large glass desk. There were three computer screens on it and two phones. Behind him you could see all the City of London through the floor-to-ceiling window, which was dark to cut out the sun. He was on the phone as they came to his desk, he put his hand over the phone and said, 'Sit,' and pointed to two leather chairs on their side of the desk.

Manjitt smiled, looked at Jordan and walked over to a sofa that had a small coffee table in front of it and sat down and picked up a magazine which was lying on it. Jordan sat in one of the leather chairs. It was one you could spin round on, which he did, spinning a full 360° to return facing Sir Mark, whose face registered surprise. Manjitt held the magazine up covering her laugh after watching Jordan.

Sir Mark put the phone down, looked at Jordan in front of him and across at Manjitt. 'You have five minutes so what do you want to know?' he said.

'Manjitt, do you have your notebook?' Jordan said. Manjitt held it up. He looked at Sir Mark. 'I think we should introduce ourselves. I am Detective Sergeant Rhodes, and this is my colleague, Detective Constable Virdee.'

Sir Mark looked at his watch. 'Yes, yes, I said you have five minutes. I am a busy man.'

'Is your view south-west facing?' Jordan said. 'I bet you get some glorious sunsets.' Sir Mark's face showed confusion and annoyance.

Before he could answer, Manjitt said, 'No, I think it's facing east, you would have to be the other side of the building to get a good sunset.'

Sir Mark looked at Manjitt and back at Jordan. 'What are you two on about?' He turned to Manjitt. 'Come and sit here.' He pointed to the chair beside Jordan.

'No, thank you, Sir Mark, I am quite comfortable where I am,' Manjitt said.

'Manjitt you should, these chairs are great,' Jordan said and proceeded to do another 360° spin. When he stopped he looked directly at Sir Mark and said, 'You may have five minutes, Sir Mark, but we will decide when we have finished asking our questions. We are investigating a murder, not some parking offence, and the only person who tells us what to do is our boss.'

Sir Mark sat back in his chair. He smiled and pressed a button on his desk. 'This interview is over. I shall be lodging a complaint about your behaviour and attitude.' The door opened and the two large men who had brought them up entered the office. 'These two are leaving,' he said, waving his hand in Jordan and Manjitt's direction. Manjitt stood up and came around the coffee table to face the two men.

Jordan remained in his chair and said, 'Sir Mark, we can question you here or ask you to come to the station. Now we are trying to be helpful and not cause you too much trouble.'

Sir Mark took no notice of Jordan and said to the two men, 'They are leaving, escort them from the building.'

One of the men stepped forward and put out his hand and took Manjitt's left arm. She looked up at him and said, 'That could be taken as an assault of a police officer.'

He pulled her slightly towards the door. He didn't see her right arm pull back. Her hand formed a flat fist, palm facing down and it shot forward, driving into the sternum of the man holding her. It happened quickly. The only sound was the man making a gurgling noise. He stood still holding her arm for a few seconds, then sank slowly to his knees, gasping for breath and holding his chest. Manjitt stepped around his curled-up body to face the second man, whose face registered surprise and confusion, Manjitt winked at him but said nothing.

Sir Mark was trying to take in what was happening. He looked at the man who Manjitt had struck laying on the floor making louder and louder gasping noises.

Jordan, who had not moved, said, 'Now, Sir Mark, before we were interrupted I was going to ask you a few questions.'

Sir Mark looked back at Jordan, his face was like thunder, 'I could have you thrown out,' he said.

Jordan looked over his shoulder at the man on the floor and Manjitt standing facing the second man, and said, 'Sir Mark, I think we have seen you could try, but is it worth the aggravation? We will ask our questions and be gone before you know it.'

Sir Mark sat silent, staring at Jordan. 'Okay, leave,' he said to the two men.

Manjitt helped the second man lift his partner up from the floor, 'Just get some ice and place it on your chest and lie flat on your back. You will be able to breathe comfortably in a short while,' she said. The second man helped his still gasping partner from the office, shutting the door. Manjitt walked over and took the seat beside Jordan. 'They look pretty fit, your security men,' she said.

Sir Mark looked at her. He saw the stitches over her eye and the swelling and bruising around it. 'They are ex-royal marines, what did you do to him?' he said.

'Me, nothing. He walked into my hand,' Manjitt said.

'What happened to your eye?' Sir Mark asked.

It was Jordan who spoke. 'She was sparring with our Olympic karate gold medal-winner. He doesn't look too good either. Now, if I can ask you about Gerald Parkin.'

Sir Mark nodded, but he looked back at Manjitt and said, 'So you do a lot of karate. I am a black belt.'

'Yes, since I was a small child. My level is Rokudanm' Manjitt said.

'I would bow to you if I was standing,' Sir Mark said. 'Sixth dan, I'm impressed, now I see how my man ended up on the floor.'

'If I could just interrupt your sporting conversation and get back to Gerald Parkin,' Jordan said. 'Sir Mark, you had dinner with him the evening before he was killed. Did he seem worried about anything?'

'No, he told his usual stories, made people laugh. He was a great one for the gossip.' Sir Mark said.

'Did you see much of him. Did you ever go to his house?' Manjitt asked.

'No, never been to his house. I saw him on other occasions, at the cricket at Lord's or at another dinner party. You know, just generally around.'

'No, he wasn't a close friend?' Jordan said.

'No, he's not someone I would class as a friend, more an acquaintance.'

'Did he ever ask you for money?' Manjitt said.

'Money, no why should he?' Sir Mark asked.

'We believe his murder may have been to do with blackmail,' Jordan said.

'Blackmail? He was being blackmailed, or was he blackmailing someone?' Sir Mark said.

'We think he may have been blackmailing someone. So he didn't try and blackmail you?' Manjitt asked.

'Me, what could he blackmail me about?'

'Well, we have heard stories that you were among a number of people who attended a more adult type of party,' Jordan said.

Sir Mark smiled at Jordan. 'Yes I did, and very enjoyable they are and I don't worry if people know about them or not. I am a single man and can do what I want.'

'But there where other people at those parties who may have been open to blackmail,' Jordan said.

'Is that a question? Because if it is, you will have to ask them,' Sir Mark said.

'Can you give us the names of the people you think may have been susceptible to blackmail?' Jordan asked.

'No, I don't think I can. From your questioning you would seem to know who else attended those parties so you will have to ask them. But I don't know all their personal situations,' Sir Mark replied.

'Did he ever ask you for any business advice?' Manjitt asked.

'No, he never spoke to me about business. He occasionally mentioned something that concerned me that he had heard and would pass on the gossip, but business advice, no,' Sir Mark said.

'Who organised the parties?' Manjitt said.

'I think you know that already, but I never personally asked who organised them,' Sir Mark said.

'Did you hold any of the parties at your house?' Jordan asked.

'Yes, I did.'

'Who asked you to hold them at your house?' Manjitt said.

'I can't remember. I think I may have said at one party that I could hold one at my house,' Sir Mark said.

'And Gerald Parkin, did he attend the parties,' Jordan said.

'No, he was never at them. He was not amongst, how would you say, the right crowd,' Sir Mark said.

'Do you know Angela Cook?' Manjitt asked.

'I don't think that name rings a bell,' Sir Mark said. 'Who is she?'

'It's a name that has come up in the investigation,' Manjitt said.

'Sorry, not a name I know.'

'Thank you for giving us your time today, even if we got off on the wrong foot,' Jordan said.

'It's been interesting seeing how our great police force work, especially when put under pressure.' Sir Mark looked at Manjitt, smiling. 'If you ever give lessons, I would love to become one of your pupils. Or if you decide that police work is not for you, I could guarantee you a very well paid job on my close protection staff.'

Manjitt smiled back. 'That's a tempting offer, Sir Mark, but I don't think I would have half the fun I get out of my job now.'

'Well, that job offer will stay open.' Sir Mark stood. 'I hope I have been helpful.'

Jordan and Manjitt stood. 'Thank you, Sir Mark, if we need to speak to you again we will be in touch,' Jordan said.

Sir Mark pressed the button on his desk. The door opened and one man appeared. 'Just phone my office,' Sir Mark said. 'Show my guests out.'

Jordan and Manjitt left the office with the lone man who escorted them to the reception area. They walked from the building, passing the first security man they had met when they arrived. 'Thank you for all your help,' Jordan said as they passed him.

When they got to their car, they noticed there were five cars parked behind them along the road. All had parking tickets on their windscreens.

'What a silly place to park,' Manjitt said.

Charlie and Danny were seated opposite Stanley Moore in his office in Pall Mall not far from St James Palace. There was no sign on the building, and if you walked past you would not know inside was one of the most powerful private banks, not just in Britain, but across the world. Its main operation was run from this building. The office itself was wooden panelled. It had a quiet feel about it, like you might get in an old library.

'Thank you for seeing us today,' Charlie said. 'We just want to talk to you about Gerald Parkin. How well did you know him?'

'I wouldn't say he was a close friend. I met him at dinner

parties and generally around, you know an opening at a gallery or at the opera,' Stanley Moore said.

'On the night before he was killed,'Charlie said, 'you were at dinner given by Lord Dorres. Gerald Parkin was there, do you remember him saying anything or behaving in a way that you thought was different from normal?'

'No, not really, he was his normal self. He did turn up later than everybody else,' Stanley Moore replied.

'Did you speak to him alone at all during the evening?' Danny asked.

'No, it was general talk around the table,' Stanley Moore said.

'Did anyone ever say anything about Gerald Parkin to you. You know, how they felt about him?' Danny said.

Stanley Moore look quizzically at Danny. 'How do you mean, how they felt about him?'

'Was he well liked amongst the group?' Danny said.

'I wouldn't say Gerald Parkin was part of the group as you put it. I saw him on occasions. As I said, he was someone who was invited along to various events for his gossip and stories,' Stanley Moore said.

'But did anyone ever express an opinion about him, did anyone ever say they didn't like him?' Danny asked.

'He was not someone who came up in conversations when he was not there,' Stanley Moore replied. 'As I said, he was invited along when people wanted to hear some gossip.'

'So he was just there to entertain,' Charlie said.

'I suppose you could look at it like that, he was not missed if he was not present at a dinner,' Stanley Moore said.

'And you can think of no reason why anyone would want to kill him?' Charlie asked.

'No, nothing. I'm sorry, would you gentleman like some tea or coffee? I should have asked you when you came in.'

'No, thank you, sir,' Charlie said. 'Did you ever go to his house?'

'No, I have never been to his house. I don't think I even know where he lives,' Stanley Moore said.

'And since we have been looking into Gerald Parkin's background, we have discovered that he may have been blackmailing some of the people he knew. Can I ask was he blackmailing you?' Charlie said.

Stanley Moore looked at Charlie. 'Blackmail, Gerald? Why would he be blackmailing me?'

'Well, we have found out that he knew about some private parties, that maybe people would prefer not to be made public,' Danny said.

Stanley Moore said nothing. 'Did you ever attend any parties you might think could cause you embarrassment if it got out?' Danny asked.

Stanley Moore still said nothing.

'Do you know Angela Cook?' Charlie asked.

Stanley Moore looked from Charlie to Danny but still remained silent. Charlie could see by his face he was confused.

Finally he spoke. 'Private parties, I am not sure what you mean?'

Charlie smiled. 'I think you know what we mean, sir. I can assure you we are not interested in what went on at the parties, but it would give people a reason to be blackmailed. And what you say to us in this room goes no further.'

Stanley Moore sat a little more upright in his chair and leaned forward, his hands coming onto the table. 'I did not kill Gerald Parkin,' he said.

'That's nice to know, sir,' Danny said, 'but we asked if you attended any of those private parties.'

Again the room was quiet. Charlie saw Stanley Moore lick his lips.

'Are you sure you would not like some tea or coffee?' he asked.

Charlie and Danny shook their heads no. Stanley Moore pressed a button on the telephone and asked for a coffee to be brought in. He sat back in his chair. Charlie could see he was trying to work out just how much they knew and what he should say.

'I just want to assure you again that anything you say to us will not be repeated to anyone else,' Charlie said. The silence was only broken by a knock at the door and Stanley Moore's secretary entering with a cup of coffee. She placed it on the desk and left. Stanley Moore picked it up took a small drink.

'And if I did attend some of these private parties, what of it?' he said as he put the coffee cup back on the desk.

'Is that a yes, you did attend them?' Danny asked.

'Yes, I did go to some.'

'Did Gerald Parkin approach you and say he knew about them, and ask for money or he would expose you?' Charlie said.

Again the room was silent. 'I did not kill Gerald Parkin,' Stanley Moore said.

'I understand that, sir, but did he demand money from you to keep quiet about what he knew?' Danny said.

Stanley Moore picked his coffee back up and took another drink. Putting the cup down he said, 'Yes, he did.'

'And how much did you pay him?' Charlie asked.

'Two hundred and fifty thousand pounds,' Stanley Moore said.

'And how did he approach you to ask for it?' Charlie asked.

'I was at the opera one evening and ran into him at the interval,' Stanley Moore said. 'I was there with my wife and some friends. I was at the bar when he came up to me. He just stood there talking generally, then out of the blue he told me what he knew and demanded the money to keep quiet.'

'Did he want the 250 thousand pounds in one go?' Danny asked.

'Yes, he just said he wanted 250 thousand or it would appear in the papers. I have a reputation to keep and the bank does not need publicity like that,' Stanley Moore said.

'How did you pay him?' Charlie asked.

'He said I should give him a banker's draft for that amount. He told me he was going to a dinner party at Sir Martin Oliver's house the next week where he knew I would be, and I should give it to him there.'

'And after you gave him the money, did he ask you for any more?' Danny said.

'Yes he did come back again and say he needed some more money,, but I told him no,' Stanley Moore said.

'Are you being truthful about that?' Charlie said. 'If you didn't give him some more money, what was to stop him getting the story into the papers?'

Stanley Moore sat for a quiet for a moment, then said, 'Yes, okay, I did give him some more money.'

'How much more did you give him?' Danny asked.

'Another hundred thousand, by banker's draft like before, but I told him that was all he was getting,' Stanley Moore said.

'And was he satisfied with that? He didn't come back and ask for more?' Charlie asked.

'I told him he would get no more money out of me and up to now he had not been back for more. And he won't be asking for any more now, will he?' Stanley Moore said.

'People might think that is a good reason to kill him,' Danny said.

'But I didn't kill him, I told you that. But I am not sorry he's dead,' Stanley Moore said. 'I never really liked him, he was always so full of himself and his stories. Although they could be funny, they did seem to be a bit spiteful towards people.'

'I asked you before if you knew Angela Cook,' Charlie said.

'No, never heard of her, who is she?' Stanley Moore said quickly.

'It's a name that has come up in the investigation. We might have to speak to you again, sir, but if you can have someone take us to speak to your wife now,' Charlie said.

Stanley Moore pressed a button on his phone and told the secretary that she should come into the office and take the police along to Mrs Moore's office.

Charlie and Danny stood. 'Thank you for taking the time to see us, sir,' Charlie said.

Stanley Moore nodded. Charlie and Danny left the office. The secretary took them along the corridor to Mrs Amanda Moore's office. She knocked and they followed her in.

Mrs Moore was seated at her desk. 'Come in gentleman, and take a seat.'

The secretary left, closing the door. Charlie and Danny sat down opposite her.

'Now, I understand you want to talk to me about Gerald Parkin. What is it you want to know?' she said in a soft American accent.

Charlie introduced themselves. 'We are looking into Gerald Parkin's background, trying to get an idea of who he was and why someone would want to kill him.'

'Okay, what can I tell you?' Amanda Moore asked.

'Well, you were one of the last people to see him alive,' Danny said.

'Yes, and your point is?' Amanda Moore said, looking at Danny, a smile at her lips. She had the look of a very self-assured woman.

'Can you tell us how he seemed? Did he mention he was worried about anything?' Danny asked.

'He was his usual self, and no, he never said he was worried about anything.' Amanda Moore leaned back in her chair.

'Did you know him well?' Charlie said.

'No.' She turned to look at Charlie.

'So you would not class him as a friend,' Charlie asked.

'No,' she repeated.

'I can see you're a person of few words,' Charlie said.

Amanda Moore smiled as she said, 'I answered your question.'

'Yes, I can't fault you there,' Charlie said. 'But how did he get on with the other people at the dinner?'

'The same as always, jokey.' Amanda Moore sat forward, her hands resting on the desk.

'Did anyone seem upset with him?' Danny asked.

'No, not that I could tell,' she said, turning to look at Danny. 'I have to say your fashion sense for a police officer is one of the most amazing I have seen. Do you work undercover?'

Charlie spoke before Danny could answer. 'That's how he normally turns up for work,' Charlie said and continued. 'Since we've been looking into Mr Parkin's background, we believe he may have been blackmailing some people. Did he approach you, threatening blackmail?'

'What could he blackmail me about?' Amanda Moore said to Charlie. She half laughed at the question.

'That's what I am asking you,' Charlie said. 'Was he trying to blackmail you?'

'No, as I said, what could he blackmail me about?' Amanda Moore said with a confident tone in her voice.

Charlie could only smile. Mrs Moore was sharp. He watched as she opened a drawer in her desk and took out a wooden box. She opened the box and took out a cigar. 'Can I offer you one?' she said. Charlie and Danny shook their heads. 'You don't mind if I smoke, do you?' she said.

Charlie shrugged. 'It's your office.' He watched as she went through the ritual of lighting it, finally leaning back in her chair and slowly blowing the smoke into the air.

'Is that a Cuban cigar?' Danny asked.

'What would a good American girl be doing with a Cuban cigar. No, this is the finest cigar you can get. It's from the Dominican Republic, a Fuente Opus X.' She looked at the cigar. 'Was Parkin blackmailing my husband?' She looked up at Charlie as she said it.

'We have not found any evidence he was,' Charlie said. Amanda Moore smiled at Charlie, She knows something, Charlie thought.

'Did you ever go to his house?' Danny said.

'Whose house?' she asked.

'Gerald Parkin's Danny said.

'No.' She rolled the cigar between her fingers. 'It seems that we did not know Gerald as well as we thought.'

'Do you know Angela Cook?' Charlie asked. He saw a slight hesitation. He knew from the log in Angela Cook's building that an Amanda Moore had been signed in on a few occasions.

'Angela Cook.' She was silent for a moment after saying the name. 'Yes, I do know her.'

Charlie sat forward. 'How do you know her?'

Amanda Moore smiled at Charlie. She put the cigar to her lips, took a long drag on it, before slowly blowing the smoke out. 'I met her at Sir Martin Oliver's gallery in Brook Street, she was working there. I was looking for a nice piece of art. Martin was not in the gallery at the time. Just as well, he would have guided me to the most expensive, but Angela was very helpful and knowledgeable. She found me a lovely piece.'

'Apart from meeting her at the gallery, did you meet her on any other occasions?' Danny asked

Amanda Moore did not take her eyes from Charlie, even on hearing Danny's question. 'Yes, I did see her.' A smile was on her lips as she said it.

'Can I ask you where and when you saw her?' Danny asked.

She finally turned her head towards Danny to answer. 'I can't give you exact dates,' she turned to look back at Charlie, 'but I went to her flat on a few occasions, I am sure you know that.' She tilted her head slightly, and the smile came back to her lips. 'And she came to our house in London on a couple of occasions.'

'Yes, we did know you had been to her flat. Can you tell us why you went there?' Charlie asked.

'I could say it was to discuss art, but you would not believe that, would you?' she said, looking at Charlie. 'After I met her at the gallery I had dinner with her a couple of times, and we became lovers. Oh, I see I have shocked your young officer.' Amanda Moore laughed as she said it.

'That might be a good reason for you to be blackmailed,' Charlie said.

'That might well be a good reason, but my husband knows that I am bisexual. He has since before we were married. My family know and most of the people I work with know, so if anyone thought they could blackmail me they would not get very far.'

'So Gerald Parkin never approached you and threaten to blackmail you over your affair with Angela Cook?' Charlie said.

'I thought I answered that at the beginning of our interview, Chief Superintendent.' She took another slow drag on her cigar.

'Did Angela Cook ever mention Gerald Parkin when you were with her?' Danny asked.

She turned to Danny, blowing the smoke in his direction so he was engulfed in a blue haze. 'No, she never did.' Charlie suppressed a laugh as he watched Danny wave a hand to clear the smoke. 'It has a beautiful aroma, don't you think?' she asked Danny,

'I much prefer Lynx body spray,' Danny said, as he continued waving his hand to clear the smoke.

'Do you have any idea who else Gerald Parkin was blackmailing?' Charlie asked.

'As I had no idea he was blackmailing anyone, I could hardly know, could I, Chief Superintendent?' Amanda Moore smiled at Charlie and he smiled back. She is sharp, he thought. 'If there is anything else I could help you with, and I know it doesn't seem like it, but I am very busy.'

'No, you have been very helpful,' Charlie said, standing. Danny stood up too. 'If there is anything else we need to ask, we will be in touch'.

'Just call my office, but I don't think I have anything else I can help you with,' Amanda Moore said.

Later that day the team were all seated around Charlie's desk at the Yard. They had all related how they had got on with the questioning of the people at the party. 'So let me just run through what we think,' Charlie said. 'Jordan and Manjitt, you interviewed Sir Mark Coale, who says he wasn't being blackmailed, and you believe him.' They both nodded. 'But if he was, you don't think he would hesitate to kill or have someone kill for him to get rid of the problem, and he employs a lot of ex-marines, so he has the capacity to do it. Harry, Cramer, you questioned Lady Dorres. She admits to being blackmailed over her affair with a drugs dealer, but says that when she got her drug dealer friend to warn Parkin off, he was himself given a severe beating by two men who Parkin had with him, so Lady Dorres continued paying. You also questioned the butler, but don't have him down as a killer. Danny and myself questioned Stanley Moore and his wife, Amanda. Stanley Moore admits to being blackmailed, but kept saying he didn't kill Parkin. His wife says Parkin was not blackmailing her, but she admits to having an affair with Angela Cook.' Charlie sat back. 'The floor's open for anyone who wants to chime in.'

'It would seem to be a bit of a spider's web Parkin had going for himself,' Harry said. 'Noone spoke about Parkin to each other, so he merrily went about his little blackmail business. You have to hand it to him, he was a sly one.'

'The amounts of money he has blackmailed people for don't begin to come anywhere near what we found in his Swiss bank, or cover his share-buying,' Manjitt said.

'So he could have had another little side operation going. We need to find out what it is,' Charlie said.

'Lady Dorres was meeting her lover at a flat in the same apartment block as Angela Cook,' Harry said. 'It would appear that's where Parkin got the video of her enjoying herself. We found a set of keys at Gerald Parkin's house, I think we might find they are for that flat. We will have to check that out. And she gave us the name of a friend who was also using the flat, she needs to be spoken to.'

'If we believe Lady Dorres about her boyfriend being beaten up by two large men when he approached Parkin, Sir Mark Coale employs some very big men, according to Manjitt and Jordan,' Danny said. 'Could he have a connection to Parkin we don't know about?'

'Well I don't know if we are any closer to catching our killer, but we have a good idea how some of the high society spend their time,' Harry said.

'I don't think you have to be worried about being asked to

join in,' Jordan chimed in bringing laughter from the rest of the team.

'Let's try and clear a few things up, so we can concentrate on the main picture,' Charlie said. 'Danny, you find out how we got on with Tim Green's Jaguar.' Danny nodded. 'Manjitt, you and Cramer check out Tim Green's finances and those of his fiancée. We need to know how much he was involved, or was Parkin just using him. Jordan we want to know who got the solicitor in for Tim Green, also we are still missing the jewellery we know Parkin bought. See if the jewellers have any pictures of what they sold to Parkin. If they do, circulate them to all pawn shops and jewellers, tell them that they are very very hot and we want to know if they turn up. Everyone back here at nine tomorrow to see how far we have got.' The team rose and left Charlie and Harry.

'I want to bump into our friendly drug dealer, Micky Adams tomorrow,' Harry said. 'Cramer got an address for him. I'll speak to a couple of the drugs squad and find out what up-to-date intelligence they have on him. We will see if Lady Dorres has tipped him off that we know about him.'

'I will go over to the flat Lady Dorres was using with your drug dealer, and give it a search,' Charlie said. 'I can call in on Angela Cook at the same time to ask her about Amanda Moore, and if she spoke to her about Parkin. And we still have the third set of fingerprints from Parkin's house that we need to identify.'

'There are no hits on the system for them,' Harry said, 'and I got a call from the inspector searching for the murder weapon, they've had no luck. It looks like whatever was used went with the killer.'

'We have to question Lord Dorres again,' Charlie said. 'We didn't know about the blackmail when we first spoke to him. Who do you think we should send along to ask the questions?'

'I would love to pay a second visit boss, but I want to chase down our drug dealer. What about sending Jordan and Danny? I know how much Lord Dorres would appreciate a Hippie and a big black man turning up on his door step,' Harry said.

'Harry, haven't you ever been to any police equality training programmes? That is not how we describe people from ethnic backgrounds,' Charlie said.

'But Jordan's from south London,' Harry replied, looking shocked.

Charlie nodded and laughed. 'That's true, and everyone knows south Londoners are dodgy.' Charlie stood. 'Come on then Harry, let's go. We don't want Maggie's roast lamb to burn.'

Harry stood picking up his overnight bag. 'I've thought of nothing else but dinner all day boss, lead on.'

Julian squires was seated at the table on Charlie's patio at the back of the house. He took a drink from the wine glass he was holding. 'Charlie, you have done it again, absolutely wonderful,' he said, holding the wine glass up and looking at the colour.

'I have a few bottles for you to take away,' Charlie said. 'I thought you would like it. A vintner who has some good connections told me he had laid his hands on some of the best wine to come on the market in the last twenty years, and got me a couple of cases, so my cellar is filling up nicely.'

Maggie came onto the patio. 'I'm off now, Charlie,' she said.

'Thank you, Maggie, that was a great dinner,' Charlie said.

'Maggie, if you ever feel like leaving Mike, I will take good care of you,' Harry called to Maggie.

'I will let Mike know he has to give me breakfast in bed more often or I will leave him for you, Harry,' Maggie said, laughing.

'It was a lovely meal, Maggie,' Julian said. 'Thank you.'

'Let Mike know Julian will be leaving later, but Harry is staying till the morning,' Charlie said.

Maggie turned and walked to the gate at the side of the house, Charlie's three greyhounds trotting along beside her looking for any treats they thought she might have for them.

'You're not a wine drinker, Harry?' Julian said. Charlie laughed out loud.

Harry, with a glass of lager in his hand, looked at Charlie laughing and said, 'No, Julian, never been much of a wine drinker, but like you the boss occasionally gets me some good lager he has come across. It's usually a six-pack from the local off-licence.' Julian joined in with Charlie's laughter. The three greyhounds came back after seeing Maggie through the gate and not getting any treats. They all lay down on the grass in front of the patio.

'Harry said you were going to have a swimming pool built,' Julian said.

'I think it will be nice in the summer. I'm having it built next to the garage, so it will be facing the south-west and will get the sun for most of the day. The ground runs away so the views should be great.' Charlie had fifty acres around the house, and it could not be seen from any roads in the area. Mike and Maggie lived in the old gatehouse that stood by the electric gates Charlie had installed at the start of his driveway. Anyone wanting to enter had to press a bell and Mike would check who they were. All around and inside the house was a state-of-the-art security system, courtesy of a firm from Switzerland that Julian had arranged. Charlie took a sip of his wine and said, 'So, Julian, what did you find out for us.'

Julian put his wine down and picked up a black folder from by his feet. 'I put a couple of people onto it, Charlie, and it was quite a chain with some surprising findings.'

'The way this case is going, Julian, I don't think we would expect anything else,' Harry said, taking a drink from his glass. Julian opened the folder. 'We have looked at all the company names you gave me. We have ruled out any that just seemed to be normal run-of-the-mill businesses that didn't come up often, and any of the people whose names you gave us we did the same thing with. We put your Mr Parkin at the centre and worked from him. He seemed to have the Midas touch in buying his shares, and it doesn't look like he made too many mistakes. The two front companies he used to buy and sell the shares were then channelling the profits back through a bank in Luxembourg, which turns up again later, but it returned the money back to each front company but swapped it over, so A got B's money and B got A's money. They then sent any money back to the Swiss bank account. I hope you're following me so far,' Julian said.

Harry nodded. Charlie said, 'He was swapping the money between the two companies, but not actually doing anything with it.'

'Yes, that's it, but that's not the best. When we were looking into the company he had registered in the British Virgin Islands, it turns out that he is only a nominee name.'

'What's that?' Harry asked.

'Well, if you're just looking at the register, it would appear he's the owner, when in fact he is just a front himself,' Julian said. Harry nodded. 'The company is in fact owned by another that is registered in the Cayman Islands. It got a little difficult then to work out who owned it, but its name turned up on a few registers of share ownerships. It had in fact been using your Mr Parkin's firm to short shares in a company here.'

'What do you mean, short shares?' Charlie asked.

'It's called shorting.' Julian said, 'Basically it's a bet. Say the share price of a company is a pound, you borrow shares for an agreed period, paying a small fee to the company or person who's lent them, and you sell them straight away for the pound, hoping the price will fall say to ninety pence. You then buy the shares back at the lower price of ninety pence, return the shares you borrowed and pocket the profit of ten pence per share. But it's a risk. If the price were to rise, you would have to buy the shares back at a higher price to return to the owner, and it could cost a lot of money to cover your position.'

'I understand,' Charlie said, 'but what was the company Parkin was shorting the shares in?'

'It's your friend, Sir Mark Coale's oil company,' Julian said.

'Why would they be doing that?' Harry asked.

'It might become a little clearer in a few minutes, Harry,' Julian said. 'Now it looks like a tidy profit was made. We checked when we saw a pattern, and there were a number of other companies who were holding a similar position. It turned out that some of them had ties to the Cayman Island company. I won't bore you too much with the trail we had to follow, but the two main companies who seem to be in control of most of what has been going on are a trust that is controlled through lawyers in New York and surprise, our bank in Luxemburg that was moving Parkin's money about.'

'So to what end do you think they are doing this?' Charlie asked. 'And who's behind it?'

'Well let me say first, your Mr Parkin was not running it, although from his share-buying he must have had connections to someone who was close to the centre and knew what was happening,' Julian said.

'I hate to say this, boss,' Harry interrupted, 'but I get the feeling we may have just discovered another reason someone might want Gerald Parkin dead.'

Charlie nodded. He poured some more wine into Julian's

glass and some into his own. 'Go on, Julian,' he said.

'I had a check run on Sir Mark Coale's company, because that seemed to be at the centre of most of the short selling. According to people we spoke to in the market, if the shares were to fall any lower it could be ripe for a takeover. Now there are only a few companies in the world that would be able to raise the finance to launch a takeover of that size, but with the shares falling it becomes more and more possible. Rumour has it that one of the big American oil companies is sniffing round.'

'But I thought if there was rumour of a takeover the share price would go up,' Charlie said.

'That's true, Charlie,' Julian said, 'but in the last few months Sir Mark's company has had a run of bad luck. Apart from losing a contract just today with the British government to build a pipeline from the new Irish oil fields, they have also had trouble with negotiations to drill for oil in Burma. They raised money in the market on the back of drilling starting this year, but it looks like it won't get started. They've had trouble in central Asia. 15% of their revenue comes from there, apparently two of their top executives have been accused of bribery and are in prison, but that's not the worst of it, the people they bribed ended up losing out in the elections, so the lot who won are not too happy that Sir Mark's company seemed to be backing their opponents.'

'So how does that tie into the bank in Luxembourg and the trust in new York?' Harry asked.

'Each have been building a stake in Sir Mark's company over the last couple of years, not buying big but slowly building up their holding, and they always manage to come in and buy at the right moment when the shares have fallen.' Julian took another drink of wine. 'We checked the share register today. The trust in New York owns 8% of Sir Mark's company. Now if you're looking at that it seems reasonable, but the bank in Luxembourg owns 11%. Put together they control nearly a fifth of the shares. That could be decisive if there was a takeover launched, and they would be in line to make hundreds of millions out of it.'

'So if Sir Mark thought Gerald Parkin was involved, he might not be to happy about it,' Harry said.

'That's true Harry, but someone else must have been feeding him info,' Charlie said.

'And don't forget,' Julian said, 'that one of his front companies was not actually his, so whoever helped set it up must have sat down with Parkin and sorted it all out. And there is one more strange thing we uncovered, the trust in New York is impenetrable, but the bank in Luxembourg has a few strange coincidences, the chairman and CEO is a man called Vincenzo Gallo. He took over at the bank five years ago. Before that the bank was not very exciting, just a normal off shore bank that didn't do too much.'

'Now Mr Gallo has been in banking a long time. He worked mainly in the Far East, Hong Kong, Singapore and Japan. He has some connections to some big investors in China. The one thing that might be of interest is that he worked as the chairman of an investment bank in Singapore. That bank was fully owned by another bank with connections to a name on your list, that is one Stanley Moore.'

'Mr Gallo left the bank in Singapore to take over at Luxemburg, now we didn't find anything to connect Stanley Moore to the bank in Luxemburg, but that's not to say there isn't one.'

'So we have Sir Mark Coale and Stanley Moore with hundreds of millions involved. If someone thought Gerald Parkin was in the way, they wouldn't hesitate to have him killed,' Harry said.

'So it might not just be the blackmail,' Charlie said. 'Julian, it's been another education.' Charlie raised his glass.

CHAPTER ELEVEN

Charlie had just returned to the office from his daily update-meeting with Assistant Commissioner Crick. He found Harry on the phone. Harry put his hand over the mouthpiece and said, 'Just talking to the drugs squad.' Charlie nodded, sat down and started to sort through some of the files on his desk. He found the one for Angela Cook and began to reread it so when he saw her later he would not forget anything she had said to him previously. He looked up from reading to see Danny wander through the office door. Charlie waved him over. 'How did you get on with the car?' he asked.

'Nothing, the boys checking it out said it looked as if it had just been valeted,' Danny replied.

'Maybe he just likes a very clean car,' Charlie said, 'or someone thought he should have a clean car. I think we need to speak to his fiancée. She must know who cleaned it. Tim Green was in custody so he didn't. Let's see what Manjitt and Cramer turn up with their checks on the pair.'

Harry put down the phone and said, 'Glad you walked in, Hippie, do me a favour. Pop downstairs to the drugs squads office, go and see an old friend of mine, Chief Inspector Best, he will give you a file for me, and don't get sidetracked.'

'What do you mean, sidetracked?' Danny said.

'That new detective constable they have on their team, I understand you have been seen getting close to her,' Harry said, a smile on his face.

'What's this?' Charlie said. 'You haven't asked my permission to fraternise with another officer.'

'Harry, how do you find these things out?' Danny said, walking away and shaking his head.

'Is his hair longer than hers?' Charlie said. Harry nodded. Charlie laughed, Danny looked back over his shoulder as he left the office, seeing Charlie and Harry both waving him goodbye.

'Had a good meeting with Crick this morning. He was pleased with my daily report,' Charlie said as he put down Angela Cook's file. 'I think it may have something to do with him appearing on the television tonight and not with the report's contents.'

'I thought the report covered all that's gone on so far,' Harry said. 'Crick on the television, what programme? I have to watch it, just to see how his tan looks in high definition if nothing else.'

Charlie laughed. 'He's on the local news programme at seven. The BBC want to do a big update on Gerald Parkin, although I think when all we have found out about him sees the light of day, they might not want to do many more programmes on him.'

The other members of the team came into the office chatting, and walked over to Charlie and Harry. 'Morning,' Charlie said. 'I hope you lot have some good news to help this case along.' No one said anything. 'That good? Well sit down, and you can start, Jordan.' The three of them sat down.

'I have spoken to the jewellers, they will get pictures from their files of the jewels and send them over. When I get them I will send out copies to all pawnbrokers and jewellers about them. I checked out HDS Group Solicitors, I spoke to a few people in the fraud squad and our legal department and checked their web site. They are specialists in company law and corporate finance; they have ties to some of the banks and some

companies who are specialised in mergers and acquisitions.'
Harry and Charlie looked at each other. 'So why they
would come down here to get Tim Green out I have no idea,
as no one I spoke to said they got involved in criminal
law.' Jordan shrugged his shoulders and sat back.

'Okay, you two give us something,' Harry said to Manjitt
and Cramer.

'We went through Tim Green's and his fiancée's bank
accounts,' Manjitt said. 'Nothing out of the ordinary, his wages
go in every month, she doesn't work, she's doing a university
course, the house they live in is on a mortgage, they don't
appear to be big spenders. The only strange thing we found is
they have a standing order for a safe deposit box.'

'I ran a check on it,' Cramer said. 'It's a bank in the City of
London, a long way from where they live.'

'I have spoken to the bank and told them we need to be
informed straight away if Tim Green or his fiancée turn up to
use it,' Manjitt said.

'Anything else?' Harry said. They both shook their heads.

'We are definitely going to have another chat with those
two,' Charlie said. Danny came back into the office, walked
over and gave Harry a file. 'Sit down, Danny, we are just going
over what the others have been up to.' Danny pulled a chair
over and sat next to Jordan.

'Jordan, what you have told us links into something Harry
and I learnt last night.' Charlie then explained to the team their
meeting with Julian and all they had found out. 'So you see it
may not be that blackmail is the reason Gerald Parkin was
killed. We need to bear that in mind when we question anyone.
We are talking hundreds of millions. If someone thought
Parkin was a threat, it's a good reason to kill him. Now what
have we got lined up today, Harry?'

'Jordan and Hippie, you two are going to track down Lord

Dorres and question him. He needs to give some answers on the blackmail, remember his wife was being blackmailed, and according to the butler he thought she had an idea about the sex parties Lord Dorres was attending.'

Danny rubbed his hands together. 'I will look forward to this. Jordan, you have not met His Lordship, he will love you and your style.'

'Boss, you're going to check the flat that Lady Dorres was using and pop in on Angela Cook.' Harry passed over the keys found in Gerald's house.

'Cramer, you will come with me,' Charlie said.

'Manjitt, you and I...' Harry said, '...are going to pay a visit to our drug dealer friend, Micky Adams.'

Harry and Manjitt were parked in a squad car in east London across the road from Micky Adams' house. His Porsche sports car was parked outside. 'Are we going to go in?' Manjitt asked.

Harry looked at his watch. 'My friends in the drugs squad say Micky is like clockwork. He will be leaving his house in about ten minutes. If they're right, he will go and have some breakfast. I fancy a fry-up, so we will follow him and join him for a chat while I eat.'

'So if they know his movements why don't they nick him?' Manjitt said.

'Come on Manjitt, you know how sly these drug dealers are. He has his stuff stashed all over the place. He's not silly enough to have it at his house. He will tell one of his dealers what's needed and the dealer will arrange things. That's the hard part; putting them and Adams together, they change phones all the time so it's hard to get a connection. When Adams has a big shipment coming in, that's when he will try and disappear under the radar. That's what the drugs squad are aiming to catch him with.'

'This case is getting more complicated as we go along,' Manjitt said.

'Keeps us on our toes though. By the way, how are you getting on with Detective Sergeant Cramer?' Harry asked.

Manjitt turned in her seat to look at Harry. 'Okay, why do you ask?'

'No reason,' Harry said. 'Just wondered how you enjoyed your drink with him the other night?'

Manjitt had a half-smile on her face. 'Harry, how do you find these things out?'

Harry tapped his nose, 'I like to look out for the welfare of my officers.' He sat up. 'Here we go.'

Manjitt looked across the street to see a tall well-built black man leaving the house and walking towards the Porsche. As the car pulled away, Harry pulled out and followed. Ten minutes later they watched as Micky Adams parked and got out of the car in a sidestreet off Chapel Street market. Harry locked up the squad car and he and Manjitt followed Adams. He walked into the market and made his way to a café. Harry and Manjitt waited five minutes, then crossed the road and entered the café. They saw Adams seated at a table with his breakfast in front of him, reading a paper. Harry went up to the counter ordered a full English breakfast and tea. Manjitt just wanted toast and tea, they walked over to the table Adams was seated at. He had not noticed them. Harry sat down opposite Adams, Manjitt sat in the seat beside him.

Adams looked up from his paper and said, 'This table's taken.'

Harry smiled at him, slowly seeing Adams' face recognise who was sitting opposite. Adams turned to look at Manjitt and back to Harry. 'I see you have a much more attractive sidekick working with you these days, Mr Davis.' He put his paper down.

'Don't let me interrupt your breakfast,' Harry said.

'I have gone right off food,' Adams said.

Harry's breakfast arrived. He rubbed his hands together. 'An honest workman should always have a good breakfast,' Harry said. 'Maybe that's why you can't eat yours, Adams.' Micky Adams just stared at Harry.

Manjitt's toast was brought over, she picked it up and started to eat. 'Pass me the sauce,' Harry said to Adams.

'Why don't you get it yourself?' Adams replied.

'Do I detect some hostility in your tone?' Harry asked.

'I have finished my breakfast and was just going,' Micky Adams said. 'So if you will excuse me...' He pushed his chair back and began to stand. Harry reached over and picked up the sauce.

'Don't go, Adams, I hate eating alone,' Harry said.

Adams stood up straight. 'Can you move?' he said to Manjitt. She turned slightly in her chair, moving her right leg around as she went to get up. Standing up straight, she lifted her right boot up and brought the spiked heel down on the left shoe of Micky Adams. A strangled cry escaped his lips as he sat down quickly, trying to grasp his foot.

'You've broken my foot,' he said through gritted teeth.

'No, maybe a toe or two, but not the whole foot. I can show you how to break a whole foot if you want,' Manjitt said.

'I'm glad you decided to stay for a chat,' Harry said as he tucked into his breakfast. Manjitt went back to eating her toast.

'I can feel my foot swelling up in my shoe,' Micky Adams said.

'Don't you be taking your shoe off while I'm eating, or my officer here...' Harry pointed at Manjitt, '...will break the toes on your other foot. Did you read about the murder of the BBC man, Gerald Parkin, in the papers?'

Micky Adams had a look of pain on his face. 'I don't remember reading anything in the paper about it,' he said.

Harry looked at him and said, 'Listen, I think we got off on the wrong foot.' Harry and Manjitt laughed. 'Just my little joke. Now you know me, Adams, I don't like to be messed about, so I am going to eat my breakfast, you will answer my questions, we will go away and you can hobble off to some doctor.' Harry looked up. 'You understand?'

Micky Adams nodded. Harry went back to eating. Manjitt reached across Micky Adams and picked his newspaper up and started to glance through it.

'Is that right, you're a close friend of Lady Natalie Dorres?' Harry said.

'Who, I don't think I know that name?' Micky Adams said.

'If you put me off my breakfast with one more lie, I am going to get annoyed,' Harry said. 'I have it on good authority that you and her are stars in a video, so let's cut out the rubbish, shall we? I know you have been supplying her with drugs.'

'I have…' Adams began, but Harry cut him off before he could finish.

'Don't you dare,' Harry said, pointing his fork with half a sausage on it at Adams. 'I am interested in Gerald Parkin's murder. You can fight it out with the drugs squad when they catch up with you about supplying drugs. I am not stupid enough not to think Her Ladyship has told you we questioned her. But I want your half of the story, because Adams, I have you down as a prime suspect.'

'Not me, you are barking up the wrong tree, Mr Davis, I didn't kill him,' Micky Adams said.

'Well, let's look at the evidence,' Harry said. 'According to Her Ladyship, she told you about the blackmail. You arranged a meeting with Gerald Parkin where you apparently got a severe beating. Now in my book and knowing your background, I think you would have wanted revenge for that. You don't want people on the street thinking they can get away with anything, and if they were to hear you had got a beating and did nothing about it, your street cred would be dead. So I think you went to Gerald Parkin's house and killed him.'

'That is a plausible story,' Manjitt said. 'I think a jury could buy that.'

Micky Adams looked at Manjitt, who still had the paper in front of her but was now filling in the crossword. He turned back to Harry, who pushed the empty plate into the centre of the table. 'I enjoyed that,' Harry said. 'Do you want another cup of tea, Manjitt?' She shook her head. Harry turned in the chair and called the man behind the counter to bring him another tea. He turned back to Micky Adams. 'So you see, Adams, I have reasonable cause to take you in and lock you up. I would probably get you remanded while we carry out further enquiries before the case comes to trial. I reckon at least eight or nine months. So what do you say? You tell me what you know and I will leave you in peace.'

Micky Adams lifted his foot onto the chair, pressing down with his hand trying to ease the pain. 'Okay, what do you want to know?' he said.

'When did you meet Parkin?' Harry asked.

'I never met him,' Adams said.

'But you told Her Ladyship you met him at the zoo and got a beating,' Harry said.

'Come on, Mr Davis, do you think I care if she was being blackmailed over some video of me giving her one? The zoo thing was just some story I spun her to stop her whining. If the video got out it wouldn't do my reputation any harm would it. As far as I'm concerned, she was just some posh slapper. I was just her bit of rough, didn't bother me, she was a good customer and I got some extra benefits from her. She even put me in touch with a few of her friends who like a bit of powder.'

Harry's cup of tea arrived, he took a drink. 'So where did you meet Her Ladyship?' Harry asked.

'Some friends of mine work the doors at a posh club in Chelsea. I wander down there sometimes to drop of the odd bit of gear and have a couple of drinks with them. I was there one night and I bumped into her. She was very drunk. I ended up in the gents' toilets with her. She snorted a few lines and I took her in one of the cubicles and shagged her. She loved it, her old man don't look after her right, and I was not going to complain.'

'You know how to give a girl a good time, don't you?' Manjitt said.

'Well, if you ever want to…' Micky Adams started, but Manjitt reached over and took his hand that was pressing down on his foot, turned it quickly and bent it backwards. Micky Adams twisted in his chair, getting lower and lower till his head was level with the table.

Harry shook his head and said, 'She is not a person you want to upset, Adams. I thought your foot would have been telling you that.'

'Can you ask her to let go, she's breaking my hand?' Micky Adams said through gritted teeth.

'Now where was I?' Harry said, looking down at Micky Adams' face resting on the table. 'Oh yes, you were telling me you didn't know Gerald Parkin, so if I believe you, who have I got as a suspect?' A groan escaped from Micky Adams. 'Do you have any ideas for me?' Harry said, taking a drink of tea.

'What about her old man, she told me he went to some naughty parties,' Micky Adams said out of the corner of his mouth, the rest of his face pressed into the table.

144

'Did she tell you he was being blackmailed?' Harry asked.

'Yes, she said Parkin was blackmailing him,' Adams said. He was clearly in pain now. 'Can you ask her to stop, my hand is killing me, she's breaking it.'

'Did Lord Dorres know that she was being blackmailed?' Harry asked.

'No, please ask her to stop, Mr Davis,' Adams said.

'I think she is waiting for an apology for your rudeness,' Harry said.

'I'm sorry,' Micky Adams said, turning his head slightly towards Manjitt. She let go of his hand. He slowly sat up, rubbing his fingers, but his foot was still killing him so he was at a loss as to which to rub to try and ease the pain.

Harry took another drink of his tea as the door to the café opened and a small well-built man entered, walked past them, glancing quickly in their direction and then away as he went to the counter. Harry saw Micky Adams eyes look at the man as he went past and showed recognition.

'Do you know Angela Cook?' Manjitt said.

'No, it's not a name I know,' he said.

'Are you sure?' Harry asked.

'No honest, never heard of her,' Adams replied.

'What about Tim Green? Ever come across him?' Manjitt said.

'No, don't know him either,' he said.

Harry stood up. It's been nice seeing you again, Adams. I would get that foot looked at.' Harry turned to the man behind the counter and called out, 'Our friend here, he's paying our bill.' The man nodded at Harry, who turned back to Adams. 'Thanks for the breakfast.' Manjitt stood and followed Harry out the café.

As they strolled back to the car, Harry asked, 'What do you think?'

'He's a real work of art,' Manjitt said. 'He was quick enough to drop Her Ladyship in it, but I don't think he was being totally honest.'

They got to the car and climbed in, 'You left an impression on him,' Harry said, 'and he made eye contact with a bloke who walked into the café.'

'Was that the small well-built white man?' Manjitt asked.

'Yes, may just be someone after drugs, but I will give our friends in the drugs squad a ring, see if they can give us a name from the description, he might be a known associate of Adams.' Harry started the car. 'Let's get back to the Yard.'

Jordan and Danny had been trying to track Lord Dorres down. After a visit to his house where they got no help from the butler, Cameron, or Lady Dorres, they had made plenty of phone calls and with a bit of arm twisting had finally tracked him to a private gentlemen's club in St James Street. It was one of the oldest clubs in London, if not the oldest, and had a very exclusive membership. Jordan had phoned Charlie to check whether they should wait till another time to speak to him. Charlie told Jordan that answers had to be had now.

They'd parked the squad car right outside the club and walked up the stairs. Two large black doors were open and they walked through. They had only just got through the inner glass doors when they were stopped by a grey-haired man dressed in a dark uniform.

'I am sorry sir, this is a private club,' he said as he put his arms out. 'If you would leave please, thank you.'

Jordan, who stood at least five inches taller than the man, said, 'It's okay we're the police.' He took his warrant card out and showed it to the man.

'Would you mind stepping over here away from the doors please?' the man said, leading them to one side where a sliding glass window in the wall showed a small office. Another man was seated in the window. The first man spoke to the man in the window, turned and said to Jordan, 'He will deal with you, sir,' and walked away to stand just inside the glass door again.

'Can I help you?' the man behind the window asked.

'Yes, we are here to see Lord Dorres,' Jordan said.

'Is he expecting you?' the man asked.

'No, but we do need to speak to him,' Jordan replied. The man nodded and picked up the phone.

'I will see if he's available, if you wouldn't mind just waiting over there.' He pointed to a window beside the main doors. Jordan and Danny walked over and stood by the door.

'What do you make of this place?' Danny asked.

'One thing's for sure, you will never be a member,' Jordan replied.

'By the colour of all the people coming and going…' Danny pointed to another set of doors, that when opened appeared to lead to a dining room. '…I have more chance than you of being a member.' Danny laughed. 'And by the look of all the paintings on the wall, even with my hair and great fashion sense I won't stand out as much as you.'

'I have always thought of myself as someone who breaks down barriers,' Jordan said.

Danny smiled and said, 'You would need a nuclear bomb to break into this place. I do believe our friend at the window is waving at us.'

Jordan turned and saw the man signalling for them to come over. They walked to the window. 'I am sorry, sir, but Lord Dorres is not available. He said you could phone his house and make an appointment.'

Jordan shook his head. 'It's very important that we speak to him now, we can't wait.'

'I am sorry, sir, but that's the message I got,' the man said.

'I understand,' Jordan said, 'and the last thing I want to do is cause any embarrassment to you or the club, but I have to speak to Lord Dorres now.'

'I'm sorry, sir, I just pass on the messages,' the man said. Jordan nodded, turned away and spoke to Danny.

'Well, Hippie, what do you reckon?' he said.

'We are never going to be members, are we,' Danny said, 'so if we upset a couple of people it's no skin off our noses.'

'It's a shame,' Jordan said. 'I could see myself popping in here for dinner after a night at the theatre.'

'Yeah, I can just see that,' Danny said. 'Why don't we try that door? It looks like it leads to the dining room.' He indicated the doors where all the people had been coming and going from.

'That's a good start,' Jordan said. He and Danny started to walk towards the doors. They had nearly reached them when the first man they met when they entered stepped in front of them. 'Sorry, sir, you cannot go in there,' he said.

Jordan took one of the man's arms, lifted him slightly so his feet were barely touching the ground, and said, 'I am afraid we have to, and it's nice of you to take us.' He carried on walking to the door, the man tiptoeing along beside him. Danny turned the handle and opened the doors. When they entered they saw about twenty dining tables; some were occupied, others laid out waiting for diners. A number of waiters were dotted around the room. 'Can you point out where Lord Dorres is dining?' Danny said.

'He's not in the dining room,' the man said. They noticed a few heads had turned in their direction.

'Well, you take us to where he is please,' Jordan said, squeezing the man's arm slightly, so he saw him wince.

'Okay, those doors over there, it's a bar, I believe he's in there,' he said.

Jordan and Danny made their way towards the other set of doors, passing the tables, diners faces giving them strange looks. Danny mimicked forelock tugging as they went. Jordan smiled but said, 'Turn it in, Hippie.' They reached the other doors with the man jammed between them. They were just about to enter when they heard a voice from the other door call out, 'Stop there.' Jordan looked to see four men dressed in the same uniform as the man he had by the arm. He pushed open the door and went in. The lighting was quite low inside. He scanned the room, letting go of the man's arm. 'Thanks for your help,' he said, 'Hippie, over there.'

Danny looked to where Jordan was pointing. Three men were seated at a table playing cards. Each had a drink in front of them. One was Lord Dorres. Danny and Jordan made their way towards them. They reached the table just as the other men caught up with them.

'Lord Dorres,' Jordan said, but before Lord Dorres even answered, one of the men who had chased Jordan and Danny into the room said, 'Come with us, please, sir,' and took hold of Jordan's arm.

Jordan saw a smile on Lord Dorres' face and that of the two men sitting with him as they watched. Another of the men took hold of Danny's arm. Jordan felt the man trying to pull him. He turned his head to face the man who was nearly Jordan's height, then screamed at the top of his voice, 'LET GO OF MY ARM!' The man took a step back, letting go of Jordan's arm, his face showing shock. The room had gone deadly quiet.

'Thank you,' Jordan said to the man in a normal voice. 'If you put your hand on me again, I will charge you with assault.' Danny shrugged the other man off. 'Now, I am going to speak to Lord Dorres here, and I know he doesn't want his private business being discussed amongst the staff, so if you can give us a few minutes.'

Lord Dorres laughed. 'Just wait by the door,' he said to the men. 'You can show these two out in a second.' The men retreated back to the door. 'Whose go is it?' said Lord Dorres, looking at his cards.

One of the players said, 'Yours,' but before Lord Dorres could play, Jordan put his hand on the table and said to Lord Dorres, 'You won't win with a hand like that.'

Danny, who had been standing behind one of the other men looking over his shoulder, said, 'My man's got a flush, what's he got?'

Jordan laughed and said, 'His Lordship only has three kings.'

Lord Dorres threw the cards onto the table. 'I have had enough of your impertinence.' The other two men threw their cards onto the table as well.

One of the men playing cards said to Lord Dorres, 'David this is too much, can't you get rid of these two?' He waved his hand at Jordan and Danny.

'Sorry for spoiling your game,' Jordan said, 'but we really do need to speak to His Lordship urgently. I am Detective Sergeant Rhodes, and this is Detective Constable Kane.'

'I have seen you before somewhere, I think,' Lord Dorres said to Danny.

'Yes, sir, I came to your house,' Danny replied.

'I remember, you were with that jumped-up inspector who thought he was important,' Lord Dorres said.

'He's talking about Harry,' Danny said to Jordan, who laughed out loud.

Jordan turned to the other card players and said, 'Now if you gentlemen would kindly leave us, it won't take long and you can get back to your game.' Neither made any move.

Lord Dorres said, 'Let me introduce you to my friends, this is Sir Michael Crisp.' He pointed to the man on his right. 'He works in the Attorney General's office. And this is Lord Smart, he is a Permanent Secretary at the Foreign Office.' He pointed to the second man, then turned back to look at Jordan.

Jordan shrugged and said, 'Well, I am sure you are both really nice people, and if I had more time I am sure we could have a good chat, but I am only here to see Lord Dorres today.' He knelt down so he was level with Lord Dorres. 'I am getting a little tired of this, you can talk here or down the police station.'

Lord Dorres sat back slightly, still smiling. 'Are you going to arrest me?'

'If I have to,' Jordan said.

The man called Sir Michael Crisp said, 'You can't do that.'

Danny, who was standing behind him, leaned down so his head was level with Sir Michael's ear and said, 'Do you want a bet on that?'

Lord Dorres looked at his two friends, a big smile on his face, and said, 'This is what we have as a police force now, a long-haired thing and this…' he did not finish the rest of the sentence as Jordan lifted him out of the chair, spun him around, and had his hands in handcuffs before he knew what was happening.

In a loud voice which could be clearly heard across the whole room, Jordan said, 'Lord Dorres, I am arresting you for allowing your home to be used for the consumption of drugs.' Jordan then told Lord Dorres his rights. The other men at the table were stunned and had not moved.

Danny leaned back down and said to Sir Michael Crisp, 'You would have lost your bet.' He joined Jordan and took Lord Dorres' other arm, and they started to lead him to the door of the bar, which was barred by the four men. Danny said to them, 'You can stand out of the way, or all you lot can come to the station as well.' They moved aside.

Lord Dorres finally found his voice, 'You two are in deep trouble, I will make sure you are thrown out of the police.'

Jordan turned to him, put his face within an inch and said, 'I am fed up with you, shut your mouth. You can whine all you like when you get to the station.' He bent Lord Dorres' arm up and forward so Lord Dorres was now walking bent over. They took him through the dining room and out into the reception area, through the front doors and to the car. Danny opened the car door, Jordan pushed Lord Dorres into the back. 'Put his seat belt on him, Hippie,' Jordan said. 'I am going to ring the boss to put him in the picture.'

After Jordan got off the phone from speaking to Charlie, he said to Danny who was leaning with his arms on the roof of the car, 'The boss wants us to take him...' Jordan pointed at Lord Dorres seated in the back of the car, '...to his home address. He is organising some friends from the drugs squad to meet us there.'

Danny nodded and said, 'I think his friends are stirring things up.' He pointed to the front of the club, Jordan turned to see the two men Lord Dorres had been playing cards with on their phones.

'Dare say the boss's phone will get hot later,' Jordan said. 'Come on, let's take His Lordship home.' They both got into the car.

'You two are finished in the police, you know that, don't you?' Lord Dorres said from the backseat as Jordan pulled out into the traffic.

Danny turned to look back at him. 'Are you comfortable in the back, the handcuffs not too tight are they?' he said. Lord Dorres scowled at him. 'When we get you back to the station you can talk all you want, but we are going to your house first, so if I could just ask Your Lordship to kindly to shut up.'

It took them about fifteen minutes to drive through the

London traffic and arrive outside Lord Dorres' house. Jordan and Danny climbed out. Across the road were two marked police cars, one was a dog unit. Jordan approached one and spoke to the officer inside. He came back and said to Danny, 'Get him out the back, we are all set.'

Danny opened the back door of the car and pulled Lord Dorres out. 'Hope your journey home wasn't too unpleasant,' he said. Lord Dorres made no reply. Jordan waved his hand and three officers crossed the road, one holding the lead of a cocker spaniel whose tail was wagging furiously. They followed Jordan and Danny to the front door of the house. 'Do you have your door keys?' Jordan said to Lord Dorres. He made no reply. 'Okay, let's have a look.' Danny held Lord Dorres' arms while Jordan searched his pockets, finding a bunch of keys.

Jordan looked at the keys, selected one tried it but it didn't fit. The second one fitted and the door opened. Jordan walked in and shouted, 'It's the police, anybody in?' Danny followed with Lord Dorres and the officers. Jordan saw Cameron, the butler, appear, he walked towards them.

'It's the butler,' Danny said to Jordan. 'Hello, we are here to search the house.' Cameron's face showed shock.

'Are you alright, sir?' Cameron said to Lord Dorres, ignoring Danny.

'Call my solicitor and tell him what's happening,' Lord Dorres said to Cameron.

'Yes, sir, right away,' Cameron said.

'Just a second,' Jordan said, grabbing Cameron's arm as he went to turn away. 'Is there anyone else in the house?'

'Her Ladyship is in her room upstairs,' Cameron replied.

'Okay, you can join us in the front room.' He pulled Cameron towards the door to the front room, followed by Danny holding Lord Dorres.

Once inside, they sat Lord Dorres down, with Cameron seated beside him. 'Can I call His Lordship's solicitor?' Cameron asked.

'Yes, go ahead,' Jordan said. 'Danny, you stay in here with these two. I will go and get Her Ladyship up and get the search started.'

CHAPTER TWELVE

Charlie turned the key and the door opened. 'Well, it's the right place,' he said to Cramer as he pushed the door open. 'Remember Parkin was letting this place be used by different people, so put some gloves on. We want to see if we can get some good prints from in here.' Cramer followed Charlie's lead and pulled some gloves on as they entered. Charlie saw the layout looked the same as Angela Cook's flat. 'We will start in the bedroom, let's see if we can find his camera.'

Once in the bedroom they started their search. It took a couple of minutes before Cramer called Charlie. He was holding up a clock radio. Charlie came across to look. 'This looks a sophisticated piece of equipment, sir,' Cramer said, passing it to Charlie, who looked over it.

'You can hardly see it, can you?' Charlie said, examining the clock. 'Okay, put it in a bag, we will get someone to have a look at it when we get back to the Yard. Let's keep looking.' They carried on their search.

'The place is pretty clean,' Cramer said.

'Parkin must have had a cleaner come in once or twice a week,' Charlie replied, walking through to the front room.

'No clothes in any of the cupboards or drawers,' Cramer called out from the bedroom. Shutting them, he followed Charlie into the front room.

Charlie opened the drawers. They were all empty. On the side he noticed some bottles of drink, most of them open. 'Get all these bottles checked for prints.' Cramer nodded. 'Have a

155

look in the kitchen, see if the cleaner left anything about unwashed. We might get some prints or DNA.' Cramer went off into the kitchen. Charlie walked to the windows that led to the balcony, slipped the lock and slid the doors open. He checked, but found nothing outside, came back in and relocked the doors.

Cramer came out of the kitchen. 'Nothing in there, just a few washed-up glasses sitting on the side,' he said.

'Oh well, we got the camera, it might tell us something. Give forensics a ring to get a team over here straight away. Tell them we will leave the keys with the porter at the desk,' Charlie said.

Cramer took his phone out to make the call as he and Charlie left the flat. Angela Cooks was two floors above so they took the lift. Outside her flat Charlie rang the bell. After a minute he rang again.

'Doesn't look like she's in,' Cramer said.

Charlie nodded, 'We will come back again. Let's go down and leave the keys with the porter for forensics and go back to the Yard.' Charlie got a phone call from Jordan as they made their way down. After he spoke to Jordan, he made a call to the Yard. They took the lift down and walked into the lobby area and walked up to the desk.

'Did you find anything, sir?' the man behind the desk asked.

'No, nothing,' Charlie said. 'We are leaving these keys.' Charlie handed him the set Parkin had for the flat. 'Some more officers will be turning up, when they do, give them the keys.' The porter nodded. Charlie was just going to turn away, when he stopped. 'Has anyone been in to see Angela Cook over the last few days?' The porter opened the log book. 'No visitors until this morning when she had a parcel delivered at 9.10 and the driver left the building at 9.20.' He turned the log so Charlie could look at it.

'Have you been on all morning?' Charlie asked the porter.

'Yes, sir, I started at seven,' the porter replied.

'Is that the name of the parcel delivery company in the book?' Charlie said. The man nodded. 'Have you seen Miss Cook leave the building this morning?'

'No, sir, not today.'

'What if she went straight to the car park?' Charlie asked.

'She would still have to walk by the desk, the door over there...', he pointed, '...leads to the underground car park. It's the only way to enter and leave the building from the car park.'

'Do you keep spare keys to all the flats?' Charlie asked.

'Yes, sir.' He opened a cabinet behind the desk.

'Give me the spare keys for Miss Cook's flat, it's 114.'

The porter took the keys from the cabinet and gave them to Charlie, who turned to Cramer. 'Let's go and see if she was pretending she was out, that parcel might have been something interesting.'

They retraced their steps to the lift and took it up to the fourteenth floor, then walked along the corridor till they were outside Angela Cook's flat. Charlie rang the bell again, waited but there was no answer. He put the key in the door and opened it. 'Angela,' Charlie called out as he entered, 'It's the police.' There was no reply. Cramer followed Charlie into the flat.

There was a box sitting on the table in the middle of the room, but nothing else looked out of place. Charlie walked over to have a look at the box. It was about a foot square with brown tape around it. Angela Cook's address was clearly written on the top. It had not been opened. 'Check the other rooms,' Charlie said Cramer walked away. Charlie picked the parcel up, it was very light.

'Sir, in here,' Charlie heard Cramer call him from the bedroom. When Charlie entered, he saw Cramer standing beside Angela Cook. She was lying across the bed on her back. 'There's no pulse, sir,' Cramer said. 'The marks on her neck,' Cramer pointed. 'Looks like she's been strangled.'

Charlie stared at the body. 'What a shame,' he said. 'Get the forensics team who were coming over to look at the other flat diverted to this first. Let's have a look around, but our murderer might have taken anything we wanted to get a look at.'

They started to search the bedroom. 'She had lots of clothes,' Cramer said as he opened a closet that was filled with dresses. Charlie opened a drawer in the bedside table. Inside was a paperback book, a couple of photographs, one of Angela Cook holding a drink in front of a bar, another of her and a girl with drinks looking like they were standing in front of the same bar. He also took out two cigars.

'I might have an idea who these belong to,' Charlie said, holding them up. He took a bag from Cramer and dropped the cigars inside.

'We have to assume the man who delivered the parcel is our killer. I will phone Harry, put him in the picture. You get some more officers over to knock on all the doors in this building. We might get lucky, someone may have seen him, but I won't hold out too much hope. And question the porter, get a description from him. The company name in the log book is probably false but get it checked. I can't believe this block doesn't have any CCTV. You get on with that, I will stay and look around the flat.' Cramer left the bedroom. Charlie heard him go out the front door. Charlie got up from the bed and walked into the front room, he took his phone out and called Harry.

Harry had just got off the phone from talking to Charlie. He was at his desk at the Yard having got back from questioning

Micky Adams. Manjitt was sitting across the desk from him. He looked at her and said, 'That was the boss. He and Cramer are at Angela Cook's flat. They just found her body, it looks like she's been strangled. The boss is organising things over there. As soon as he can he is coming back, he wants everybody here for a meeting, so get on to Jordan and Hippie, let them know.'

Manjitt rose and went to phone Jordan. Harry picked up the phone and called a friend in the drugs squad to see if he could get a name for the man they had seen in the café that morning. As he put down the phone it rang immediately. He nodded a few times and said, 'Yes sir. I will find out and get back to you. Yes, sir, right away.' He put down the phone just as Manjitt sat down. 'You are never going to believe what Jordan just told me,' Manjitt said.

Harry looked at her. 'Let me guess, they've arrested Lord Dorres.'

'How did you know that?' Manjitt asked.

'That was the Commissioner's Office on the phone. They want to know what we are playing at, arresting Lord Dorres in the middle of his club,' Harry said.

'Well, Jordan is on his way back, he said he had arrested Lady Dorres too,' Manjitt said, a smile on her face.

Harry cupped his hands and put them behind his head and leaned back in his chair. 'It could get very interesting later today. Did Jordan say what he had arrested them for?'

'He said they've recovered some drugs from Lord Dorres' house,' Manjitt replied.

'Well at least we have something.' Harry's phone rang again. He picked it up. 'Yes, sir, I have heard. No, sir, the Chief Superintendent is not in the office at the moment. Yes, I will get him to call you as soon as he gets back.' Harry put the phone down. 'That was Assistant Commissioner Crick.

Someone must have rattled his cage about Lord Dorres. He wants the boss to call him right away.'

'You know Harry, that Sir Mark Coale offered me a job,' Manjitt said, 'but it wouldn't be half as much fun as this.'

'Well, while we are waiting for the sparks to fly, let's try and tidy up a few loose ends,' Harry said. 'You can phone Tim Green and let him know he can pick up his Jaguar anytime he wants. Get a time and date from him so we know when he's turning up, we can ask him a couple of questions at the same time.' Manjitt got up and went to find the phone number for Tim Green. Harry started to write up the notes from their meeting with Micky Adams.

It was about half an hour later when Jordan and Danny came into the office. 'Ho, ho, you two have stirred up a hornet's nest,' Manjitt said.

Harry looked up from writing, waved Jordan and Danny over. Manjitt got up from her desk and followed. 'You'd better have something on Lord what's-his-name,' Harry said.

'Lord Dorres,' Manjitt said.

'Thank you, Manjitt,' Harry said. 'Well sit down you two, fill me in on what you have been up to.'

Manjitt took a seat too, smiling. She said, 'I have got to hear this.'

Jordan told Harry all that had happened at the club and what they had done once they got to the house, and that he and Danny had booked them into custody. They had been put in separate cells.

'Well, what did you get from the house?' Harry said.

Danny held up an evidence bag and said, 'The dog discovered this in Her Ladyship's bedroom.' Inside was a smaller bag filled with white powder. 'And we got this from a drawer in the front room.' He held up another evidence bag, inside which was a smaller bag, again filled with white powder. 'I would guess it's cocaine, I will get it off for tests.'

'That's good, anything else turn up?' Harry asked.

'Well, Her Ladyship and His Lordship have separate bedrooms,' Jordan said.

'Well, we know she didn't rely on His Lordship for all her needs,' Harry said. Manjitt filled Jordan and Danny in on the questioning of Micky Adams.

'It's a different world,' Danny said, shaking his head.

'Don't worry, Hippie,' Harry said. 'You will get used to it, the boss should be back shortly.' He told them about Cramer and Charlie finding Angela Cook murdered. Harry's phone rang and he picked it up. 'Yes, sir, no, the officers have not come back to the office yet, no, the Chief Superintendent is still out, yes, as soon as he's back.' He put down the phone. 'That was Assistant Commissioner Crick again. You two will be legends in your own lifetime,' he said, looking at Jordan and Danny. 'Has His Lordship got his solicitor with him yet?'

'Not yet, but I think they will be here soon,' Jordan said. Danny nudged Jordan in the side.

'You tell him,' Danny said.

Harry looked from one to the other. 'Well what is it? Don't keep me in suspense.'

Jordan looked at Harry. 'When we got back here and had them in the custody area booking them in, the sergeant asked me if I wanted them strip-searched.'

'You didn't?' Manjitt said.

Smiling, Jordan said, 'I couldn't resist it, Harry, I wouldn't want to be accused of being biased. I just followed normal procedure.'

Harry sat for a moment shaking his head. 'I suppose procedure has to be followed and I can't blame you for that. Having met His Lordship, I would've done the same thing'.

'That's good,' Danny said. 'We also confiscated the clothes they were wearing for drug checks. They are sitting in the cells in white paper suits.'

Manjitt laughed out loud and said, 'He must have really wound you two up.'

'As soon as custody ring up that their solicitor has arrived, let me know,' Harry said. Jordan nodded. 'Get me some tea, Hippie, and I will consider whether your career is worth saving.'

The team were sitting around the office chatting and writing up reports from the day's work when Charlie and Cramer came back into the office. 'Everyone, my desk,' Charlie called out. When they were all seated, Charlie went over what had happened at the flats at Chelsea Harbour, the search of the flat Parkin had the keys for and how they had found Angela Cook's body. He held up the camera they had discovered. 'Cramer is going to get it checked out by some of the technical bods, but it's a sneaky piece of equipment. We left the forensic team going over Angela Cook's flat, but we got these from her bedside table.' He held up the two cigars.

'They're like the ones Amanda Moore smoked when we saw her,' Danny said.

'They're the same,' Charlie said, 'same brand.'

'Lord Dorres smokes cigars,' Jordan said.

'Well check out what brand. These are very exclusive, according to Amanda Moore,' Charlie said.

They were interrupted by three men entering the office, two in uniform and one in plain clothes.

'Heads up,' Harry said. 'The top brass are here.'

The three men approached the team, who all stood. 'Hello, Charlie,' Assistant Commissioner Crick said. He was dressed in full uniform. Charlie nodded. 'This is Deputy

Commissioner Macready.' He indicated the other man dressed in uniform, 'and this is Superintendent Haig from Special Branch, ' he introduced the other man with him. 'We have come over because there have been numerous complaints about your officers and the detention of Lord and Lady Dorres.'

Macready spoke. 'My office has phoned on a number of occasions trying to get some answers to what is going on. We have also tried to contact you, but with no success,' he said, looking at Charlie.

'I took those phone calls,' Harry said before Charlie could answer. 'I told whoever phoned I would get back to them whenever I could, and would tell my boss when he got back to contact your office.'

'And who are you?' Macready asked.

It was Charlie that spoke. 'That is Chief Inspector Davis. He did inform me about the phone calls but we have a fast-moving inquiry going on. My team have just got back to the office and we were catching up.'

'That's very interesting Chief Superintendent,' Macready said, 'but if you go around invading private clubs where some of the most powerful people in the land are, and arrest one of them in front of everyone, you have to have answers and a good reason for doing so. I have had phone call after phone call about it.' Charlie said nothing. 'Well, what have you got to say about it?'

'Sorry, sir, I didn't know you had finished.' Crick's eyes went heavenward at Charlie's answer.

'Who where the officers who went to the club?' Macready said.

Jordan and Danny spoke to say they had. Macready looked at them. 'I hope you had good reason to behave the way you did. It sounds like you were over-zealous, and from what I have heard you could be facing a charge of false arrest or assault.'

'Who says they arrested anyone falsely?' Charlie asked.

Macready turned back to Charlie. 'There were a number of witnesses to the arrest whose background makes their complaints most believable.'

'I know my officers, and I would stand their word up against anybody, regardless of who they are or what they did for a living,' Charlie said.

'I shall remember you said that,' Macready said, looking hard at Charlie. 'Now I am sure we can get this sorted out. Firstly we need to release Lord and Lady Dorres. I will speak to them personally and apologise. It won't stop a formal enquiry into the circumstances of the arrest, there will have to be one. I am afraid your two officers will have to be suspended while the enquiry is going on. I don't make any promises; we will see if we can save their careers.'

'I am sorry, sir,' Charlie said. 'You said Lord and Lady Dorres have to be released. I can't do that, and as for my officers being suspended, if you don't mind me saying so, you are off your head.'

Assistant Commissioner Crick winced at Charlie's words and quickly said, 'I am sure we can sort this out to everyone's benefit.'

Charlie turned to Crick. 'I appreciate your words, sir, but Lord Dorres is not going anywhere. If someone wants to make a fool of themselves then go ahead and release him, but I am sure the newspapers would have a field day about it.'

'Are you threatening me, Chief Superintendent?' Macready said. 'The newspapers would not know anything that's gone on.'

'The newspapers have a way of getting stories, from where no one knows,' Harry said.

Macready looked at Harry, then back to Charlie. 'I see your officers have an attitude problem.'

'Can we just get back to the false arrest bit, please, sir,' Charlie said. Crick again pulled a face that showed he wished Charlie would choose his words more carefully. 'You said he was falsely arrested. Who told you that?'

Macready looked a little confused. 'Are you telling me you have arrested him on hard evidence?'

'Thank you, sir, for asking the right question,' Charlie said, ignoring the silently mouthed words coming from Crick. 'You see my officers were under my orders. We had been trying to talk to Lord Dorres on a number of occasions. He refused to talk to them when my officers finally caught up with him. They had no alternative but to arrest him as he refused to comply with their requests to come with them nicely. They had to handcuff him as he resisted a bit, but they used the minimum amount of force.'

'That is a very good story to cover your officers,' Macready said. 'But you said evidence, and so far I have not heard any.'

'That's because you never asked,' Charlie said. The room was quiet.

It was Macready who broke the silence. 'Well, what evidence do you have. It better be good or you might be joining your officers on suspension.'

'I would hate for a senior officer to make a fool of himself, sir,' Charlie said more loudly than normal. 'And if you were to release Lord Dorres before we can question him, I think there might be a lot of questions asked why you did. If you had come in here and asked why we had arrested Lord Dorres, instead of assuming we don't know our jobs and we pull people in just for fun, it could have saved a lot of trouble. As for my officers being suspended, you have no chance.'

Crick butted in quickly. 'If you could just tell us, Charlie, what are the reasons?' Charlie looked at Crick, whose usual tan seemed a lot paler than normal.

Charlie turned back to Macready. 'Lord Dorres was involved with a group of men who went to sex parties where high-class prostitutes were supplied by a friend of his. He also knew the murdered BBC man Gerald Parkin, who we believe may have been blackmailing him. We know Parkin was blackmailing his wife and a number of others, which would be a reason to murder Parkin. One of the girls who attended these parties was also found murdered today, and to top it all...' Charlie took the two bags of white powder and dropped them on the table, '...we recovered what we believe to be cocaine from Lord Dorres' house today. Now in my book Lord Dorres has a few questions to answer, but if you want to release him go ahead, but I will put a complaint in about your interference in a double-murder investigation, sir.'

The room was quiet again. It was Crick who spoke first. 'It seems that you have uncovered a lot Charlie. We perhaps didn't know the full extent of the inquiry.'

'I don't believe anyone asked,' Charlie said. He stared at Macready. 'And if I can just ask, why are Special Branch here? Is Lord Dorres working for them or something?'

'No, they had phone calls about his arrest from some important people,' Crick said. Haig smiled and winked at Charlie.

'So, do you want me to phone down and release him or not?' Charlie said. 'As I am trying to run a double-murder inquiry.'

'You go ahead with the investigation, but I want to be kept informed of any developments,' Macready said. He turned and walked away. Crick followed with Haig.

The team stood silent, till Charlie said as he sat down, 'Now where was I before we were interrupted.'

'Cigars,' Harry said.

Charlie nodded. 'Yes, find out what cigars Lord Dorres

smokes, and after that little chat with the gods, Danny, I could do with a cup of tea.'

'Seeing as I still have a job, boss, it will be a pleasure,' Danny said.

'What do you reckon on Lord Dorres?' Harry asked Charlie.

'I doubt if he's our killer, but he has avoided our questions for long enough, so we want some answers. Manjitt, I want you and Cramer to go and pick up Sir Martin Oliver. As Angela Cook was working as one of his girls, we need to ask him about her. Bringing him in here might shake him up a bit.'

'What about Lady Dorres?' Harry said.

'I will take Danny in with me to speak to her,' Charlie said, 'although I don't think there is much more she has to tell. But I will let her know you spoke to her lover. Okay Manjitt, you and Cramer get off.' Manjitt and Cramer left.

'They enjoy working together, don't you think so, boss?' Harry said, watching them leave. Charlie looked at Harry then at the leaving pair.

It was Jordan that spoke. 'Harry, you don't think...'

He was stopped by Charlie saying, 'You don't think anything, Jordan, if you want to keep all your limbs in working order. Manjitt might take exception to you saying anything.' Jordan nodded. Danny came back with Charlie's tea. 'Have I missed anything?' he asked. Harry and Charlie looked at Jordan.

'Not a thing,' Jordan said.

A while later Jordan took a call that Lord Dorres' solicitor had arrived. 'Harry, you and Jordan can do the questioning. I know how well you two get on with him,' Charlie said, 'but remember we want answers.'

When Harry and Jordan entered the interview room they found Lord Dorres sitting next to his solicitor. It was Harry who spoke as he sat down. 'You have been told your rights, I am going to turn the tape on now and we will formally begin the interview.' Harry switched the tape on, said who was present and then began. 'Lord Dorres, would you like to tell us all you know about Gerald Parkin?'

Lord Dorres looked at Harry. His face showed some confusion. 'Gerald Parkin? What has he got to do with my arrest?'

'If you could just answer the question,' Harry said.

'I told you all about him the first time you came to my house,' Lord Dorres said. 'I remember you now.' He turned to his solicitor. 'This was one of the officers who came to my house the first time, make a note of him. I want a complaint against him as well as this one,' he pointed at Jordan. 'He was one of the two who assaulted me.'

'I'm sure your solicitor has got all that. Now getting back to Gerald Parkin, do you want to tell us about your relationship with him?' Harry said.

'I told you all I knew about him. There was no relationship, he was someone who came to dinners, he was not a friend.'

'But if he wasn't a friend, why did you continue to invite him to your house for dinner?' Jordan asked.

'He kept people entertained, no other reason.'

'So you had no other dealings with Gerald Parkin?' Harry said.

'I will give you the same answer to the same question, and I would like to add I did not kill Gerald.'

'Thank you, sir, I hear that from a lot from people who turn out to be guilty. But I repeat, did you have any other dealings with Gerald Parkin?' Harry said.

Lord Dorres turned to his solicitor. 'Do I have to keep repeating myself?' he said.

The solicitor spoke. 'I think His Lordship has answered that question.'

'That's nice of you to point that out,' Harry said to the solicitor 'but His Lordship has not answered my question to my satisfaction.' Harry turned back to Lord Dorres. 'Did you have any other dealings with Gerald Parkin?'

Lord Dorres sat back in his chair, his paper suit rustled as he did. 'No, I did not, are you happy now?'

'Yes, sir, thank you.' Harry smiled across the table at Lord Dorres.

'Do you know Sir Martin Oliver?' Jordan asked.

'Yes, of course I do, and you know that. I remember giving him...' he pointed at Harry, '...Martin's name when he came to my house.' Lord Dorres shook his head. 'What is the point of all this?'

'During our investigation into Gerald Parkin's murder, we have had to look into his background,' Harry said. 'Now apart from his television work, it turned out he had quite a profitable sideline going. Would you like to guess what else he did to earn money?'

The solicitor spoke. 'Is that a question for my client?'

'If your client wants to have a guess,' Harry said.

'I have no idea,' Lord Dorres said.

'He was a blackmailer.' Harry saw Lord Dorres' face change. 'Does that surprise you?'

'Yes, it does. Gerald, a blackmailer, that is a shock.'

'So he wasn't blackmailing you over anything?' Jordan asked.

'No, what could he blackmail me over?'

'Well, there was your wife's drug habit. He might have threatened you over that,' Jordan said.

'He was not blackmailing me,' Lord Dorres said, leaning forward. His face had a worried look.

'Could I just ask what type of cigars you smoke?' Jordan asked.

Lord Dorres looked a bit perplexed. 'Cigars, why do you want to know that?'

'If you can just tell us,' Jordan said.

'I smoke Cuban cigars, I get them from Harrods. I can give you the name of the salesman there if you like,' Lord Dorres said.

'That's very kind of you to offer,' Jordan replied.

'Now, your good friend, Sir Martin Oliver,' Harry said. 'How close a friend would you say he is?'

'You can't suspect Martin of Gerald's murder,' Lord Dorres said. His face showed confusion at the questioning.

'I don't think that was my question,' Harry said. 'I asked you how close a friend Sir Martin is?'

'He's a close friend. I have known him for many years, but I could not imagine him murdering anyone.'

'That's nice to know. I will make a note of your character reference for him,' Harry said.

'Do you know this girl?' Jordan put a picture of Angela Cook in front of Lord Dorres, who leaned forward to look at it. Both Harry and Jordan picked up a flash of recognition in Lord Dorres' eyes.

'No, never seen her before. Who is she?' Lord Dorres said.

'Have you known for a long time about your wife using drugs?' Harry asked.

The solicitor spoke. 'Lord Dorres knew about his wife's drug habit, but had told her she should stop. He had tried to get her to go to a drug clinic for treatment and had said she should not have drugs in the house. He did not know any drugs were in the house when he was taken there earlier today, and has never supplied his wife with drugs.'

'Thank you for clearing that up for us,' Harry said. 'So where did you think she was getting her drugs?'

It was the solicitor who spoke again. 'His Lordship has no idea where she gets her drugs.'

'I just want to make sure of something,' Harry said. 'Gerald Parkin never tried to blackmail you,' Harry said.

'His Lordship has answered that question,' the solicitor said. Harry nodded.

'Okay, we will take a break now.' Interview suspended. Harry switched the tape off. 'Would you like some tea or coffee?' The solicitor asked for two teas. Harry said he would get them brought to them by the constable. He told the solicitor they would be back in fifteen minutes. When they left the interview room Harry turned to Jordan. 'What do you think?'

'He's got himself in the corner now. Did you see his face when I showed him Angela Cook's picture?' Jordan said.

'Yeah, I clocked that,' Harry said, 'and his denials of blackmail are starting to look hollow. We will leave him for a while. I think he was starting to look quite smug with his solicitor doing his talking. When we go back in we will hit him with everything. Let's go and get a drink.'

Manjitt and Cramer had arrived outside the Brook Street gallery of Sir Martin Oliver. 'That was a bit hairy this morning with the Deputy Commissioner,' Cramer said.

'Just another fun day in the Serious Crime Squad,' Manjitt said as they got out of the car.

'I think the Deputy Commissioner was fuming when he left,' Cramer said. 'Won't the Chief Superintendent be worried?'

'The boss, why should he? Everything he said was right,' Manjitt replied.

'What about Jordan and Danny? They could be in trouble,' Cramer said.

'I don't think so. The boss made it clear he backs them, so they would have to out him if they tried anything with Jordan and Danny. Anyway, let's sort out Sir Martin,' Manjitt said.

They entered the gallery and were met by a young woman. They asked to see Sir Martin. The young woman asked them what for. Cramer said they were interested in buying the large work of art in the front window. The girl phoned the office; she told them Sir Martin would be down in a minute. Manjitt and Cramer strolled around looking at the artwork.

They saw a man with jet-black hair approach them. 'Can I help you?' he said, holding his hand out. 'I am Sir Martin Oliver, I understand you are interested in the piece in the front window.'

'Hello, sir, we are from the police,' Cramer said, introducing themselves and holding up his warrant card. 'We need to ask you a few questions.'

'What about?' Sir Martin asked.

'A friend of yours, Angela Cook,' Manjitt said.

'Would you like to come back to my office, we can talk privately,' Sir Martin replied.

'No, I have to ask you to come to the station with us,' Cramer said.

'I'm sure there's no need for that.' Sir Martin's face had a worried look on it.

Cramer took hold of Sir Martin's arm. 'Sorry, sir, it's not up for debate.'

'Can I give my assistant the keys to lock up?' Sir Martin asked. Cramer nodded.

Sir Martin spoke to his assistant, gave her the keys and left with Manjitt and Cramer.

Harry had walked into the office with Jordan to find Danny and Charlie sitting going through some paperwork. Charlie looked up and asked, 'How is it going with Lord Dorres?'

'He's painted himself into a corner and he doesn't know it yet,' Harry said. 'What about Her Ladyship, how did it go?'

'Pretty straight forward, she knows no more than she already told us,' Charlie said 'She was a bit upset when I told her about her boyfriend, think he might be losing a customer.'

'Has anything come up from the drugs squad about the man we saw come into the café when we where questioning Micky Adams?' Harry asked.

'Nothing yet, Harry, but Danny got a call from Tim Green, he will be picking his car up tomorrow morning so we will surprise him with a little chat. We will need to speak to Amanda Moore again about Angela Cook, and Manjitt and Cramer are on their way back with Sir Martin Oliver,' Charlie said, 'and I had a thought about that Harry. Once we have Sir Martin here and in the cells, perhaps we should take a spin over to his gallery and house, give them a good search after all he has motive, if he knew she had passed on information to Gerald Parkin it would mess his little vice ring up, also he's running a string of prostitutes so there won't be any comebacks.'

'That's good for me, boss, when did forensics say they will get back to you about anything they find at the flats?' Harry asked.

'I buzzed them a while ago, they have lifted a few different prints from Angela Cooks place, they've not started on the second flat yet, so it might be the morning before they can give us anything,'

Harry nodded, 'Fingers crossed we get something, come on Jordan let's go back and rattle His Lordships cage.' Jordan followed Harry back out of the office.

Charlie took a call from Assistant Commissioner Crick asking him for a full, up-to-date report, as he needed to see the Deputy Commissioner in the morning, Charlie told him he would have it first thing. Charlie told Danny to find out from the company that Angela Cook was renting the flat from, about her tenancy agreement and get all her bank details.

As Harry and Jordan got to the custody area on their way to the interview room, they saw Manjitt and Cramer booking Sir Martin Oliver in. Harry pulled Manjitt aside and told her what Charlie had planned for later.

Harry and Jordan sat back down opposite Lord Dorres and his solicitor, he went through the procedures after turning the tape recorder on. 'Now, Lord Dorres, if we could just start with Sir Martin Oliver, you said he was a very close friend is that right?'

Lord Dorres looked at his solicitor who nodded, 'Yes, he was a close friend.'

'You saw him at dinner parties, did you see him anywhere else?' Jordan said.

'I told you, I can't believe Martin would be involved with Parkin murder,' Lord Dorres answered.

'That was not the question, apart from the dinner parties did you see him anywhere else?' Jordan repeated.

'Yes, of course, at gallery openings, he came up to my country houses for shooting weekends, we might go to the theatre, various places,' Lord Dorres shrugged his shoulders.

'Did you go to any special parties Sir Martin organised?' Harry said.

'What sort of special parties?' Lord Dorres said, but Harry saw as he said it his face was beginning to realise what they meant.

'You don't know anything about Sir Martin's special parties, is that what your telling me?' Harry said.

It was Lord Dorres' solicitor who leaned in and spoke quietly to Lord Dorres who whispered back to him.

'Could I ask for a slight break at this time, I need to consult with my client, maybe 15 minutes?' the solicitor asked.

'Yes, of course, but I hope when we come back he will start being a bit more cooperative with us.' Harry suspended the interview and turned the tape off, he and Jordan left Lord Dorres and his solicitor to chat alone.

Sir Martin Oliver looked across the table at Manjitt and Cramer. 'Now are you sure you don't want a solicitor present?' Manjitt said.

'No, I will answer all your questions,' Sir Martin replied. 'I would like to keep this problem as quiet as possible. I spoke to one of your officers before, I told him all I knew.'

'We will be recording all this interview for the record,' Cramer said, Sir Martin nodded.

'Do you know this girl?' Manjitt put a picture of Angela Cook on the table.

'Yes, that's Angela,' Sir Martin said.

'She worked for you,' Cramer asked.

'She worked in my gallery for a few months, then, well you know became a regular at the parties I organised. Why, is she in trouble?' Sir Martin asked.

'Her body was found at her flat this morning, we believe she was murdered,' Manjitt said.

Sir Martin sat quietly for a moment looking at Angela Cook's picture on the table, he looked up at Manjitt and Cramer and said, 'You don't think I had anything to do with her murder, do you?'

'Can you tell us where you were from eight o'clock this morning?' Cramer asked.

'Yes, I left home about 7.30,' he said, 'got to the gallery about eight or a little after and have been there all day, I have nothing to do with Angela's murder, why would I want to hurt her?'

'Do you have witnesses to your movements?' Manjitt asked.

'The girl working in the gallery today, got in about 8.45 she will tell you, but the CCTV should show when I arrived.'

'If you didn't murder her can you think of anyone who would want to?' Cramer said.

'She was a very nice girl, no I can't,' he said.

'She was a regular at your parties, did she spend time with anyone in particular?' Manjitt said.

' What do you mean?' Sir Martin asked.

'Was she particularly friendly with anyone, do you know if she met anyone away from your parties?' Manjitt said.

Sir Martin hesitated for a second. 'Well I understand she was seeing one of people she had met at the parties privately but I had no part in that arrangement.'

'Who was that?' Cramer said.

'Sir Mark Coale.'

'How do you know that?' Cramer asked.

'I had dinner with her and another girl one evening, they both got tipsy and I think they forget I was there for a time and where chatting between themselves and I heard Angela telling the other girl about going to Sir Mark's house.'

'We will need the other girl's name and an address, just to check that,' Manjitt said. 'The other girl, was she one of your party girls?'

'Yes.' Sir Martin wrote down the name of the girl on a piece of paper Manjitt had put in front of him and pushed it back across the table. 'I haven't seen her for a few months, she stopped coming to the parties. Angela said she was involved with someone and wanted to settle down, I don't have an address for her.' Manjitt picked up the paper and looked at the name.

'Did you know Angela Cook was seeing Gerald Parkin?' Cramer asked.

' I had no idea,' Sir Martin said, a surprised look on his face.

'Did Gerald Parkin ever try to blackmail you?' Manjitt said.

'Blackmail, no.'

'We know Gerald Parkin was blackmailing a number of people and you're telling us he was not blackmailing you?' Manjitt said, 'After all you were organising all these sex parties, he would see you as a ripe target.'

'He was not blackmailing me,' Sir Martin said.

'We believe Angela Cook was supplying Gerald Parkin with information about who attended the parties and what was said, now if you weren't being blackmailed, were you working with Gerald Parkin to blackmail people?' Manjitt asked.

'I had no knowledge of what Gerald was up to and was certainly not working with him.'

'Did you ever go to Angela Cook's flat?' Cramer asked.

'No, never,' Sir Martin said.

'We will have to check out what you've told us, so we are going to keep you here for a little while but as soon as we are happy you have an alibi for this morning we will release you. Are you sure you don't want a solicitor?' Manjitt asked.

'I would like to keep this as discreet as possible, will it take long?' he asked.

'We will be as quick as we can,' Manjitt said turning off the tape recorder.

'Before we continue with the interview,' Lord Dorres' solicitor said, ' he wants to make it clear he had nothing to do with Gerald Parkin murder or the supply of drugs to his wife, but he is willing to answer all your questions.'

Harry and Jordan sat listening to the solicitor, Lord Dorres looked a bit tired in his white paper suit next to his solicitor, he was leaning on the table staring at them.

'Thank you,' Harry said, he turned to face Lord Dorres. 'Let's start with blackmail, was Gerald Parkin blackmailing you?'

Lord Dorres hesitated for a second then said, 'Yes, he was.'

'What was he blackmailing you over?' Jordan asked.

'My wife's drug habit,' he said.

'Is that all?' Harry asked, 'After all he knew you were attending the sex parties organised by Sir Martin Oliver.'

Lord Dorres had a pained expression on his face when he answered, 'yes, he was blackmailing me over the parties too.'

'How did he approach you?' Jordan said.

'He turned up out of the blue at my house one day, as calm as you like, over coffee he demands £200,000 or he would let the papers know what I had been doing.'

'What did you say to him?' Harry said.

'I told him to get lost but he put some photographs on the table, taken at parties,' Lord Dorres said.

'He had photographs?' Jordan asked.

'Yes, what was I to do? I gave him the money,' Lord Dorres said with dejection in his voice.

'Did he ask you for anymore money apart from the £200,000?' Harry said.

'Not money, but I gave him tickets for all the first nights at the opera and ballet and made sure he had passes to go backstage to meet the stars and would be invited to any parties or events that took place.'

'This girl,' Harry put Angela Cook's picture on the table, 'do you know her?'

'Yes, I have seen her at some of the parties.'

'Have you slept with her?' Jordan asked.

'Yes, why what has she done?' he asked.

'She was found murdered this morning,' Harry said.

'Are you accusing my client of involvement in this girl's murder?' the solicitor said interrupting.

'Well did you murder her?' Harry asked.

'No, I did not,' Lord Dorres said.

'Can you account for your movements from eight o'clock onwards today?' Harry asked.

'Yes, I was at home till 9.30, then at my club, I have witnesses to that,' Lord Dorres said.

'We will need to check that out, but you are free to go, we will be releasing your wife as well, we may need to ask you a few questions just to confirm some things, but we will take into account your cooperation when we consider if charges should be brought against you or your wife over the drug possession,' Harry said.

The solicitor sat forward, 'My client is willing to be helpful in anyway to aid your investigation, and we are most grateful for your consideration on the drug charges.'

Harry and Jordan left the room, told the custody sergeant that Lord and Lady Dorres were to be released without charge.

The team were all gathered in the office. 'It's been a long and busy day,' Charlie said to everyone, 'and after listening to what we have managed to discover, I have to admit we are no closer to discovering who killed Gerald Parkin or if its the same person who murdered Angela Cook or someone else, so let's start eliminating who we don't think is mixed up in the murders.'

'Lord Dorres and his wife are out of the picture,' Harry said.

'I agree, boss,' Jordan joined in. 'Lord Dorres would not dirty his hands.'

'What about the butler?' Charlie asked.

'Not for me,' Harry said.

'No, the butler seemed to straight to me,' Cramer said.

'What about the drugs charges we had them in on?' Charlie asked.

'I have let them go without charge pending inquiries,'

Harry said. 'I will give it a couple of days, then let their solicitor know we won't be pressing any charges, I would love to, but it's a bit flimsy.'

'Ok, who else can we rule out?' Charlie asked.

'Sir Martin Oliver,' Manjitt said. 'I don't get him as a murderer, and I believe him when he says he did not know about Parkin's blackmail and he seemed genuinely surprised when we told him Angela Cook was dead.' Cramer nodded in agreement.

'Ok, let him go before you leave tonight, we will pass on all our evidence to the vice squad once our investigation is finished, what about Sir Mark Coale?' Charlie asked.

'Well, when me and Manjitt went to see him,' Jordan said, 'I got the impression if he wanted someone to be killed he could make it happen.'

'He has a lot of ex-military types working for him, so he could get one of them to do it for him,' Manjitt said, 'but I believed him when he said he was not being blackmailed. He did lie about not knowing Angela Cook, Sir Martin Oliver said Angela Cook was seeing him privately and we have a name of one of the girls Angela spoke to about Sir Mark, so we will need to speak to her, although he didn't have an address so we will need to do some digging.'

'So we keep him in the frame, he will have to be questioned again and we need that girl spoken to,' Charlie said.

'I don't think Stanley Moore is our man,' Danny said. 'He seemed a bit to sheepish to me, although his wife Amanda is a different kettle of fish.'

'I will go along with that Danny, but we have to bear in mind his connections to Vincenzo Gallo at the bank in Luxembourg, there are 100 million reasons to have Parkin shut up,' Charlie said. 'His wife is another one we have to speak to again, her connection to Angela Cook needs to be checked thoroughly, anyone else we can rule out.'

'I don't think Micky Adams was involved,' Harry said. 'He was just using Her Ladyship for a good time, and the face we saw in the café will probably be one of his fellow drug dealers. But I will chase the drugs squad up in the morning just to be sure.'

'Okay, tomorrow morning I want us to get rid of any more dead ends,' Charlie said. 'Danny, you have Tim Green coming to collect his Jaguar tomorrow. Have a chat with him, Jordan, you work with Danny. I know we ran a check on him and his fiancée's bank details and that they have a safe deposit box in the city, but let's dig right into their backgrounds, find out more about the two of them. Gerald Parkin didn't just give him a Jaguar because he liked him. Also he had some posh law firm with him last time, find out how he ties in with them.' Danny and Jordan nodded. 'Cramer, you dig into Angela Cook's background. Who was she? Chase up the letting agents for her flat. Did she pay the rent or was it paid for her? Don't forget to phone the technical boys about the camera we found at the other flat.'

'Okay, sir,' Cramer said.

'Manjitt, you and I will go out and question Sir Mark Coale and Amanda Moore, and I think we should have another word with her husband. He never mentioned photographs when I spoke to him,' Charlie continued. 'Harry, you see if you can kick a few backsides. Get all the forensics we are waiting for.' Harry nodded. 'Now we know from Harry and Jordan's questioning that Gerald Parkin had photographs taken at the parties. Who was taking them? Angela Cook maybe? Where are the pictures now? Was it the blackmail over the parties that got Gerald Parkin killed, and is his death connected to Angela Cook's? We still have lots of questions to be answered before we can start to get a handle on this enquiry. Check that girl out who Angela Cook spoke to about Sir Mark Coale. On a lighter note, Assistant Commissioner Crick is on the television tonight at seven, talking about how well the case is going, so if we all watch it we might find out who our killer is. Now get out and I will see you all in the morning.'

The team all got up and left Charlie and Harry alone. 'This is a tough one, boss,' Harry said. 'We have plenty of suspects, but it might not be just the blackmail that got him killed.'

'Well, put that in tomorrow's report for Crick, that should throw him even more,' Charlie said.

'Shall I put our chat with the Deputy Commissioner in it?' Harry asked.

'My reports to Assistant Commissioner Crick never leave anything out, do they Harry?' Charlie smiled as he said it. 'And I know you will word it in your usual tactful way.'

'Leave it to me, boss,' Harry said.

'I'll be seeing him in the morning, so he will be able to tell me what I put in it,' Charlie said. 'While I am up in his office, get Manjitt to find out where Amanda Moore and Sir Mark Coale are going to be, so we can drop in and ask them a few more questions.'

The squad, minus Charlie and Harry, were sitting in the Feathers pub just along the road from Scotland Yard. All had a drink in front of them. 'Well, that was an eventful day,' Jordan said.

'Do all your investigations go like this?' Cramer asked.

'No, some are not as easy as this,' Danny said.

'What about the Deputy Commissioner? Bet he's fuming,' Manjitt said.

'Won't the Chief Superintendent worry about that?' Cramer asked. The rest of the team laughed.

'That's nothing, the boss has had some right bustups with the gods,' Jordan said.

'It's because of the cases that come our way. The boss has always told us, do what's right, not what someone else thinks is right. So if we have to tread on toes we always know the boss will tread on them with us,' Manjitt said.

'But he can't have many friends amongst the senior ranks, don't you think that bothers him?' Cramer asked. 'He won't be in line for promotion'

'The boss loves his job. I don't think promotion comes into his thoughts, he just loves catching the bad guys,' Danny said. The rest of the team nodded.

'What about the Chief Inspector? Working with the Chief Superintendent can't have done his promotion chances much good,' Cramer said.

Danny and Manjitt leant back laughing. Jordan nearly spilled his drink and said, 'Harry, promotion? And Cramer, you have to stop calling them by their rank. It's Harry and the boss. Then we know who you're talking about.' Jordan took a drink and continued. 'Now Harry is as sharp as a knife, he knows everyone, got friends tucked away all over the place and knows where lots of skeletons are hidden. He's worked with the boss for years. I sometimes think they're telepathic. You will never get anything past him, and if you think something's a secret Harry will know it. Like for instance, you and Manjitt meeting up for drinks.' Manjitt looked at Cramer as he turned to look at her. 'See, nothing gets past Harry, does it Hippie?'

'What you asking me about?' Danny said.

'Come on Jordan, you have just thrown my private life onto the table. Dish the dirt on him,' Manjitt said, pointing at Danny.

'I can't tell, Harry would kill me,' Jordan said. Danny picked up his glass, a smile on his face. 'Oh alright, there's a certain young female detective constable working in the drugs squad that the Hippie has been getting friendly with.' Danny had lost the smile from his face.

'Hippie has a girlfriend! And I thought you were training to be a monk,' Manjitt said, laughing.

'Ha ha, my round, who wants another drink?' Danny said standing up.

CHAPTER THIRTEEN

'I thought you came across well on the television last night,' Charlie said to Crick.

'Did you?' Crick said. 'I tried to convey how the investigation was going without giving away too much.'

'I don't know how much you could have given away, sir,' Charlie said, 'as we are no closer to finding out who the killer is.' Charlie sat back in his chair.

Crick as usual was dressed in full assistant commissioner's uniform, his hat on his desk. Charlie had come straight to Crick's office for the morning briefing.

'I got your daily report,' Crick held up a sheet of paper. 'You know I will be passing this on to the Deputy Commissioner. Are you sure you don't want to change any of it before I send it up?'

Charlie wondered what rich language Harry had put into the report. 'No, sir, I think it covers everything that has happened so far.'

Cricked looked at Charlie. 'Well, if you're sure, I won't change anything then.' He put the paper back on the desk. 'The girl who was murdered – you say in the report you think it's linked to Gerald Parkin's murder. Are we going to put that out to the press?'

'Not yet, we still have a couple of people I want to question,' Charlie said. 'You should be able to include it in your press conference tomorrow.'

'Gerald Parkin's body has been released to his family. I understand the funeral is in two days' time. I will be going as a police representative, I will want you accompanying me,' Crick said. Charlie nodded. 'I am glad you are not bringing any charges against Lord Dorres or his wife, it would have created a real media circus.'

'We're not bringing charges because it's too minor. It would take valuable time away from the main investigation. What the press think has no bearing on what we do,' Charlie said. 'I think they both appreciate now they need to treat the police with a bit more respect.'

'I am sure you're right, Charlie. What about the vice ring you uncovered?' Crick asked.

'Once we have cleared up our inquiry I will pass everything on to the vice squad, let them sort it all out,' Charlie replied. 'If there's nothing else sir?' Charlie stood.

'No, that's all. Are you sure you don't want me to change any of your report before I send it upstairs?' Crick asked.

Charlie thought, I must read what Harry has written when I get back to the office. 'No, sir, I'm fine with it.'

'Okay, Charlie, keep me up to date with anything new,' Crick said.

On the way back to the squad's office, Charlie got a phone call from Julian. He told Charlie there were rumours in the city of a takeover being launched for Sir Mark Coale's oil company. As soon as he heard anything else he would get in touch.

Charlie walked into the office and over to Harry. 'Morning Harry, anything new?'

'Morning boss, a couple of things. How was Crick? I watched him on the telly last night. I thought he looked more orange than I can remember, I suppose it was the make-up.'

'He sounded like he enjoyed his appearance on the programme and I don't think it was make-up. I reckon he had an extra hour under the sun lamps, he was glowing this morning,' Charlie said. 'But first things first Harry, can I read my report that I sent up to him this morning. He kept asking me if I wanted to change anything,' Harry took a sheet of paper from a folder on his desk and passed it to Charlie.

'I think it covers everything, boss,' Harry said.

Charlie slowly read through the report and handed it back to Harry. 'Yes, I think you got everything in. I especially like the bit about how the squad are happy to have the backing of senior officers during a difficult investigation and them not being swayed by outside influences and trying to interfere. Upholding the best traditions of Scotland Yard, a wonderful turn of phrase.'

'Your reports are always second to none, boss.' Harry smiled.

'Right, what news have you got for me?' Charlie asked.

'I spoke to forensics first thing. They have Gerald Parkin's prints on the camera and from the second flat, so we know he's been there. We also have Micky Adams' and Lady Dorres' prints, and a few others.' Harry paused; he was smiling at Charlie.

'Come on, Harry, don't keep me waiting. You have something else,' Charlie said.

'It's not a breakthrough, boss, but it's very interesting. The outstanding set of prints we found at Gerald Parkin's house also appear in the second flat,' Harry said.

Charlie thought for a second. 'Do you think he was working with somebody else?'

'He could have been. I reread the book we found at his house. I can't see any mention of anyone else in it, but we know he had pictures from the camera and we don't know where they are. And according to Cramer, who has spoken to the technical boys, the camera in the flat could be viewed remotely by wireless. So Parkin could have been sitting at home watching what was going on in the flat. The camera had a movement alarm that would send a message to alert him when anyone was in the bedroom. Apparently it was top of the range, very expensive. Cramer is trying to track down where it was bought.'

'That gives us something to look into,' Charlie said, looking at Harry, who was still smiling. 'You have something else.'

'Forensics found a couple of prints in Angela Cook's house. Apart from Angela's they have a set on the bedside table. Now they are the same as on the cigars.'

'My betting is on Amanda Moore,' Charlie said. Harry nodded. 'When I see her today I will ask her if she will let us take her prints to eliminate her.'

Harry sat back. 'One more thing boss, whoever killed Angela Cook didn't leave any prints. Probably wearing gloves.'

'It was too much to ask, Harry,' Charlie said.

'But…' Harry said pausing, 'the parcel that was left on the table, forensics got a print from the tape it was fastened with.'

'Do we have a match on the system?' Charlie asked.

'Not one who we can put a name to, but we have it on the system. It's the same as the ones we got from Gerald Parkin's house and the second flat,' Harry said.

Charlie rubbed his hands together. 'Now that's interesting. It looks like we have one killer. What about the description the porter at the flats gave us of the delivery driver, does that give us anything?'

Harry opened the file on Angela Cook that was on his desk, pulled out a sheet of paper. 'Not a lot, white, between 5ft 6 and 5ft 10, wearing a hat, not sure of the hair colour, in fact a rubbish description. And the company that was put in the log doesn't exist.'

'Well, we know Gerald Parkin, and whoever our killer is

has been in those flats before,' Charlie said. 'We need to get all the logs over the last year from the porters and go through them, see if there are any people booked in to visit those two flats that we can't account for.'

'I will send someone over to get them,' Harry said.

'I got a call from Julian,' Charlie said. 'He told me there are rumours Sir Mark Coale's company might be taken over. It might tie in with us. We know Parkin's companies were mixed up in the share-buying. Julian will ring me if he hears anything more.'

'You can ask Sir Mark about it, when you see him later,' Harry said.

'I will do,' Charlie said. 'Has Manjitt arranged the interviews for today yet?'

'She was on the phone this morning trying to sort them out, but she never said anything. I think she went out to check up on a few things. The rest of the team are clearing up the loose ends we spoke about last night. Oh I nearly forgot, I got a call from the drugs squad. They nicked Micky Adams last night, they caught him as he drove out of a warehouse. He had two kilos of cocaine in the boot of his car and sitting beside him was the other face Manjitt and I saw from the café. So Lady Dorres will have to get a new supplier.'

'Well, that's one good thing to come out of this so far,' Charlie said.

Danny had taken a call from the front desk to tell him Tim Green had arrived to pick up his car. Danny told them to get an officer to take him down to the car park and he would meet him there. He waved Jordan over and they both left the office. When they got to the car park they found Tim Green and a constable standing beside the Jaguar. Jordan told the constable they would take care of things and he left. 'It looks like new,'

Danny said. 'Do you want to have a walk round and a check inside to make sure it's not been damaged?'

Tim Green didn't answer but walked around the car and then unlocked it, had a look inside and said, 'Yes, it's fine.'

'Well if you just come over to the office, there are a couple of papers for you to sign before you can take it,' Jordan said.

The three of them walked across the car park to an office tucked away in the corner. Once inside, Jordan asked the police mechanic for the release papers for the Jaguar.

He pulled a folder from the desk drawer, took out some forms and asked Tim Green to sit down. He passed the papers to him and said he should read through them carefully, then sign them if he was happy with everything. Danny signalled the mechanic to leave, he stood up and said he had to go and check on a car, closing the office door as he went out.

'While you're here, Tim, could you just answer a couple of questions to clear up a few things. We don't believe you killed Gerald Parkin, but what you tell us might help us catch whoever did and could save us valuable time,' Jordan said.

Tim Green looked up from reading the papers. 'My solicitor told me I was not to answer any questions unless he was present.'

'We realise that,' Jordan replied, 'but as I said, we don't believe you killed Gerald Parkin and we just want to tie up a few loose ends. Have you always used those solicitors? I checked the last time you were in trouble, you had a local firm, so how did you end up with these new ones? Did the company you work for arrange them?'

'My fiancée got them, and I won't say anymore unless they are here. Now if there's nothing else,' he signed the papers and stood up, 'I want to go now.'

'Yes, of course, we might have to speak to you again,

because like it or not, you are mixed up in this investigation. It would be simpler if you just sat down with us to answer all our questions, then we would leave you alone,' Danny said.

Jordan opened the door to the office. 'Just follow the signs and that will lead you up to the exit barrier.'

They watched Tim Green walk across the car park, get into his car and drive away. 'He's a bit frightened of something,' Danny said.

'You're right there, Hippie. Let's get back to the office and have a good look at his and his fiancée's background, and we will check his solicitor out see if there's a direct link to anyone else whose name has come up.'

Manjitt came back into the office and over to Charlie and Harry. 'Well, Manjitt, how did you get on?' Charlie said.

'I got Sir Mark Coale's office. He's in Brussels till this evening, meeting some people from the EU energy committee. And Stanley and Amanda Moore are at Ascot races. Apparently their bank is sponsoring the big race of the day, they are presenting the trophy.'

'Oh well, we can't fly to Brussels, but we can go to Ascot,' Charlie. 'Harry, you know anyone so we can get in and around without any hassle?'

Harry opened a drawer in his desk and took out a black diary, flicked through a few pages, stopped and began to dial a number on his phone. Charlie and Manjitt watched in silence as Harry spent five minutes on the phone. When he put it down he said, 'All sorted boss, you go to the owners' and trainers' car park. When you get there, give them your name and a man called Cyril Holborn will come and meet you. He will arrange for you to have passes that let you go anywhere on the course without being stopped.'

'If I want tickets to a West End show Harry, can you get them for me?' Manjitt asked.

'He's an old friend, used to work in the fraud squad, boss,' Harry said, ignoring Manjitt. 'He's with the British Horse Racing Authority now, works for their integrity department rooting out corruption and making sure that racing is clean and honest.'

'Your black book, Harry, I hope you have left it to me in your will just in case anything happens to you,' Charlie said.

Harry put his book back into his drawer, 'And no, Manjitt, West End tickets are not on the list.'

'Oh well, it was worth a try,' she said.

'Come on, let's go,' Charlie said, standing up.

'Don't I get to go home and change into something smart?' Manjitt said.

Coming out of the office they bumped into Danny and Jordan. 'Did you get anything out of Tim Green?' Charlie asked.

'Not much, he kept saying his solicitor had to be there if we wanted to speak to him,' Jordan said. 'We are going to have a good look at his and his fiancée's background.'

Charlie nodded. 'Speak to Harry, I will see you later.'

'The boss is treating me to a day at the races,' Manjitt said as she followed Charlie to the lifts.

'Well?' Harry said as Jordan and Danny sat down in front of him. 'What did you get out of Mr Green?'

'Nothing,' Jordan said. 'He keeps saying he won't speak to us without his solicitor, so unless we get something on him there's no way we can sit him down.'

'He did say one thing though,' Danny said. 'When Jordan asked about his solicitor, he said his fiancée arranged them for him. So maybe she has some connections we don't know about.'

'That's something you need to check out,' Harry said. 'Also, we think we have one killer, the same fingerprints from Gerald Parkin's house turn up at Angela Cook's flat, and the flat that was used to film Lady Dorres and Micky Adam. Get on with it then, I know I can rely on you two ferrets to find something. I'm going to pop over to the flats at Chelsea Harbour and have a look around for myself.'

As Harry made his way from the office he met Cramer. 'Cramer, how are you doing with the background checks on Angela Cook?'

'I've found out quite a bit,' Cramer said.

'That's good, well you can tell me on the way to Chelsea Harbour, I'm going over there to pick up all the logs and have a look around.' Cramer followed Harry to the lifts. The doors to the lift opened and Harry got in. Cramer followed. There were two officers already inside, one in the uniform of a commander the other in that of a superintendent. 'You going down?' the superintendent asked.

'Lower-ground floor please,' Harry said.

'It's Davis, isn't it?' the commander said, looking at Harry.

'Yes, sir, that's right,' Harry replied.

'I remember you, I had you on my staff in the West End, I'm surprised you're still in the force. Who are you working with now?' the commander asked.

' Chief Superintendent Smith, sir,' Harry said.

The commander looked at the superintendent and raised his eyebrows. 'Oh well, I suppose someone has to work with him, and I guess it's the last place that was left for you to go.'

'It's not all bad, sir,' Harry said as the doors opened on the ground floor and the superintendent and commander got out. 'At least I know he's not bent.' The commander turned just as the doors were closing. All he saw was Harry waving goodbye.

Cramer said nothing until they were walking across the car

park to the squad car. 'I have found things very interesting working alongside the squad.' They climbed into the car.

'That's good to know,' Harry said.

'It's completely different from my usual work.'

'I hope it will come in handy in the years to come. I don't think you will be a detective sergeant for too long,' Harry said as they pulled out into the London traffic.

'It has been a real education. One thing I have found that I've not in other departments is an honesty when speaking, not just amongst the team but to anyone,' Cramer said.

They stopped at some traffic lights. 'Cramer, let me tell you something,' Harry said, turning his head. 'If you want to get on in the police force and I mean promotion, working for the boss is not the best way to get it.' The lights changed. Harry put the car into gear and pulled away. 'But if you want to be involved in some real police work, be trusted to make decisions for yourself, knowing you will be backed up right or wrong, then you can't be in a better place.'

'I think I am getting that impression,' Cramer said.

'Well, hopefully after this investigation is finished and you go back to your department, you can take some of what you've learnt and use it,' Harry said.

Cramer laughed out loud. 'I might need to come back and ask for a job if I do.'

'So tell me about Angela Cook,' Harry said.

'I reread the file we had on her,' Cramer started. 'I then got in contact with her parents, who are both working. Her father works for the local council, her mother is a receptionist for a doctor. She has one brother. They are still very upset, but I had a long chat with her mother. She told me Angela did quite well at school and the family were very proud when she got to university. Her mother said Angela studied art and business, she got good degrees in both. As far as they know she had a job working in an art gallery in London. I never said anything about what we had found out she had been doing.'

'Best thing,' Harry said. 'Bad enough their daughter being murdered.'

'Angela did tell one lie when the Chief Superintendent questioned her,' Cramer continued, 'she said she paid rent, but she didn't. All her rates and rent were paid. I checked her bank details. Not since the day she moved in has she paid anything and she's lived there for just over eighteen months. I'm still trying to find out where she lived before moving in. Her mother said she would try and find the old address she had for her. I did discover a couple of funny things, the flat she was living in is owned by the Jersey registered company owned by Gerald Parkin, which also happens to own the second flat as well. I ran a check on the whole block just in case he owned any others, but it was just those two. I've sent a request to the Land Registry to find out when they were bought and how much was paid for them. Her bank account shows she was doing quite well out of the parties. Sir Martin Oliver's company shows monthly payments to her in the form of wages, but no two months were the same. Her lowest payment was two thousand pounds, other months it was up to ten thousand, so the party business was very good. She also got a few one-off payments of twenty-five thousand, they came from a different account. I am waiting for information of whose account they came from.'

'Could be Gerald Parkin paying her for information,' Harry said. 'When you get the information, check it against the bank details we have for Parkin, see if you can marry them up. If you can, see if Parkin was making any similar payments to other bank accounts. After speaking to Jordan and Danny I get the feeling Tim Green is hiding something. Although his bank account doesn't show anything, he might have access to an account we don't know about.' Harry turned into Chelsea Harbour and parked the squad car.

'There's some nice boats moored here,' Cramer said, looking across the marina.

'Never been one for the water,' Harry replied. 'Come on, let's go get the logs and I want to have a look around the flats.'

Charlie eased the Bentley along Ascot high street. The traffic was pretty heavy. On his right he saw a sign for the Owners and Trainers' car park. It was situated opposite the imposing new grandstand. He turned into the entrance behind another car.

One of the security staff who was stationed there came to his window. Charlie lowered it and said he was here to meet Cyril Holborn, and gave the security man his name. He was told to park on the far side, and if he came back to the entrance, Mr Holborn would be along shortly to meet him. Charlie parked the Bentley amongst a lot of other expensive cars. He and Manjitt joined the throng of people making their way back towards the car park entrance. 'Look at all those lovely dresses,' Manjitt said, watching all the fashionably dressed women. 'You should have let me go home to get changed, boss, I have never been to the races before so I've missed a chance.'

'Manjitt, we are here to do some work,' Charlie said.

'I know, boss, it's alright for you, you have your Armani suit on, so you fit in,' Manjitt replied.

'Manjitt, you look fine,' Charlie said, 'apart from your black eye.'

'Boss, that's the nicest thing you have ever said to me. The rest of the team will be jealous when I tell them,' Manjitt replied, smiling.

They got to the entrance and saw a tall well-dressed man standing next to the security guard. He approached them, holding out his hand. 'Chief Superintendent Smith,' he said. 'I'm Cyril Holborn.' He shook hands with Charlie, who introduced Manjitt. 'I have some badges for you if you want to put them round your necks.' He handed over two passes on nylon straps. 'These will allow you to go anywhere on the course without being stopped by security staff. I have a map of the course and grandstand for you. Here's a race card too if you get time for a bet, all the races are in it.' He passed them to Charlie. 'Now, if you want to follow me I will take you into the course.'

Charlie thanked him and he and Manjitt followed Cyril Holborn across the road towards the main entrance of the grandstand. 'You spoke to Harry, did he tell you we wanted to speak to Stanley and Amanda Moore,' Charlie asked.

'Yes, he did, their company have sponsored the big race, they've hired one of the large boxes for their party. I think they have about 75 guests for dinner. They've sponsored the race for the last five years so are valued customers. Their box is on level two of the main grandstand.' They walked through the main entrance past the people queuing up to get in. 'How is Harry? I haven't seen him for a few years.'

'Harry is fine, enjoying his job,' Charlie said.

'He was a good policeman, kept me out of a few scrapes when I could have got into trouble, saved my career,' Cyril Holborn said. 'I will leave you now, but if you have any problems or you need to ask me anything here's my mobile number.' He passed a business card to Charlie.

'Thanks for your help, Cyril,' Charlie said, shaking his hand.

Cyril turned to walk away, stopped, half-turned and said, 'I like the eye,' to Manjitt, then walked off into the crowd.

'There you go, boss, I don't even have on a lovely dress to take people's minds off my eye,' Manjitt said.

'Well give up the karate,' Charlie said. 'Come on, let's have a wander round, get a good look at the place.'

Harry and Cramer were standing in the small office behind the porter's desk in Angela Cook's block of flats. 'You will be returning all the logs when you have finished with them?' the porter said, placing six large books on the table.

'Yes, don't worry,' Harry said. 'We will get them back to you. Cramer, go and put them in the car.' Cramer picked up the books and left the office. 'Were you on duty the morning the girl's body was found in flat 114?'

'Yes, I saw her a few times, seemed a lovely girl,' the porter said.

'You worked in the job long?' Harry asked.

'Over four years now, I worked in another block of flats before coming here.'

'Why don't you have any CCTV in the flats?' Harry asked.

'We did have a couple of years ago, but the residents' committee voted to have them taken out. They said it was to much of an intrusion. They might change their minds after what's happened.'

'The description you gave of the person who delivered the parcel is not great,' Harry said. 'Do you remember anything else that might help us?'

'Not really, they just came in, signed the log and took the lift up,' the porter said. He thought for a moment. 'That was a bit strange, I suppose. Thinking about it now, he seemed to know he had to sign the log. Maybe he had delivered to the block before.'

'So you didn't have to ask him to sign?' Harry said.

'No, now I think about it, he said, "Do you want me to sign in?" like he knew.'

'Did he have a London accent?' Harry asked.

The porter thought for a second. 'No, I think it was foreign.'

'Can you say where it was from?' Harry said.

'No, European, I think,' the porter said.

'You said he was between 5ft 6 and 5ft 10, can you narrow that down a bit?' Harry asked.

'I think maybe 5ft 8 tops, but might have been smaller.'

'You didn't give much of a description of the face. Can you remember what colour eyes or what type of complexion they had?' Harry asked.

'He was wearing a hat and he didn't look directly at me, kept looking down as he signed the log. I would say he had fair skin though.'

Cramer came back to the office after putting the logs in the car.

'We're going to go up to have a look round the flats,' Harry said to the porter. 'If you can try and think of anything else before we come down, it would be helpful.' He and Cramer left office and took the lift to the twelfth floor to have a look round the flat Gerald Parkin had used to film Lady Dorres and Micky Adams. Cramer showed him where the camera had been. 'Was there nothing else in the flat?' Harry asked.

'No, nothing, it looked like it was just used as a meeting place,' Cramer replied.

'Expensive meeting place,' Harry said. 'But if he was earning so much from the blackmail, I suppose it was worth it. Did we get any joy from any of the neighbours?'

'Nothing at all, nor from Angela Cook's floor, some had said they saw her but not to talk to, and no one saw anyone else coming or going.'

'Let's hope the logs give us a bit more.' Harry looked around the flat. 'Come on, let's go up to Angela Cook's flat,' he said.

Charlie and Manjitt turned right away from the main entrance, walking around the parade ring where a number of horses for the first race were being led round by their stable hands. They followed the curve of the white railed fencing that surrounded the parade ring and past the bandstand to their right where a jazz band was playing. Charlie recognised the tune, 'Stardust'. His grandfather loved listening to Artie Shaw, it was one he always heard when he went to his grandparents' small house in Dagenham for Sunday dinner with his mum. They walked into the main grandstand building and stopped. 'This place is massive,' Manjitt said, looking around the vast structure.

'Let's walk through and see it from the racecourse side,' Charlie said.

They passed out into the sunshine, seeing the lush green racecourse laid out before them. 'You get a great view,' Manjitt said.

'I think it's even better from up there' Charlie said, pointing up at the grandstand. Manjitt turned her head to look up.

'It's magnificent, this is where they have that big ladies' day isn't it boss, during Royal Ascot?' Manjitt said.

'Yes, you better be good to Harry, he might get you a ticket,' Charlie said. 'Now let's go and find Stanley and Amanda Moore.' They went back into the grandstand, found the lifts and went up to level two. As they got out of the lift a security man gave them a look, but seeing the passes said nothing. 'Let's find someone who can tell us which box their company's in.'

Manjitt saw a well dressed man who was directing some waitresses carrying trays of drinks. 'Hold on, boss, I will go and ask him,' Manjitt said, pointing. She approached the man and spoke briefly to him. When she came back to Charlie she said 'It's this way, their box is one of the large ones towards the finishing line.' Charlie followed Manjitt. She stopped outside a double set of doors, the name of the bank was on the outside.

'Here we are.' Manjitt pushed on the door and opened it. Just inside stood two well-dressed men who moved in front of them as they entered. 'Can I help you?' one of them said. He looked at the pass round Manjitt's neck. 'Oh sorry, I didn't see your pass, is there anything we can help you with?'

'Can you get Mrs Moore for us, we need to speak to her,' Manjitt said. The man nodded and walked off. 'This is all very nice, boss,' Manjitt said as she turned to Charlie.

'Looks very nice,' Charlie said, looking at the tables all laid out before them. Waiters and waitresses were scuttling between them serving champagne. Charlie saw the security guard stop at a table by the big panoramic window, he saw Amanda Moore stand and look in their direction. She seemed to lean down and say something, then she came walking towards them. the security guard falling in behind her.

'She's a good-looking woman, boss,' Manjitt said. 'That dress she has on must have cost my yearly wage.'

'Don't go asking for a clothing allowance,' Charlie said.

When Amanda Moore reached them she said in her soft American accent, 'It's Chief Superintendent Smith, isn't it? This is a pleasant surprise, were you just passing or have you come along especially to see us?' She smiled at Charlie.

'We came all the way just to speak to you,' Charlie said.

'I am honoured, will you join us for a glass of champagne? You don't have to rush off, I hope,' she said.

'I do need to ask you a couple of questions,' Charlie replied.

'Well, come to my table. Do you need to speak to Stanley? He's downstairs looking at the horses. One of our guests owns a horse in the next race, he will be back up to watch the race from here, so you can speak to him then.' She turned away before Charlie could answer and made her way between the tables. Charlie looked at Manjitt, shrugged and they both followed. Amanda Moore stopped at different tables to speak to people as she made her way past them. She reached her table and turned just as Manjitt and Charlie got there.

'You haven't introduced me to your friend,' she said, looking at Manjitt.

'This is Detective Constable Virdee,' Charlie said.

'It's nice to meet you,' Amanda Moore said, holding out her hand which Manjitt shook. 'What happened to your eye? The Chief Superintendent hasn't been knocking you around, has he?'

'No, it was a sporting accident,' Manjitt replied.

'Let me get you some champagne, you will have a glass with me, won't you?' she said, looking at Charlie.

'I don't think one glass would be considered a bribe,' Charlie said. Amanda Moore waved her hand and a waiter appeared within seconds. Charlie took two glasses, passing one to Manjitt. Amanda Moore held up her glass. 'Here's to our magnificent and incorruptible police.' She smiled at Charlie as she took a drink. 'If you give me a moment, I will just see if my guests are alright, then we can talk.' She moved away to another table.

'Boss, don't get me wrong, but is she flirting with you?' Manjitt said.

Charlie looked at Manjitt. 'I get the impression she is sizing me up for dinner.'

Manjitt laughed. 'This must have cost a pretty penny to lay on,' she said, looking around the box.

'The race their company is sponsoring is worth three hundred thousand to the winning horse, according to the race card,' Charlie said. 'I dare say there's some tax dodge they use to put it down as entertainment expenses.'

'Do you think we could get something like this as our Christmas party?' Manjitt said, smiling.

Amanda Moore returned. 'Do you want to follow me?' She

led them through some glass doors onto the balcony. There was a number of seats which overlooked the racecourse. 'It's a wonderful view from here, don't you think?' Amanda Moore said as she sat down.

'Yes,' Charlie said taking a seat in the row in front and turning to look at her. Manjitt stood by the door.

'So what do you want to ask me?' she said.

'Angela Cook was found murdered in her flat yesterday,' Charlie said, looking at her. She didn't make any response for a moment.

'That's terrible news, who would want to do such a thing?' she said.

'That's what I want to ask you. We found some cigars in her bedside cabinet. I want to know if you will give us your fingerprints, we are trying to work out who's been in the flat' Charlie said.

'I told you I had been to her flat, and the cigars are probably mine, but if you want my fingerprints and it will help catch whoever killed her I have no objections,' she said.

'When I spoke to you last time, you said you never spoke about Gerald Parkin with Angela,' Charlie said.

'Yes, that's right, why would I?'

'Well, we believe she may have been helping Gerald Parkin with his blackmail, passing on information to him,' Charlie said. He watched Amanda Moore's face, her expression didn't change.

'I am shocked,' she said, but she was smiling as she said it. 'Angela, mixed up in blackmail?'

'You said before that Angela had been to your house. Were you alone together or was it for a dinner with other guests?' Charlie asked.

'No, we were alone. My husband was out somewhere, I don't know where,' she said.

'Did you ever visit any other flat in the block Angela lived in?' Charlie said.

'I don't know anyone else who lives there,' Amanda replied. 'Shall we go back in? My husband should be back by now and the first race is due off. Have you had a bet?' Amanda stood up, not waiting for an answer. Taking Manjitt by the arm she said, 'Come on, Detective Constable Virdee, let me introduce you to my husband.'

Charlie stood and followed them inside. The box was full with people and the noise of their voices filled the room. Amanda Moore called her husband's name out. He was talking to some people, but turned when he heard his wife and walked over to join them.

'Stanley, I have someone you must meet. This is Detective Constable Virdee.' Stanley Moore looked confused but shook hands with Manjitt.

'Very nice to meet you,' he said.

'And of course, you already know Chief Superintendent Smith,' Amanda Moore said. He looked at Charlie and nodded in recognition, but didn't hold his hand out.

'What do you want?' he asked.

Before Charlie could answer, Amanda Moore said, 'He's here to ask us some more questions.' She turned, smiling at Charlie. 'I think he suspects us of murder.'

'That's nonsense,' Stanley Moore said.

'Let's watch this race. I'm sure the Chief Superintendent doesn't mind waiting a few minutes,' Amanda Moore said. 'Come on, Chief Superintendent.' She took Charlie's arm. 'Let me show you a good place to watch the race from. Stanley, look after Detective Constable Virdee.' She led Charlie back out through the glass doors and onto the balcony. They walked down four steps to the front. 'It's a beautiful view from here' Charlie looked back over his shoulder to see Manjitt, champagne in hand, standing with Stanley Moore. She raised her glass in a toast to him. He turned back to look at the course.

'Yes, it's a wonderful view' he said.

'We have been coming here a few years now. It was one of my husband's better ideas. Are you married, Chief Superintendent?'

Charlie looked at her, she was smiling at him again like she could read his mind. 'No, I'm not married,' he said.

'That's interesting,' Amanda Moore said, still smiling.

'What's interesting about that?' Charlie said.

'Well, I always imagined you policemen had a good woman sitting at home waiting for you to get back after a hard day.'

'Sorry to disappoint you,' Charlie said.

'Oh that doesn't disappoint me,' she said taking a drink from her glass, looking over it at Charlie. They heard the course announcer say the race had started and they both turned to watch the horses making their way up the course towards the finish. As they got nearer the noise from the grandstand grew louder. Charlie turned as he heard someone screaming, 'Come on boy,' at the top of their voice. He saw Manjitt watching the race, Stanley Moore was beside her jumping up and down with a man next to him doing the same, screaming at the horses. He turned back to see the race as it flashed by beneath him towards the winning post. The colours of the jockeys were a blur, the noise was deafening. He could just about hear the racecourse commentator describing the finish. A loud cheer went up.

Amanda Moore turned to face him. 'Our guests' horse won,' she said. 'Come on, let's go back in.' She took Charlie's arm and they walked back up the stairs and into the box. Stanley Moore was shaking the man's hand who had been jumping up and down beside him. Amanda Moore led Charlie to them. 'Well done, Jeremy,' she said. 'What a great race.' He kissed her and said thank you, then he excused himself, said he had to get his wife and some friends and go and collect the trophy, but would share the champagne when he got back.

'He's a very good client of ours,' Amanda Moore said, 'has a shipping business. Now Chief Superintendent, you and Officer Virdee must stay and have dinner with us.' She turned to her husband. 'Don't you think the nice police officers should stay and have dinner, Stanley?'

'If you like,' he said, but in a tone that said he rather they didn't.

'We just need to get some answers to a few questions,' Charlie said. 'I don't think we have time to stay.'

'Oh you must, I am sure Stanley and I will be able to answer all your questions over dinner.' She waved her hand and a waiter came over. 'Can you put two more places on my table please,' she said without waiting for Charlie to answer. 'Now you must have another glass of champagne.' Charlie found the glass in his hand swapped for a full one. Manjitt was standing beside him. Charlie leaned close to her and whispered, 'No more drink after that one.'

She nodded. 'I am looking forward to dinner, boss, first you tell me how good I look, now dinner, the rest of the team are going to gossip about this.'

'You can sit next to my husband,' Amanda Moore said to Manjitt, pointing to a chair at the far end of the table. 'I'm sure he can answer all your questions. Superintendent, you can sit here next to me.' Charlie saw Manjitt smile and wink at him as she turned away to go to her chair. Stanley Moore was beside her. 'Don't worry, Stanley will look after her.' Charlie turned and saw Amanda Moore was already seated; he sat down beside her. 'It's a couple of races before the big one we have sponsored, so we have plenty of time to chat. Dinner will be served in a moment.' People were sitting down all around the box. 'Now I can't keep calling you Chief Superintendent, you have to tell me your name.'

Charlie looked at her, she had that smile on her face again. He knew how she had become such a powerful woman in banking. The smile hid a sharp operator who he thought was as tough as nails. 'It's Charlie.'

'Well, Charlie,' Amanda Moore said. 'You must call me Amanda.' She placed her hand on his and raised her glass. 'Here's to success in everything we do.'

Harry was standing next to the bed in Angela Cook's flat. 'So she was lying on her back across the bed when you found her?' Harry said to Cramer.

'Yes, Chief Superintendent Smith was in the front room. I walked in here and found her,' Cramer replied.

'And nothing else was out of place?' Harry asked

'No, nothing.'

'So there was not much of a struggle. Forensics said there were no drugs in her system, so why did she walk into the bedroom with whoever killed her without putting up a fight?' Harry asked.

'Maybe they had a knife or something,' Cramer said.

'In that case they could have stabbed her in the front room or in here,' Harry replied. 'But they strangled her. Forensics didn't find anything under her fingernails, but they did say she had bruises on the top of her arms. So we have to think the killer got her in here for whatever reason, she sat on the bed quite happily, the killer then pounced, forcing her back, pinning Angela with their knees on her arms and strangling her.'

'But why come in here in the first place?' Cramer said.

Harry walked around the bed. 'There was nothing else found in the flat apart from the cigars and the photographs.'

'Just a paperback, it was in the drawer along with the other things,' Cramer replied.

'Did it look like someone had been searching the flat?' Harry asked.

'No, not really, it was tidy, it didn't look like someone had been going through the place,' Cramer said

'So our killer strangles her and leaves straight away, doesn't even pick up the parcel they brought. If I remember the log said that the delivery driver was here for only ten minutes,' Harry said.

'Yes, ten minutes,' Cramer replied.

'So our prime suspect is the delivery driver. The print we got off the parcel is the same as the ones we got from Gerald Parkin's house and the flat downstairs, so our killer certainly knew Gerald Parkin. Where does that lead us, Cramer?' Harry said.

Cramer looked at Harry. 'Angela Cook knew her killer.'

'Well done, Detective Sergeant,' Harry said. 'So now we know why Angela walked into the bedroom without any struggle. She must have felt safe with whoever it was. It's a pity the description we have is so bad. Although the porter told me whoever it was had a foreign accent and was fair skinned, they must have been here before. The porter said they knew the signing in procedure.' Harry walked back around the bed. 'Let's hope her mum comes up with her last address, and we need to find the other girl who was at dinner with her and Sir Martin Oliver, when she was talking about Sir Mark Coale. I wonder if it was the girl in the photograph with Angela we got from the bedside table?' Harry looked at Cramer. 'When we get back to the Yard, dig it out of the evidence bag and take it round to Sir Martin see if he identifies her. Let's go.'

They left the flat and took the lift back down. They got out of the lift at the ground floor and saw the porter was seated behind his desk. Harry stopped and said, 'I just had a thought, you take the car back to the , get the photograph, take it over to Sir Martin. See if he can put a name to the girl, don't let him fob you off with I'm not sure or something, remind him how close to going to prison he is. I am going to have a look round the harbour.' Harry gave Cramer the keys to the car and watched him leave. Harry walked over to the porter and asked, 'Does the harbour itself have security?'

'Yes, their office is in the big glass building on the other side. If you turn left out of here, just follow the path around the marina,' the porter said.

'Thanks, remember if you think of anything else that might help us, give me a ring.' Harry handed his card to the porter. 'Anything at all.' The porter nodded. Harry left the building, making his way to the marina security office.

Charlie looked up the table at Manjitt who was in conversation with Stanley Moore. He had a worried look on his face, Manjitt must be giving him a grilling. His thoughts were disturbed by Amanda Moore saying, 'Don't worry about your officer, Stanley's pretty harmless.'

Charlie turned back to face her. 'I'm not worried about her, she's more than capable of looking after herself,' he said. The dinner things had all been cleared away, he had a glass of water in front of him, declining any wine during the meal despite Amanda Moore's urging to have some. Their conversation over dinner had been very general, about the police and banking. Charlie found her a fascinating woman. Amanda Moore leaned back in her chair and looked at her watch. 'The big race goes off in fifteen minutes,' she said. 'Stanley and I have to go down and present the prize to the winning owner.' She leaned forward. 'So do you have any suspects for the murders apart from Stanley and me?'

'I am hoping your fingerprints will rule you out, I will have to take your husband's as well,' Charlie said.

'Will we have to come to the police station?' she asked.

'No, I can send someone along to your office if you like,' Charlie said.

'Yes, that's fine with me,' she said. 'Although I don't think Stanley would kill anyone, he won't even shoot pheasants when we go down David and Natalie's house in the country.'

'Is that Lord and Lady Dorres?' Charlie asked.

'Yes, are they suspects too?' Amanda Moore asked

'How do you get on with them? Have you known them long?' Charlie asked.

Amanda Moore smiled at Charlie, picked up her wine and took a drink. 'So you're not going to tell me who's a suspect.' she put her drink back onto the table. 'Yes, I get on well with them, he can be a bit tiresome sometimes and she's, how would you say it, highly strung.' She smiled at Charlie and said 'Maybe it's to do with the medication she takes on occasions.'

Charlie smiled back. So she knew about Lady Dorres' drug habit. 'What about Sir Mark Coale, is he a close friend?'

'Mark's a friend, but not close. I know Stanley likes him, he's very intense, has a lot of bodyguards around him. I think it gives him a sense of importance,' she said.

'I hear on the grapevine his company is in a little bit of trouble.' Charlie saw her expression change just for a moment.

'I didn't know the Financial Times was required reading at Scotland Yard,' she said.

Charlie picked up his glass of water and took a drink. 'I also hear rumours that a takeover might be in the wind.' Amanda Moore smiled at him.

'I can see you're very well informed about the workings of the city.' She stood up, placing her hand on his. 'Not a policeman to be underestimated.' Charlie looked up at her, she smiled and said, 'Now, I have to go and get ready for the presentation, I hope we can continue our talk when I get back.' She ran her hand up his arm as she walked away. He watched her as she went to her husband and spoke to him. He rose and followed her from the box. Charlie waved Manjitt down to join him at his end of the table. She took the seat vacated by Amanda Moore.

'You look like you're having a very nice time, boss,' Manjitt said. 'I could swear she thought you were the afters to the main meal.'

'She is a sharp woman. It feels like a fencing match, she doesn't give much away,' Charlie said.

'I get the impression she would give you as much as you like if you wanted it,' Manjitt said, laughing.

'Thank you for that assessment, what did you get out of her husband?' Charlie asked.

'He has admitted Gerald Parkin showed him pictures of him at the parties,' Manjitt said. 'I showed him the photograph of Angela Cook; he recognised her from the parties but said he had never been to her flat. I don't get the feeling he's our killer, but he knows something. What about his wife?'

'Well, she knows more than she's letting on,' Charlie said, 'but just how much I don't know. She said we can have her fingerprints and those of her husband. We will arrange a time to go to their offices and get them.' They heard the announcement that the race was about to start and stood up and went out onto the balcony to watch.

Harry had found his way to the harbour security office, introduced himself and asked to see the head of security. The man in charge turned out to be an ex-officer who had worked with some policeman Harry knew. He chatted to him about the force and how things had changed for a while. 'I was hoping you might be able to help us. We are investigating the murder of the girl in the block of flats on the other side of the marina,' Harry said.

'Yes, of course, what do you want?' he said.

'They don't have any CCTV in the block, I was wondering if you have any that covers it at all?' Harry asked.

'I might be able to help. Why don't you come through to the control room.' He led Harry into an office behind the main room. There were twelve screens on one wall, two operators were sitting in front of them. 'We have full coverage of the marina from here, and we've got eight security staff wandering around the harbour who are in radio contact. If we see something suspicious we can be in touch with them right away and vice versa.'

'I was hoping you might have some recordings of yesterday from between nine o'clock and nine thirty,' Harry said.

The head of security told one of the operators to get up yesterday's recordings from all the cameras from 8.45 to 9.30. 'If we put it to fifteen minutes earlier we can see if anyone was hanging around,' he said. 'What are we looking for?'

'A delivery driver carrying a small parcel,' Harry replied.

One of the screens went blank, then flickered back on. 'Right, this is from 8.45 on camera one, I will fast forward it, if you think you see anything call out,' he said.

Harry watched till the time 9.30 came up at the bottom. 'Nothing on that one, here's camera two.' They went through that one. Nothing. It wasn't until camera six that Harry shouted, 'Stop, wind it back a little.' The CCTV was wound back slowly. 'There, look, walking along the path.' A person was clearly seen carrying a parcel. They had a cap on, the time read 9.07. 'Can you tell where they have come from?' Harry asked.

The security man checked the camera's position. 'Camera six, yes, that's over towards the main road. If I get camera nine up, that covers the street outside.' He tapped the computer keyboard and the picture changed to the street outside. 'I will fast forward again, just shout out.'

Harry watched the screen carefully. Lots of people and cars were whizzing through the picture. 'Stop,' Harry cried out. He looked carefully at the still picture on the screen. 'Look, walking along the street towards the gate.'

The security man studied the screen. 'Now I know what I'm looking for, do you want to leave it to me? I will go through all the cameras and make a CD up from all of them, showing whoever that is...' he pointed to the screen, '...coming and going from the marina. Might take me an hour or so, but as soon as it's done I will get it couriered over to you.'

'That would be great,' Harry said. 'Here's my card, it's got the squad room number on it. And if there's anything you think I can help you with in the future, just give me a bell.' They shook hands and Harry left to get a taxi back to the Yard.

Manjitt and Charlie walked back into the box after watching the race. There was a large-screen television on the wall at one end; they watched Amanda Moore present the trophy to the winning owner, and a silver salver to the jockey who had ridden the winning horse.

'We will see how much more we get out of them, then make a move. I want to catch up with everyone back at base,' Charlie said. 'Ask Sir Stanley about Sir Mark Coale, how well he knows him. See if he has any idea about who might have taken the pictures at the parties, and did he meet any of the girls privately.' Manjitt nodded.

The box began to fill up again with people, and Charlie saw the Moores arrive back. They made their way towards Charlie and Manjitt, stopping to take congratulations from people as they passed them. When they reached Charlie, Amanda Moore said, 'That went very well. The winning owner has interests in banking in Australia. I have invited him to come to our house for dinner next week, we might be able to do some business.'

Stanley Moore said, 'My wife never stops working.'

Amanda Moore looked at him. 'It's just as well that I do, isn't it Stanley?' Her husband didn't answer, but his face told a story of resentment.

'Could we just finish asking you a few more questions? We really do need to get off,' Charlie said.

'You go off with the beautiful officer, Stanley,' Amanda Moore said. 'I will let Charlie interrogate me.' Manjitt walked away with Stanley Moore, Amanda turned back to Charlie, 'But first let me have a glass of wine.' She signalled to a waiter, who came over with a tray. 'Can I tempt you to have another glass, Charlie?'

'It's kind of you but no thanks. I have to drive back to London and it wouldn't be good if I got stopped for drinking and driving, would it?'

She took a drink from the glass. 'That's better, now where do you want me, on the chair or out on the balcony?' She smiled at Charlie as she said it.

'Where would you be most comfortable?' Charlie said, smiling back at her.

'Let's do it on the balcony.' She took Charlie's arm and guided him through the glass doors and down the stairs to the front of the balcony. She took a seat and Charlie sat down next to her. 'Now where were we, Charlie?'

'We were discussing Sir Mark Coale and the rumours surrounding his company,' Charlie said.

'Oh yes, I had heard the odd whisper that all was not well, but Stanley deals with that side of things, although not very well at times,' she said.

'Is he doing any business with Sir Mark now?' Charlie asked.

'He and Sir Mark have been discussing some work. I have told Stanley not to get involved, but he knows best sometimes,' she said.

'Did Gerald Parkin ever ask you about investments or shares?' Charlie asked.

Amanda Moore took a slow drink from her glass. She's measuring her answer carefully before she says anything, Charlie thought. 'He might have, he was always asking about one thing or the other,' she said.

'Did business get discussed much at the dinner parties?' Charlie asked.

Amanda Moore smiled her smile at Charlie. He saw her dip her finger into her wine glass, and lick the wine off her finger. 'We discussed lots of different things, but not all the guests were as fascinating as you.'

'I will take that as a compliment. Fascinating is not something I get called a lot,' Charlie said. She never answered the question. 'Do you know if Gerald Parkin discussed with Sir Mark Coale about investments and shares?'

'You will have to ask Mark about that,' she said. 'So what do you get called if not fascinating?'

'Nothing I could repeat in front of a lady,' Charlie said. Amanda Moore smiled at him. 'Do you know if your husband discussed investments with Gerald Parkin?'

'Gerald discussed a lot with my husband, which I am sure you're more aware of than me.' She looked at Charlie waiting for an answer. He stared back. 'You're not going to give anything away then. As for financial advice, I couldn't tell you. So why are you not married, Charlie?'

She's trying to move the conversation away again, Charlie thought. 'I guess I never got round to it, the job keeps me too busy. Did you ever meet any of Angela Cook's friends?' He saw a look of surprise in her face for a split second, then her features went back to a smile. She took another drink from her glass. Charlie knew her mind was working out an answer, but couldn't work out what she was trying to hide. She had already said she had an affair with Angela Cook.

'I don't believe I met any of her friends,' she said.

'But you would remember if you had?' Charlie said. It was he who smiled now.

Amanda Moore placed her hand on Charlie's arm. 'I think I would, but even I forget things. I know you will remind me if I have.' Charlie saw the smile widen on her face. 'Are you going to remind me, Charlie?'

'Does the name Tim Green mean anything to you?' Charlie asked.

Amanda Moore lightly rubbed Charlie's arm before taking her hand away. 'Tim Green.' She repeated the name then took another drink from her glass, which she emptied. 'I can't say the name rings any bells with me, who is he, a suspect?'

'It's a name that's cropped up,' Charlie said.

Amanda Moore stood up. 'Shall we go back in, or do you want to have me out here to yourself?' She smiled down at Charlie 'There's one more race and anyone might come out and catch us.'

Charlie stood up. 'I'm sure we wouldn't want anyone coming out and putting them off the race.' He stood aside and let her lead the way in. She looked back over her shoulder as she walked up the stairs.

'You haven't complimented me on my dress, Charlie, do you think it suits me?' Amanda Moore stopped at the top step just before going back into the box.

'It's not a question a policeman gets asked a lot,' Charlie said.

'But do you think it suits me? It's not too tight on me, is

it?' She smiled at Charlie. He knew she was trying to make him feel a little uncomfortable and get his mind off asking any more questions.

'You look stunning in it,' Charlie said, 'but I'm sure you know that.' He joined her on the top step.

She took his arm. 'That's a lovely thing to say, Charlie. You're a fascinating and handsome man, but I suppose we'd better go and rescue your officer from my husband.' She led Charlie in and over to where Manjitt was sitting with Stanley Moore. Manjitt stood up when she saw them coming over.

'I hope you've finished with my husband,' Amanda Moore said.

'Yes, thank you, he's been very helpful,' Manjitt replied.

'I will walk down with you two,' she said, turning to Charlie. 'I want to have a cigar and you can't smoke in here, so if you just wait a moment.' She wandered off. Stanley Moore stood up. 'Goodbye,' he said to Manjitt, 'it was nice meeting you.' He said nothing to Charlie as he turned and walked away.

'I can see you have worked your magic on him,' Charlie said, watching Stanley Moore walk away.

'Not half as much as you have on his wife, boss,' Manjitt said.

Amanda Moore came back. She had a large cigar in her hand. 'Well, shall we go?' She took Charlie's arm. Manjitt caught Charlie's eye, winked at him, a big smile was on her face. They left the box, taking the lift to the ground floor.

'Have you enjoyed your day at the races?' Amanda Moore asked Manjitt as they walked towards the main entrance.

'Yes, thank you, it was lovely,' Manjitt said. They crossed the road to the car park entrance. Amanda still had Charlie's arm. He took his pass off and Manjitt took hers off and they gave them to the security guard.

'One moment,' Amanda Moore said. She put the cigar to her

lips and produced a lighter she must have had in her other hand. 'Do you mind lighting it for me, Charlie?' She passed him the lighter, he lit it and held it to the cigar. Amanda Moore took three or four puffs, before blowing out a long stream of blue smoke 'That's better,' she said. 'Do you like cigars?' she said to Manjitt.

'No, they're not something I have ever tried,' Manjitt replied.

'Where are you parked, Charlie?' she said. Charlie pointed over towards the far side of the car park. Out of the corner of his eye he saw Manjitt with a broad smile on her face. They walked through the parked cars till they came to the Bentley. Amanda Moore looked at it and said, 'I didn't know the police had cars like this.'

'This is the boss's own car,' Manjitt said. 'He doesn't use police transport, you can't have the top down.' She looked at Charlie, smiling.

'There's more to you than meets the eye, Charlie,' Amanda Moore said. Charlie unlocked the car and Manjitt got in. 'I hope I have been helpful and answered all your questions today.'

'You have been helpful,' Charlie said.

Placing her hand on his arm, she smiled at him, leaned forward and lightly kissed him on the cheek. 'Tomorrow I am having some friends to dinner. Sir Mark Coale is going to be there, you could have a chat with him if you want to come along. You could bring your young officer if you want.' She placed the cigar to her lips.

'I will check my diary, but it would be good to meet him,' Charlie said.

Amanda Moore blew out some smoke. 'Do you know our address?' She smiled and said, 'Of course you do, you're a policeman. I will look forward to seeing you.'

Charlie climbed into the Bentley and started the car. 'Are we having the top down, boss?' Manjitt said.

'No,' Charlie said, putting the car into gear and slowly moving forward. Amanda Moore waved to them as they passed her.

It had taken Harry about half an hour to get back to Scotland Yard by taxi. When he walked into the office, he found Jordan and Danny at their desks. 'Has Cramer been in?' he said.

Jordan and Danny looked up. 'Yes, been and gone again,' Jordan said. 'How did you get on?'

'Interesting,' Harry said. He waved the two of them over to join him at his desk. He sat down in his chair. Jordan and Danny walked over and sat down in chairs opposite him. 'I think Angela Cook knew her killer, so we have to assume whoever it is was, they were mixed up in this whole thing. How have you been getting on with Tim Green and his fiancée?'

It was Danny who spoke. 'We went over what we had and apart from his brush with the law when he was a bit younger, there's not much on him. Before the Jaguar he had a small Ford Fiesta, so he stepped up in the world, but there's nothing exceptional, Harry.'

'But you said after questioning him you think he is not telling us all he knows,' Harry said

'I do, but there's nothing in his background or what shows up now that tells us anything,' Danny said.

'What about his fiancée?' Harry asked.

'Her name is Rebecca Rosen, 27,' Jordan said. 'She's from Israel, came to the country three years ago. I have put a request in to the Israeli police for any information they have on her. One strange thing, she was down as going to university but I checked. She did do the first year but has not been since. The two of them have lived in the house for eight months.'

'I wondered what her accent was.' Danny said.

'Is that it?' Harry asked.

'Nothing else out of the ordinary,' Jordan said.

'It doesn't ring true,' Harry said. 'Tim Green gets a Jaguar from Gerald Parkin, what did he do to get that?' Harry sorted through the paperwork on his desk, which as usual was piled up. He pulled a file out and opened it, read a little bit of it and said, 'When you questioned him, he said he got it for helping with Parkin's contract, but then he says he went to Gerald Parkin's house to tell him he couldn't accept it. No, there's more to it than that. Danny, you ring up the firm Tim Green works for. Ask them how much work he did on Gerald Parkin's contracts. The house they are in, is it on a mortgage or being rented?'

Jordan sorted through some papers. 'It's on a mortgage.'

Harry leaned back in his chair and said, 'Right, get onto the mortgage people. 'Find out what addresses they gave when they took it out, and how much deposit they put down. Let's see where they used to live. Surely Tim Green's not earning enough on his own to pay the mortgage. And don't forget he said his fiancée arranged the solicitor for him, so we need to know how she ties into this.'

'By the way, a call came from Angela Cook's mother,' Danny said. 'She gave an address for where Angela lived before she moved to her flat.' Danny pushed over a note.

Harry picked it up. 'Well, she was not living in luxury before she moved to Chelsea Harbour,' Harry said. 'She was in a flat in Peckham. I will get Cramer to check it out.'

'Where did he go when he rushed off earlier?' Jordan asked

'I sent him over to Sir Martin Oliver's, to show him the photograph we got from Angela Cook's flat, the one with her and the other girl, to find out if he knows the girl's name and if she was the one at the dinner when Angela Cook let slip she was seeing Sir Mark Coale. It's the only picture we have of Angela Cook with any other girl, so it's worth a try. I also had a wander round the marina while I was there and called in at the security office. The chief of security is an ex-copper. They have CCTV covering the place. I had a quick look through what they had from yesterday morning and saw our delivery driver, so he is going to look through all the cameras and make a CD up for us with any that show our driver.' Harry then explained what the porter had told him about the delivery driver's accent and height. 'Okay, get on with chasing up some of the loose ends.'

It was just after five when Charlie and Manjitt got back to Scotland Yard. They walked into the office and found the rest of the team seated round a television. 'What are we all watching?' Charlie asked

'We got some CCTV from Chelsea Harbour,' Harry said. 'We are just watching our delivery driver, where he went and came from.' Charlie and Manjitt sat down and watched along with the others. When it was finished, Harry said, 'It's not great, but it gives us something to go on.' Harry told Charlie about what the rest of the team had been doing during the day.

'Sounds like we're moving along a bit,' Charlie said.

'Cramer got the name of the girl in the photograph with Angela Cook that we got from her flat,' Harry said. Charlie looked over at Cramer.

'Sir Martin Oliver said her name is Jayne Cavill, we have an address for her,' Cramer said.

'That's a strange thing,' Harry said. 'It's the same address as Angela Cook's old flat her mother sent over to us.'

'So they were living together before Angela moved into Chelsea Harbour,' Charlie said.

'We got a number for the flat and rang it, but there's new tenants at the flat now,' Harry said. 'Cramer is going to get onto the letting company see if they have a forwarding address for her.'

'I had a look at Gerald Parkin's bank statement. He paid Jayne Cavill a total of £75,000. I have been onto the bank to get her records. Gerald Parkin was also the one paying money into Angela Cook's account,' Cramer said.

'How long had she worked for Sir Martin?' Charlie asked.

'He said Angela brought her along about two months after she started working for him,' Cramer replied.

'We don't have anything on the system about her.' Harry said. 'But we need to find her. She could be the next victim if someone is trying to clear up a trail that leads to the killer.'

'On a lighter note,' Charlie said. 'We had a good day at the races, didn't we Manjitt?'

'A great time, boss. Harry, I want to ask you about tickets for Royal Ascot,' Manjitt said.

Harry sat back. 'I will see how good you are.'

'Harry, you're not asking me on a date,' Manjitt said. The team all started laughing.

'Very good, Manjitt,' Harry said. 'I will find you a few nice jobs to do.'

'I think we have a new teamaker,' Danny said, smiling at Manjitt.

'One thing I can say is the boss has a new girlfriend,' Manjitt said. All the team turned to look at Charlie.

'That's very funny, Manjitt,' Charlie said.

Jordan chipped in. 'Come on, tell us more, Manjitt.'

Charlie held up his hand. 'She's just pulling your leg.'

'Oh come on, boss,' Manjitt said. 'Amanda Moore was all over you.'

Harry turned to Charlie. 'Do I hear wedding bells?' Everyone joined in the laughter and Charlie's embarrassment.

'Okay, settle down,' Charlie said. 'You lot finish up with what you're doing now, then clear off. Tomorrow I want you all to concentrate on what's outstanding. You all know what we need answers to.' The team all left Charlie and Harry sitting alone.

'Did you get much out of Amanda Moore?' Harry said.

'She's a real smart one,' Charlie said. 'She was grilling me as much as I was her. I get the feeling she knows a lot more than she's letting on, just how much...' Charlie shrugged his shoulders, '...I don't know.'

The phone on Harry's desk rang and he picked it up. He listened, took his pen and wrote something down. He talked for a minute, said, 'I owe you one,' and put the phone down. He looked at Charlie and said 'Boss, have you been to Brighton today?'

'Brighton, no. Manjitt and me have been at Ascot, Harry, you know that,' Charlie said. 'Why?'

'That was a friend of mine. You know I like to be informed if anyone is sniffing around members of the team, so I keep in touch with old friends. Well, that was a mate of mine. He's at the national police computer centre. He phoned to tell me someone just ran a check on your car registration number.' He pushed the paper over to Charlie he had written the information on. 'Apparently you were driving strangely in Brighton.'

Charlie picked up the paper and read it. 'Do we know anyone on the Sussex force?' Charlie asked. Harry opened his drawer and took his black diary out. 'What about MM?' Harry said, looking up at Charlie.

'Is Maggie down there now?' Charlie asked.

'According to the last scribble I put in the book she is. I'll give her a bell.' Harry picked up the phone looked at the number in his book and dialled.

'I thought you would have stayed in touch with her, Harry. She had a soft spot for you,' Charlie said.

Harry smiled. 'The job got in the way, boss.' He shrugged, the phone was answered at the other end, he asked to be put through to Chief Inspector Maggie O'Dowd. He waited a second. 'Hello Maggie, its Harry. Yes fine, how are you?' He listened for a minute. 'Well I'm ringing to ask a favour. No, I'm not after a dirty weekend in Brighton. Someone ran a check on the boss's car. They where based in Brighton, but he's been on a case in Ascot today so there's no way he could have been down there. Yes the boss is sitting here with me. Maggie says, "Hello." Yes, he is still the same old slave driver. I have the name of the officer who ran the check. It was a Detective Sergeant Dawson. We're investigating a double-murder at the moment that has a few delicate people involved. Yes, I know, we always upset someone. Thanks, Maggie, yes we'll be in the office for a while yet.' Harry put down the phone. 'She's going to check it out for us, you know Maggie, boss, she will get an answer.'

Charlie nodded. 'You will have to invite her up for a weekend, Harry, be nice to catch up with her, you could come over to the house for dinner.'

'I'll think about it,' Harry said.

'We still have a lot of loose ends to tie up, Harry,' Charlie said.

'I know, boss, but as soon as we get an answer to one thing it throws up another question. I have got six log books from Angela Cook's flat. I will have a look through them, see if any names we have or any we don't know come up as visiting her.'

'Don't forget the other flat, Harry, see who used that. What about Angela Cook's car, have forensics done anything with it yet?'

'I will chase them up.' Harry cleared a space on his desk, found a notepad and wrote a reminder to himself.

'We also need to track this Jayne Cavill down,' Charlie said. 'She may have something to tell us about Angela Cook's relationship with Sir Mark Coale. And talking of him, he is going to be at a dinner at Stanley and Amanda Moore's house tomorrow. I have an invite, you will be coming with me.' Charlie held up his hand as Harry went to speak. 'Don't go saying you don't have anything to wear.' Harry laughed.

'We can question Sir Mark while we're there, and I want you to meet Amanda Moore, I think you will find her an interesting woman.'

'Do I detect a soft spot for her?' Harry said.

'I find her fascinating,' Charlie said.

Harry raised an eyebrow but went back to the case. 'What did you make of the CCTV?'

'We need a bit more, it nails the time down but the pictures are not very clear,' Charlie said. 'Give it to Danny to follow up in the morning, you know how he likes playing with videos. He can get on to some of his techno mates, see if they can do anything with it. I want Jordan concentrating on Tim Green and his fiancée, they keep popping up, I want to get a handle on them. Cramer can work with him as he's already looking at his fiancée, what's her name, Harry?'

Harry looked down at his desk and pulled some papers out. 'Rebecca Rosen.'

'Yes, that's it, well let those two chase everything they can get on them,' Charlie said, 'and send Manjitt over to the Moores' offices tomorrow to take their fingerprints, they have agreed to give them to us. When she's done that she can help with the log books.'

'By the way, boss, we got a call from the people who sold the camera that we found at the flat. It was bought online. The address it went to was Gerald Parkin's,' Harry said.

'Ah well, it was too good to expect it would lead to the killer. We agree that it's one person who's the killer,' Charlie said. Harry nodded. 'Well, they were looking for something at Gerald Parkin's house as it was a mess, and we know they didn't get what they were looking for as we got his books and things. But Angela Cook's flat was tidy, we didn't find her phone or any diaries or anything. So we can assume whoever it was took those. The question is, Harry, why kill them?'

Harry's phone rang. He picked it up. He put his hand over the phone. 'It's Maggie.' Harry listened for a minute. 'That's great, Maggie, I will tell the boss.' Harry wrote something on his pad. 'Yes, we will have to get together. The boss tells me he's having a get-together soon at his house, perhaps you can come up for the weekend. Yes, I will give you a bell with the date, okay speak soon.' Harry put down the phone. He pushed the pad over to Charlie, who picked it up and looked at it. 'Our Detective Sergeant Dawson was doing a favour for a private detective agency. The name's on the pad. Maggie said she's suspended him, she will let us know if anything else turns up. I will run a check on the agency, we can drop in and see them,' Harry smiled. 'Always nice to meet face-to-face.'

Charlie put the pad back onto the table. 'I will leave that with you, Harry, don't forget Crick's report.'

Harry held up a sheet of A4 paper. 'Nearly finished, just got to add a few things on.'

'I will read it in his office in the morning when he moans about it,' Charlie said standing. 'Don't forget, Harry, we're going to the Moores' house for dinner tomorrow, so wear a nice suit.' Harry glanced down at the one he had on. 'Bring one in you can change into. No, on second thoughts, when we're out and about tomorrow I will treat you to one.'

'I should get invited to dinners every week,' Harry said, smiling.

'See you in the morning, Harry,' Charlie said.

CHAPTER FOURTEEN

Harry had got into the office early and had spent the time sorting out what needed to be done and by whom. He had taken photographs and names off the whiteboard who they now thought were not involved in the murder, and replaced them with other pictures and names that had come to their attention. Jordan came in. 'Morning, Harry, you redecorating?' he said, seeing Harry rearranging the whiteboard.

Harry turned. 'Jordan, what's up? Couldn't you sleep, or are you trying to get in my good books because you want a favour?' Harry said.

'Harry, I'm just a hard-working copper,' Jordan said, stretching his arms.

'Yeah right,' Harry answered. 'I'm putting Cramer with you today, I want to get to the bottom of Tim Green's connection to this investigation. We need to know if he's really mixed up in it or not. And I want his fiancée fully checked. Chase up the Israeli police for the report on her, see if you can find anything that ties her to the solicitor Tim Green had. Check their mortgage, previous addresses, re-check their bank accounts. I want those answers today.

'Will do, Harry,' Jordan said. 'Do you want some tea?'

'You are after something,' Harry said and nodded yes. Jordan walked off to make the tea. Harry went back to re-arranging the white board.

Jordan and Harry were seated at Harry's desk drinking their tea. 'You know, you make the worst tea I have ever tasted,'

Harry said. They were looking at the whiteboard, discussing if anyone else needed to be added or taken off, when Danny walked in.

'Good God,' Jordan said when he saw him.

'Morning,' Danny said, walking towards them.

'Hippie, are you going to a rave or something?' Jordan asked.

Danny stopped by the desk. 'I don't understand you,' he said to Jordan. 'I think I set the standard when it comes to keeping up to date with new fashion.'

Jordan turned to Harry, who was looking at Danny and shaking his head. 'Well Hippie, I have to say there is no doubt you set some sort of standard,' Harry said. He leaned round the table looking down at Danny's feet then slowly raised his eyes. Danny had on a pair of yellow velvet trousers and what appeared to be a silk shirt. Its colour was turquoise with big green leaves over it. 'I'm wondering about the sandals, are they covered under health and safety?'

'Police issue, Harry,' Danny said.

Harry sat back, shaking his head. 'Oh well, at least that's okay then. Grab a chair, Hippie, I will tell you what I want you to do today.'

As Danny got a chair Cramer came in. 'Morning, everyone,' he said, walking over to join them, his eyes drawn to Danny. He turned to Harry and was about to say something.

Harry held up his hand. 'Don't say anything, we have all ready been there. We can't explain it either. You're working with Jordan today.' Jordan stood up and he and Cramer went off.

Harry had sent Danny on his way and was on the phone when Manjitt walked into the office. She came over and sat down in front of him. Finishing his call he put the phone down and said, 'Nice of you to drop in today.'

'Harry I had a tough day yesterday, the horse races really take it out of you,' she said.

'I have some good news for you today, you're working with me,' lifting up the six log books from Angela Cook's flats. We are going to go through these and find out all the names of visitors to her and the other flat Gerald Parkin owned.'

'Harry, I can see why you have a reputation for giving a girl a good time,' Manjitt said.

Harry smiled. 'That's not all the treats I have for you. The boss wants you to go over to the Moores' offices and get their fingerprints.'

Manjitt smiled. 'It will be nice to see the boss's girlfriend again.'

'I'm going to meet her tonight,' Harry said. 'What is she like?'

'She's American, very, very attractive and very, very confident,' Manjitt replied. 'I got the impression she likes to be in charge of everything. I don't think her husband tells her what she should do. When we questioned her she was flirting with the boss all the time, but was not giving too much away in her answers and asking questions back herself. She was dressed beautifully and carried herself with an assurance of power.'

'Manjitt, that was a good appraisal of her, not any jealousy in it though, was there?' Harry asked.

Manjitt smiled. 'Maybe about her wardrobe, Harry.'

'I will bear it in mind for this evening.' Harry said. 'The boss is taking me to dinner at her house, Sir Mark Coale is going to be there, so we can ask him a few questions.'

'Is it a black-tie affair?' Manjitt looked at Harry's suit.

'Very funny,' Harry said. He took two of the logs and put them in front of Manjitt. 'Get reading.'

'I have had the top brass onto me, Charlie,' Crick said. 'They want to hear about some progress with the investigation.' He held up the daily report. 'There's not much in this.' He pushed it across the desk to Charlie, who picked it up.

'I think it says everything that has gone on so far,' Charlie said, scanning it and putting it back down.

'I have been told that the BBC Crimewatch programme want to run a section on Gerald Parkin's murder. After all, he was working for them when he was killed. So we need to put together something. It will mean you going on the programme to ask the public for help,' Crick said.

'I don't think that would be a good idea,' Charlie said. 'We believe it's more complicated than it would seem, and the last thing we need is lots of phone calls leading us off in the wrong direction.'

'We don't have any choice,' Crick said, 'it's been decided upstairs, so put something together. I'll sit down with you and go through it. Make sure you have everything correct for the television.'

'That's very kind of you, sir,' Charlie said.

The sarcasm was lost on Crick. 'It's no problem,' Crick said. 'We also have a meeting with the Deputy Commissioner tomorrow. He wants to hear from you personally about the investigation. I think he was a little upset about how things went the last time.' Crick sat forward in his chair. 'I can rely on you to be on your best behaviour.'

Charlie suppressed a smile. 'Of course, sir, whenever have I not been?'

Crick sat back and said, 'Remember Charlie, we don't have a lot of friends amongst the top brass, we don't want more enemies.'

'I'm sure they will come to love us in the end,' Charlie said. 'If that's all, I will be getting back to the office.' Charlie stood up.

When Charlie got back to the office he found only Harry and Manjitt in there. 'Where is everyone?' he said.

'They're all off chasing down leads.' Harry replied. 'Manjitt volunteered to read through the logs with me.'

Manjitt looked up. 'You know me, boss, always reliable.'

Charlie sat down with them and told of his meeting with Crick. 'Doesn't he think we are busy enough?' Harry said.

'I think he has had his ears burnt by the top brass and is getting a bit worried,' Charlie said.

'I phoned Maggie earlier,' Harry said, 'and told her we would be calling in to the private detectives later. She said to let her know how we get on, she will then get the officer in and decide what to do with him.'

'Where is the private detective based?' Charlie asked.

'Covent Garden. They seem quite an upmarket outfit, but I'm sure we will be able to persuade them to be helpful,' Harry said.

'That's handy,' Charlie said. 'Covent Garden, we can do a bit of shopping for you, Harry.'

'Shopping?' Manjitt said. 'You never take me shopping, boss.'

'Did you dig Amanda Moore's address out, Harry?' Charlie said, Manjitt's words not even acknowledged.

Harry tore a page from his pad and passed it to Charlie.

'Nice area,' Charlie said, looking at the page. He folded it and put it into his pocket. 'Give me one of those logs over, Harry. I will help to get through them.'

An hour later, after sorting through three of the log books, Charlie told Manjitt, 'Get off to Stanley and Amanda Moore's office, take the mobile fingerprint-scanner.'

Manjitt stood up. 'Oh boss, I was just starting to enjoy trawling through those books.' Manjitt stretched and started to smile. 'What do you want me to tell Mrs Moore if she asks after you?'

Charlie looked up. 'That I have gotten rid of a nosey officer.'

Manjitt waved as she left the office. Harry watched her go and said, 'When will we hear about her Detective Sergeant's test?'

'The results should be in any day now,' Charlie said.

'I think she will have walked it,' Harry said.

Charlie nodded, 'I agree Harry; let's get these logs finished, then we can pay a visit to the private detective and get you a suit.'

They still had one more log left to sort through when Danny came strolling into the office. Charlie looked up. 'What is that?' he said.

Harry looked up and started to laugh. 'I forgot you hadn't seen Hippie today.'

'Morning boss,' Danny said, ignoring Harry's laughter.

Charlie sat silently looking Danny up and down. 'Words fail me,' he said.

'You like the outfit?' Danny said. 'I was out shopping last night, I saw this shirt and couldn't resist it.'

Charlie shook his head. 'You have a style no one else can put a claim on.'

'That's nice of you to say, boss, Harry doesn't appreciate the trouble it takes to look this good,' Danny said.

Charlie turned to Harry and said, 'I dread to think what the rest of the Yard think of us with him strolling around.'

Harry, still smiling, said, 'Well, Hippie, what have you and your techno mates got from the CCTV?'

'Have a look.' Danny pulled the television over and slid the CD in the player. 'We messed around with it a bit, so it's only a couple of minutes long now, but I think you will be happy with it.' Danny pressed play and stood back. Charlie and Harry watched in silence. After a couple of minutes the screen went blank.

It was Charlie who spoke first. 'You can wear whatever shirt you want Danny, great job. What do you think, Harry?'

'I don't know about the shirt, boss,' Harry said, 'but Hippie you done good. Can you get a few stills off that?'

'Yes, no problem,' Danny said.

'Blow them up,' Charlie said. 'We might have something to put out, Harry.'

'Well, it would be the first break if we have,' Harry said.

Charlie stood up. 'Seeing as you've done so well, Danny, once you have got the pictures off the CD, I am entrusting you with an important job.'

'What's that, boss?' Danny said.

Charlie handed over the log book. 'You get to go through this. Any names that come up as visiting Angela Cook or the other flat that Gerald Parkin owned, write down.'

Harry stood up. 'I second that.' He handed the other log book to Danny.

'We will see you when we get back. If you haven't finished going through them when Manjitt gets back, she can help you finish off.' Charlie and Harry left Danny holding the logs, watching them leave the office.

It didn't take Charlie too long to get to Covent Garden. Finding a parking space was another problem. He drove round the block twice. He was driving the Ferrari Daytona, as the Bentley had been picked up by the dealers for its yearly service that morning.

Harry said, 'Boss, why don't we call in to Bow Street nick, leave the car there and walk.'

'Harry, good idea.' Charlie drove past Covent Garden Opera House, down a side street and came to the back gates of

Bow Street Police Station. Harry got out and went to the intercom. The gats started to open and Charlie drove in, found a parking space, parked up and joined Harry at the back door of the police station. 'Who's here we know?' Charlie asked.

'I think Bernie Thompson is working the drugs squad out of here,' Harry said.

'That's okay, we had Bernie working for us a while back,' Charlie said. 'Let's pop in and see him while we're here.'

They made their way into the station, stopping at the duty sergeant's desk to tell him they had parked the car up and would be back in a couple of hours, but they had to speak to Detective Inspector Thompson. The duty sergeant told them where Thompson's office was. They made their way up to the second floor and walked into an office that was busy with officers on phones and sitting in groups talking. A few of them looked up when they entered. Harry asked one of them where Thompson was. They were pointed to the back of the office. As they neared the back, they saw two men standing at a desk talking to a third sitting down.

'Bernie,' Harry said. The man seated looked up.

'Harry, you old devil,' he said standing up. He was a large black man who was even taller and larger than Jordan.

He spotted Charlie and smiled, 'Boss, how are you, what you doing down amongst the low lifes?'

Charlie held out his hand. 'How are you, Bernie? Looks like a fair team you got here.'

'Doing good, boss. This is my number two, DS Brown. Brown, this is Chief Superintendent Smith.' Charlie shook Brown's hand, 'and this is Chief Inspector Davis.' Harry shook hands. 'Well, what are you doing over here, boss?'

'We are off to check on a lead,' Charlie said. 'We couldn't find anywhere to park, so Harry said we should call in. He reminded me you were here, so I thought we would come up and see you.'

'Anything I can help you with?' Bernie asked.

'No, we're investigating the Gerald Parkin murder,' Charlie said.

'Oh yeah, I saw Crick on the television the other night. God, he gets more orange every time I see him,' Bernie said.

Harry laughed. 'The make-up he had on dulled the colour a bit, he's even worse now. What you got happening, Bernie?' Harry asked.

'We have a mob working out of a couple of clubs, big heroin dealers. We're trying to set up a deal with them so they think we're big buyers. But you know what they're like, scared of their own shadows.' Bernie looked at Charlie. 'Boss, I just thought. We've been trying to make an impression on them, you know flash the cash, act the part, but as I said they are wary. We know they're meeting at a restaurant one of them owns in Soho in an hour.'

'What can we do to help?' Charlie said.

'Did you come in your Bentley?' Bernie asked. DS Brown looked shocked at the news the Chief Superintendent drove a Bentley.

'Sorry, Bernie, it went in for a service today,' Charlie said.

'Ah that's a shame,' Bernie said. 'I thought if we turned up in that, the dealers would think we were the real deal.'

Charlie went into his pocket taking his car keys out. He threw them to Bernie, 'I hope the Ferrari will do just as well.'

'Boss, that's brilliant,' Bernie said. 'What time are you getting back here?'

'About three hours I think, we have to get Harry a new suit after we have spoken to our lead.'

Bernie looked at Harry. 'Has someone died?' he said, laughing.

'The boss is forcing me to get one,' Harry said, laughing back.

'Don't go doing any car chases and break it,' Charlie said. 'There's not many of them of them left in the world.'

'No worries, boss,' Bernie said.

'Catch up with you later,' Charlie said, as he and Harry left.

'Is he for real, Bernie?' DS Brown said. 'A Bentley and a Ferrari?'

Bernie turned to his number two. 'He taught me everything I know, you won't get a better chief than him.' He rubbed his hands together, picked up the car keys and said, 'Let's go and catch some drug dealers.'

Charlie and Harry left Bow Street nick, crossed the road and over to the main Covent Garden shopping area. 'I remember this when it was still the fruit market,' Charlie said, as they walked past all the boutique shops.

'Yeah, I remember chasing some robbers through it when I was a constable,' Harry said. 'I slipped and went crashing into a load of orange boxes, they went everywhere. Never did catch the robbers, but the grocer put a claim for £25 for damage to his stock. My chief at the time gave me a right telling off.'

They passed the underground station on their left and stopped in front of a black painted door that was tucked between a phone store and a modern furniture shop that had chairs in the window that looked like they would be a pain to sit in. Charlie read the brass plaque to the side of the door. 'They're on the first floor,' he said to Harry, and pushed the bell. They waited and a voice came from the intercom, asked them what they wanted. Charlie said they needed the help of a private detective. The door buzzed and Charlie pushed it open and entered. Harry followed him in. They made their way to the first floor and pushed open the door with the private detective's name on. Inside a young woman was seated at a desk and a man at another. The man asked them what they could do for them. 'Are you the boss here?' Charlie asked.

'No,' the man said, 'but if you tell me what the problem is, I will see if it's the sort of case we take. If it is, I will get one of our detectives to see you.'

Harry took out his warrant card and flashed it at the young man. 'Why don't you get the boss, we will tell him our problem personally.'

The man looked at the warrant card and stood up. 'Wait here,' he said, walked away and went through a door behind the girl's desk. Harry and Charlie walked over to her. She looked up as they stopped, standing right in front of her.

'You're very busy?' Charlie asked.

'We have been these last couple of weeks,' she said.

Before they could say any more the young man came back out of the door. 'Mr Hammond will see you,' he said, holding the door open. Harry and Charlie walked past him into a corridor. 'It's the second door on the right.' They walked along the corridor, came to the door and opened it without knocking. A middle-aged man was seated behind the desk. He stood up and came round from behind it.

'Hello gentleman, I'm Dave Hammond, it's always nice to see the police.' He held out his hand, shaking Harry's and Charlie's. 'What is it I can help you with? Come and sit down.' He moved two chairs so they were by his desk, then walked back around the desk sitting down again. Charlie and Harry sat down opposite him.

'Are you the owner?' Harry asked.

'No, I am a senior representative, so I'm sure if you need any help I will be able to sort things for you,' Hammond said.

'Were you in the police force?' Charlie asked.

'No, I was in the army before I joined the agency,' he said. 'What is it you want?'

'We wanted to speak to your boss really,' Harry said. 'Is he in?'

'I am not too sure, I have been quite busy so he may have gone out,' Hammond said. 'You didn't tell me your names.'

'I am Chief Superintendent Smith, this is Chief Inspector Davis, and we would really like to speak to your boss.' Charlie looked at his watch. 'We don't have a lot of time, so if you could get him for us.'

Hammond looked at Charlie. 'As I said. I'm not sure if he's in.'

Harry stood up. 'Mr Dave Hammond,' he said. 'My boss just asked to see yours, now either pick up the phone and call him,' Harry walked around the desk to stand next to Hammond, 'or get up and go and get him. But don't say you don't know if he's in again.'

Hammond looked up at Harry. 'I will check.' He stood up, walked to the door and left the office,. Harry quickly crossed the floor to the door, pulling it slightly open and looking through the gap.

'Next door along on the right,' Harry said, looking back over his shoulder at Charlie, who stood up.

'Let's go and say hello' Charlie said. Harry held the door open, they walked along the corridor and pushed open the door Harry had seen Hammond go into. As they entered Hammond was standing talking to two men. One was seated on a sofa by the window, the other behind a desk. Hammond turned when he heard the door open.

'Sorry, we got bored waiting,' Charlie said, walking into the office. The man on the sofa stood up.

'You can't just barge into offices,' he said.

'And who might you be?' Harry asked. 'You seem to know what we can and can't do.'

He didn't answer but sat back down on the sofa. The

man behind the desk told Hammond to leave. He went out closing the door. 'Please gentleman, take a chair. Mr Hammond was just being careful, we can get some strange people in here.'

Charlie took a chair. Harry went and sat next to the man on the sofa. 'I will sit with my friend over here,' Harry said. 'I think we can become good friends.' He smiled at the man as he sat down; the man moved slightly away.

'So, who are you?' Charlie said to the man at the desk.

'Desmond Carrington. I am the owner of the agency, and you are?'

'Chief Superintendent Smith, what's your friend's name?' Charlie pointed at the man on the sofa.

'He's a friend, just called in during his lunch break for a chat,' Carrington said.

'I don't remember asking for his daily routine, the clue was in the question,' Charlie said, staring at Carrington.

'What's this about?' Carrington said. 'I think we may have got off on the wrong foot. If there's anything I can help you with, I would be only too pleased to.'

'So what's your name?' Harry said to the man on the sofa, ignoring Carrington. The man on the sofa looked at Harry, then back towards Carrington.

'He's a client,' Carrington said. 'I don't think we need to embarrass him by asking his name. Is it all right if he were to leave?' Carrington stood up.

'I don't think he would be embarrassed telling the police his name. After all, we don't know why he would be embarrassed, do we?' Charlie said. He turned to look at the man on the sofa next to Harry.

It was Carrington who broke the silence. 'Robert Jones.'

'Now that wasn't too hard, was it?' Harry said. Carrington sat back down.

'What did you do before you started this agency up?' Charlie said.

'I was a colonel in the army,' Carrington answered. 'We don't need Mr Jones here. Do we?'

'No, I don't see any reason for him to stay,' Charlie said.

The man on the sofa stood up. Harry stood up with him and held out his hand. 'Sorry we interrupted your meeting, Mr Jones,' he said.

Jones took Harry's hand and shook it. Harry, smiling, said 'Do you have any identification on you to prove who you are?'

The man withdrew his hand. 'I don't have to prove who I am to you,' he said.

Harry shook his head. 'Another one who knows the law. You don't have to tell me who you are, but now you have, I am quite entitled to ask you to prove it.'

Charlie smiled at Carrington. 'This could have been so much easier, I would have asked my questions and been gone. But now you have got my Chief Inspector's radar going. One thing he doesn't like is people telling him the law. So would Mr Jones just show some identification, then I can get on with talking to you.'

Carrington looked over at the man standing next to Harry and back at Charlie. 'He is a client, but his name's not Robert Jones.'

'Thank you,' Charlie said. He turned to the man. 'Could you show some identification please, and we will forget you gave us a false name.'

The man slowly put his hand to his back pocket and pulled out a wallet, opened it, taking his driving licence from it, and gave it to Harry. 'Thank you,' Harry said, looking at it, making a couple of notes in his notebook and giving it back.

'Can I go now?' the man said.

'Yes, fine,' Harry replied. 'It was nice meeting you.' The

man quickly left without saying another word. Harry wrote another couple of things in his notebook then came over to the desk and took a chair beside Charlie.

'Now, Mr Carrington, perhaps we can get down to what I came to see you about,' Charlie said.

'Yes, of course,' Carrington said. 'What is it you wanted my help with?'

Charlie sat back in his chair and said, 'Yesterday a check was run on a car in Brighton. That check was carried out by a Detective Sergeant Dawson. He said he did it for your agency.'

'I don't believe anyone here would ask a police officer to do something like that,' Carrington said, 'that's against the law.' He smiled at Charlie.

'The man who just left,' Harry said. 'His name's Turnball, right?'

Carrington turned to Harry. 'Yes, that's right.'

'Have you known him long?' Harry asked.

'Why do you ask?' Carrington said.

Harry sighed. 'Have you known him long?' he repeated.

'A few months, why?' Carrington asked.

'So you're saying no one in your agency asked Dawson to run a check on a car in Brighton?' Charlie said.

'Yes, no one would do that, as I said it's against the law. We're an agency that abides by the law,' Carrington said.

'That's good to know, don't you think Harry?' Charlie said. Harry nodded. 'Detective Sergeant Dawson has been arrested on corruption charges. Now, if it turns out that someone in your agency was asking him to do some checking for them and you were not helpful, I would have to come back here and maybe arrest you too. So do you want to do a bit of checking amongst your staff before you put your reputation on the line?'

Carrington sat looking at Charlie. Before he could answer, Harry said, 'Mr Turnball, how do you know him?'

'What?' Carrington said, looking at Harry.

'Mr Turnball, how do you know him?' Harry repeated.

'I met him at a dinner given by the Association of Detective Agencies,' Carrington said.

'So he's a private detective. I thought you said he was a client,' Harry asked.

'I was a bit confused, he does freelance work,' Carrington replied.

'So do you want to check up before you make a statement, or deny all knowledge of someone corrupting a policeman?' Charlie said.

Carrington turned back to Charlie, slightly confused. 'I will check with all my staff to make sure no one has been silly,' he said.

'That's the wisest thing to do,' Charlie said. 'What sort of clients do you have. Are they all divorces and adultery?'

'No, not at all,' Carrington said. 'We work for companies who want background checks on staff, or other companies they're dealing with to make sure they're sound.'

'So do you have a phone number for Mr Turnball?' Harry asked.

Carrington turned to Harry. 'I think I have one here.' He opened a small phone book on his desk, he read out a mobile phone number to Harry.

'Do you have an office number for him?' Harry asked, writing the number down.

'No, sorry, I only have his mobile,' Carrington said, shutting the phone book.

'Now I don't want to press you,' Charlie said. 'But I want an answer to that question by five o'clock this evening.'

'But not all my staff are in the office,' Carrington said.

'Well, you'd better find them and speak to them. Whoever it is, we will have to arrange for them to come in and make a statement. I'm sure you don't want lots of policemen turning up here with a search warrant looking for information on payments to corrupt policeman, do you?'

'I will do my best to find out,' Carrington said.

Harry took out his phone and dialled a number, shook his head. 'Oh dear,' he said. 'That number you gave me appears to be dead.' Looking at Carrington, Harry said, 'you don't want to look in your little book, make sure you didn't give me the wrong one by mistake.'

Carrington slowly opened his phone book, read out a number to Harry. 'Oh silly you,' Harry said, 'you gave me the wrong one. I'm sure it was a genuine mistake.' Harry dialled the number, waited a second, listened, then pressed end call. He looked at Carrington, but said nothing.

Charlie stood up. 'It's been a pleasure meeting you, Mr Carrington.' He held out his hand. Carrington slowly got to his feet and shook Charlie's hand. 'Five o'clock, or I will have your offices swarming with policemen.' Charlie smiled, turned and walked towards the door. Harry smiled at Carrington and followed Charlie,.

When they were back in the street, Harry said, 'Not a man to be trusted.'

'I think he will put someone up to take the blame for the car check,' Charlie said. 'He will claim it was a oneoff and he never knew it was going on. You will have to ring Maggie, fill her in, she can take it on from here. What about our Mr Turnball?'

'The number Carrington finally gave me was answered by a John Russell, so we will have to run a check on him as the man with three names. He needs looking at, but is it to do with the murders, boss? The driving licence he showed me as Turnball was counterfeit. Quite a good one, but a wrong un.' He passed the piece of paper from his pad he had written the name on to Charlie, who looked at it. The date of birth and the licence number were beside Turnball's name.

'When you speak to Maggie,' Charlie said, 'make sure she finds out who they were running the check on the car for. It might not be connected to the murders, Harry, but there have been so many strange connections in this case you never know. Now let's go and get your suit.' They walked down Long Acre towards Leicester Square.

'I'll call her now, get things moving,' Harry said. He called Maggie, gave her all they knew about Carrington and said he would be back in touch as soon as he heard anything from him, hopefully by five.

When he got off the phone, Harry said, 'I have been thinking about that CCTV that Hippie has messed around with,' They crossed Leicester Square, heading for Piccadilly. 'The face of the killer is not too clear, and maybe it will be a bit better when he gets some stills from it, but I'm sure I have seen it somewhere before.'

'What, in another case, Harry?' Charlie asked.

'I'm not sure boss, but it's bugging me. There's something in the face I have seen before.' They came out of Coventry Street and into Piccadilly, crossed over and into Regent Street.

'As you say, Harry, when Danny's got some stills from it, it might jog your memory.' They walked up Regent Street, crossing over to turn into Vigo Street then right into Savile Row.

'Here we are, Harry,' Charlie said, stopping in front of a shop whose sign read, 'Bespoke Tailors'. Charlie pushed open the door and let Harry go in first. Inside was a haven of peace from the traffic noise of central London. The shop had a quietness about it. A short, rather rotund man came towards them. His face broke into a smile as he got closer.

'Chief Superintendent,' he said. 'How are you?' He held out his hand and Charlie shook it.

'Very well thank you, Mr Katz,' Charlie said. 'I hope you got my message I left for you yesterday, I think I spoke to one of your sons.'

'Yes, I have your new suit ready,' Mr Katz said. He stood back and looked Charlie up and down. 'You don't look like you have changed much, so it should fit as good as always.'

'This is Chief Inspector Davis,' Charlie said, introducing Harry. 'It's him who needs the suit for tonight, I hope it's possible.'

'I have a cutter on standby and two of my best seamstresses ready to go to work,' Mr Katz said. 'Do you want to follow me Chief Inspector, I will take all your measurements, get things started. One of my boys will bring you a cup of tea, Chief Superintendent.' He took Harry's arm, guiding him to the back of the shop. 'This suit you have on, what shop did you get it from?' Mr Katz felt the material, 'I think you'd better not go back there.' Charlie smiled as he watched Mr Katz take Harry away. He sat in a chair by the window and took out his phone and called Manjitt.

'Hello, boss,' he heard Manjitt say.

'Manjitt, we will be back in the office in an hour or so, but I want you to check out a couple of names,' Charlie said. 'The first is John Russell, he might be a private detective. The second is Michael Turnball.' He gave Manjitt the date of birth and driving licence number and the mobile telephone number. 'They are the same person, so check the date of birth against John Russell's when you run him through the computer. Find out as much as you can.'

'Will do, boss,' Manjitt said. 'Is he on the radar for the murders?'

'I don't know, but check him out for me,' Charlie said. He put down the phone just as a cup of tea was brought to him. He sat watching Harry being measured up for his suit, smiling at Mr Katz, who was shaking his head when he looked at some of the measurements on his tape and called them out to his assistant. When he had finished, a large book of materials was brought over for Harry to look at. Harry stopped at one or two, rubbed the material, he looked at Mr Katz who shook his head. Mr Katz left Harry looking in the materials book and came over to speak to Charlie.

'Chief Superintendent, the suit...' he pointed at Harry, '... what is it for?'

'We're going to a dinner this evening, it's not black tie but very distinguished people will be there.' Charlie said. Mr Katz nodded, turned and went back to Harry. He took the book Harry was looking in off him and said something to his assistant, who brought a new one over. Harry opened it, looked through stopped at a couple he liked but when he looked at Mr Katz, he got the shake of the head no. He carried on looking, stopped at another one, looked at Mr Katz, who beamed at him and told him what a good choice he had made. He passed the book back to his assistant and guided Harry back to Charlie.

'Everything sorted, Mr Katz?' Charlie said.

'I think your colleague has an eye for style,' Mr Katz said.

Charlie stood up. 'If he has, Mr Katz, he has kept it hidden for years. You will have the suits delivered to Scotland Yard for me by six?'

'Of course, Chief Superintendent,' Mr Katz said.

'Put them both on my account,' Charlie said, 'and if you can, put in a couple of nice silk shirts that will go with the suits for both of us.'

'Of course, not a problem, you will need ties, I will sort them out too,' Mr Katz said, shaking Charlie and Harry's hand. They left the shop.

'I have no idea what sort of suit or material I have chosen,'

Harry said, as they walked down towards Vigo Street, retracing the way they had come.

'I think you will be alright, Harry,' Charlie said. He told Harry about his conversation with Manjitt.

'While I was being measured up,' Harry said, 'I was thinking about the killer's face. I'm sure I've seen it somewhere in this investigation already.'

Charlie looked at Harry and said, 'When we get back, we will go through every picture we have. If Danny's got some good stills from the CD it might make it a little easier.'

It took them about twenty minutes to walk back to Bow Street Police Station. Once inside they made their way up to the second floor to see Bernie Thompson. When they entered his office, he was seated on his desk, talking to a number of officers standing in front of him. Charlie and Harry stopped, waited a couple of minutes till he finished, then walked over.

Bernie saw them. 'Boss, it worked a treat,' he said. DS Brown stood next to him.

'Glad to hear it, Bernie,' Charlie said.

'They even came outside the restaurant to have a look at the car and talk motors,' Bernie said. 'We have set up a buy off them in a couple of days, three kilos of heroin. They think we are South London gangsters.' Bernie laughed. 'I should've had Jordan with me, it might have been true then.'

'I will let him know you're thinking of him,' Harry said, smiling.

'I've put them under observation now, we'll watch them till the buy, see where they go, who they meet, then hit any places we think are of interest the same time we bust them at the buy,' Bernie said. 'How did you get on, boss?'

'We did all right, don't know if it will lead us anywhere or further the investigation though,' Charlie said.

'Did Harry get a new suit?' Bernie asked.

'I did,' Harry said, 'although I'm not too sure what it will look like on yet.'

'Oh you took him to your tailor's boss, wait till word hits the grapevine. Harry has a new suit, people will think the end of the world is coming,' Bernie said. Charlie laughed.

'Bernie, now I know why I always knew you would be a useless copper,' Harry said, joining the laughter.

Bernie passed Charlie the keys to the Ferrari. 'Thanks again boss, and you know any time you need a favour you only have to call.'

'I will do, Bernie.' Charlie shook hands, he turned to DS Brown. 'It was nice to meet you too, Brown, you're working with a good copper, learn well and you'll be alright in this job.'

'You take care, Bernie,' Harry said, shaking hands.

'Good luck with the case, Harry,' Bernie said.

'I have been meaning to ask you all day,' Manjitt said. She was seated across from Danny. The logs they had been through were piled up on the table between them. 'How are you getting on with your detective constable from the drugs squad?'

Danny looked at Manjitt suspiciously. 'Okay, why?'

'No reason, I just worry about your welfare,' Manjitt said, a smile on her face.

'What are you not telling me?' Danny said.

'Nothing, I was just thinking about you bringing her along for a drink one evening,' Manjitt replied.

Harry and Charlie walked into the office. 'Okay you two, I can see you are working hard,' Harry said.

'Harry, we haven't stopped,' Manjitt said.

'Get out of my chair, Hippie, and make me and the boss some tea,' Harry said.

'It's at times like this I realise why a career in the police is so fulfilling,' Danny said, standing up.

'I'll have a cup while you're at it,' Manjitt said. Danny aimed a slap at her head as he went by, but missed.

Harry sat down in his chair. 'Well Manjitt, what have you found out for us?' Charlie sat on the edge of Harry's desk. He had to push a pile of files to one side to find space.

'Well I got the fingerprints from Mr and Mrs Moore,' Manjitt said. 'She was quite pleasant, she told me she was looking forward to seeing you again, boss.' She looked up at Charlie, smiling.

Charlie smiled back. 'You're not working in a dating agency.'

'Just passing on information, boss,' Manjitt said.

'Get on with passing some more on,' Harry said.

Manjitt turned back to Harry. 'I ran their prints through the system, his are clear, but hers come up on the bedside table and the cigars.'

'That's how we saw it,' Harry said. 'What else have you got?'

Manjitt turned to Charlie. 'I checked those names out you gave me, Turnball and Russell. I can't find any one called Turnball on the system, and no driving licence has been issued. On the other hand, using the same date of birth and the mobile number, I got a hit on John Russell. He's ex-army, has two convictions for dangerous driving and threatening behaviour. He also has a driving licence, I pulled his picture up off it.' Manjitt picked up a file from in front of her, pulled out a photograph and passed it to Charlie.

He looked at it, passing it to Harry. 'That's our Mr Turnball, or Russell.'

Harry took it and nodded. 'I will add it to the whiteboard later. We don't know if he's involved, but he can stay up there till we're sure one way or the other. Did you get an address for him too?' Manjitt took another piece of paper from the file and passed it to Harry. Danny came back with three cups of tea and passed them out. He pulled over a chair and sat down.

'I also followed up on Jayne Cavill,' Manjitt said. 'I went over and saw the letting agents on the way back from the Moores' office. I showed them the photo of the girl and Angela Cook. Two of the people at the agents confirm that's Jayne Cavill. They told me a bit about her, she didn't move in at the same time as Angela Cook, she moved in with Angela about four months later. They gave me the address Jayne Cavill had given them as where she lived before. I checked it out, it's a really nice place, upmarket. She went downhill when she moved to Peckham. I can't find any trace of her before that.'

'Well we're getting somewhere with her,' Harry said.

'I wouldn't speak too soon,' Manjitt said. 'I re-checked Jayne Cavill's bank account to find out who she was paying rent to at the other flat. In fact she owned it, she sold it and moved out to join Angela Cook in her pokey flat in Peckham.'

'This girl is getting more interesting,' Charlie said. 'How much did she sell that place for?'

Manjitt looked at the paper in front of her. '£450,000, so she was not short of a few bob. But why move in with Angela Cook?'

Harry looked at Charlie. 'If she was worth that much, why did she go and work for Sir Martin Oliver as one of his girls?'

'She was also getting money off Gerald Parkin, remember,' Charlie said.

'That's the good news,' Manjitt said. 'The bad is the address for her bank account was the old flat in Peckham.'

'Well, she must still be using it,' Harry said. 'We can maybe trace her through it.'

'The bad news gets worse, Harry,' Manjitt said. 'Yesterday morning, she cleared most of her money out of the account – in total, £655,000.'

'She didn't go into the bank and do that, did she?' Harry asked.

'No, she phoned in. She paid the money to a diamond merchant in Antwerp,' Manjitt said. 'She left £12 in her account.'

'I don't think she will be coming back for that, but why suddenly close the account? Are we getting close to her, but we don't know it yet?' Charlie said.

'That's it,' Harry cried out. ' Hippie, get me the pictures from the CD. Manjitt, pass me the photo of Jayne Cavill.' Danny went to his desk and got a couple of pictures of the killer, and brought them over and passed them to Harry who took them, looked at both and put one aside. He cleared a space on his desk in front of him. He took the picture of Jayne Cavill that Manjitt passed him and laid them down side by side. 'Look, boss.' Charlie came round to stand beside Harry, he looked at the two pictures.

'You could be right, Harry,' Charlie said, picking the pictures up.

'I know we can't see the hair of the killer, but look at the face, it's the same,' Harry said.

Charlie studied them. 'I think you have it, Harry,' Charlie said. He passed the pictures to Manjitt and Danny, who studied them.

'I agree with Harry, it could definitely be her,' Manjitt said. 'It's the same person.'

'It would explain how Angela Cook let the killer into her bedroom without any worry, and Gerald Parkin knew her so he would have let her in too,' Harry said.

'The porter said she had a foreign accent,' Harry said. 'Hippie, ring up Sir Martin Oliver, ask him if Jayne Cavill was foreign.' Danny was looking at the pictures.

'Okay Harry.' He put the pictures down slowly.

'What's wrong, Danny,' Charlie asked.

'I don't know, it's something about the pictures now I have seen them close up,' Danny said. He laid them on the table. 'I will call Sir Martin and ask him about Jayne Cavill.' He got up and went to find the file on Sir Martin Oliver to get his phone number.

'Well, now we know why she cleared her bank account out,' Charlie said. 'Manjitt, get those pictures out to all ports and airports with her name. She might have slipped the net, but let's see.'

'It's a breakthrough, boss,' Harry said.

'Your sharp eyes, Harry, but we still don't know why she killed. She wasn't poor, was she?' Charlie said. 'We need to try and clear these pictures up a bit, get Danny to work on them with his techno mates. Manjitt, do we have the address of the diamond merchant?' Manjitt nodded. 'Get on to the Belgium police, explain the case and ask them if they can check the diamond merchant out, and if the diamonds are still waiting to be collected or they are sending them on. And most of all, who are they for?' Manjitt got up and went off to her desk.

'A chink of light, boss,' Harry said.

'Let's hope someone doesn't switch the light off again, Harry.' Charlie said.

Danny came back over. 'According to Sir Martin, she had a foreign accent. He doesn't know exactly where she was from though.'

'That's good,' Harry said. 'Hippie, take the two pictures we have of her and see if you and your weird techy mates can make them a bit clearer.'

'Harry, you're too kind about the technical photography department,' Danny said. 'I will see what we can do.' He picked up the two pictures and left. As he went out off the office door Jordan and Cramer came in. 'Hey, Hippie, how are things going?' Jordan asked.

Danny held up the pictures. 'Getting exciting, see the boss.'

Jordan and Cramer came over to Harry's desk. Charlie was still perched on the edge. 'Well you two, what have you got to add to our pot?' Charlie said.

'Sit down,' Harry said to them, pointing at the empty chairs in front of his desk. 'Come on then, let's have it.'

It was Jordan who spoke first. 'We went right back to the beginning with Tim Green like we had just discovered him. We know about his affray charge and his suspected fraud. He lived with his mother and father before he bought the house he's in now. On the mortgage application it's the same address given by Rebecca Rosen. We haven't spoken to his parents yet to check that out.'

'Might be something we need to do,' Harry said.

Jordan continued. 'The bank account is normal, the only strange thing is, his fiancée as we know was not working. She was on a university course, but we know she only did that for a year, so for the last couple we don't know what she's been doing. Now with the mortgage, normal household bills, Tim Green's wages hardly cover it. So she has an account, Cramer got the details of that.'

Harry and Charlie looked at Cramer, who had a piece of paper in his hand. 'She had an account. Every month £2000 was transferred into it from a bank in Israel. It may be her parents or something. I got a reply back from the Israeli police on her, she went into the army at 18 like all Israelis have to. It said she left the army when she was 24. I did some checking because I thought that conscription for the army was three years. It turns out I was wrong, it's three for men but only two for women, so Rebecca Rosen stayed in four years longer than she needed to.'

'Perhaps she liked the army,' Harry said.

'Do we know what she did in the army?' Charlie asked.

'No, the information I got from them just gives dates, nothing on what she did,' Cramer said.

'What course was she down as doing at the university she was supposed to be going to?' Harry asked.

Jordan sorted through her and Tim Green's file. 'Business degree course,' he said.

'Well, she must have had some references, so get on to the university and find out about them,' Harry said.

'I checked with Tim Green's company about how much work he did on Gerald Parkin's contracts. They told me he did not have too much to do with them, so he's been lying about that,' Jordan said.

'Why is it that Tim Green keeps popping up with unanswered questions?' Charlie said.

'I checked the solicitor he had,' Cramer said. 'I can't find any connection to him or his fiancée, there's no payment from their account, to the solicitors and we can't go along to the solicitors and ask them.'

'Well, that's one thing that will have to wait,' Charlie said. 'We now believe Jayne Cavill and the delivery driver are the same person. Harry put them together, they look alike. Danny has gone to see if he can get the pictures cleaned up so we have a definite match.'

'Well that's a start, but the porter never said the driver was a woman,' Jordan said.

'No, the porter said the driver had a hat on and just came in and signed the book,' Charlie replied. 'So apart from telling us the driver had a pale complexion and a foreign accent, he didn't get a good look. But some of the stills from the CCTV give us a full look at the face.'

'It doesn't get better,' Harry said, and explained what Manjitt had found out.

'Where do we go from here?' Cramer said.

'Okay, this is what I want you to do,' Charlie said to Cramer. 'Get onto the university about Rebecca Rosen's references, get onto the Israeli police about the account that was sending her money every month. Speak to Tim Green's parents, check that they both lived there before they moved. Jordan, I want you to ring those solicitors and tell them we want Tim Green here at midday tomorrow for an interview. Let's see how they react to that. Let them know if he doesn't turn up we will issue a warrant for his arrest. Then put together a file on him of all we have, he has questions to answer. Get on with things, then.'

'But if we think Jayne Cavill is the killer, should we spend so much time on Tim Green?' Cramer asked.

'Do you think he's involved, boss?' Jordan said.

'I don't know, but let's look. He's been in this investigation from the start, he got a car from Gerald Parkin. Angela Cook got a car, she's dead. Could he be a target, or could he be involved in the killing? We need to clear him one way or the other,' Charlie said. Cramer and Jordan got up and left.

Manjitt came over and said a message from a Mr Carrington had come in for Harry. She passed it over and went away. Harry looked at it, 'I will call Maggie with these details.'

Charlie's phone rang. He took the call, stood up and signalled to Harry to carry on, and walked away talking.

When Harry had finished his call to Maggie, he got up, stuck the two pictures on the whiteboard, taking others off and redrawing some lines to make connections. He went and sat back down and watched Charlie, who was still talking animatedly on his phone. Charlie walked towards him shaking his head. Harry heard him say, 'Yes, sir,' and saw Charlie come off the phone.

'You're not going to believe this,' Charlie said. 'That was Crick on the phone. I was supposed to have a meeting with him and the Deputy Commissioner tomorrow morning at 9.30.

He now tells me that the Deputy Commissioner has decided he wants the whole team there for the meeting. Apparently he thinks we need a full debrief so he can gauge how everyone thinks the case is going. Crick said the top brass are under pressure from the media, especially the BBC, for faster progress.'

'Sounds like they're angling to move someone in to oversee us,' Harry said.

'You could be right, Harry. Crick was all a-fluster, he must have had a right telling off.' Charlie said.

'Well, that Deputy Commissioner Macready would jump at the opportunity to stick it to us,' Harry said. 'He was embarrassed that we put him in his place.'

'Let's see if anything turns up before we go to the meeting,' Charlie said. 'If not we will play it by ear.' Charlie looked at his watch. 'How was Maggie?'

'She's well, I let her know what Carrington had said. You were right, boss, he has put up someone to take the blame. Maggie will let us know who they say the check was being done for,' Harry said.

Charlie nodded. 'Our suits should be arriving soon. We can get a shower and change in the police gym downstairs and drive straight there from here.'

'That's okay with me,' Harry said. 'How do you want to play the questioning later?'

Charlie looked at Harry and smiled. 'I have had a thought about that.' He then explained to Harry what he wanted them to do.

Jordan looked up from putting together the file on Tim Green ready for the interview tomorrow and turned to Cramer. 'How are you getting on with his fiancée?' he asked.

Cramer was bent over his computer screen. 'I got an email back from the Israeli police. The bank account sending her

£2000 pounds each month was in her name.' He looked up. 'I did get something interesting from the university she was supposed to be attending. She had a reference from the Israeli Army Education Department, that you would expect. But the other reference was from a bank. I'm just trying to find something out about it. Maybe she worked there before going to the university.'

Jordan stretched his arms. 'Did you find out why she stayed in the army for six years instead of two?'

'I did ask, but they told me they don't discuss army personnel records,' Cramer said.

'We will ask Mr Green tomorrow how he met his fiancée,' Jordan said, making a note in the file. 'Did you manage to get hold of his parents?'

'I got a number for them but they weren't in, so I left my number asking them to call.' Cramer sat back in his chair. 'Do you think Tim Green and his fiancée are mixed up in the killings?'

'The boss is right about them being in or around the investigation from the start, so we need to eliminate them one way or the other,' Jordan said.

Manjitt strolled into the office, picked a note up from her desk and came over to Jordan and Cramer. 'How's things going with you two?' she asked.

'We're getting there, did you get anything from the Belgium police?' Jordan asked.

'The diamond merchants check out, they are all above board. Apparently the diamonds were picked up by a courier in line with instructions they had received from Jayne Cavill,' Manjitt replied.

'Do we know where the courier took them?' Cramer asked.

'No, well not yet. I have asked the Belgians if they can find out for me, as the diamond merchants would not tell me anything.' She sat down on the corner of Cramer's desk. 'The boss left a message on my desk for all of us.' She waved the piece of paper. 'We are to be in the office no later than nine tomorrow morning, he says there is a meeting with Deputy Commissioner Macready and all the team must be there.'

'Sounds ominous.' Cramer said. 'He was not best pleased the last time we saw him.'

'Let's wait until the morning and see what the boss and Harry have to say,' Jordan said.

Manjitt stood up. 'Are you all done?' she said to Cramer.

'Yes, as much as I can until I get some phone calls back,' he said, standing up.

Jordan looked at them. 'Where are you two off to?'

Manjitt tapped her nose, Cramer just smiled as they both left Jordan sitting alone in the office.

About an hour later Jordan had finished the report on Tim Green to aid the questioning tomorrow. He closed the file and stood up and stretched just as Danny came into the office. 'Hey, Hippie, you still here?'

Danny waved a couple of photographs as he walked towards Jordan. 'Been downstairs trying to get these cleaned up.'

'Well, give them here. Let me have a look,' Jordan said. Danny passed over the pictures, Jordan put them side by side on the desk. 'You've done a good job, Hippie, I can see what Harry saw now. They are the same person. Have you sent them out to all police stations, ports and airports yet?'

'No, not yet, I am just going to,' Danny said.

'Well, don't forget to remind them to throw away the old pictures they have of her.' Jordan looked at Danny. He didn't seem to be his bubbly self. 'Is there something bothering you, Hippie?'

'I don't know.' He picked up the pictures from the desk. 'It's these photos. There's something...' he shook his head, '... but I can't put my finger on what it is,'

'What, you don't think they're the same person?' Jordan asked.

'No, they're the same person alright,' Danny said. 'It's just something else, but for the life of me I can't think what it is.'

'Well get them out, we might catch her trying to get on a plane to Belgium,' Jordan said, explaining what Manjitt had found out about the diamonds. He also told Danny about the meeting tomorrow. 'I will see you in the morning, Hippie.'

'Okay, Jordan,' Danny said as he walked away towards his desk. Jordan watched him sit down, put his feet up and stare at the pictures.

CHAPTER FIFTEEN

Charlie was driving the Ferrari through the late evening traffic heading for Elstree in Hertfordshire. Harry was seated beside him on the way. They had been discussing the case. Charlie turned the Ferrari into a wide tree lined road on each side large houses were just visible behind high hedges or trees. The further they went along the road, the houses became fewer but bigger. Charlie swung the Ferrari off the main road onto a driveway, stopping in front of high gates that barred the way. He saw a buzzer attached to a pole and got out and pressed it. Security lights came on and a few seconds later the gates started to open. Charlie walked back to the car, got in and drove through the gates.

'Very nice place,' Harry said, as Charlie drove along the drive, coming to a large Georgian style mansion. It was three storeys high and every light appeared to be on in the house. Cars were parked all along the front of it. The main doors were wide open, a woman and a man were standing in the doorway. In front of the house was a lake. 'Wonder if they go fishing in there?'

'I think they would have someone to do that for them,' Charlie said as he parked the Ferrari. 'That's the Moores standing in the doorway.'

Harry looked at the couple. 'She looks a very attractive woman, boss.' Amanda Moore was dressed in a long black dress that hugged her body, her blonde hair was up, showing the long diamond earrings that matched the necklace she wore.

'Don't you start, Harry,' Charlie said. 'I had enough from

Manjitt.' They both got out of the car and made their way towards the front door. They heard music coming from inside.

'Sounds like Beethoven's *Piano Concerto Number Five*,' Harry said, as they reached the Moores.

Amanda Moore stepped forward, 'Charlie, I am so glad you came. I was looking out for your Bentley, but I see you have a different car and a classic Ferrari. You are an intriguing policeman.' She leaned forward and Charlie lightly kissed her on the cheek. 'And who is this you have with you?' she said.

'This is Detective Chief Inspector Davis,' Charlie said.

Amanda Moore held out her hand. Harry shook it. 'Pleased to meet you, do you have a first name?' she asked. 'I suppose Charlie never introduces you by your first name to anyone.' She looked at Charlie.

'It's Harry.'

'Well, Harry, I hope you enjoy yourself tonight, but my husband will be disappointed.' She turned to her husband, who had stood silently in the doorway. 'Charlie has not brought that beautiful policewoman for you to chat to, Stanley.' She turned back to Harry. 'This is my husband. Stanley, this is Harry, he's another policeman, so mind what you say, he will write it all down.' She smiled as she said it, but Harry heard the meaning she put into it. She took Charlie's arm and guided him inside, Harry followed. It was a large entrance hall that rose to take in the height of the building. Two chandeliers hung above them lighting up the whole hall. A grand piano was to the side of a sweeping staircase, with a woman playing. 'I have to leave you and greet the rest of my guests,' Amanda Moore said, 'but I am sure we will have lots to talk about later. If you go into the main drawing room, everybody is having a drink before dinner.' She pointed to the room on the right, the double doors were wide open. She left them and went back to the main entrance of the house.

Charlie and Harry slowly made their way to the drawing room, stopping at the doors and scanning the crowd inside. There were about twelve people in the room talking in groups.

'What do you make of our hostess?' Charlie said.

'I think I will have to keep an eye on you, boss, I think she wants her wicked way with you,' Harry said.

Charlie laughed. 'I will hold you to that Harry, look who's over there.' Charlie indicated with his head. Harry looked over and saw Lord and Lady Dorres talking to another couple.

'I bet they will be happy to see us here,' Harry said. A waiter came up and offered them a glass of wine, they each took one.

'A maximum of two glasses,' Charlie said.

'That's the rule,' Harry replied. They made their way into the room, walking towards the big fireplace that had a painting above it. The painting was of Amanda Moore. 'She's a very good-looking woman, boss.'

'She is that, Harry,' Charlie said as they both gazed up at the picture. They turned and looked back at the rest of the people in the room.

'I will ask her to introduce us to Sir Mark Coale when she comes back in,' Charlie said.

'I recognise the fat guy with the grey hair standing over there talking to that woman,' Harry said.

'Harry, the word is not fat,' Charlie said, turning to look. 'Haven't you read the latest police handbook? It's large or rotund. Fat is a non-PC word,' He saw the deputy Mayor of London. 'We are in exalted company, he is a bit fat, you're right, Harry.'

Harry nudged Charlie. 'We're going to meet some old friends,' he said quietly.

Charlie turned to see Lord and Lady Dorres approaching them. His Lordship's face did not show any sign of affection.

'Don't you think you could organise your questioning without gate crashing someone's party?' Lord Dorres said.

'We are here as guests for the evening,' Charlie replied.

'It's so nice to see you outside work,' Harry said to Lady Dorres.

They both turned away and went back to the group they had been standing with. 'Do you recognise anyone else?' Charlie asked.

'No, nobody,' Harry replied. They stood watching the crowd and noticed another couple enter. After a few minutes Stanley and Amanda Moore entered with another man, he was tall and thin. A waiter approached them and they all took a glass of wine. The doors were shut behind them as the waiter went out. Stanley Moore walked away from his wife and joined the group Lord Dorres was amongst.

'I bet we are the topic of conversation,' Harry said.

'It will give them something different to talk about,' Charlie said. They watched as Amanda Moore took the tall man over to the Deputy Mayor and the woman he was talking with. After a couple of minutes a man entered the room, walked over to Stanley Moore, whispered in his ear and went away. Stanley Moore moved to the centre of the room and announced everyone should make their way to the dining room. The doors were opened and Charlie and Harry followed the rest of the guests out and across the hall into another large room.

A long table had been set for dinner. There were three tall candlesticks on it, each holding four large lit candles. The main lights in the room were dimmed, and two waiters stood either side of the doors as they passed through. Amanda Moore was pointing and telling everyone where to sit. Stanley Moore was seated closest to where they were standing at the head of the table. At the other end, the tall man was seated. She came to

Harry. 'I have put you here, Harry.' She pointed to a chair halfway along; she took his arm and guided him to his chair. 'Let me introduce you to your neighbours,' she said. 'This is Christine Williams, she works for Channel Four News, I know you will have a lot to talk about. And this is Grant Sherman, he's the Deputy Mayor.' Harry exchanged handshakes. 'This is Harry.' Amanda Moore introduced him. 'He's a policeman, so be careful what you say to him.' Harry took his seat between his table companions.

Amanda Moore came back to Charlie. Taking his arm, she said, 'You're at the other end of the table, Charlie.' She guided him down the room on the opposite side of the table to Harry. She showed Charlie the last seat on the end; Charlie sat down. Amanda leaned into his back, placing her hands on his shoulders, her head close to his ear. 'Charlie, let me introduce you to Sir Mark Coale.' The man at the head of the table held out his hand. 'Mark, this is Charlie, or should I give you your official title, Chief Superintendent.' Charlie shook hands.

'She loves to try and wind people up,' Sir Mark said.

'Oh, don't be nasty,' Amanda Moore said, feigning being upset. 'Is everybody seated? You can start to serve dinner now,' she said to the waiters standing at the door. She took the empty seat to Charlie's left. 'I hope you don't mind having me sitting next to you, Charlie.'

Charlie turned his head. 'The pleasure's all mine.'

'You never know, Charlie, it might be,' Amanda Moore said, and took a drink from her wine glass. The waiters started to serve dinner. The food was very good and Charlie kept the conversation light, not asking any questions or mentioning the case. When all the dinner things had been cleared away, Amanda Moore asked for brandy and a box of cigars to be brought in. Two waiters, one with the cigars and one with the brandy went around the table offering them to the guests.

Charlie refused both, but he saw Harry take a cigar. Harry looked over at Charlie, held the cigar up and waggled it between his fingers.

Charlie's thoughts were interrupted by Amanda Moore speaking, 'Could you light my cigar, Charlie?' She handed him her lighter, she licked her lips looking at Charlie and slowly put the cigar to her mouth. Charlie flicked the lighter and held the lighter steady as she puffed away, finally leaning back and blowing out a long stream of cigar smoke. 'Thank you, Charlie.' She held out her hand and Charlie gave her lighter back. Speaking across Charlie to Sir Mark, she said, 'Mark, Charlie is a very unusual policeman.'

Sir Mark took a puff on his cigar. 'In what way?' he asked.

Amanda half leaned across Charlie, speaking to Sir Mark in a conspiratorial way. 'He drives very expensive cars, don't you Charlie?' she said looking back at Charlie. He felt her hand on his leg.

'So what car do you drive?' Sir Mark asked.

Before Charlie could answer, Amanda Moore said, 'He has a brand new Bentley, although he turned up in a Ferrari tonight.' He felt her hand squeeze his leg. 'Do you think he takes bribes?' She smiled at Charlie, putting the cigar to her lips.

'I don't think that's something you should accuse our police of,' Sir Mark said, 'although it is a bit unusual, granted.'

Taking the cigar from her lips, Amanda Moore said, 'So come on Charlie, tell us your secret.'

'I put all my spare pennies in a jar and save up,' Charlie said.

'Charlie, you won't tell me, will you?' Amanda said. Charlie felt her hand start to run up his thigh and down again. 'Charlie came down to Ascot for our big race.'

'Do you go racing a lot?' Sir Mark asked.

'No, not really,' Charlie said.

'When we were talking there, Charlie mentioned your business,' Amanda Moore said. She continued to run her hand up and down Charlie's thigh. 'He said he heard rumours of a takeover.' She picked up her brandy, she was leaning into Charlie. 'He might even be a shareholder.'

'Are you a shareholder, so what did you hear?' Sir Mark asked.

'No, not a shareholder,' Charlie said.

Before Charlie could answer, Amanda Moore said, 'He told me your company was in a bit of trouble.' He felt her hand squeeze the top of his leg, he was finding it hard to concentrate on the conversation.

'We've had a few bad breaks lately,' Sir Mark said, 'and we have noticed some strange share-buying. But no one has made any formal bid, and I think I still have the backing of the board and our banks to carry on with the business strategy we are pursuing.'

'I don't know if you can trust bankers,' Charlie said, turning his head to look at Amanda Moore. 'You can never tell what they're likely to do next.'

Amanda Moore smiled back at Charlie. She leaned closer and he felt her body pressing into him. 'Charlie, I can assure you I always know what I am doing.' He felt her hand run up his leg, her eyes looking directly at him.

'So, what do you do in the police, Charlie?' Sir Mark said.

'Oh didn't Charlie mention, he's in charge of Gerald Parkin's murder case.' Amanda Moore said.

Sir Mark sat back, taking a drink from his brandy glass. 'I had two of your officers come and question me about that at my office.'

'Yes, I know,' Charlie said.

'Did you know one of your officers knocked out one of my security guards?' Sir Mark asked.

'I'm sure it was an accident,' Charlie said.

Sir Mark laughed. 'Accident, I don't think so. Amanda, you should have seen it. I had been having a bad day, and if you can forgive me Charlie, I called security to have your officers thrown out of my office. When they came, in this policewoman, I can't recall her name now…'

'Detective Constable Virdee,' Charlie said.

'Oh I met her at Ascot,' Amanda Moore said, 'a very attractive girl.'

'Yes, that's her name,' Sir Mark said. 'Anyway, one of my ex-royal marines goes to get hold of her and the next thing you know he's lying on the floor in agony. It happened so fast I didn't even see what she did.' He shook his head. 'I offered her a job but she turned me down, said she had too much fun being a police officer.'

They all turned when they heard the tapping of a glass coming from the other end of the table. It was Stanley Moore, who was standing up with a glass in his hand. We are going to go through to the drawing room to relax now,' he said. The guests round the table started to rise.

'I hope you enjoyed your dinner, Charlie,' Amanda Moore said as she stood.

'It was lovely, I don't think I've had better company at a dinner in a long time, who knows how to make you feel so comfortable,' Charlie said.

She took Charlie's arm and followed Sir Mark. Charlie saw Harry walking through the door talking to the Deputy Mayor. They left the dining hall and crossed the hallway again. The girl who had been playing the piano was gone. When they got to the drawing room Amanda Moore said, 'I have to go and talk to my husband about a few things and speak to a few other people, but I hope we can get together for a chat before you go.' She ran her hand up Charlie's arm as she said it.

'I won't go before saying goodbye,' Charlie said. 'But there is one thing, is there somewhere I could take Sir Mark for a private chat?'

'Yes of course, you see that door over in the corner,' she pointed, the cigar still between her fingers. 'That's the snooker room, you won't be disturbed in there.'

'Thank you,' Charlie said and watched her walk away towards her husband. He couldn't help but notice how the dress clung to her body.

'Did you enjoy the meal?' Charlie turned to see Harry standing beside him.

'It was dinner, Harry, we have a meal in the canteen,' Charlie said.

'I thought she was going to get on your lap a few times,' Harry said, indicating Amanda Moore. 'She couldn't have got any closer.

'It's what her hands were doing under the table. I think I could have nicked her for sexual assault quite a few times,' Charlie said.

'I can't remember seeing you protest too much,' Harry said, a grin spreading across his face. Charlie said nothing. 'Had a nice conversation with the woman from Channel Four news. Apparently I'm to blame for most of the things that's wrong with the country. I say me but I mean the police. I think I upset her a little when she asked me if I watched Channel Four and I said never, because it was full of posers and has-beens. She never said much after that, although the Deputy Mayor seems alright, if a little slow.'

'The bloke who was at the end with us is Sir Mark Coale. Amanda said we can use the snooker room to speak to him.' Charlie pointed at the door in the corner. 'We won't be disturbed in there, but we have to get him away from this lot.'

They looked for Sir Mark and saw him talking to Lord

and Lady Dorres. 'Let me go and see if I can break up that happy gathering,' Harry said and walked away. Charlie watched him approach the group; after a minute Lord and Lady Dorres walked away with faces like thunder, leaving Harry with Sir Mark. Charlie watched as Harry guided Sir Mark towards the door that led to the snooker room. Charlie moved in that direction too; he reached the door just after Harry and Sir Mark went in, he went through and closed it behind him. A snooker table was in the centre and a number of chairs were around the wall; in the corner there was a drinks bar.

It was Harry that spoke first. 'Thank you for giving us the time to have a chat this evening, Sir Mark. It's just a couple of things we wanted to clear up from when our officers questioned you. We didn't want to bring it up within earshot of anyone else.'

'That's okay,' Sir Mark said, taking one of the seats. He looked at Charlie. 'So what is it you want to know?' Charlie was leaning with his back to the snooker table in front of Sir Mark.

'When my officers spoke to you, they asked you if you knew a girl called Angela Cook. You said the name didn't mean anything to you. I wondered if you wanted to think about it again,' Charlie said.

Sir Mark took a smoke from his cigar. 'I take it from that question you don't believe me.'

Harry took the seat next to Sir Mark and said, 'It's not a question of belief, we know you're lying, we just want to know why.'

'I like your officers Charlie, none of them tend to beat around the bush,' Sir Mark said.

'So you do know her?' Charlie asked.

'Yes, it came to me after your officers left. I meant to get in touch and tell them I had remembered but I have been so busy it slipped my mind.' He was smiling when he said it.

'Well, putting that aside, would you like to tell us what you know of her, because she has been murdered,' Harry said.

'I had heard the news,' Sir Mark said.

'Who told you about it?' Charlie asked.

'Oh I can't remember,' Sir Mark said. 'Someone mentioned it in passing.'

'You do seem to have a bit of a problem remembering,' Harry said.

Sir Mark turned in his seat to look at Harry. 'I have been very busy lately.'

'You said that already, so do you want to tell us a bit about her,' Harry said.

'What's to tell, I met her at the parties. She was a lovely girl – she could hold a conversation, but very sexy,' Sir Mark said.

'You can't remember anything else about her?' Harry said.

'No, not really,' Sir Mark said.

'I think your memory is playing tricks on you again,' Harry said.

'What do you mean by that?' Sir Mark said.

'Sir Mark, I don't mean to sound rude, but so far you have been telling us a load of rubbish. Now I wanted to drag you off to the police station and have you questioned, but my boss stopped me.' Harry looked at Charlie. 'So if you want to put your mind into gear and start giving us some truthful answers, it would save us a lot of time and we can all go back to the party.'

'I don't understand what you mean,' Sir Mark said.

'Well let me give you a hint,' Harry said. 'I think you knew Angela better than you've let on so far. Ring any bells yet? I will give you a clue, it wasn't only at the parties you saw her.'

Sir Mark took another smoke from his cigar and looked

back and forth between Harry and Charlie. 'You don't think I had anything to do with her killing, do you?' Harry and Charlie just looked at him without saying anything. 'I had nothing to do with it,' he said.

'Well, if you want us to believe that, you'd better start being open and straight with us. Because you're coming across as someone who has something to hide,' Charlie said.

'I have nothing to hide. I suppose in the business I'm in, you don't give much away and it's a hard habit to get out of,' Sir Mark said.

'So let's start again,' Harry said. 'Tell us all you know about Angela.'

Sir Mark sat back in the chair, placing one arm on the back and half turning to face Harry. 'I met her at the parties, she was very vivacious and I spent a lot of time with her. I asked her if she would like to meet away from the parties and have some fun together on our own. She was happy to.' He stopped for a moment then continued. 'Just let me say I know she got paid to attend the parties, but I never gave her any money when she was alone with me. We went out to dinner together and to the theatre, but I never gave her any money and she never asked for any. I found her really good company when I needed to unwind without any complications.'

'Did she ever ask you any questions about the other people who attended the parties?' Charlie asked.

'No, we talked about them generally, she told me a few stories of what the other, shall we say gentleman, liked her to do at the parties. So if anything she told me their secrets,' Sir Mark said.

'Did she talk about Gerald Parkin?' Harry said.

'No, did she know him? He was never at the parties,' Sir Mark said.

'Yes, we know that, but she did know him. We believe she

was passing on information about people at the parties so he could use it to blackmail them,' Harry said.

'That does surprise me. I told your officers Parkin never approached me, she must have told him not to bother. Or maybe she liked me.' He smiled as he said it and took another smoke on his cigar.

'Did she ever speak to you about your business?' Charlie asked.

'No, not really,' Sir Mark answered.

'Did you ever meet any of her friends?' Harry asked

'What do you mean?' Sir Mark said.

'Well, Angela wasn't the only girl at the parties, did you take any of the other girls who knew Angela out alone?' Harry said.

'Well no, not really,' Sir Mark answered.

'I hope we are not getting another memory problem,' Harry said.

'I get the feeling you know a lot about what's gone on,' Sir Mark said.

'Well, you just keep telling us all you know and answer our questions honestly. It might help us catch her killer,' Charlie said.

'So her friends…' Harry said.

Sir Mark moved in the chair again. The ash from his cigar fell onto the floor. 'Oops, I will have to tell Amanda to get the cleaners in here,' he said and continued. 'Angela was a very, how should I say this, she seemed to enjoy everything she did, in and out of bed. I mentioned one time that I would love to be with two girls at once, doesn't every man?' He looked back and forth at Harry and Charlie. Getting no response he carried on. 'Well, one evening when we had arranged for her to come to my house she turned up with a friend. She told me she liked making me happy.'

'What was her friend's name?' Harry asked.

'I think it was Julia or Julie, no Jayne. That's it, Jayne,' Sir Mark said.

Harry took the picture of Angela and Jayne Cavill from his inside pocket and gave it to Sir Mark. 'Is that her?' he asked.

Sir Mark looked at it. 'Yes, that's her.' He looked up at Charlie. 'Is anything I'm telling you helping? Because you seem to have a lot of the answers.'

'Sir Mark, you are being very helpful. We don't know everything, we just want to build some background on Angela and who she knew. Something you might tell us could help, so if you want to go on, what was her friend like?' Charlie said.

Sir Mark gave the picture back to Harry. 'Her friend, well, she was different from Angela. As I said, Angela seemed to enjoy herself all the time in and out of bed. For her friend it seemed more like work, if you understand.'

'You paid her to join you and Angela,' Harry said.

'No, no that's not what I meant, I never paid her,' Sir Mark said.

'But she was at the parties too?' Charlie asked.

'Yes, she was, although I never slept with her at the parties. You should speak to Stanley, he seemed to spend a lot of time with her at the parties,' Sir Mark said.

'You mean Amanda's husband?' Charlie asked.

'Yes, but I'm sure you know he was at them.' He looked at both Charlie and Harry waiting for a response, but none came.

'You were telling us she was different from Angela,' Harry said.

'Yes, you know we had fun the three of us in bed. After, Angela and I would generally just chat about everyday things, art, theatre or what was happening in the world, but when her friend was with us she was different,' Sir Mark said.

Harry interrupted him. 'So she came along with Angela more than once.'

'Oh yes.' Sir Mark smiled. 'Quite a few times. She said she was doing a business degree or something, I can't remember exactly. We always had quite a bit to drink before and after if you know what I mean. Anyway, she always wanted to talk about what was going on in the business world and how things happened around companies. Angela would get bored most times and say she wanted more fun.'

'Did you speak to her about your business?' Charlie asked.

'Yes, I did, I got the impression she might have been after a job,' Sir Mark said.

'She asked you for a job?' Harry said.

'No, it's just the feeling I got. The way she talked I think she will get her business degree easily, she certainly understood how things worked.' Sir Mark took another smoke from his cigar.

'Did you tell her about any of the problems your company was having?' Charlie asked.

'Well, I think I may have in a general way, comparing it to other things that were going on at the time,' Sir Mark replied.

'Did you say how you could get out of your problems and what you had planned?' Harry asked.

'I'm not sure. As I say, sometimes we had a lot to drink, so I might have,' Sir Mark said. 'Why, do you think she was passing anything I said on to Gerald Parkin? But what would be the point, he didn't try to blackmail me?'

'Now you told me over dinner that you think there had been some suspicious share-buying in your company. What did you mean by that,' Charlie said.

'It's just that a few foreign-based businesses have been buying up blocks of shares,' Sir Mark said.

'Don't all businesses do that?' Harry asked.

'Yes,' Sir Mark said, 'but our financial director brought it to our attention at a board meeting a few months ago. He said they always seemed to come into the market and buy when the shares were low and they never sold off when the price went up. Now if they were speculators, you would expect them to bale out with a profit when the shares rose.'

'Do you know who was behind the share-buying?' Harry asked.

'We did get some investigations done, because the blocks of shares they had been buying over the last couple of years were mounting up to quite a large shareholding in the company,' Sir Mark said. 'We traced some of the buyers to America, but we don't know who's behind it as they haven't broken cover yet.'

'Was there anyone else?' Charlie said.

'There were a few smaller holdings, but nothing very big, except one. We traced it to a bank in Luxemburg. I tried to get a meeting with the head of the bank when I was in Brussels yesterday but the meeting never happened,' Sir Mark said.

Harry exchanged a look with Charlie. 'It's funny you should mention Luxemburg,' Charlie said. 'It came up when we were looking into a couple of things.'

'In what way?' Sir Mark asked.

'If it affects you I will say,' Charlie replied, 'but go on with what you were saying.'

'Well I really wanted to get a meeting,' Sir Mark said. 'You mentioned over dinner about rumours of a takeover, Charlie. Well, the board of the company have heard them too, so we need to contact all the large shareholders, to see if they will back us if someone was to launch a takeover. Anyway, when the meeting fell through I called Stanley, he knows everyone in banking. He did me a big favour, he got the head of the bank to come over and meet me.'

'So what happened?' Harry asked.

'I haven't spoken to him yet, he's here at the dinner. Stanley has arranged that I can meet him when everyone is gone,' Sir Mark said.

'What's this man's name?' Charlie asked.

'I don't understand,' Sir Mark said. 'What has my meeting got to do with Gerald Parkin's murder?'

'Don't forget Angela,' Harry said.

'Well, what has my meeting got to do with anything?' Sir Mark asked.

'Just indulge me a little,' Charlie said.

Sir Mark looked at Charlie quizzically, shrugged his shoulders and said, 'His name's Vincenzo Gallo.'

'Sir Mark, thank you for being so helpful tonight,' Charlie said.

'Is that it?' Sir Mark stood up.

'Yes, I can't think there's anything else, can you Harry?' Harry shook his head.

'That's okay,' Sir Mark said, 'but I wouldn't have harmed Angela, and as for Parkin I didn't give him too much thought.'

'No, you have been more than helpful,' Harry said.

'Shall we go and re-join the party?' Charlie said. All three made their way to the door, opened it and went back into the drawing-room. Guests were sitting and standing in groups talking. Charlie took Sir Mark's arm and said, 'One more thing, can you point out Mr Gallo to us?'

Sir Mark scanned the room. 'That's him over there talking to Amanda.' Charlie and Harry looked at the man with Amanda Moore. He had jet-black hair, olive skin and stood about six foot tall.

'Do you know where he's from?' Harry asked.

'I think he's Italian, but I'm not too sure,' Sir Mark said.

'Well, thanks for your help,' Charlie said, 'and I hope your meeting with him goes well.' Sir Mark walked off; they saw him join Stanley Moore who was talking to a the Deputy Mayor.

'That was quite interesting,' Harry said.

'It was,' Charlie said. A waiter came over to them with a tray of drinks. They refused the wine but asked if they could both have orange juice. The waiter went away to get them some. 'There are a couple of strange coincidences from what Sir Mark told us, our Jayne Cavill would seem to have used Angela to get to know Sir Mark , but why, he tells us Gerald Parkin wasn't blackmailing him?'

'I believe him on that score,' Harry said.

'Was Jayne Cavill working with Gerald Parkin?' Charlie said. 'But what would be the point of taking the trouble to become involved with Sir Mark?'

'If she was, did Angela know?' Harry said. The waiter returned with two glasses of orange juice; they took one each. 'There is one other thing, boss. Sir Mark was in Brussels which is the capital of Belgium. We know that Jayne Cavill brought her diamonds in Antwerp, which just happens to be in Belgium.'

'Good point, Harry, but I think we agree Sir Mark's not involved with the murders,' Charlie said.

'Yes, I agree there, boss,' Harry said. 'We need to speak to Stanley Moore though, about his relationship with Jayne Cavill. From what Sir Mark said, he spent time with her.'

'We'll have to try and do that discreetly,' Charlie said. 'I don't think he's too happy about us being here, and I would love to have a word with Mr Gallo about Gerald Parkin funnelling his money through his bank.'

Harry looked at his watch. 'It's getting late, boss, we don't know how much longer this is going to go on. Do we try and speak to Stanley Moore tonight?'

'I think we should give it a try,' Charlie said. 'You get him to one side. I know he doesn't want his wife to know too much about him being blackmailed, even if I get the impression she already knows. Tell him you don't want to bring up anything in front of his wife. I think that will spook him enough, you concentrate on him, I'll see if I can get a word with our Mr Gallo.'

Harry walked off in the direction of Stanley Moore. Charlie watched him go, he turned to look for Vincenzo Gallo, he scanned the room but couldn't see him anywhere. He had been talking to Amanda Moore, but she was nowhere to be seen either. Charlie checked that Sir Mark was still in the room, he was standing talking to Stanley Moore and the Deputy Mayor; the group of them had been joined by Harry.

Charlie walked to the doors of the drawing room and walked through to the hallway. No-one was there. He saw the doors to the dining room were slightly open so walked over to them. He pushed slightly and was able to look inside; it was empty. He turned to go back to the drawing room. As he did, Amanda Moore and Vincenzo Gallo appeared at the top of the stairs. Charlie walked to the bottom and watched them as they came down. As they reached the bottom Amanda Moore said, 'Charlie, what are you doing wandering about? I will have to ask to see your search warrant.'

'I wanted to use the bathroom,' Charlie said.

'Oh, you can use the one on the first floor, turn left at the top of the stairs, it's the second door on your left,' Amanda said.

'Thank you,' Charlie said, and began to climb the stairs. He looked back over his shoulder, Amanda Moore and Vincenzo Gallo were watching him. He made his way to the bathroom. It was strange Amanda never introduced him to Gallo, all night she had been introducing him to people at the party.

When Charlie went back downstairs and entered the drawing room he looked around for Harry. He was nowhere to be seen, nor was Stanley Moore, so Harry had got him away somewhere for a chat. A waiter approached him and asked if he wanted a drink. Charlie refused, he looked around to find Vincenzo Gallo. He spotted him, he was still standing with Amanda Moore. Charlie glanced around for Sir Mark and spotted him talking to Lady Dorres and another woman. Charlie walked over to speak to Amanda. As he approached he saw her saying something to Gallo. He smiled as Charlie got to them. 'Charlie, I hope you have had a lovely evening.'

'Yes, thank you,' Charlie said. She seemed a little hesitant, which was strange for her. 'Aren't you going to introduce me to your guest?'

'Oh yes, of course, I didn't know you hadn't been introduced,' she said. 'This is Vincenzo Gallo.' Charlie held out his hand. 'Vincenzo, this is Chief Superintendent Charlie Smith.' Charlie shook the man's hand.

'How do you do, Mr Gallo,' Charlie said. 'What do you do?'

'He's in banking, but I'm afraid his English is not very good,' Amanda Moore said.

'That's a shame, I would have liked to ask him a few questions,' Charlie said.

'Charlie, are you going to question all my guests?' Amanda Moore said. 'Vincenzo has only just come to the country, are you going to ask him about his immigration status?' She laughed.

Charlie smiled back. 'No, its strange but Mr Gallo's name came up during the investigation.'

'Really?' Amanda Moore said. She then turned to Gallo, speaking in Italian. He nodded and looked at Charlie. He turned back to Amanda, and answered in Italian. When he had finished, Amanda spoke to Charlie, 'He says he doesn't understand how his name could have come up in your investigation, as he's never been to England.'

'You'd be surprised what we turn up,' Charlie said.

'If you would like, Charlie, I will translate for you,' Amanda said.

'I don't know if that would be a good idea. Mr Gallo might not like someone knowing about things I would ask him, and it's information that is private to the investigation,' Charlie said.

'Well he speaks a little English. I would just help if he wasn't too sure of what you meant. You know the nuances of the English language can be confusing,' Amanda said. She turned to Gallo and spoke to him in Italian.

Gallo turned to Charlie. 'I will try and give you answers,' he said in very broken English.

'Shall we go and find somewhere to talk privately?' Amanda said. Charlie thought for a moment, he didn't want to let on to Amanda too much of what they knew in the case. But he wanted to see if Gallo could give him some answers to Gerald Parkin's bank accounts. It was a risk worth taking. He turned to Amanda.

'I will be relying on your discretion, Amanda,' Charlie said.

'Charlie, I can assure you I won't repeat a word of what's said, not even to Stanley,' she replied.

She stood between them, taking their arms, and led them into the hall. As she passed a waiter she asked him to bring some brandy and three glasses to the library. She crossed in front of the stairs, past the dining room doors and along the hallway. They came to a door and she opened it and went in. Gallo and Charlie followed her. It was not a big room, one wall consisted of a bookcase which stood from floor to ceiling, it was filled with books. There was a large fireplace which was unlit, with two chairs either side of it. 'You two sit by the fireplace. I will bring a chair from over by the window and join you,' she said.

'No, let me get that for you,' Charlie said. He went and

picked up a chair from the window and brought it over to the fireplace. Gallo had already taken a seat. 'Where do you want me to put this?' Charlie said.

'Put it next to Vincenzo, it will be easier for me to explain anything he is not sure of then,' she said. Charlie put the chair down and went and took the chair opposite.

The door opened as they made themselves comfortable and a waiter brought in three glasses on a tray. He came over and they each took one, then he turned and left, closing the door behind him.

'This room is lovely when it's cold outside,' Amanda Moore said, taking a drink of brandy. 'I like to have the fire lit. With the big logs burning, it's a lovely place to sit at the end of the day and unwind with a drink after work.'

'Yes, you can't beat a nice open fire to make a room feel cosy,' Charlie said as he made himself comfortable.

'You have one in your house, Charlie?' Amanda asked.

'Yes, I do,' Charlie said. He turned to Gallo. 'Mr Gallo, I only want to ask you a couple of questions. Do you know a man called Gerald Parkin?'

Gallo looked at Charlie then at Amanda. He struggled to answer in English. He spoke to Amanda in Italian, she turned to Charlie. 'He said he doesn't know him.' Gallo held the brandy glass in his hand, moving it in a circular motion, swilling the liquid around.

'He was quite famous, had a television programme but was found murdered. Are you sure you have never heard of him?' Charlie said.

Gallo turned to Amanda and spoke Italian. She replied then turned to Charlie and said, 'He says he has never heard of him. It's the first time he's been to Britain, he wants to know why you think he should know Gerald?'

Charlie looked at Gallo who was sitting back in the chair;

he looked totally relaxed and at ease. Charlie continued. 'You see, Mr Gallo, we have found out that Mr Parkin was channelling money through an account at your bank.' Gallo remained relaxed, he spoke in Italian to Amanda. She replied to him, and they had a short conversation, then she turned to Charlie.

'He said, he was not aware of Gerald Parkin having an account with his bank, and in any case he would have nothing to do with the opening of accounts. He runs the whole thing; account management is left to staff much lower down the management structure.'

'We aren't talking small sums of money,' Charlie said. 'Would he be alerted if the account was moving money – say between Switzerland, Luxemburg and the British Virgin Islands?' Charlie noticed Amanda's face show surprise for a second then return to its usual smile. She took another small drink from her glass.

Amanda Moore spoke to Gallo. Charlie saw him shrug his shoulders and reply. He noticed they seemed very comfortable in each other's company. Amanda turned back to Charlie and said, 'He says he would only be alerted if it was thought it was money laundering, otherwise he would not be kept informed. He says he can check it out for you.'

'That would be good of him if he could,' Charlie said.

Amanda Moore spoke to Gallo. He took a drink from his glass and sat forward. In broken English he said, 'Do you think it is funny money?'

Charlie smiled at the term. 'Yes, funny money, we believe it could be the proceeds of crime.'

Amanda spoke in Italian to Gallo who nodded and replied to Amanda. She turned back to Charlie. 'He will get it looked into first thing tomorrow for you. Do you have a card for him, Charlie, so he can contact you with any information he gets?'

Charlie took a card from his inside pocket and passed it to Gallo. 'Thank you for your help, sir,' Charlie said.

'You're not drinking your brandy,' Amanda said to Charlie.

'No, I have to drive home,' he said.

'Well, if you have no other questions for Vincenzo, shall we go back and join the rest of the guests?' Amanda said. She stood up, said something in Italian to Gallo, who stood too. She took Charlie's arm. 'I hope that was helpful,' she said.

'If Mr Gallo can supply us with any information he finds out, it might be,' Charlie said. She took hold of Gallo's arm, and between the two men took them back to the drawing room.

When they had entered the drawing room, Amanda Moore said she was taking Vincenzo Gallo to meet someone and left Charlie by the door. He looked around for Harry, and spotted him sitting in a chair on the far side of the room. Charlie made his way across to Harry, who he noticed had the large cigar he took at dinner lit. 'You enjoying that?' he said.

Harry looked up from his chair. 'Boss, I was just thinking, it might be a good idea if we kept a box of these in the office. You know, when we have a get together you can pass them round, it might be a good touch.'

Charlie ignored Harry. 'Did you speak to Stanley Moore?'

'Yes, I did,' Harry said. 'I take it the cigar idea is a no-no.'

'Well tell me in the car, it's about time we left,' Charlie said. Harry stood up. 'Let's say goodbye to our hosts.'

'They're over there,' Harry said, 'having a chat.'

Charlie turned his head. 'Let's go, Harry.' The two of them started across the room, towards Amanda Moore, her husband, Sir Mark Coale and Vincenzo Gallo, who were in conversation. As they approached the group, the three men left Amanda and walked towards the doors of the drawing room and went out. 'We are leaving now,' Charlie said as the two of them reached Amanda.

'Oh Charlie, do you have to?' she said. 'I was hoping to show you around the house.'

'I'm afraid so, we have a meeting early tomorrow,' Charlie said.

'Well let me walk you out to your car.' She took Charlie's arm. 'It was nice to meet you Harry, even if you have upset my husband.'

Charlie exchanged a quick look with Harry. 'I hope I haven't,' Harry said.

'Well, he says you were rather rude to him a little while ago,' she said as they walked through the front door. The night air was a little chilly. 'Oh, it's getting cold.' She held Charlie's arm tighter, they walked to Charlie's car. 'It really is a lovely car, Charlie.'

'Thank you, I don't drive it too often,' Charlie said as he unlocked it.

Harry walked around to the far side of the car. 'He keeps it for special occasions, it was nice meeting you, Mrs Moore.'

'Harry, call me Amanda please,' she said.

'Thanks for a lovely evening,' Harry said and got into the car.

'It was a lovely evening,' Charlie said, 'and thanks for helping us get to question Sir Mark and Mr Gallo.'

'I'm glad I could help.' She moved round to face Charlie. She was still holding his arm. She moved in closer and he felt her press her body to his. 'Perhaps you will reward me.'

Charlie smiled. 'Amanda, you have a lovely way of getting what you want.'

'Charlie, I would like to have the chance to talk to you alone, I think I might have some information,' she said.

'Is it about the investigation?' Charlie said.

She took Charlie's hand in hers. 'Yes, something that came to me when you were speaking to Vincenzo.'

Charlie took a card from his pocket. 'Here's my card, ring me tomorrow and we can sort something out.'

She leaned forward, pressing herself against Charlie, and kissed him quickly on the lips. 'I do hope so, Charlie.'

Charlie was caught off guard by the kiss. He looked at her. She was smiling at him. 'Are you going to Gerald's funeral tomorrow?' she asked. Charlie remembered that Crick had told him he would be going with him.

'Yes, I am,' Charlie said.

'Well I will see you there perhaps. We could have a private get-together after,' she said.

'That's a good idea.' Charlie stood back. 'Until tomorrow, Amanda.'

'Goodbye Charlie,' she said as Charlie got in the car. He started the engine and pulled away.

'Boss, I have known you for many years,' Harry said as Charlie drove out of the main gates and onto the road. 'In all those years I thought I knew all your interrogation techniques, but that was a new one on me, kissing the subject.' Harry waved his cigar about.

'You're not smoking that in this car,' Charlie said, he pressed the window down on Harry's side.

'It's okay, boss, it's not lit now,' Harry said and pressed his window back up.

'She says she has something to tell me', Charlie said. 'I have to go to Gerald Parkin's funeral with Crick tomorrow. She will be there. What do you make of her, Harry?'

'Manjitt described her to a tee, very very attractive and sharp. I know she wants to get you into bed,' Harry smiled, 'I could say I have no idea why,' Charlie laughed, 'but with a woman like that, there must be a motive behind it.'

'Harry,' Charlie said, 'are you saying a woman wouldn't want me just for this body?'

'All I know is, Amanda Moore doesn't seem to do anything that isn't in her interest,' Harry replied.

'I think you're right, Harry. Even during dinner I got the impression she was asking the questions not me. But I have to admit I do find her very attractive.'

'Steady, boss, I might think you're going soft,' Harry said.

Charlie smiled. 'So how did you get on with her husband?' he said.

'He was a bit reluctant to start with,' Harry said. 'I showed him Jayne Cavill's picture and he confirmed it was her. He did spend time with her at the parties, tried to say no more than anyone else. In the end he said he saw her a couple of times away from the parties.'

'Where did they meet?' Charlie asked.

'That's what's surprising, they met at the Moores' house. I thought it would have been Angela Cook's place or the other flat,' Harry said.

'Well you can bet Amanda knew all about it, she wouldn't miss something that was going on under her own roof,' Charlie said.

'He seemed to think she didn't know, but I agree, boss, she is too sharp for that. Anyway, our Jayne made Stanley a happy man. He said he gave her some presents and money, not a lot according to him. Do you think he and his wife have the same bedroom? After all, as you know, Amanda is a very attractive woman.' Harry glanced sideways at Charlie.

'I'm not going to rise to the bait Harry, get on with the story,' Charlie said.

Harry smiled. 'Anyway, she liked to talk about business, same as with Sir Mark. He said that he found it nice to be able to unwind with someone who listened to him. Says a lot for the marriage.'

'So he might have told her anything,' Charlie said.

'It would seem so, but it doesn't tell us why she killed,' Harry said.

'Well, she lived with Angela for a while, how she met Parkin I'm not sure unless Angela introduced them. But why? Jayne must have thought she was working for Martin Oliver,' Charlie said.

'Perhaps Angela might have told her about her deal and introduced her to Parkin,' Harry said.

'Maybe, Harry, but don't you feel Jayne Cavill knew everything she was doing for a reason? After all, she has cleared out her bank account, the only two people she seemed close to have been murdered, she doesn't want to leave a trail,' Charlie said.

'It does seem planned, but why now?' Harry said. 'You might say it was professional. How did you get on with the banker?'

'Mr Gallo, his English wasn't very good, so Amanda translated for me,' Charlie said.

'Boss, you are a lucky man,' Harry said.

Charlie cast Harry a sideways glance. 'Anyway, he says he doesn't know anything about Gerald Parkin or that he had a bank account with his bank. But he's going to look into it tomorrow and get back with anything he finds out.'

'I bet he doesn't discover anything,' Harry said. 'I did ask her husband about Mr Gallo, apparently he's known him for years. Have you got to wear your uniform tomorrow for the funeral?' Harry asked.

'I don't know, Crick never said it was a must. Why?' Charlie said.

'Nothing boss, but I've heard some women like a man in a uniform,' Harry said, leaning back and laughing at his own joke.

CHAPTER SIXTEEN

Jordan had got into the office first. He was making himself a cup of tea when he heard 'I'll have a cup.' He turned and saw Harry making his way to his desk. Jordan brought the tea over to Harry and sat down opposite. 'Nice to see you in early Jordan, how did you finish up yesterday?'

'I wrote up a full report on Tim Green.' He stood, went to his desk and came back with a file, gave it to Harry and sat back down. 'I have put a list of questions in there that he needs to answer to.'

Harry opened the file and glanced through it. 'Did you get on to those solicitors?'

'Yes, I told them he gets here for an interview at twelve, or he will be arrested. They're due to get back to me this morning to confirm,' Jordan said.

'Who are you going to take in with you to do the questioning?' Harry asked.

'I thought Manjitt, she can be pretty good at getting an answer.' Jordan replied.

Harry nodded. 'Yeah good choice, you know I have persuaded her to go for her detective sergeant's exam.'

'No, she never said anything. I'll give her a few tips,' Jordan said.

Harry picked up his tea. 'Do you think that's a good idea?'

'Harry, aren't I one of the best detective sergeants you have worked with?'

'Well, you're a detective sergeant, that's for sure.' Harry took a drink from his cup.

'Jordan, you make the worst tea in the squad.'

'It's practice, Harry. How did you and the boss get on last night?' Jordan asked.

'Interesting,' Harry said. He then went through what they found out. They were still chatting when Manjitt and Cramer came in.

'Morning Harry,' they both said. Harry told them to take a seat and bring him up to speed with what they had been doing.

Jordan looked over at the two of them. 'Harry only wants to know about work.'

Manjitt gave Jordan a long stare, Cramer's face went red. Manjitt explained what she had learnt and she was waiting for the Belgians to come back to her.

Cramer went over what he had been doing. Harry asked about the reference from the bank, Cramer told him the name.

Harry sat back took a drink from his tea, made a face. 'God that's disgusting,' he said.

'I take it that's one of Jordan's teas,' Manjitt said.

'You're right there,' Harry said. 'Now Cramer, what you told me is a funny coincidence. Last night the boss got to talk to the head of that bank at Amanda Moore's dinner party.'

'How did the boss enjoy it?' Manjitt said smiling. 'Did his girlfriend look after him?'

Harry looked at Manjitt, who still had a big smile on her face. 'You can ask the boss when he gets in, I'm saying nothing. Now these coincidences, we know Gerald Parkin was using the bank, we believe its mixed up in an attempt to take over Sir Mark Coales oil company, now we have our killer getting a reference to obtain a place at university, so she gets into the country without any hassle. Think we might have to have a closer look at that bank.'

'Morning everyone,' They all turned to see Charlie walking towards them. 'Nice to see you're all in early.' He looked around. 'No Danny yet.'

'I left him here late when I went last night, he was sitting looking through those pictures,' Jordan said.

'Okay bring me up to speed,' Charlie said as he pulled a chair over and sat down with them. Everyone went through what they had done. 'Now that's very interesting,' Charlie said. 'Harry, when we get out of this stupid meeting this morning, I want you to organise everyone to try to get to the bottom of that. I need a cup of tea.'

'I'll get you one, boss.' Jordan went to stand up.

'No, you stay where you are,' Harry said. 'Cramer, it's about time we tasted your tea.' Harry passed him his cup. 'Throw that away and make me a fresh one.' Cramer got up and went to make the tea.

'I have to go to Gerald Parkin's funeral this afternoon with AS Crick. Jordan, I want some answers from Tim Green. I don't care if you have to keep him here all night, understand?' Charlie said.

'Yes boss, I am taking Manjitt in with me,' Jordan said.

'Someone give Danny a ring, see where he is. Don't want him late when we go up to see Macready,' Charlie said.

Manjitt stood up. 'I will give him a bell.'

'Did you send a report up to Crick?' Charlie asked Harry.

'Yes, you sent it first thing this morning,' Harry said.

'We need to go over everything that we know about Jayne Cavill,' Charlie said. 'She must be living somewhere, and someone must know.'

'That's if she hasn't already got out of the country. After all, she had the brains to buy diamonds abroad,' Harry said.

'That's true Harry, but where did she come from. We can only trace her to the flat she had and sold for a lot of money.

Where was she before that? It might give us a clue to where she might be,' Charlie said.

'Do we release her picture to the press?' Harry asked.

'I've been thinking about that,' Charlie said. 'I think we may have to. I just worry about getting snowed under if false sightings come in. Let's see if we can get anymore information about her. Manjitt and Jordan are going to be tied up with questioning Tim Green, so put Danny and Cramer on it.'

Manjitt came over. 'Danny's on his way, ten minutes he said.'

'Okay, thanks Manjitt,' Charlie said. 'Oh and by the way I'm glad you're going for your detective sergeant exam.'

'Thought it was about time,. I didn't fancy having to take orders from Jordan for ever,' she said. Jordan looked over and smiled.

'Heads up boss.' Charlie turned to see Assistant Commissioner Crick coming into the office.

'Morning Charlie,' he said. Everyone stood up.

'Morning sir, what do we owe the pleasure of your visit?' Charlie replied.

'I just thought I would see how things are progressing before we go to the meeting with the Deputy Commissioner.' He looked at Harry's desk. 'Do you know where everything is?'

'Everything is only an arm's length from me,' Harry said.

'I got today's report, Charlie,' Crick said. Charlie cast a look at Harry. He had not seen what Harry had sent up.

'I hope it kept you up to date with everything' Charlie said.

'It was its usual informative read.' Crick looked at Harry then back to Charlie. 'Are all your team here, they do know they have to attend the meeting?'

'Yes they're all here, but I don't think we should be doing this. We are at a critical time in the investigation, the last thing we need is to be sitting around listening to DC Macready telling us what needs to be done,' Charlie said.

'I hope you will keep those thoughts to yourself during the meeting,' Crick said.

'You know me sir, discretion is my middle name,' Charlie said. Crick raised his eyebrows.

'Okay, bring your team up to my office at about 9.20, we can all go up to the ninth floor together. And don't forget, Charlie, we have to attend Gerald Parkin's funeral, we will leave here at one o'clock.' Crick turned and walked away. As he got to the door he met Danny coming in. Charlie and Harry saw Crick stand to one side, look Danny up and down, shake his head and leave the office. Danny came walking over to them.

'Nice of you to put in an appearance, Hippie,' Harry said.

'Morning Harry, boss. Sorry I was late, I didn't sleep well last night,' Danny said.

'You're not ill, are you?' Charlie said.

'No, nothing like that, it's just these pictures.' He reached into his pocket and pulled out the folded-up copies of the photographs of Jayne Cavill.

'What about them?' Charlie said.

'That's it boss, I don't know, its been bugging me ever since we had them cleaned up yesterday. It's just something, I can't put my finger on it,' Danny said.

'Do you have an iron at home, Hippie?' Harry looked at Danny's clothes.

'I just grabbed something and put it on this morning. Didn't have time to iron anything,' Danny said.

Harry and Charlie looked at the creased clothes Danny was wearing. 'Are you actually telling us you don't usually just grab something and put it on. That is news to everyone,' Harry said.

'Well, you just keep your mind on the case,' Charlie said.

'Cramer's making some tea, get yourself a cup.' Charlie turned to Jordan and said 'There won't be anyone in the office for a couple of hours. Let someone know to take any calls for us and pass the messages on.' Jordan nodded.

All the squad were standing in Assistant Commissioner Crick's office. 'It's nice to see you all together,' he said. He was sitting behind his desk in full uniform. 'Now I don't know how much Chief Superintendent Smith has told you about the meeting with the Deputy Commissioner.' He looked around the squad but no one said anything. 'Well, the DC wants to reassess the investigation. We have been under a little pressure from the media, particularly the BBC, so we want to show that we are making progress.' He waited a moment but the squad still remained silent. 'Now he may ask you individually about the case. I'm hoping you will be able to give him concise answers.' He waited again, looked around, but no one made any move to reply. 'Shall we go up to the DC's office?' he said, getting no response.

When they entered the Deputy Commissioner's office, Charlie saw Macready was seated in the middle of two other people. One he recognised as a commander from meetings he had been to on policing strategies. The other was a woman he didn't know. There were two rows of seats set out in front of the desk. Macready stood up. 'Will you all take a seat.' The squad all sat. Charlie was next to Crick in the front with Cramer, Harry and the rest sat behind them. 'Now, I have asked you all here to go over the investigation into the murder of Gerald Parkin,' he said.

'Don't forget Angela Cook,' Harry said.

Macready shot Harry a look. 'Yes Angela Cook too. Now let me introduce Commander Suchet,' Macready indicated the man sitting next to him. 'He is going to help me decide any course of action we need to take that may improve the speed of the investigation.' He looked around everyone. 'And this is Ms Danbury, she is from the BBC. I asked her here so she will get an idea that we are giving this investigation top priority. I have told her she may hear some confidential information, and she has given me her word, along with the BBC chairman, that nothing she hears will be divulged. Now I will ask Assistant Commissioner Crick to give us an overview of how things are progressing.'

Crick stood up and began to talk about the investigation from the start. After about ten minutes of talking he sat down. Macready stood up, thanked him and explained that Commander Suchet had been going through all the paperwork on the case and would now give his opinion. Suchet stood and started to talk. He went over everything he said he had seen from the investigations, mentioned things he thought could have been done better and some ideas on what they needed to do to get things moving. After twenty minutes he sat down.

Macready thanked him, said he thought some of his ideas were excellent. He looked at Charlie as he was speaking. He then said he would go over everything he thought was wrong with the investigation and what he thought could put it back on track. He had been talking for about half an hour. Manjitt, who was only half listening, glanced to her left. Jordan was beside her and Danny was next to him on the end. She saw Danny was asleep. She nudged Harry to her right, who looked at her. She signalled to him with her head and he looked by her. He saw Danny, his arms folded, his head leaning forward and his long hair hanging down. Harry made a gesture to Jordan, who looked at Harry. He indicated Jordan to look at Danny. Jordan turned to his left, saw Danny asleep and dug his elbow into him.

Danny sat up with a start. 'What, what?' he said loudly.

Macready stopped talking and looked at Danny. The rest of the team suppressed laughing. Crick turned around giving Danny a stare. Macready started talking again, when suddenly Danny stood up. 'That's it, he said.' The team all turned to look at him.

Macready stopped, was about to speak to Danny, but Danny continued. 'Boss, I got it, I knew those pictures meant something. It's been bugging me since yesterday,' he said excitedly, looking at Charlie.

'Could you sit down,' Macready said. 'You will get your say later.'

Completely ignoring Macready, Danny carried on addressing Charlie. 'The pictures. When I had them cleaned up, I thought I recognised something in them. It's just come to me, I know who it is.'

Charlie stood up. 'I'm sorry sir, but I think we may have a breakthrough with the case. Everyone back to the squad room,' he said.

The team all stood up, and started to make their way to the door when Macready said 'Everyone stay here.' They all stopped. 'I decide when this meeting is over.'

Charlie looked at him. He noticed Crick was still sitting in his chair. 'Sir, you want this case cleared up. So do we. It would seem one of my officers has made a breakthrough. Now I know you wouldn't want our friend from the BBC to think we didn't react straight away when we have new information.' He turned without waiting for an answer and led the team out of the office.

As they all hurried into the squad's office a uniformed sergeant caught Jordan and passed him a number of messages that had come through while no one was about. Charlie sat down at his desk. 'Now Danny, tell us what you were shouting about in Macready's office.' The rest of the team all gathered round.

'Boss, all yesterday and last night, those pictures that Harry had me clear up, there was something about them that was bugging me. I had seen the face somewhere before,' Danny said.

'Well don't keep us waiting, who is it?' Harry said.

'It's Tim Green's fiancée, Rebecca Rosen,' Danny said.

'We don't have any pictures of her,' Charlie said.

'No, but I searched their house. It's her, boss. The hair is different, maybe she coloured it. She's got a lot more make-up on, but I know I'm not wrong,' Danny said.

Charlie turned to Jordan. 'You saw her, what do you think?'

Harry took the pictures from the white board and passed them to Jordan. He looked at them. 'I don't know boss, I only saw her for a minute. It was Hippie that searched the house,. I saw her at the front door when we were looking for Tim Green, but I will take Hippie's word for it.'

Charlie looked at his watch, it was nearly elven o'clock,. 'I think we should pay them a visit.' Charlie stood up. 'Harry, organise a search warrant.' Harry picked up his phone.

'Someone pass me Tim Green's file,' Harry said.

'It's on my desk,' Jordan said. Danny went over and got it and gave it to Harry.

'Boss, there's a message for you,' Jordan said. He gave Charlie a piece of paper. 'Harry, there's a couple for you.' He put them down beside Harry's phone, while he sorted out the search warrant.

Harry got off the phone as the team stood around waiting. 'All sorted, the warrant will be at the main desk for us to pick up.'

'This is interesting,' Charlie said, holding up the message Jordan had given him. 'It's from the bank where the safe deposit box is.' He looked at the message. 'This came in at twenty to ten. They were letting us know someone had turned up to use it. Cramer, phone them, see what they say, and ask them who it was. If we hadn't been at that stupid meeting we could have gone there and caught them.' Cramer went away to get the bank's number. 'Harry, get back on the phone, I want a warrant to search that safe deposit box.' Harry picked up his phone again. 'Now everyone, let's look at this. Is Rebecca Rosen our killer?'

'I say yes,' Danny said.

'Okay Danny, we believe you,' Charlie said. 'But why. How has she planned it, and it seems a bit strange that their safe deposit box is used today, just like Jayne Cavill or Rebecca Rosen cleared her bank account out just when we were getting close.'

Harry put his hand over the phone. 'She must have been working with someone,' Harry said. 'Perhaps Tim Green has been in it from the start and had us fooled.'

'We're supposed to have Tim Green in here at twelve for an interview, boss,' Jordan said.

'Did the solicitors get back to you?' Charlie asked.

'No not yet, and there's no message. Shall I ring them see if they've spoken to Tim Green?' Jordan asked.

'Ye,s do it now. Manjitt, pull all we have on Rebecca Rosen and Jayne Cavill, let's see if we can piece anything together, I'm sure we're missing something. Then we can go over to arrest her,' Charlie said. Manjitt walked away to get the files.

Cramer came back. 'I spoke to the bank, they say it was Rebecca Rosen who used the safe deposit. As we never got back to them they had no reason to do anything but let her use it.'

'That stupid meeting,' Charlie repeated.

'The warrant for the safe deposit is sorted,' Harry said,. Manjitt returned with the files.

'Right everyone, let's have a good read, see if there's something we're missing,' Charlie said.

'I spoke to the solicitors,' Jordan said. 'They will be here at twelve, but they said although they had told Tim Green, he's not been in touch since, but they expect him to attend.'

'Somehow I don't think so,' Danny said, looking up from reading.

'Grab a chair, Jordan, we;re looking for some connection between the two,' Charlie said.

They had all been reading for ten minutes in silence. Charlie put down the part of the file he had and looked around everyone at the table. 'Well, there's nothing I see, except a few coincidences.' The rest of the team looked at Charlie. 'We have no knowledge of Jayne Cavill before she bought and sold the flat she had, and moved in with Angela Cook. We have no knowledge of Rebecca Rosen until she moves in with Tim Green. Anyone else see anything?'

'If she was going out to these parties,' Harry said, 'surely Tim Green must have had an idea of what was going on.'

'We don't know too much about how they met,' Manjitt said, 'and from what we do know, I would say Rebecca Rosen was a smart cookie. After all she has managed to create a second identity, a third if you include the delivery driver. We only got on to her through Danny. If we didn't get any pictures of her face from the CCTV at Angela Cook's flat, we might not have even known it was her.'

'Okay let's go and pick her up,' Charlie said, 'Tim Green too.'

All the team stood. 'Cramer, you go to the bank, have a look in the safe deposit, get any CCTV of her they have.'

'The search warrant should be at the main desk downstairs,' Harry said. 'I will go down there and pick up the one for Tim Green's place and meet you outside, boss.'

Just as they were about to leave, Deputy Commissioner Macready entered the office with AS Crick and the lady from the BBC. 'Well, have we got the murderer?' Macready asked, looking at Charlie.

'We have a suspect,' Charlie replied. 'We are just going to the address now.'

'That's something at least, but don't you have a funeral to attend?' Macready said.

'I think that will have to wait,' Charlie said. All the team were stood behind Charlie watching.

Macready turned and spoke to Crick. The lady from the BBC looked on. When he turned back to Charlie, Macready said 'I think it would not be appropriate for the head of the investigation into the murder of Gerald Parkin not to be at his funeral. I'm sure your team will be able to handle anything without you for an afternoon, after all I'm continually informed by Assistant Commissioner Crick that you have the most efficient team behind you.'

Charlie knew Macready was testing him, but he would play his game. 'I have full confidence in my team.' He turned to Harry. 'Get on with things, but keep me up to date.' Harry nodded and led the team out of the office.

'I want to be kept informed of any developments as they happen, do I make myself clear?' Macready said to Harry as he passed.

'Yes sir, you do,' Harry said, without turning to acknowledge him.

'I will expect a report later,' Macready said to Crick. He took the arm of the lady from the BBC, and left Crick standing looking at Charlie.

It was Charlie who spoke first. 'Do you think this is right? I should be out with my squad,' Charlie said.

'I know Charlie, but I think he was trying to show our visitor from the BBC who's in charge, he was a bit upset about how you all left his office,' Crick said.

'He was a bit upset, well I'm a bit upset,' Charlie said. 'I will make sure it goes into the final report when it's written up, about Macready's interference in this case.'

'I don't know if that would be a good idea,' Crick said.

Charlie looked at Crick. 'Well that's the way I feel. When do we leave for the funeral?'

Crick looked at his watch. 'We will leave in fifteen minutes. I have a car that will take us.'

'No, I will go in my own. Once the funeral is over I want to catch up with Harry and the rest of the squad,' Charlie said.

Crick nodded. 'Alright Charlie, I will see you there.' He turned and left. Charlie walked back towards his desk and sat down, he was fuming from Macready's instructions. He picked up the file on Jane Cavill, scanned through it and picked up the one on Rebecca Rosen. He had an idea. He went to Harry's desk and started to sort through all the files and paper on it, trying not to move too much around, because although it looked messy, Harry knew where everything was. He found what he was looking for, took it back to his desk, picked up the phone and dialled. He waited and the phone was answered; he heard the soft American voice of Amanda Moore say hello.

'Hello Amanda, it's Charlie.'

Charlie, it's nice to hear your voice,' she said. ' I didn't know ,I had given you my mobile number.'

'You didn't,' Charlie said.

'I shall have to remember nothing is secret from you,' she said. 'Are you still going to the funeral?'

'Yes, but I was hoping you could do me a small favour,' Charlie said.

'Yes of course Charlie, anything to help,' Amanda said. 'But you will owe me one.'

'As long as it's not against the law,' Charlie said.

'It won't be, but what is it you want?' she said.

'I would like to speak to Vincenzo Gallo again,' Charlie said.

'Oh I don't know if he's still in the country. He said when he left the house last night that he would be leaving early for Belgium,' Amanda replied. 'I can check for you if you like.'

'If you wouldn't mind,' Charlie said. 'It's just a question about something that came up this morning that he might be able to help with.'

'Is it about Gerald Parkin?' she asked.

'Yes, to do with the case,' he said.

'Okay I will see if he's still in London and let you know,' she said. 'Do you want to give me your mobile?' Charlie gave her his mobile number. 'I will let you know as soon as I find out.'

'Thank you Amanda, I will see you later.'

'Don't forget I want to have a private word with you after the funeral,' she said.

'Yes, that's fine.'

'Bye for now, Charlie.' She rang off.

One more call, he thought. He phoned the front desk, told them if any solicitors turned up to represent Tim Green, the desk should call Chief Inspector Davis. Charlie looked at his watch. It was time to leave.

Harry and the rest of the team had made their way to Tim Green's address, and parked their cars on the opposite side of the road. Danny was in the car with Harry, Jordan and Manjitt in the other. They got out and came together.

'Well, his car's parked there,' Jordan said.

'You and Manjitt make your way to the back,' Harry said. 'When you get there, call me.'

Rebecca Rosen looked from the upstairs bedroom window. She had seen the two cars arrive and knew it was the police. They had come quicker than she thought they would. They were standing on the far side of the road, she recognised the long haired one as the officer who had questioned her when Tim was arrested. The phone call last night had told her they were getting close and she should disappear. She was surprised there was no challenge at the bank when she went to open the safe deposit box, but that was the last instruction she had got, to clear everything out. It was worth it though, there had been another £160,000 in it, plus the photographs she had got from Gerald Parkin's house. Once clear of the bank, her next stop had been the post office where as instructed she posted the pictures to the address she was given. She had checked that the diamonds had been delivered and were safely stored, and the money promised for doing the job had been paid into the Swiss bank account. The two million pounds had been deposited.

It had not worked out how she had planned it. Complications with Gerald Parkin started when he discovered she was up to something. A phone call had come, telling her he was asking questions that would interfere with the plan and was getting greedy. She should do something about him. It had been easy, what a vain man he was. All she did was tell him she needed to see him, as something that she had overheard would be worth a fortune. One quick blow was all it took. The pictures were a bonus; they had been in a briefcase and not expected. But she wasn't interested in them, and had sent them all on as instructed.

She saw two of the police officers walk off, going around the back she thought. She made her way out of the bedroom, it was clean. She walked down the stairs, stepping over the body of a man in the hall and into the front room. Poor Tim, he was lying on the sofa. The drug she had given him would leave him out for at least six hours. He should have been killed like the others, but she couldn't bring herself to do it.

He had fallen in love with her and had been like a puppy. It had been a surprise to her when she discovered he actually worked for a company that had dealings with Gerald Parkin. All she had been after was a safe place to live when he had chatted her up in a bar one evening.

She had been out with Angela when she met Tim. Angela had got her own place, so she needed somewhere to live. Tim had been easy to manipulate, and he was soon in love with her, saying they should buy a place together, and he asked her to marry him. She got Gerald Parkin to buy him a Jaguar. Tim was for ever going on about how great the car was, and she felt sorry for him, but knowing she couldn't just buy it without raising suspicions she got Parkin to pay for it, like it was a present for Tim for work he did. Parkin had taken the money out of what she was owed, but that didn't matter as she had it all now.

Parkin thought he could use the information that her boyfriend didn't know what she was doing at the parties, to try to get her to do other things for him. A smile came to her lips; it was a pleasure killing him. They had played out the charade that he should take the car back, which poor Tim had been fooled by. It had been a bit of a problem when the police had called. It was lucky that Tim's firm had phoned saying what had happened. She had cleared out her lap top and any paperwork that was about, gone to his work and picked up the car. When the police had called, she put on a brave display of not knowing anything and how poor Tim was innocent. He was, but it kept the police busy trying to work out what had been going on.

She had one more look around. Nothing was left. Leaving the front room, she went back into the hall. She glanced towards the front door; the man was lying face down. It was Tim who had answered the door to him.She did recognise him though, he had been following her for over a month. At first she thought he was a policeman and had worried, but one evening when he had followed her home, she waited till she saw him pull away and quickly took the car and followed her follower to his house. She had made a phone call giving the address; a day later she had been called back, he was a private detective. It didn't bother her then.

It was a surprise when he called at the house. She knew he had followed her from the bank, but she had not expected him to knock on the door. Tim had called her to come and see a man who was asking for her. The man had smiled at her, said could he come in as he knew what her game was. Tim had looked mystified, but she had let him in. As he followed Tim towards the front room, she had grabbed the man, pulling his neck back and twisting it. The crack had made Tim jump; he had turned to see her dropping the man to the floor. Tim didn't say anything, she had pushed him into the front room, said she would explain and sat him on the sofa. His face was white with shock.

She had told him she would get some water for him, but had got some strong tranquilisers from her handbag, mixed them into some orange juice and brought it back. She told Tim to drink it, and she would explain to him what had been going on. It took only a minute from him drinking the orange juice to the tranquilisers taking effect. She had one more look around the hall, grabbed her handbag and went upstairs.

While Harry was standing with Danny watching the house, he took a call from Cramer, who told him the safe deposit box was empty. He had checked the CCTV, Rebecca Rosen had been alone. When she left the bank, she was carrying a large bag over her shoulder. Harry told Cramer to go back to the Yard and man the phones, then he told Danny what Cramer had said.

Danny nodded. 'I notice all the curtains are drawn in all the rooms,' Danny said.

Harry looked at the house. 'Bit late to be having a lie in, especially as Tim Green is supposed to be coming to the Yard for an interview,' Harry replied.

'You reckon they've already gone,' Danny asked.

'We'll know that in a little while,' Harry said.

Rebecca Rosen climbed the ladder into the loft, turned and pulled the ladder up. She put it down across the floor of the loft, then she closed the hatch and switched on her torch. Bending double so she didn't bang her head, she made her way to the far side. The large holdall with the money in was there, next to a hole she had made the previous week. She opened the holdall and put her handbag inside with the money.

She had checked out all her neighbours. Most of them worked so were out most of the day, except the old couple three houses down, but it was a risk she took that they would not go into their loft.

It was an escape plan backup she had learned when she was in the army, funnily not from the army but the enemy. It was just as she was coming to the end of her two years' service. When she was first conscripted she imagined it would be horrible, but to her surprise she loved it, found she learned so much. A captain who she didn't know approached her and asked if she would be staying on or leaving the army. Leaving, she had said. He sat her down said her reports were excellent. If she joined up full time, he could guarantee her an exciting time. She had thought about it for a day, decided there was not much to look forward to out of the army, so took the captain up on his offer. She was sent away to a training camp in the south of the country. It was much harder than the training she had already been given, lots of hand to hand combat and small arms training. She learned covert techniques for tracking suspects to spotting and losing anyone tailing her. It's how she spotted the private investigator who was following her. She spent six months in the camp before being transferred to an anonymous office block in Netanya up the coast from Tel Aviv. Here she spent months learning about different Palestinian organisations and individuals who were suspected of involvement in terrorism at home and abroad, being tested on photographs and names, how to forge documents, and break into houses or offices without being detected. The time there flew; it was about a year since she was first approached by the captain when he turned up again. She had been called from a class to the office of the colonel in charge. When she entered his office the captain had been sitting in there. She was told that her progress had been first class, he asked if she was prepared to go on an under-cover operation. She hadn't asked what it might be but had said yes. The captain had taken her to Tel Aviv. In an office opposite the Charles Clore gardens she met two other men both in normal clothes. Neither introduced themselves.

For two hours it was made clear what would be expected of her, with no frills and nothing hidden. Anything that had to done she must do it; she was asked once if she was prepared to do it, without hesitation she had said yes.

She had been given a week off to visit her mother, her father had been dead for three years. The week went quickly; when she returned to the office on the Monday morning the captain had met her. He told her what she would be doing. That evening she found herself on plane to New York, and she was met there by a man from the embassy who took her to the house of a Jewish husband and wife in Queens, where she stayed for another six months. In that time the husband of the family, who was a retired executive from a national photographic company, taught her all there was to know about cameras and photography, how to take pictures, angles, sunlight and exposures, everything and anything,night and day he filled her head. She had been given an American passport in the name of Liza Clinton, with a file filled with information on Liza Clinton's family and background which she learnt by heart. She became Liza Clinton, a photographic journalist. The husband showed her national and international magazines in which photographs had been placed beside written articles with the name Liz Clinton on the pictures. The wife was a ex-teacher of Italian; when she wasn't learning about cameras she learned a grounding in Italian. One evening the man from the embassy came; he brought a bag filled with brand new cameras and lenses, also a file on what her mission was. She was to make contact with the Palestinian organisation in Rome. Her cover was she wanted a story on the troubles in Palestine, to get help in meeting groups on the West Bank and getting some pictures of the troubles there; in the file were pictures and names of all the important Palestinians she should contact.

A week later she was in Rome. It went much easier than she thought and it came naturally to her. She found that most of the Palestinians where pretty macho. After sleeping with a couple they trusted her and she spent time in their company. She raised the prospect of doing a photoshoot on the West Bank about the troubles and getting it into some international magazines. The eldest and the leader was a man named Badran. He was about fifty and boasted of his part in terrorist attacks. He handled all the financial and logistics for the organisation in Italy. It was through him she actually met the father of one of her current employers whose bank the Palestinians used. Funny how life works out.

Harry got the call from Jordan. They were at the back of the house. He told him to stay on the line. Harry and Danny crossed the road to the door and knocked. There was no reply. Danny banged harder, still nothing. He bent down to call through the letter box, and he shouted for Tim Green. He looked to see if he could see any movement. He stood up quickly. 'Harry, there's a body in the hallway.'

Harry bent down to look. He spoke to Jordan, told him to see if he could break into the back of the house. Danny ran back to the car and got the heavy battering ram out, came back and started to smash at the lock.

Rebecca Rosen heard the banging start. She knew it would take some time as she had put every lock on. She grabbed the holdall and crawled through the hole into the loft next door, crossed that then through the hole to the next house.

It was in the West Bank when she had infiltrated a Palestinian group that she learned this trick. There had been a riot, and one of the group she was with fired a gun at the Israeli police. When they had been chased the group had entered a house, gone up to the first floor and through a hole into the next house. They had gone through six houses, came out of that one and nonchalantly walked off down the road, mingling with the crowd like nothing happened. She had tipped off the police so next time under-cover officers were waiting and the whole group were rounded up. Her cover had been blown when one of the Israeli police had congratulated her within earshot of the Palestinians.

After that she was sent to work abroad, mainly spying on or identifying potential terrorists, breaking into offices and homes, sleeping with foreign diplomats to loosen their tongues or to get compromising pictures which could be used to make them spy for Israel. It was a few years later, when she was in Italy on a mission that she met the father of her current employer again. They had struck up a genuine friendship. She had warned him that the Israelis were pressuring the Americans to blacklist his bank for doing business with a terrorist organisation. She should not have done it, but he reminded her of her father. He was grateful as it saved his bank from being bankrupted. When she had been told to leave the army he offered her a job, so she went to work on his personal security staff; that was when she met his son.

She crawled into the loft of the old couple, taking her time to make sure she made little noise, then into the next house. After two more she stopped, prised the hatch open and dropped the holdall through. It landed with a thud on the landing. She wasn't worried, she knew the couple who lived there were at work. She dropped through the opening and landed beside her bag.

Danny had been battering at the door for over three minutes. Harry could hear banging from the back of the house too. The lock on the front door started to give, and it finally flew open. Harry went in first, Danny dropped the battering ram and followed. Harry knelt down beside the body, checking for any life. 'He's dead,' he said. 'Go to the back see if you can let Jordan and Manjitt in.'

Danny went off down the hallway and into the kitchen. He saw Jordan and Manjitt kicking at the door it was halfway off the hinges. He went over and pulled as they pushed. The door collapsed in nearly falling on top of Danny, Manjitt and Jordan stepped over the door, 'There's a body in the hall,' Danny said. 'Don't know who it is.' The three of them walked into the hallway, looking at the body.

'Harry!' Manjitt shouted.

'In here' Harry called from the front room. When they went in, Harry was kneeling beside Tim Green.

'Is he dead?' Jordan asked.

'No, but he seems to be out for the count,' Harry said. 'You and Danny have a look upstairs, see if his fiancée is up there.'

Jordan and Danny left. 'Who's the dead man?' Manjitt asked.

Harry stood up. 'That's our Mr. Russell or Turnball, whatever name he was using. don't ask me how he comes to be here. Call an ambulance, Manjitt, get some locals over here and forensics.'

Harry put a call through to Charlie, but had to leave a message on his voicemail as his phone was off.

'The ambulance is on its way,' Manjitt said, coming back into the room. 'I have the local force on their way and forensics, what do you think happened here, Harry?'

'That's a good question,' Harry said. 'He might be able to tell us,' Harry looked at Tim Green, 'when we can get him to talk.'

Jordan and Danny came down the stairs and into the front room. 'No-one hiding up there, looks like his fiancée is missing,' Jordan said.

'You reckon she killed the guy on the floor,' Danny said.

'His name's Russell,' Harry said. 'A private detective, and if I had to put money on it, I think she probably did.'

'So where does he fit into this,' Jordan asked.

Harry shrugged. 'Another lead to follow. Let's have a quick look around, see if there's anything that might be useful to us. Manjitt, phone Cramer, tell him to get an all ports and police forces red notice out on Rebecca Rosen. Make sure they know she is to be approached with extreme caution and remind them she has a foreign accent. Jordan, search the body out there.'

Rebecca Rosen made her way downstairs to the front door, opened it slowly and stepped out into the street. The banging had stopped; they must be in the house she thought. She pulled the bag onto her shoulder and walked down the path to the road. She took a quick look up the road in the direction of the house, no-one to be seen. She turned in the opposite direction and walked. There were only two more houses till she reached the corner. She kept her pace unhurried. Turning the corner she saw the second hand car she had brought last week. It was one that would not attract any attention, there were thousands of its type on the roads. It was parked on the other side. She crossed, opened the car, threw the bag into the back, climbed in herself, started the car and drove off. She smiled slightly. Just one more little job to clear up.

The funeral had finished and people were streaming out of the crematorium. Charlie stood beside Crick watching. He hadn't noticed anyone from the investigation, except the Moores. A few faces from the television he knew, but no-one else. He took his phone out and switched it on. It buzzed and he saw he had a voicemail; he was about to check it when Stanley and Amanda Moore approached. 'Charlie, how are you?' she said. 'It was a lovely service, don't you think.'

'Yes, very nice,' Charlie replied. He introduced them to Crick and they exchanged pleasantries. Crick said he was going and Charlie should phone him later with an update. Stanley Moore said he had a meeting to get to in the city.

Amanda Moore said Charlie would drop her at the office so her husband needn't worry. She turned to Charlie and said 'You don't mind, do you Charlie?'

'No, not at all,' Charlie said. 'It's on the way to Scotland Yard.' Stanley Moore shrugged, gave Charlie a dirty look and walked off.

'I get the impression your husband doesn't like me,' Charlie said.

'Oh he doesn't like you, he told me that,' Amanda said, taking Charlie's arm. 'Now where is your car parked?'

She and Charlie joined the others walking along the crematorium road going to their cars. 'You wanted to tell me something,' Charlie said.

'Yes, but when we get in the car,' Amanda replied. When they reached the Ferrari, Charlie opened the passenger door to let her climb in.

'Always the gentleman,' she said as she slid into the seat. She was looking up at Charlie. She allowed her dress to ride up as she swung her legs in. Charlie noticed the tops of her black stockings. He looked back at her face, she was grinning.

'Charlie, I hope you weren't looking at my legs.' He closed the door, shaking his head, and walked around the car. He got in, started the engine and pulled away.

'This is a very lovely car Charlie. I have a Porsche, did it cost you much?' she said.

'I've had it a long time now, it's a classic car, I can't remember what it cost,' Charlie said as he turned onto the main road. 'What is it you wanted to tell me?'

She turned sideways to look at Charlie. 'It's about my husband. He's been acting strangely ever since you questioned us first time around.'

Charlie stopped at some traffic lights. He turned his head to look at her. 'In what way, strange?' he said, noticing she was displaying a lot of leg. 'And could you put those legs away?'

She laughed. 'Charlie, are you immune to my charms?'

'Not immune, I just don't want to crash this car. Now you were telling me about your husband,' he said. The lights changed and Charlie pulled away.

'Well, as I said he has been acting strangely, and after you came down to Ascot he seemed to get worse,' she said.

'In what way?' Charlie said, keeping his eyes on the road.

'It's not something I can put my finger on, but he's not his usual self. I do have a small confession myself though,' she said.

Charlie glanced over at her then back to the road. 'Go on' he said.

'I do hope you will forgive me.' She put her hand onto his leg. 'When you first came to the office, you asked questions about Gerald blackmailing people.' Charlie turned his head to look at her. 'No, I wasn't being blackmailed.' He turned back to look at the road. 'One evening when I was in bed with Angela, she told me about going to parties and thatmy husband was at them. She was a lovely girl, very attractive, don't you think so?'

Charlie stopped at another set of traffic lights. 'Yes she was, did she say what went on at the parties?'

'It doesn't bother you that she was my lover?' she asked.

'Why should it bother me?' Charlie said.

'That's good to know, I have never met a man who wasn't intimidated by my power and wealth, but I see that neither seem to worry you. I like that.' She ran her hand up Charlie's leg.

Charlie smiled. 'Amanda, I said I did not want to crash the car.'

She laughed and took her hand away. 'Yes, she told me all that went on at the parties. She also told me who else was at them. I think she was glad to have someone to talk to, but anyway a little while later I was in a meeting with one of our financial officers. He happened to mention my husband had asked for a couple of banker's drafts. I didn't know anything about it at the time, so I checked. They were worth in total £350,000. When you told me about blackmail, I could only assume that my husband was paying Gerald.'

'Did you ask your husband about the money?' Charlie asked.

'No, I wanted to wait and see if he told me anything,' she said.

'I asked you if you ever met any of Angela Cook's friends.'
He glanced at her, she was still sitting with her legs pulled up.

'No, I never met any of her friends,' she said.

'Did she mention any of them when she was talking, girls
who were also at the parties?' Charlie asked. He drove away as
the lights changed to green.

'Not that I can remember,' she said.

'And Angela never mentioned she was passing on
information to Gerald Parkin?' Charlie said.

'No, he never came up in our conversations,' she replied.

'Did it bother you that your husband was at the parties?'
Charlie asked.

'Not in the least,' Amanda said. She placed her hand on
Charlie's leg. 'We don't have a sexual relationship, haven't for
many years. He's been working on something at work we have
disagreed on too. I worry that he could damage the bank, I
know some of the shareholders are worried, but he's got us in
too far now. I honestly think as a couple we have gone as far as
we can.'

'Do you know if your husband met any of the girls from
the parties privately?' Charlie said glancing at her. She
continued to rub his leg with her hand, sliding it onto the top
of his thigh. 'Amanda although I find what your hand is doing
to my leg very nice, if you get any higher I will crash this car.'

She laughed out loud. 'Well, at least I know you enjoy it.'

'What about your husband?' Charlie said.

'Well, I know he brought a girl to our house a few times. It
hadn't happened before, anytime he wanted to meet someone
he would disappear, find a hotel I assume,' she said.

'Do you know the girl's name?' Charlie asked.

'No, why should I?' she asked.

'I suppose not, but she was a friend of Angela Cook's'
Charlie said.

'Was she? I don't know what my husband will do now, he has none of those parties to go to.' she said.

They had reached Amanda Moore's office. Charlie pulled the car over to the kerb, he turned in his seat. 'Do you think your husband was mixed up in the murder of Gerald Parkin and Angela Cook?' he asked.

'I honestly don't know,' Amanda Moore said. 'He could be. It's a lot of money he was being blackmailed for. Maybe he found out Angela Cook was involved. Although if he was involved, it really would surprise me.'

Charlie got out of the car and walked round to open the passenger door. Amanda Moore swung her legs out. Her dress had ridden up again. Charlie knew she was doing it on purpose. 'Charlie, are you looking at my legs again. Do you think I have nice legs?' she said, smiling at him. Charlie smiled back. He purposely took a long look at her legs, then held out his hand. She took it, got out of the car and stood up. 'I hope what I told you has been helpful, Charlie.'

'It could be,' Charlie said.

She still had Charlie's hand. 'Give me your card, Charlie. I can't remember where I put your last one. If I think of anything else, I will call you.' Charlie took a card from his inside pocket and gave it to her. Charlie shut the passenger door, Amanda squeezed his hand. 'I would like to know more about you, Charlie,' she said.

'I will bear that in mind,' Charlie answered.

'Perhaps we could have dinner one evening, just the two of us,' she said.

Charlie smiled. 'I will see how long this case takes.'

She lent forward and Charlie went to kiss her cheek, but she turned her head at the last moment, so her lips met his. She held the kiss for a few seconds. He felt the tip of her tongue brush his lips, then she pulled back smiling. She let go of his hand, 'Goodbye Charlie,' She turned and he watched her walk up the stairs and into her office. Charlie went round and got back into the car, took his phone out and listened to his voicemail. He phoned Harry straight away.

After he had spoken to Harry, he drove quickly to Scotland Yard. When he reached the office Cramer was there. 'Any more news yet?' Charlie asked.

'Nothing yet,' Cramer said.

'Dig out the address from the files for John Russell. He's the private detective whose body they found at the house,' Charlie said. 'When you have it I want you to go over there and search the place, see if you can find anything that links him to Rebecca Rosen.' Cramer went off to look for the address. Charlie picked up his phone and called Crick. He told him of the latest developments, he then put a call through to Julian Squires.

They had found nothing in the search of the house, and the body had nothing on it. 'She cleaned up well before she cleared out,' Manjitt said. Harry nodded. The local force had arrived, Harry had kept them outside searching the garden and doing house to house. One of the local officers came in and told them an ambulance had arrived, Harry said to send them in.

'Manjitt I want you to go to the hospital with Tim Green. Stay beside him, and as soon as he wakes we need answers.' Manjitt nodded, the rest of the team moved into the kitchen when the ambulance personnel came in, so they had space to treat Tim Green.

'Harry, there's one thing that's strange,' Danny said as they stood in the kitchen.

'Go ahead, Hippie,' Harry replied.

'Well, we had to smash our way in the front door,' Danny said. 'All the bolts were on, so it was locked from inside. Manjitt and Jordan had the same trouble getting in the back door because all the bolts were on that. So whoever locked up the place should still be here'

'But we searched every room in the house,' Jordan said.

They all looked at each other and nearly said in unison, the loft. They left the kitchen to make their way upstairs, seeing Manjitt leave the house beside the stretcher-borne Tim Green as they did. Standing below the hatch to the loft, Harry said quietly 'Now if she's up there, this is one dangerous woman, so let's be very careful. Is there a ladder or something up here so we can get in?' They looked in all the rooms and found nothing. 'Hippie, you get on Jordan's shoulders, you can open it.'

'Thank you Harry, for the honour of going first,' Danny said.

'Well unless you can lift Jordan up, it's the only way,' Harry replied.

Jordan knelt down. 'Come on Hippie, get on,' he said. Danny swung his legs over Jordan's shoulders.

'Just try to push it gently at first, see if it gives,' Harry said. Jordan straightened up, moving to stand directly below the loft entrance. Danny placed his hands on the hatch and pushed gently. He felt it move, he looked down at Harry and said quietly 'It's moving.'

'Well shove it open. Jordan, as he does, move out of the way,' Harry said.

Danny braced his hands on the hatch and gave a hard quick shove. The hatch flew inward. Jordan jumped to one side, his momentum swung Danny on his shoulders violently, Danny's head banged into the top of the wall. Harry called up at the loft, saying it's the police. They heard nothing. He called again, still no reply, 'Hippie, pop your head up and have a look,' Harry said to Danny, who was rubbing the back of his head where he had banged it on the wall. Jordan moved back under the opening.

'If there's any sudden noises Harry, tell Tarzan here…'
Danny pointed down at Jordan, '…just to bend down and not
throw me against the wall again.'

'Just stick your head up and look, Hippie,' Harry said.

Danny quickly popped his head into the open hatch and
out again, then up slower a second time. He called out but
heard silence.

'Doesn't look like anyone's up here, Harry,' he said.

'Get right up and have a look around, see if you can find
anything,' Harry said.

Danny put one leg onto the Jordan's shoulders, lifted
himself up and through the hatch. Harry saw him disappear,
then his head appeared at the hatch.

'Have we got a torch Harry, I can't see a thing up here,'
Danny said.

Harry sent Jordan downstairs to get one of the local officers,
he came back a minute later and passed the torch to Danny who
disappeared back into the darkness. Harry and Jordan stood
waiting. They could hear Danny moving about, he came back
to the hatch. 'There's a hole through to next door's loft and I
think there's a hole from that one to the next house,' Danny said.

'Check it out, see how far it goes,' Harry said. 'We will go
outside, see where you come out.' Danny went away again.
Harry and Jordan went downstairs and into the road; they saw
local officers knocking on the neighbouring doors to ask if
anyone had seen anything.

'This escape route was well planned,' Harry said.

'She does seem to be one step ahead of us,' Jordan said. 'Do
you think she was in the house when we turned up?' Jordan
asked as they both looked down the street waiting to see where
Danny appeared.

'I think she may have been when we started to break in. I
think she then escaped through the loft,' Harry said.

'So we were in the house and she slipped away under our noses,' Jordan said.

'Well above our heads at least,' Harry said. 'She is a cool customer, we need to find out more about her.'

They suddenly saw Danny appear about six houses down. He came walking back towards them. 'She knew exactly what she was doing,' Jordan said.

'Yes, but where is she now?' Harry said as Danny came up to them.

'The holes were neatly cut into the far corners of the lofts,' Danny said. 'So if you put your head up looking for something, you wouldn't see there were holes.'

Harry put a call through to Charlie and told him what else they had discovered. Charlie told him Cramer was on his way to the private detective's house to see if anything that could help them was there. He told Harry to come back to the Yard, so they could have a talk about their next move.

When Harry got off the phone he made another; when he finished that he turned to Jordan and Danny.

'Jordan, you're coming back to the Yard with me. Hippie, I have just spoken to an inspector I know on the local force, he is going to come over and oversee the investigation for us here. You wait for him, tell him everything we know that's gone on here. Make sure he gets forensics into the lofts, you never know she might have left something, but I doubt it. As soon as you have him fully briefed, follow us back to the Yard and make sure the car is taken in for a check.'

When Charlie had got off the phone to Harry, he knew there was a man with a few questions to answer, and he wasn't going to take any more evasions. He picked up the phone and rang Detective Inspector Bernie Thompson. The phone was picked up on the second ring. Charlie heard the voice say 'Thompson here.'

'Hello Bernie, it's Charlie.'

'Boss, how's things? You didn't find any scratches on the car you are trying to put down to me are you,' Bernie said.

'No Bernie, you're safe. I wanted a favour if you're not too busy,' Charlie said.

'Anything boss, just ask,' Bernie replied.

Charlie then explained he wanted a man named Desmond Carrington picked up. He gave Bernie the address, said to nick him on suspicion of perverting the course of justice for now, and drop him to the Yard. Bernie said consider it done and rang off. Charlie had no sooner put down the phone when it rang again. It was Julian Squires, Charlie spent ten minutes talking to him.

CHAPTER SEVENTEEN

Rebecca Rosen had driven up the road three times in different directions. She was sure there was no one watching the house. She parked around the corner, locked her bag in the boot and walked along the road till she came to the house. She didn't hesitate but went straight up the path. She scanned the outside walls for burglar alarms, there wasn't one on view. She got to the door and used the keys she had taken off the man's body. The door opened, she stepped in quickly closing it. She stood and listened, heard nothing. She knew time was short as the police would surely get this address soon. There would be no time to search thoroughly so it would have to be a bit of destruction.

Going to the kitchen first and looking through the cupboards, she found a bottle of white spirit. Taking it out she took the top off, left the kitchen and went to the front room. She began to douse the furniture in the white spirit. When the bottle only had a tiny amount left in it, she went back to the kitchen. Picking up a newspaper that was amongst a pile by the back door, she walked over to the cooker and turned on one of the rings, holding the ignition button in. When it was alight she rolled the newspaper up, emptying the last little drops of white spirit onto the end of the newspaper. She held it over the cooker, it caught fire straight away. She turned the gas ring off then back on again without lighting it, then switched all the other gas taps on. The hissing was quite loud. Moving quickly back to the front room, she went round the furniture holding the lighted newspaper against them. Soon most were well alight. The white spirit had soaked in and all were burning. Throwing the newspaper down and walking back to the front door, she left, walked along the road got into her car and drove off. It would only be about five minutes before it went bang, she thought.

Charlie was sitting listening to Harry, who had arrived back at the office with Jordan telling him exactly what they had found when they got to the house. 'Well, the floor's open to ideas,' Charlie said when Harry had finished.

'It looks to me…' Jordan said, '…that she is one step ahead of us all the time. I don't think it's luck.'

'I agree with Jordan,' Harry said.

'Well, I don't think we have a leak in the squad,' Charlie said.

'No neither do I,' Harry said. 'I just think someone has a fair idea what we are up to and has been letting her know.'

'Harry's right, boss,' Jordan said. 'Rebecca Rosen as Jayne Cavill cleared her bank out just when we got onto her and disappeared. Now Rebecca Rosen empties her safe deposit and does a runner.'

'Maybe she was spooked when she knew we were going to pull Tim Green in and question him,' Charlie said.

'No boss,' Harry replied. 'The escape route must have been planned well in advance, and she waited till we turned up to make her escape.'

'So we are dealing with a cool but ruthless customer,' Charlie said. 'Do we reckon then that she was working with someone, or for someone?'

'There's no evidence of anyone else being at the murder scenes,' Jordan said. 'So if someone else was working with her they just helped out. They found out Gerald Parkin's blackmail racket and decided to kill him and take all his money.'

'I think she was working for someone,' Charlie said. 'Parkin didn't have that much money lying around, most of what he had was in a Swiss bank or in shares. No, I think it's deeper than that.'

He then told them about the phone conversation he had with Julian. A takeover had just been launched for Sir Mark Coale's company that morning. Julian had said a consortium of banks was backing a large American oil company in its bid. He was going to phone back when he got news of who was involved. He also went over the conversation he had with Amanda Moore after the funeral.

'So you think it's the share-buying Gerald Parkin was doing that got him killed,' Harry said.

'That's my guess, Harry,' Charlie said.

'But what about the blackmail?' Jordan asked.

'I think a number of people would have liked to kill him over the blackmail,' Charlie said, 'but remember he had pictures, so they couldn't be sure they wouldn't get out even if they did. Also they didn't know if he was working alone.'

'And we know just how much money he was making out of his share dealing,' Harry said.

'You're right Harry, the blackmail has had us side tracked,' Charlie said. 'So now we know there was a lot more money involved than a few hundred thousand pounds here and there. We're looking at hundreds of millions.'

Harry nodded. 'I think Parkin stumbled onto the blackmail as a side line when he had the conversation with Sir Martin Oliver. I get the feeling it was a game to him.'

'So who are we looking at?' Jordan said.

'I think it all revolves around Sir Mark Coale's company,' Charlie said. 'This is not something that has just been thought up. We know the secret share-buying has been going on for over a couple of years. I think Rebecca Rosen was brought in to get close to Sir Mark.' Charlie's phone rang interrupting the conversation. He listened for a minute said 'Okay, come back to the office,' he put the phone down. 'That was Cramer, he got to John Russell's house and found the fire brigade there. The fire chief told him it was a gas explosion. Cramer said there's not much left of the house, nor the ones next door to it.'

'Looks like she went there to clean up,' Harry said.

'Do you think Russell was working with her?' Jordan said, 'and she decided she didn't want to share with him or something?'

'I don't think so,' Harry said. 'He has not popped up at all till the boss and me bumped into him accidently.'

'You got room for us poor people in the posh part of town?' They all looked towards the door and saw Bernie Thompson coming towards them with his detective sergeant following.

'Bernie, good to see you,' Harry said.

'How are you, you South London low life?' Bernie said to Jordan, smiling.

'Looking at the overweight body of yours, pretty good,' Jordan said, smiling back and holding out his hand. Bernie shook it and turned to Charlie, 'I got your man for you, boss.'

Charlie told Harry and Jordan he had got Bernie to nick Desmond Carrington for them. 'Did he say anything when you picked him up?' Charlie asked.

'He wasn't happy, thought being an ex-army man gave him some kind of privilege.' Bernie said. 'He also went on about a solicitor, but you know what my hearing's like boss, not as good as it was. I thought he was going to put up a fight for a moment, but I persuaded him otherwise.' The detective sergeant with Bernie laughed.

'I won't ask how,' Charlie said, 'but thanks for that, Bernie.'

'No problem boss, anything else just call, he's in the cells downstairs,' Bernie said. 'I'll leave you lot and get back to some real police work.' He said goodbye to everyone and left.

'Harry, you and I are going to have serious chat with Mr Carrington,' Charlie said. 'Jordan, I want you to get everything we have on Rebecca Rosen.Jayne Cavill and go through it all again, also check if she has a phone. Cramer should be back soon, he can help. Also put a call through to the Israeli police. Tell them we have a triple murder down to this woman, and want everything they know about her. We haven't had much help from them. Also give Manjitt a ring, find out what the score with Tim Green is.' Charlie and Harry left Jordan sorting through files.

'Do you remember us?' Charlie asked Desmond Carrington, who was seated opposite in the interview room.

Carrington looked at Charlie and Harry. 'Of course I recognise you, I want to see a solicitor and make a complaint about the arresting officer.' He held his hand against the side of his head, holding his ear.

'We want to ask you a few questions about the man who was in your office when we called in,' Harry said.

'Did you not hear me?' Carrington said. 'I want to see a solicitor.'

'Now if I recall, you had trouble remembering the man's name, and didn't you give me the wrong phone number by mistake?' Harry carried on.

'What is the matter with you people?' Carrington said. 'Look at my ear.' He took his hand away. There was a small amount of blood seeping from it, and it had already swollen to twice its size.

'Did you have a fall or something?' Charlie asked.

'A fall, no that policemen who arrested me did this,' Carrington said, putting his hand back to his ear. Charlie knew that Bernie had a little trick he used when arresting uncooperative suspects. He had told Charlie that the nerve endings were very close under the skin of the ear, so pain was doubled. He proved it to Charlie when on an arrest of an armed robber who was a brute of a man who had been fighting three policemen to avoid arrest, Bernie had stepped in, grabbed hold of his ear, twisted it and the man had been like a lamb. 'Don't pull my ear off', he'd said, and he'd given up.

'Now the man we met in your office, can you remind me of his name?' Harry asked.

'Are you not listening? I am saying nothing until I have seen a solicitor,' Carrington said.

'Oh that is a shame, don't you think he should be more cooperative, Harry?' Charlie said.

'You'd think he would be, the trouble he's in,' Harry replied.

'Well you can't help some people,' Charlie said. 'We will charge him with conspiracy to murder, conspiracy to blackmail, and perverting the course of justice.'

'Don't forget assaulting a police officer. Bernie looked like he had some bruises coming up on his face,' Harry said.

'Wait a minute what are you on about?' Carrington said.

'That's okay Mr Carrington. If we were in your position we would not want to say anything either, but it's a shame as we could have seen our way maybe to help you if you had helped us,' Charlie said.

'I will sort out the paperwork then we can formally charge you. Then if you give us your solicitor's name we will get him down here,' Harry said.

'Now just hold on a minute,' Carrington said. 'What are you talking about, murder and blackmail?'

'Mr Carrington, I'm only going to give you one more chance. My inspector here didn't even want to bother with giving you a chance to answer any questions, just wanted to charge you. He feels you're a born liar. After all, you did give him the wrong name for the man in your office ,didn't you,' Charlie said. 'If you want to talk we can, but we will ask the questions, you answer them.'

Carrington sat back in his chair. He still held his hand to his ear. 'Okay, but I have no idea what you're talking about,'he said.

'The man we met in your office, what was his name?' Harry asked.

Carrington hesitated for a moment. 'John Russell.'

'That's a good start,' Harry said, 'a truthful answer. Keep this up and we might even let you walk out of here scot free.'

'Does he work for you?' Charlie asked.

'Not for my company, he is freelance. I get him in sometimes to do work for me,' Carrington replied.

'So he was doing a job for you at the moment?' Charlie said.

'Yes, but what has Russell done?' Carrington asked.

'Oh dear, there you go asking questions, now one last chance,' Charlie said.

'When did you last speak to him?' Harry asked.

'When you came to my office,' he said.

'What job was he doing for you?' Harry said.

'He was tracing a girl,' Carrington replied.

'What was the name of the girl, and why were you looking for her?' Charlie asked.

'Her name was Jayne Cavill…' Carrington stopped for a moment, then carried on. 'We had been asked to find her by a client.'

'And did Russell find her?' Harry said.

'Yes, he had been watching her for a while,' he said.

'So if he found her, why did he still follow her?' Charlie asked.

'We were instructed to watch her and report about anyone she met.'

'And who asked you to find her?' Charlie asked.

'A city company engaged us to find her. I got Russell in because he is good at that sort of thing.'

'I will let you off that,' Charlie said, 'and who asked you to find her?'

Carrington sat quietly for a moment. 'We got a request from the British Deep Sea Oil Company.'

'Who did you speak to, and did they explain why they wanted to find her?' Harry asked.

'I spoke to the head of security at the company, and no, they didn't tell me why they wanted her.

'Did Russell report back about any people she had been meeting,' Charlie said.

'No, but he had a dossier on her. He was going to finish it this week and bring it to the office.'

'Did he mention that the girl, Jayne Cavill, might be using a different name?' Harry asked.

'No, he never said that. Why don't you pick him up? I could give you his address and you can ask him all these questions, it would be much simpler', Carrington said.

'Giving us his address might not be very useful, as his house isn't there anymore,' Harry replied.

Carrington looked confused. 'What do you mean, his house is not there anymore?'

'Mr Carrington, seeing as you have been helpful so far and I believe you have told us the truth, I will let you off those questions,' Charlie said. 'What my inspector means is that his house blew up earlier today.'

'Blew up, how? What happened, is John alright?' Carrington asked.

'The fire brigade say it was a gas explosion, which it

probably was, but we think it was deliberate,' Charlie said. 'Mr Russell wasn't in the house at the time.'

'Well that's good,' Carrington said.

'Not really,' Harry said. 'He was murdered by the girl you know as Jayne Cavill this morning.'

'Murdered!' Carrington said. He sat up in his chair.

'Now this is the problem we have,' Charlie said. 'Russell was working for you, following a girl you tell us you know as Jayne Cavill. You said Russell didn't tell you she was using another name. Well, we know her as Rebecca Rosen, does that name ring any bells?' Carrington shook his head no. 'Well, she is a dangerous piece of work. We believe she has murdered three people so far, including your Mr Russell. Now we think after killing him she went to his house. If she found any documents with your name on, you might be next on her list,'

Carrington asked for a drink. Harry got up and left the room. Charlie sat looking at Carrington. 'I think your officer has damaged my ear badly,' Carrington said. Charlie never said anything. Carrington looked at his hand and saw the blood on it. 'Do you have something I can use to wipe it?' he asked. Charlie still sat looking at him, not answering. Harry came back into the room with a glass of water, gave it to Carrington and sat down. Carrington took a drink.

Charlie turned to Harry and said 'He thinks the officer who arrested him has permanently damaged his ear.'

Harry looked at Carrington. 'I thought we had decided you fell over.'

Carrington took another drink of water. 'Forget it,' he said.

'Now where were we? Oh yes, she could be looking for you, if she thinks Russell has passed on information about her to you,' Charlie said.

'Or she might not have been working alone' Harry said,

'She may have been tipped off by someone that she was being watched.' They both stared at Carrington.

'I have had no contact with her, John never even said where she lived,' Carrington said.

'Did anyone else ask you to find her, or mention the name Rebecca Rosen?' Harry asked.

'No, no-one,' Carrington said.

'Now you see the problem we have, don't you, Mr Carrington,' Charlie said. 'If I let you go, she might be watching your office with the intention of killing you. Or she might be meeting up to share out some of the money she has got,'

'I don't know the woman,'

'What do you reckon, Harry?' Charlie said.

'I'm willing to give him the benefit of the doubt,' Harry said. 'But let me tell you, Mr Carrington, we don't want anyone to know we have had this conversation, do you understand?' Carrington nodded. 'That includes the people who asked you to find her. If we think you mentioned our meeting, we will come down on you like a ton of bricks, understand? You tell no one.' Carrington nodded. 'If I were you, I would stay away from your office, and if John Russell knew where you lived I would not go home till we find this woman. She is highly dangerous.'

'I will get an officer to show you out,' Charlie said.

When Charlie and Harry walked back into the office, they found the whole team minus Manjitt seated around Jordan's desk going through files. 'Nice to see you're all hard at it,' Harry said. 'Come over to the boss's desk.'

They all brought chairs and sat down round Charlie's desk. Harry went over what they had learned from questioning Carrington.

'Did you speak to Manjitt?' Charlie asked.

'Yes, she said the doctors can't say when he will wake up, could still be a few more hours. He has been given some kind of tranquiliser,' Jordan said.

'So what have we got on this woman?' Charlie asked.

'We have been through everything again,' Jordan said, 'and this woman is very smart. If she leaves a trail it's false, or as in the case of Russell she gets rid of the problem.'

'What about a phone?' Charlie asked

'There is one registered to her at that the address, but it's switched off and hasn't been used for a day. I have asked the phone company to send a list of calls made to and from it over to us,' Jordan said.

'Speak to the head of the security at the phone company, Jordan,' Harry said. 'We want to know when it's switched on again and where. They can give us a fix of the area, we can narrow things down. Make sure they understand the importance of it.' Jordan nodded.

'What about the Israelis, did you get hold of them?' Charlie asked.

'Yes I spoke to an inspector over there. I explained what was going on he said he would phone me back tonight,' Jordan said.

'Well if we don't get any help from them, I will have a word with Crick, see if he can get something for us?' Charlie said.

'It solves one problem,' Danny said. 'She told me she couldn't drive when I asked her how the Jaguar got back to the house when we pulled in Tim Green. She must have picked it up, she was just causing us more confusion so we thought someone else was involved.'

'We know Sir Mark Coale had private detectives looking for her,' Harry said, 'well at least under the name of Jayne Cavill. Although Carrington said it was the head of security at the company who asked him to search for her, we can assume the order came from Sir Mark.'

'So how did the private detective end up in the house?' Danny said.

'He told Carrington he had found her. Maybe he thought he could confront her or something,' Harry said.

'So we don't think she was working for Sir Mark and double-crossed him or something,' Cramer said.

'No, I think he discovered or at least suspected she was up to something,' Charlie said.

'We will have to question him again, boss,' Harry said. 'He's not been very honest with us.'

'You're right, Harry,' Charlie said. 'This time we will have him in a cell downstairs, see if that jogs his memory.'

'Boss, didn't you say that Sir Mark said Jayne Cavill was seeing Stanley Moore privately away from the parties?' Danny asked.

'Yes she was, and from what his wife told me this morning, I suspect she was meeting him at their house, he's another one to bring in for a chat,' Charlie said.

'It doesn't get us any closer to knowing where she has disappeared to,' Jordan said.

'She seems to be well organised, so I don't expect her to just be running round looking for somewhere to hide, she's gone to ground somewhere that was sorted out earlier,' Charlie said. 'We think someone has been letting her know when we have been getting close. So who do we think that could be?'

'Are we ruling out Sir Mark?' Danny said.

'Yes, I think he was after her like us, so he wouldn't be tipping her off,' Charlie said.

'Well that only leaves two people who we have spoken to about her,' Harry said. 'Jayne Cavill. Rebecca Rosen cleared out her bank after you and Manjitt went to Ascot races, and

Rebecca Rosen was ready to go the day after you and I boss, went to the dinner party. Both times we questioned Stanley Moore and his wife,' Harry said.

'So Stanley Moore is more in this than he makes out,' Jordan said.

'Russell must have discovered her real name. Didn't he tell Carrington?' Cramer asked.

'Carrington said he didn't know the name and although I don't like him, I believe he didn't,' Harry said.

'So if she was working with or for Stanley Moore, what's in it for him?' Charlie said.

'He must be mixed up in the share dealing. Remember Sir Mark said Stanley Moore organised the meeting with that banker from Luxemburg, Vincenzo Gallo,' Harry said.

'That reminds me,' Jordan said. 'A message came through for Manjitt from the Belgian police. They traced the courier who picked up the diamonds; they delivered them to an address in Brussels, which turned out to be a business that rented out post boxes. The diamonds are well gone, someone has been and picked them up.'

'So Rebecca Rosen has friends who are working for her in Belgium,' Harry said.

'Well, we can't do anything about that, so we'll write the diamonds off.' Charlie said. 'But where to next looking for our killer?'

'There must be something we're not seeing,' Harry said.

'She may have even left the country already,' Cramer said.

'I don't think so,' Charlie replied. 'She's smart. She knows we will be watching all the ports and airports. She will have gone to ground, somewhere she will feel safe and knows the area. Now we know she lived in Peckham with Angela Cook, and she had a flat before and sold it, where was that?'

Jordan got up and went over to his desk, sorted through a couple of files and came back. 'It was in Bow, East London.'

'So she knows those areas. Harry, you get onto anyone you know in those areas who we can rely on to be discreet. If she's spotted I don't want some gung-ho copper spooking her and she disappears again. Explain we just want all eyes open for her, make sure they have the best pictures we have of her and remind them it's got to be hush hush. I don't want some paper getting a hint and running some manhunt story.' Harry got up and went to his desk and took out his black book.

'Boss, it's been bugging me,' Danny said.

'What's that?' Charlie asked.

'The way she mugged me off about not driving when I questioned her,' Danny said.

'We had no idea she was a suspect then, Hippie, don't let it bother you,' Jordan said.

'But she must be using a car now,' Danny said.

'Yes, and we have no idea what make, colour or year it is,' Cramer said. Or maybe she had someone pick her up from the house.'

'I don't think so,' Jordan said.

'No, she's driving round in a car,' Danny said.

'What's your point, Danny?' Charlie asked.

'Well from all we know about her, she plans things carefully, leaves nothing to chance. So the way I see it, she's not going to risk driving round in a car that's not taxed or insured,' Danny said.

'Good point, Hippie, but where does that get us?' Jordan said.

'She must have insured the car under a name she knows has a driving licence,' Danny said.

'Well, what are you waiting for Danny?' Charlie said.

Danny got up and went over to his desk. 'He can come up with some good ideas, that boy.'

Harry came back. 'All sorted, boss. I spoke to a couple of inspectors in those areas, they will brief all their teams, they can be relied on to be discreet. I sent the best pictures we had over to them.' Charlie told Harry what Danny had come up with.

'We need to get Sir Mark and Stanley Moore in here for questioning,' Harry said.

'We'll do that,' Charlie said. 'Jordan, phone the Israelis again. Let's pester them. I want more background on this woman. If they don't come across with something this time I will go upstairs, get some pressure applied. Cramer, I want you to contact the offices of Sir Mark Coale and Stanley Moore. We need to speak to them, don't get fobbed off.' Jordan and Cramer got up and went off.

'What do you reckon, Harry?' Charlie said.

'It's one of those so close but so far cases, boss,' Harry said. 'And now we're clutching at straws.'

'We can only hope one of the straws stick, Harry,' Charlie replied.

Rebecca Rosen knew the area, she had lived there before. She had parked the car two streets from the furnished flat on the main road. She knew sooner or later the police would get onto it, but it had a part to play. She had rented the flat a few weeks ago when she felt things were coming to a head and she might need a bolthole. The letting agency thought she was a company executive from Europe over for a month on business. The flat was on the first floor, among other modern blocks with people coming and going all the time who didn't know each other and didn't care. She had gone to the local street market on Roman Road. It had been thronged with people, so she felt invisible, but knew her appearance had to change. She called in at a beauty salon, they told her they could fit her in. When she left her hair was in a pixie cut and blonde. She looked in the mirror and inwardly smiled. I wouldn't recognise myself, she thought. After leaving the salon, a call to a couple of nice clothes and shoe shops had got her the outfits she wanted. She visited a small supermarket and brought some food, coffee and milk. Her last stop was to pick up a Daines and Hathaway executive leather briefcase. She should get most of the money in it, and it wouldn't look as incongruous as the large holdall.

Once back at the flat, the first thing she did was transfer the money from the holdall. All bar £10,000 went in the briefcase. She took two passports from her handbag, one in the name of Rebecca Rosen, the other of Liza Clinton. Tucking the Rebecca Rosen in with the money she closed the briefcase, and opened the Liza Clinton American passport. It showed a blonde haired woman; the hair was longer but that was no problem. The passport still had a couple of years to run. She left it out, putting it on top of the money that would not fit in the case. She walked over and switched the television on, then walked to the windows. The sky was dark now. Drawing the curtains and walking back, she sat down on the sofa, putting her feet up to watch the news that had come on the screen. It didn't say anything about the killings, but in the business section there was a big item on the takeover of the British deep sea oil company by an American oil giant. At the end there was a small part about a gas explosion that was being investigated by the fire brigade. She was happy to see the house looked totally destroyed. She got up and went to make a coffee.

From where she was, it would only take about twenty minutes to London City Airport. Her ticket would be waiting at the desk, the Air France flight to Luxemburg would leave at

3 pm, so tomorrow evening she would be sitting having dinner at the Mosconi, the best restaurant in Luxembourg city. She smiled at the thought. She took her coffee back to the sofa and sat down. Her only regret from this job had been Angela; she had really liked her. It was partly Gerald Parkin's fault and partly Sir Mark Coale's. Angela had worked out from questions those two had asked her that she was not who she said she was. When they had met for lunch after Gerald Parkin was killed, Angela had asked her if she was mixed up in the killing, and although she had denied knowing anything about it, she knew Angela did not believe her. Then when she got a phone call from Angela saying the police had been to question her, she knew that she had to act. After calling to find out if she should kill her, she was told to leave no loose ends.

Angela did not recognise her at first when she opened the door. She had actually invited her in with the parcel, but once in the room Angela saw through the disguise. They had spoken for a couple of minutes, she knew Angela was frightened and had made an excuse to go into the bedroom, to make a phone call, to the police she thought, but she had followed her in. She could still see the shock on Angela's face when she had pushed her back onto the bed and pinned her down. She took a drink of her coffee, the news had finished, a programme on travel came on.

Everyone had been busy in the office trying to trace Rebecca Rosen, when a shout went up. They all turned to see Danny standing with his arms in the air. 'I got her!' he said, turning towards Charlie and Harry. He walked over.

'What you got, Hippie?' Harry said.

'Last week someone took insurance out on a silver Ford Fiesta in the name of Angela Cook,' Danny replied.

Charlie looked over at Danny. 'Good work, Danny,' he said.

'Get all the information out countrywide. Make sure they know its significance and should only be noted where its is and not approached, and we should be informed straight away.'

'Give me the details, Hippie,' Harry called. 'I will get onto the Peckham and Bow police separately, as that's where we think she might be.' Danny copied the details down on Harry's pad then went off to get the details out nationwide.

'Cramer,' Charlie said. 'Give Manjitt a ring, see how she is getting on with Tim Green and bring her up to speed with what we know. And how are you getting on with finding out where Sir Mark Coale is, and Stanley Moore?'

'I have spoken to their offices,' Cramer replied. 'Both said they had gone to meetings in the city of London and they could give me no idea when they would be back.'

'I'll see if I can find out where Stanley Moore is,' Charlie said. 'You concentrate on Sir Mark.' Cramer nodded.

Jordan came over. 'I chased the Israelis up again, but I am having no luck, boss,' he said. 'They just keep saying if anything new comes up on her they will let us know.'

'Okay Jordan, I'll go and see Crick about them, I have to bring him up to speed with the case anyway. What about her phone?' Charlie said.

'I had a good talk with the security,' Jordan replied. 'It's at the top of their priority list. They have my mobile number to tell me straight away if it comes on and what area.'

'Okay, well make sure your phone's fully charged, we don't want to miss that call,' Charlie said. 'In the mean, time do something important and make some tea. I'm gasping.' Jordan walked off.

Charlie picked up his phone on his desk and dialled a number. It was answered after a few rings. 'Hello,' a soft American voice said.

'Hello Amanda, it's Charlie,' he said.

'Charlie, nice to hear your voice, you couldn't keep me out of your mind,' she said. Charlie heard her laugh.

'Something like that, Amanda, but I want a favour,' Charlie said.

'Anything I can help you with, Charlie,' she replied.

'I need to speak to your husband, it's very important but we are having a hard time tracking him down. His office say he's at a meeting in the city of London and can't be contacted,' Charlie said.

'That's right,' Amanda replied. 'Things have gone quite mad here, it's all to do with Mark's company, a takeover has been launched for it. Stanley has got his finger in the pie so to speak, do you want me to get him to phone you?'

'No, we need to sit down and talk to him face to face,' Charlie said.

'Oh, so it's serious then?' Amanda asked.

'It's important to the case that we clear a couple of things up,' Charlie said.

'Okay, give me a few minutes, I'll find out where he is and call you back,' she said.

'Thank you, Amanda,' Charlie said, putting the phone down. He looked up and saw Harry looking at him smiling. 'And what are you smiling at?'

'Nothing boss, just admiring your skills at getting information,' Harry said as Jordan brought a cup of tea over and put it on Charlie's desk. 'Jordan, I hope you haven't forgotten me when you made that,' Harry said, pointing to the cup.

'Not at all Harry, I was just waiting for you to finish your phone calls. I didn't want it getting cold,' Jordan said, walking away.

Harry turned back to Charlie. 'I spoke to the Peckham and Bow teams. They have all the info on the car, so we can only wait now and see if any patrol spot it. Mind you it might not even be in those areas,'

'We don't have many leads on this woman, so anything that might give us a break is welcome,' Charlie said. Jordan came back with a cup of tea for Harry. Charlie continued. 'I've been thinking, Harry. I know we don't want the press all over us, but if we don't get much out of Stanley Moore and Sir Mark, we might have to put her picture out to the press.' Just then Charlie's phone rang, he picked it up straight away.

'Hello Charlie.' He recognised Amanda's accent.

'Amanda, did you find out where your husband is?' Charlie asked.

'Yes he's at an office in Moorgate.' She gave Charlie the address. 'He might not be too happy if you turn up to question him. Apparently he's meeting other bankers and investors involved in the takeover.'

'Some things can't wait,' Charlie said. 'Thanks for your help.'

'That's okay, Charlie. It does mean you owe me a favour though. I will try and think of something,' she said. 'Bye for now, Charlie.'

Charlie put down the phone. 'Harry, you and Jordan get yourselves off to this address.' He passed over the details to Harry. 'That's where Stanley Moore is. If he doesn't want to answer the questions there, or if he's evasive, bring him in.'

'Come on, Jordan,' Harry said, taking a drink of tea. He pulled a face. 'God that's rotten. I don't know why I ask you to make tea.' They left the office, discussing how tea should be made.

Charlie put a call through to Crick, arranging to pop up and see him. 'If you need me', he said to Danny and Cramer, as he got up and walked across the office towards the door, 'I will be up seeing AS Crick.' Danny and Cramer looked up, both nodded then got back to their work.

Manjitt had been sitting beside Tim Green's bed for hours. Cramer had been in touch and told her what was happening, but she felt out of touch with things. A nurse came in and checked Tim's pulse and the saline drip they had him on. Manjitt asked if she had any idea when he would wake up. Could be anytime, the nurse said. At that moment Tim's head moved and his eyes fluttered. The nurse said she would get a doctor and went out. Manjitt leant closer to Tim and called his name. His eyes opened for a second then closed again. Manjitt called Tim again. His head turned in her direction and his eyes opened. Manjitt told him she was a police officer. As she did, a doctor came in with the nurse. He leaned over Tim, shone a light in his eyes and checked his pulse.

'Mr Green, can you hear me?' the doctor asked. Tim made no reply, the doctor leaned in closer and asked again. 'Can you hear me?'

Tim's eyes seemed to open wider and focused. 'Where am I?' he asked.

The doctor stood up straight. 'You're in hospital, Mr Green. Do you know what you have taken?' Tim shook his head. 'You're going to be fine, Mr Green,' the doctor said. Manjitt asked if it was okay if she spoke to him. The doctor said it would be, but that Tim could still drift off to sleep again at anytime. He left after telling the nurse to call him again if there was any change.

Manjitt leaned closer. 'Hello, Tim, I am Detective Constable Virdee. Do you think you could answer some questions?' He turned his head to look at her and went to speak, but seemed to have trouble.

'I think he needs a drink,' the nurse said. She got a glass and filled it with water from a jug beside the bed. She took

Tim's head in one hand and lifted him slightly, putting the glass to his lips. He took a small drink, then a second longer one. The nurse let his head rest back on the pillow. Tim licked his lips a couple of times, then turned his head to Manjitt.

'Where is Rebecca?' he asked.

'We don't know, Tim,' Manjitt said. 'We need your help to find her.' Tim closed his eyes again. 'What happened at your house?' Manjitt asked.

Tim was quiet for a minute, and Manjitt thought he had gone back to sleep. 'She killed the man who came to the door.' he said. without opening his eyes.

' Tim, who was the man?' Manjitt asked.

Tim turned his head again, opening his eyes to look at Manjitt. 'I don't know. He just knocked on the door and asked for Rebecca.'

'So he asked for Rebecca. He didn't ask for anyone else, or use another name?' Manjitt asked.

'Can I have another drink?' Tim said, turning to the nurse. She picked up the glass of water and held it to his lips. After taking another drink, he turned back to Manjitt. 'Another name?' he asked.

'Yes, did he ask for anyone else?' Manjitt said.

'No, he asked for Rebecca. When she came to the door she spoke to him. She told me to go into the front room, and she invited the man in. I was just about to go through the door into the room when I heard a commotion and a crack. I thought something had caught on the door, but when I turned the man was falling to the ground. I thought he had tripped.' He stopped speaking, closing his eyes.

'Go on, Tim, you're doing fine. We need to know what went on,' Manjitt said.

Tim opened his eyes again. 'The man bounced when he hit the floor, I knew something was wrong. Then I saw his eyes.

The man's head was turned towards me, his eyes were just staring blankly ahead. I knew he was dead.'

'What did you do?' Manjitt asked.

Tim shook his head again. 'Nothing, I did nothing. Rebecca stepped over the man and pushed me through the door and sat me on the sofa.' Tim closed his eyes again. 'The man was dead.'

'Did Rebecca say anything to you?' Manjitt asked.

He opened his eyes again, looking at Manjitt. 'She said she would explain everything to me, but I needed a drink. She left me sitting on the sofa. I could see the man lying in the hallway. Rebecca brought me some orange juice and I drank it. That's the last thing I remember.' He settled back again into his pillow.

'I understand Tim. Now I want to ask you about Rebecca, we need to find her,' Manjitt said. 'Can you tell me if you know any friends she might have gone to?'

Tim lay looking up at the ceiling. 'I don't know any of her friends. We never socialised that much, I think I only ever met one girl she knew,' he said.

'What was her name?' Manjitt asked.

'It was the first time I met Rebecca. I'd gone out with a couple of mates, I can't remember the name of the place, but I was at the bar getting a round of drinks in. There were two girls trying to get a drink at the same time, one of them was Rebecca.'

'Do you remember the other girls name?' Manjitt said.

'No, I don't think Rebecca ever mentioned her, and I never saw her again after that night. Can I have another drink?' he said. The nurse brought the glass to his lips and he sat up slightly, taking a drink. The nurse put the glass down and adjusted the pillows so he was sitting up.

'So you never met any of her friends?' Manjitt asked.

'No, as I said, never. We went out as a couple to the cinema or to have dinner, but never with anyone else,' he said.

'Did she go out alone with friends?' Manjitt said.

'No, not that I know of,' Tim said.

'Did she have a job?' Manjitt asked.

'Yes, a part time one. We needed it for the mortgage, so it came in handy. She had been doing a business degree course,' Tim answered.

'What was the job?' Manjitt said.

'It wasn't something she did all the time, it was in a call centre in the city that dealt in stocks and shares around the world, so they had to have twenty four hour cover. Sometimes she worked nights and weekends, but as I say we needed the money.'

'Did she say the name of the firm?' Manjitt asked.

'No. Why did she kill that man?' Tim asked.

'We don't know yet, that's why we have to find her,' Manjitt said.

'Was it to do with Gerald Parkin?' Tim said. 'Did I get her mixed up in that because of the car?'

'We don't think you're to blame, Tim,' Manjitt said. 'I would like to ask you about Gerald Parkin and the car, and what Rebecca said about it.'

Tim closed his eyes. 'I'm really tired,' he said.

The nurse said Manjitt should give the questions a rest now. 'I will come back in the morning Tim,' Manjitt said. He made no response. He had gone to sleep again.

CHAPTER EIGHTEEN

Charlie had run through things with Crick. 'So the officer with the long hair, what is his name?' Crick asked.

'Detective Constable Danny Kane,' Charlie said.

'Yes Kane, so he was right. Well, that should placate the Deputy Commissioner anyway. So you're saying this woman has killed three people.' Charlie nodded. He liked Crick but he wondered how he had risen to his position. He always seemed to be amazed at how they tracked people down. 'And you want me to get pressure onto the Israelis for more information on her.'

'Yes sir, so far they have been very sketchy about what they tell us,' Charlie said.

'Do we think there is some connection with Israel?' Crick said.

'Only that she was in the army. If we knew what she did while she was in it, we might have a better idea about her,' Charlie said.

'Okay, I will make some phone calls, see if I can get some information,' Crick said. 'So you don't think it was the blackmail now that was behind it all.'

'No sir, part of it but not the main thing,' Charlie replied.

'Are we going to tell the press we are looking for a suspect?' Crick asked.

'I don't want to, not just yet. When we have finished questioning a couple of people, I think we can go public then,' Charlie said.

'Later today or tomorrow?' Crick asked. 'I will have all the leading papers and the television in for a press conference.'

'I will phone you as soon as I know the outcome of the questioning,' Charlie said, standing up. 'I have to get back to the office, sir.'

'Okay Charlie,' Crick said. 'I will see if I can get you some answers from the Israelis.'

Harry and Jordan had made good time to Moorgate, due mainly to Jordan's driving with blue lights flashing and horns blaring. The evening traffic was heavy, but Jordan carved his way through it, enjoying himself. When they pulled up outside the office block, Harry looked across at Jordan and said 'Thank you Jordan, I really enjoyed that. Might have taken a few years off me, but glad to see the driving's improved.'

They left the car and went into the office block. The first hurdle was to get past the security, who at first refused to even say that Stanley Moore was in the building. Once Harry had made it clear he would be arresting anyone who lied or obstructed him by way of Jordan actually putting handcuffs on one security guard, they were taken to the third floor. They walked along a corridor, with a glass wall on one side which showed lots of empty offices. They came to one with the blinds down, but lights were on inside. The security guard who had showed them up asked them to wait outside a moment. He knocked and went in closing the door. The door reopened within a minute, and the security guard came out, followed by Stanley Moore and another man. Stanley saw Harry. His face was not showing happiness at the prospect. 'What the hell do you want, I am in very important negotiations,' he said.

Harry ignored his words. 'It's so nice of you to give up your time to see us. We need to ask you a few more questions. Is there another office we could use?'

'Don't you understand, we're at a delicate moment, I don't have time to see you now. Ring me later and we can arrange something then,' Moore said.

'What is it you want with Mr Moore?' the man who came out of the office with Stanley Moore said.

Harry ignored him. 'Mr Moore, I am afraid we need to ask you a few questions now, here, or I can take you to the police station.'

'This is ridiculous,' the man said.

Still taking no notice of the man, Harry said to Stanley Moore 'My time is as precious as yours, now last chance, we speak here or we go to the station now.'

The man went to step between Harry and Stanley Moore, but Jordan stuck an arm out, pushing the man back into the room. 'You mind your own business,' Jordan said. The man looked at Jordan, said nothing, and retreated back into the office.

'Okay, give me a minute to speak to the others and I will be out to talk,' Stanley Moore said, going back into the office and closing the door.

Harry turned to the security guard, 'are any of these office open' he said

The security guard checked the door of the office opposite. The door opened. 'You can use this one' he said.

'Thank you, we won't be needing you any more so you can go,' Harry said.

The security guard looked a little reluctant to leave, but Jordan said 'Go.' The security guard disappeared back down the corridor.

Stanley emerged on his own from the office, and Harry led him into the other one. 'Can we make this as quick as possible?' Stanley said.

'We don't want to take up too much of your time,' Harry

said. 'Why not take a seat?' Harry indicated one of the chairs round a large table. Stanley Moore sat down, Jordan and Harry took seats opposite him.

'Now when I spoke to you last night,' Harry said, 'you told me about your relationship with Jayne Cavill.'

'I didn't have a relationship with her,' Stanley Moore said.

'Did you know that wasn't her real name,' Jordan said.

'No, why should I care, I knew her as Jayne,' Stanley said.

Harry watched him. Stanley Moore seemed not in the least bothered. 'Do you know a girl called Rebecca Rosen?' Harry asked.

'No, never heard of her,' Stanley said,. Harry thought he was telling the truth but he couldn't be sure. He would make a good poker player.

'When you spent time with Jayne, you said you talked about business a lot,' Harry said.

'Yes that's right, what about it?' he asked.

'Did you talk about Sir Mark's company and the problems it was having?' Harry continued.

'We probably did. As I told you she is a smart girl, she had a good knowledge of business practises. I expect she read a lot of financial papers, and anyway I suppose it helped her in the work she was doing to have something to talk about after.' Stanley Moore smiled when he said it.

'Did you know she was spending time with Sir Mark?' Jordan asked.

'No, why should I?' he said.

'Well, we believe she was trying to get information on Sir Mark's company. She had been asking him questions about it, and if she was seeing you and finding more out, she could have a good idea of what was going on,' Harry said.

Stanley Moore sat quietly for a minute. 'Now I think of it, she did seem to know a lot, and thinking back she seemed to ask the right things. So her name was Rebecca, that's a nice name why didn't she use that?'

'We believe she has killed three people, so she wouldn't be using her real name,' Jordan said.

'I suppose not,' Stanley said. 'What was the point of it though?'

'We thought it was tied to Gerald Parkin and his blackmail. We now believe it's to do with Sir Mark's company, share buying and the take over,' Harry said.

Stanley Moore nodded his head. 'Ah I see now, but why would you suspect me to be mixed up with her?'

'Well, if she was finding out information on what Sir Mark was up to, you know how he was going to defend his company from a takeover, she could have been passing that information on,' Harry said. 'And you told us you gave her money and presents.'

'What, you think she was working for me?' he said and laughed.

'What you told us about her might be lies,' Jordan said. 'To cover it up.'

'I think you have got this all wrong,' Stanley Moore said. 'Why would I want to find out what Sir Mark was up to, when I could ask him myself?'

'If you were hoping to profit from the takeover of his company, it would make it worth it,' Jordan said.

'You really are wrong,' Stanley Moore said. 'I'm working with Sir Mark to prevent his company being taken over.' He looked at Harry.

'We'll have to ask Sir Mark about that,' Harry said.

'Well why don't you?' Stanley Moore said. 'He's in the meeting, we have been here trying to work on a plan to stop the takeover.' He stood up. 'Would you like me to get him, so we can clear this up once and for all?'

'If you don't mind,' Harry said,. Stanley Moore went out of the office.

Harry looked at Jordan. 'Well that throws a spanner in the works.'

'I don't get it.' Jordan said.

Stanley Moore came back into the office with Sir Mark Coale. 'Sir Mark here will verify everything I told you,' he said, taking his seat. Sir Mark sat down next to him.

'Before I get onto that,' Harry said. 'Sir Mark, did you employ a private detective agency to find Jayne Cavill?'

'Who told you that?' he said.

'Sir Mark, can you please answer the question?' Harry said.

'Yes, I did,' he replied.

'Why did you do that,' Jordan said.

'I thought she had been snooping around my house,' Sir Mark said.

'Why didn't you mention this last night when we spoke to you?' Harry said.

'It slipped my mind,' Sir Mark said.

'Well, can we just make sure nothing else slips your mind? Otherwise we will be questioning you at a police station, and I'm sure you have more important things to be getting on with,' Harry said.

'Ask away, we need to get back into the meeting,' Sir Mark said.

'Why did you think she was snooping round your house?' Jordan asked.

'Well I didn't think really. I know she was. As I told you, when Angela and I got together we had a lot to drink, well a couple of times when the other girl, Jayne, was there, she would disappear to go to the bathroom or something. I really didn't notice at the time, but my security came and saw me a few days later. I have CCTV in my office at home. Anyway, they had been checking the office tapes. There she was going through my desk. I don't know how she got in it, as it was all locked up, and if I hadn't seen the tapes I would never have known.'

'So why didn't you confront her the next time she came over with Angela?' Harry asked.

Sir Mark smiled. 'That's just it, there wasn't a next time and I knew there wouldn't be.'

'How did you know that?' Jordan asked.

'You won't believe it, but when she had finished going through my desk, she put everything back as it was, but just before she left the office she looked directly at the CCTV camera. Now remember, it's hidden, you shouldn't know its there. Well, she looked right at the camera and blew a kiss.' Sir Mark smiled. 'You have to admire her.'

'Did you ask Angela about her?' Jordan asked.

'Of course I did, but Angela said she did not know where she had moved to and didn't see her except at the parties,' Sir Mark said.

'So you got a private detective to try and find her,' Jordan said.

'Yes, but they haven't been back to me yet,' he said.

'Well, I can tell you they did find her,' Harry said.

'That's good,' Sir Mark said. 'Perhaps now when you speak to her you will find out we have been telling the truth all along.'

'It's not that easy, I'm afraid,' Harry said. 'And as for telling the truth, if you had been as open and honest from the moment we first spoke to you, we might not have another murder on our hands.'

'What do you mean, another murder?' Sir Mark asked.

'The private detective who was looking for her, he found her. He even went to the house she was living at. Unfortunately she killed him,' Jordan said.

'My god,' Stanley Moore said. 'And to think she was in my house. Do you think she had a snoop around when she was there?'

'It's a possibility,' Harry said.

'Is that all?' Sir Mark asked.

Harry looked at Jordan, who shrugged. 'Yes that's all, thank you gentlemen,' Harry said. Sir Mark and Stanley Moore got up and left.

'What do you make of that?' Jordan said.

'I don't know what to make of things. Let's get back to the office and sit down with the boss,' Harry said.

Charlie was sitting at his desk listening to Manjitt, who had arrived back from the hospital, telling him what she had managed to get out of Tim Green. Danny and Cramer were standing listening in. 'So not a lot from him, then?' Charlie asked.

'The doctor said he should be a bit more lucid tomorrow, but she had him believing everything. The part-time job covered her times when she was at the parties, or when she spent nights away,' Manjitt said.

'It doesn't look like he will be able to tell us much about her,' Danny said.

Charlie sat back in his chair and stretched out his arms. 'So we believe he was just being used.' He looked around the team and they all nodded. 'Well, she's hiding out somewhere, we have to hope she makes a mistake when she breaks cover.'

Harry and Jordan came strolling into the office. Charlie saw them and said 'Tell me you got some information that will cheer us up.'

Harry pulled a chair over to the desk and sat down. Jordan stood next to Danny. Harry went over what they had learned. 'So you see boss, we've hit a wall again,' Harry said.

'It was a complete surprise to us when Stanley Moore said Sir Mark was with him,' Jordan said.

Charlie looked at his watch. 'It's getting late, you lot get off home,' Charlie said to the team. 'We can only hope someone spots the car. Jordan, make sure you ring the phone people again, just to make sure they understand how important it is we know right away if her phone goes on.'

Jordan nodded. 'Will do, boss,' he said, walking away with the rest of the team, leaving Charlie at his desk with Harry.

'Well Harry, where do we go from here?' Charlie said.

'Every time it seems we are getting close, things change again,' Harry said. 'We can only hope she makes a mistake, whether its the car or her phone. But the way she's planned things, I wouldn't hold out much luck.'

'What about Stanley Moore and Sir Mark? We seem to have got that wrong,' Charlie said.

'It looks that way boss, but she must have been getting her information from somewhere. It's too much of a coincidence that she has been one step ahead of us,' Harry said.

Charlie's phone rang. He picked it up, it was Julian Squires. Charlie listened to Julian for a couple of minutes and put the phone down. 'Come on Harry, we're going to meet Julian for a drink. He has a few things to tell us,' Charlie said.

It didn't take them too long to get to the city of London. Charlie drove round the back of Blackfriars train station, coming to the security gates. A guard approached the car, Charlie flashed his warrant card at him and the gates were opened. He drove in and found a parking space. 'Where are we off to?' Harry said as they got out.

'Don't worry Harry, the food will be just what you like,' Charlie said, locking the car.

'That's good because I've hardly eaten all day,' Harry said.

They left Blackfriars by the back way, going down onto the path along the river Thames, turned left and walked towards the millennium bridge. Passing under it they took some stairs up and found the entrance to the High Timber restaurant. They were greeted warmly by the manager when they entered, and he asked them if they had booked. Charlie said they were meeting a friend and mentioned Julian's name. The manger smiled, Mr Squires, of course, this way please. He led them to a table where Julian was sitting. It had a great view of the River Thames through the long window that ran down one side of the restaurant. When they were settled in their seats, Julian said 'Shall we order first, then we can talk.'

Harry opened his menu read through it, looked up at Julian and said 'I think I'm going to enjoy it here.'

'Charlie said you would,' Julian replied. 'I can recommend the rib eye steak.'

Harry chuckled. 'Oh yes that will do nicely,' A waiter came with a bottle of wine and a pint of lager.

'This is a very nice wine Charlie, it's South African. Harry I know you appreciate a good lager, so I ordered for you.'

'You carry on Julian, you're doing fine by me,' Harry said, taking a long drink from the glass. 'How did you find this place Julian, I had no idea it was tucked away down here by the river.'

'Through some African friends. Since then I've been back many times. Now let's order.' Julian said.

Their meals had been served and they were all enjoying them. 'So, Julian, what did you want to tell us?' Charlie said.

'Before I left the office, news came through that the British deep sea oil company had been taken over,' Julian said.

Harry looked a little surprised. 'I spoke to Sir Mark Coale earlier,' Harry said. 'He was in a meeting trying stave off the takeover.'

'So the American oil company won,' Charlie said. 'So what happens now?'

'The repercussions have already started,' Julian said. 'Sir Mark has been removed from the board, so have many of the other board members who supported him. The Americans will move in their own people,. I expect tomorrow they will have their staff in the offices going through things,'

'How did they manage to do it so fast?' Harry said. 'I thought these takeovers took ages.'

'Some do,' Julian said. 'Some come out of the blue and happen quickly. It seems the ground was well prepared by the Americans, and this is what might interest you, the shares you asked me about threw their lot in behind the Americans straight away. With what the Americans had acquired themselves it was basically a done deal. Sir Mark should have seen it coming, there are a lot of people in the city who are annoyed with him, a good few fingers have been burnt and from what I hear, some big institutions have lost quite a bit of money through backing him.'

'How much have the Americans paid for it?' Charlie said.

'Fourteen billion pounds,' Julian said.

Harry stopped eating. 'Did I hear you right?' he said.

Julian nodded. 'Now if you remember, I told you about the trust in New York and the bank in Luxemburg who had built up a stake in Sir Mark's company over the last two years, always managing to buy the shares when they were at their lowest. Well, by backing the Americans right away, they have walked away with a profit of over a billion pounds.'

Charlie looked at Harry. 'Now that's a reason for killing.'

Harry nodded. 'Julian, when I questioned Sir Mark earlier he was with Stanley Moore. He told me he was working with Sir Mark to prevent the takeover. So how does he come out of it?'

'That's one of the other repercussions,' Julian said. 'His bank has been underwriting the defence of the oil company. Rumour has it, he has left the bank very exposed financially. They themselves could be open to a takeover now.'

'I met Vincenzo Gallo, the head of the Luxemburg bank, the other night,' Charlie said. 'He had a meeting with Sir Mark and Stanley Moore. They told me they were trying to get him not to join any takeover bid.'

'This was a well-planned raid,' Julian said. 'The Americans must have had an idea Vincenzo Gallo's bank and the trust in New York would back them, otherwise it could have been a lot more expensive and time consuming.'

'So you reckon Stanley Moore's in trouble,' Harry said.

'I would think so,' Julian replied. 'I also picked up on the grapevine his wife has filed for divorce, so it's not a good time for him.'

'Boss, that leaves an opening for you,' Harry said.

Charlie looked at Harry. 'Thank you for the advice,' he said.

'What's this?' Julian said. 'Has Charlie got a secret I don't know about. Come on Harry, let the cat out of the bag.' Charlie sat back and raised his eyebrows.

'I don't know if I should, Julian, it might cost me my job.' Harry looked at Charlie smiling. 'Ah I can always become a private detective. Stanley Moore's wife, Amanda, has the hots for the boss. She was all over him when we went to dinner at their house.'

Julian laughed, 'Charlie, you dark horse.'

'Don't believe everything this ex-Chief Inspector tells you,' Charlie said. Harry joined in the laughter with Julian.

Julian took a drink of his wine. 'She has the reputation for being a formidable operator amongst bankers.' Julian said. 'There were rumours she had a massive disagreement with her husband about backing Sir Mark's company.'

'Maybe that's what has started the divorce,' Harry said. 'Still, the boss won't mind.'

'In that case,' Julian said, 'there is one other thing you might find interesting. The major American bank that backed the bid, it's run by a man called Garfield Crane. He's also the majority shareholder in the bank. I believe he's in the top fifty richest men in the world, one of those men hardly anyone has heard of, but behind the scenes he knows presidents and prime ministers all round the world.' Julian smiled. 'You might get to know him Charlie, if what Harry tells me is true.'

Charlie and Harry looked a little confused. 'I don't get you, Julian,' Harry said.

'Well, Amanda Moore, before she married, was Amanda Crane, daughter of Garfield Crane,' Julian said.

Charlie and Harry sat quiet taking in the information. 'Julian, wouldn't Amanda know that her father was involved in the takeover?' Charlie said.

'I would have imagined she would have. Maybe that's what the trouble with her husband was,' Julian said.

Charlie sat back. 'The other night, she seemed to be on good terms with Vincenzo Gallo. Didn't you say last time we spoke that in the past he worked for Stanley Moore's bank?'

Harry looked at Charlie. 'You think she was involved with him.'

'I don't know Harry, but it's food for thought. Did you say he worked for them?' Charlie asked Julian.

'He didn't work for them, he worked for a bank in the Far East, if I remember rightly in Singapore, that had strong connections to Stanley Moore's bank,' Julian said.

'So he might have met Amanda Moore out there,' Charlie said.

'He may well have done,' Julian said ,'but I don't know, do you want me to keep looking, Charlie?'

'I don't think it would hurt to collect a bit more information,' Charlie said.

'What you thinking, boss,' Harry said.

'Well, if Stanley Moore wasn't passing on information, that only leaves one person,' Charlie said. 'And Amanda Moore seemed to know Vincenzo Gallo a lot more than she let on the other night.'

Harry took a long drink from his lager. Putting the glass down, he said 'So you think she's been playing us.'

'She pushed her husband our way,' Charlie said.

'We'll have to speak to her, boss,' Harry said.

Charlie nodded. 'Let's finish off our dinner, we can sort things out later,' Charlie said.

'Have you had the swimming pool started yet?' Julian asked.

CHAPTER NINETEEN

The phone was ringing. Harry put his hand out from under the bedcovers and located the phone. 'Hello,' he said, his eyes still shut. It was the inspector from Bow. He told Harry a patrol had just come across the car they were looking for. Harry sat up, opening his eyes. He asked about where it was parked. The inspector assured him no one had been near it since it was spotted, and that he had taken all patrols away from around the area where it was parked, except one unmarked car that was parked about a hundred s from it. Harry thanked him and said he would be back in touch soon.

He looked at the clock, four fifteen shone in the dark. He called Charlie, they spoke for five minutes about how they should work things. When he had finished speaking to Charlie, Harry rang the rest of the squad, giving them their instructions.

Danny picked Harry up from his flat. It only took forty minutes from getting the phone call, to arriving at Bow Road police station. After meeting up with the inspector and having a quick chat, it was decided that the inspector would take them out in an unmarked car to have a drive past where the suspect car was parked, so they could see the area for themselves. It was only five minutes' drive from the police station to Parnell Road. 'It's not a great place to leave a car if you don't want it found,' the inspector said. 'This is quite a busy road, especially when the market's on in Roman Road. It's just coming up on the left.' Harry and Danny saw the car as the inspector drove past, not slowing or going too fast. He came up to Roman Road

Market and turned into it, drove about fifty s then came to a stop.

'Where are your guys parked?' Harry asked.

'At the other end of Parnell Road by the traffic lights. They can just see the car, if it moves they will know,' the inspector said.

'You think its been dumped, Harry?' Danny said.

'It might be, but she doesn't know we are onto the car,' Harry said, 'so I reckon she's around this area somewhere. Let's go back.'

The inspector drove them back to the police station. When they arrived they saw the boss's Bentley in the car park. They went in and found the boss talking to a uniformed superintendent. 'Harry, have you had a look?' Charlie said when he saw him come in.

'Yes boss, the inspector took us on a drive by, it's our car,' Harry said.

Charlie nodded. Turning back to the superintendent he said 'Your inspector has really helped us out, that car is connected to three murders. This could be a big breakthrough. I'll let my Assistant Commissioner know how helpful you've been and what a great job your team here have done. Do you mind if I keep the inspector and a couple of his squad with us? We'll need their local knowledge.'

The superintendent looked very happy at what Charlie said. He told Charlie that was no problem, and if he needed any more help to just let him know. Charlie told him he would. Turning back to Harry he said 'Do we have an office.' Before Harry could speak the inspector said they could use their squad room while they were there. He led them up to the first floor. Charlie told the inspector to pop down and wait by the front desk as a couple more of his team would be arriving, and when they do he was to bring them up.

When the inspector had left the office, Danny asked 'Boss

why didn't you just tell that superintendent what to do, you outrank him?'

'Danny, we only just got here. Why upset people? He thinks he is going to get some good words said about him to the top brass at the Yard. He will go out of his way to help now,' Charlie said. 'Harry, what's the score on the Inspector?'

'He's sound, boss,' Harry said. 'I had him on a team when he was a detective constable.'

'That's good then, so what do we reckon on the car?' Charlie asked.

'Well, on the one hand she doesn't know we have the car on our list,' Harry said. 'On the other hand she has not been stupid enough to make any mistakes so far, so the car might have been dumped.'

'But if she doesn't know we're onto the car,' Danny said, 'why would she dump it?'

'We'll wait for the rest of the team to arrive, then work out where we're going to watch the car from, it's the only lead we have at the moment,' Charlie said. 'It could be a long day. I think I'll put a call through to Crick, seeing as he wants to be kept up to date with things. Be nice to get him up early.'

Harry laughed. 'Tell him his daily report might be delayed boss. While you're on the phone, I'll see if I can get us some tea. Come on, Hippie.' Harry and Danny left the office.

Charlie got his phone out and dialled Crick's number, he was smiling as he did.

About five minutes later Harry and Danny came back to the office carrying cups of tea. 'Well done, Harry,' Charlie said as Harry passed him a cup.

'How was Crick?' Harry asked.

'Very tired, by the sound of it,' Charlie said. 'I explained what was going on, so he's up to date with everything. He had one bit of news for us, he made some phone calls yesterday. I won't bother you with the trouble he said he had, but the bottom line is he has a man coming over from the Israeli embassy at one this afternoon to meet us. Crick says he will pass on what they know about Rebecca Rosen.'

'That's something, but I don't know why they just don't send it over,' Harry said.

'Maybe there's more to her than meets the eye,' Charlie replied. At that moment the Inspector came into the office followed by the rest of the team. 'Right now we're all here, take a seat and we'll sort out how we are going to work things.' The Inspector went to leave. 'No Inspector, I want you staying with us too.'

'Oh right, sir,' the Inspector said. He pulled a chair over and joined the rest of the team round the desk.

'Let me start by saying if Rebecca Rosen appears, I don't want her approached until she has got into the car,' Charlie said. 'That way we'll cut down her opportunity to run. If we can trap her in the car it's in our favour. Now Inspector, you know the area, we don't want her to have the chance to drive off. What do you suggest?'

'May I get a map, sir?' the Inspector said.

'Yes of course,' Charlie replied. The Inspector went to another desk, opened a drawer and came back with a map. He laid it out on the desk.

'Now, this is were the car is parked,' the Inspector said. He took a pen from his pocket and made a cross on the map. 'At the moment I have two officers in a car here, I will have to relieve them soon as they have been on all night. Now the car is facing east so it would have to drive past Roman Road. The market's on tomorrow so there is no way she would be able to turn into it because of all the stalls across the road. So that just leaves the two ways, going north to Old Ford Road, or she turns around and goes south to Tredegar Road. There are no other turnings she could use to get off Parnell Road.'

'So how do we get close enough to intercept her?' Harry said.

'There might be a way,' the Inspector said. 'Just here…' he pointed at the map, '…is a fire station. It's only about forty s from where the car is parked. We could put a couple of cars in there. They would be well hidden. And we could use their offices to watch the car, it overlooks where it's parked. We could put some cars along Tredegar Road to cut her off at the junction if she turns the car around to go that way.'

Harry looked at Charlie and nodded.

'I like it, Inspector,' Charlie said. 'Jordan, you take Cramer and Danny with you. Inspector, I know you have been on a long time, are you okay to stick around?'

'Yes sir,' the Inspector said.

Charlie carried on. 'That's good, Jordan, the Inspector will go with you. Make the fire station the main point to keep watch. I don't want any other cars within half a mile. Inspector, can you organise some backup in the roads you indicated that we should block off if she gets in the car?' The Inspector nodded. 'Make sure they understand we're dealing with someone who has killed three people, so they should be very careful how she is approached. But if we can catch her inside the car it will be to our benefit. I will have a word with your Superintendent, he can speak to the fire station commander about us using the place. Any questions?' No-one said anything. 'Okay, get going. I want you in position before too many people are up and about'. Jordan and the other three left the office.

'The Inspector seems a good one, Harry,' Charlie said.

'He is, boss, as I said he worked for me years ago, I'm surprised he's still only an inspector. I know he has had a couple of run-ins with some of his commanders, maybe they found him too much to handle,' Harry said.

'What's his name?' Charlie asked.

'Ankudinov. His dad was Russian, when he worked for me everyone called him Lenin,' Harry said. 'In fact I still do.'

'Harry, political correctness passed you right by,' Manjitt said. 'I hate to think what you call me,'

Harry smiled. 'It's usually beautiful.'

'Oh, in that case Lenin is fine by me,' Manjitt said, smiling back at Harry.

'Well, now you two have become great friends, Manjitt, what about Tim Green,' Charlie said.

'I will call the hospital later, see how he is. If they say he will be able to stay awake and answer questions I will go over there,' she said.

'Harry, I really want to have a chance to call in on Amanda Moore today, but it all hangs on what happens here,' Charlie said.

'Don't forget we have a meeting at one with the Israelis back at the Yard,' Harry said.

'I will pop up and see the Superintendent,' Charlie said. I will meet you two by my car in ten minutes. I fancy some breakfast, we'll go find a café.'

Charlie and Harry were back at the Yard. It was twelve thirty. They had left Manjitt with two of the inspector's officers in one of the cars parked in Tredegar Road. The hospital had told her Tim Green would not be able to answer any questions till later on in the afternoon. 'No word from Jordan yet,' Harry said.

'Nothing, she might be waiting a day or two, hoping things have calmed down,' Charlie said.

'Let's hope not,' Harry said.

Charlie stood up. 'Let's go up to Crick's office.'

Rebecca Rosen looked at her watch, twelve forty five, time to make a move. She locked the briefcase, picked up the passport in the name of Liza Clinton and put it in the pocket of the jacket she had on, then walked over to the mirror on the wall and checked how she looked. The business suit she had bought yesterday fitted the image she wanted perfectly. Walking back to the coffee table, she took three hundred pounds from the money that wouldn't fit in the briefcase, tucked that in with the passport, then picked up her phone. She was going to switch it on, but thought she would wait just a little longer before doing that. Taking hold of the briefcase and having one last look around the flat, she left.

Danny was sitting by the first floor office window of the fire station commander, which over looked Parnell Road. He could see the car clearly from his vantage point. The Inspector was sitting with him. 'Did I hear Harry say you've worked with him before?' Danny asked.

'Yes a good few years ago. I was a detective constable, Harry was my inspector, I learned a lot from him, he kept me out of some trouble too,' he said.

'What was he like back then?' Danny said.

'Well, I don't know if he's mellowed but he knew how he liked things done, didn't care who he told. I've seen him have some standup rows with senior officers. I'm surprised he wasn't kicked out of the force,' he said.

'He's not mellowed,' Danny said, chuckling. 'But you're right, he's a great one to learn from.'

'What about the Chief Superintendent? He's a bit of a legend in the force, everybody's heard the stories of his flash cars and designer clothes, and someone told me he has a big house in the country. The rumours of how he can afford them are rife,' the inspector said.

'Let me ask you something,' Danny said, turning slightly to look at the inspector. 'Do you trust Harry?'

'Yes, one hundred per cent,' he said.

366

'So if Harry told you something, you would believe him. You wouldn't doubt his word?' Danny said.

'No, I would trust what he said as true,' the inspector said.

'Well, Harry told me the boss is the best copper he has worked with and is as straight as an arrow,' Danny said.

The inspector nodded. 'That's good enough for me.'

Danny turned back to look at the car. 'Anyway, it's not a big house in the country, its massive, got over fifty acres around it. The best thing is he's having a swimming pool built, so come the summer I know where I will try to get invited.'

Rebecca Rosen stepped out into the street. She had a quick look up and down it, traffic was moving normally. She scanned the parked cars, nothing. If she turned right she would be walking up towards Tredegar Road, back in the direction of the car. She turned left and walked down Fairfield road. It was about a five minute walk before she would reach Bow Road.

Jordan came into the fire station office. 'Do you think she will show up, Hippie?' he asked.

Danny looked over his shoulder. 'My guess is as good as yours.'

'Harry and the boss have gone back to the Yard for a meeting with Crick,' Jordan said.

'Where's Manjitt?' Danny asked.

'Harry said they had left her tucked up in a car with a couple of the inspector's men,' Jordan said.

'Oh you better warn them inspector, if they want to get out of that car alive, they don't want to be chatting her up,' Danny said.

The inspector laughed. 'Hippie's not joking,' Jordan said. His phone rang, he listened for a moment and waved his hand at Danny. Okay, I will keep this line on, you feed me the details as you get them,' he said into the phone. He put his hand over it. 'Come on you two, let's go.' Danny and the inspector followed Jordan out of the office.

'What is it Jordan,' Danny said.

'Her phone's just been switched , and according to the mobile people it's in this area. They're just trying to narrow the fix down,' Jordan said.

'But the car's still parked up,' Danny said.

'She must have another somewhere,' Jordan replied.

Rebecca Rosen had reached Bow Road. The traffic was fairly busy for lunchtime, she took her phone from her pocket and switched it on. She knew they would be tracking her phone, that's what she was relying on. She stood by the traffic lights. She wanted to get to the other side of the road. She would take a taxi to the airport. The lights changed so she could cross, but she remained where she was. The traffic lights changed two more times, but she stood watching the traffic slowly moving past. Finally she spotted what she wanted. The lorry came level with her, it had an open back, there was some wood and pieces of metal piled on it. As it got close, it slowed with the traffic. She stepped into the road, moving close to the lorry, putting her hand up and over the side and dropping the phone into the back of the lorry. She carried on walking between the traffic, reaching the island in the middle of the road. Turning, she saw the lorry heading off, away from the direction she would be taking. She crossed from the island to the far side of the road, walked about twenty yards and stopped, turned and looked for a taxi.

Jordan and the others piled into the car. Jordan had his phone pressed against his ear. 'They say she's moving south of us.'

The inspector was at the wheel of the car. He pulled out of the fire station turning left. 'Hippie, ring the boss and let him know we are on the move. Cramer ring Manjitt, give her a commentary of where we are going so she can catch up.'

Assistant Commissioner Crick was just introducing Mr Dyan from the Israeli embassy to Charlie and Harry. Charlie felt his phone vibrate, he took it from his pocket, he told Crick he had to take the call as it was important. Crick sat looking at Charlie as he spoke on the phone for a couple of minutes. 'Sorry about that sir, it was to do with the investigation,' Charlie said.

'Well let's get on,' Crick said. 'Mr Dyan has kindly come here to answer some of your questions on Rebecca Rosen.'

It was Charlie who spoke first. 'Mr Dyan, we understand Rebecca Rosen was in the army. Now we have established she stayed in it for six years, but can you tell us what she did while she was in it?'

Dyan was seated next to Crick. He opened a case in front of him and took out a sheet of A4 paper. 'I will not be giving you any written information on her, but I will tell you her background. I have been assured that none of the information I give you will get out to the press.' Harry and Charlie nodded. 'If it were to appear, it could have implications for any future cooperation between our police forces.'

'I can assure you of my officers' discretion,' Crick said.

'Thank you,' Dyan said. 'She was in the army, but when her conscription time finished, she joined Shabak. You might know it as Shin Bet. It's the equivalent to your MI5. After she had spent time training, it was felt that she could do some things abroad, so she was seconded to Mossad, which is our foreign intelligence service. She was a very skilled agent. She came back and worked in Israel again, but when she was doing some further work abroad, it was felt that she had compromised a mission through passing information to someone. She was dismissed from the organisation after that.'

'Is that it?' Harry said.

'What else would you like to know?' Dyan said.

'So you're telling us she worked as a spy,' Harry said.

'She was an agent for the state of Israel,' Dyan said.

'Okay, what was this agent's training. Could you tell us about that so we have some idea of the person we are dealing with?' Harry asked.

Dyan looked at the paper in front of him. 'She was trained in the usual subjects, she's highly skilled in self defence, surveillance and counter surveillance, also breaking and entering premises.'

'She's an all round good thing then,' Harry said.

'Don't you think you might have told us all this when we first enquired?' Charlie said. 'We are dealing with someone who has now killed three people.'

'I believe your own government would not openly admit if one of their agents was mixed up in something abroad,' Dyan replied.

'So you kicked her out. I don't suppose you want to expand on that,' Harry said. Dyan shook his head no.

'You must keep track of your agents, whether they're still working for you or not,' Charlie said.

'We do our best,' Dyan replied.

'So can you tell us where she has been since you threw her out?' Harry asked.

Dyan looked at his paper again. She spent some time in Italy, then went to the Far East, then she came back to Europe.'

'Does she come from a rich family?' Charlie asked.

'No,' Dyan answered.

'Don't take this the wrong way, Mr Dyan,' Harry said. 'But trying to get an answer out of you is like pulling teeth.'

'There's no need to talk to Mr Dyan like that, Chief Inspector' Crick said, giving Harry a dirty look.

'That's alright,' Dyan said, 'I take that as a compliment.' he smiled at Harry.

'I bet you do,' Harry said, getting another look from Crick.

'So if she doesn't come from a rich family you must have paid her well, if she was jetting around the world,' Charlie said.

'The Israeli army does not pay well,' Dyan said. Charlie waited but Dyan didn't expand on his answer.

'So can you hazard a guess as to where her money came from?' Charlie asked.

Dyan smiled at Charlie. 'I believe she met some rich friends when she was in Italy.'

Charlie nodded. 'I think I am getting the hang of this now,' he said. 'Do you know who they might be?'

Dyan nodded to Charlie, smiling. 'I believe they were involved in banking.'

Harry chuckled. 'Oh I see now,' he said, looking at Charlie. 'Can I ask one, boss?' Charlie nodded. 'You wouldn't happen to know the name of these friends?'

'I understand…' he looked at the paper in front of him, '… that the family name was Gallo.'

Crick was looking a little confused and asked 'Hasn't that name come up in the investigation? I seem to remember it in one of your reports.'

'That's very observant of you, sir,' Harry said. Crick missed the sarcasm. 'Could you tell us if you know whether she got a job?'

'We understand she went to work as part of the personal security for the banker,' Dyan said.

'Was the banker's name Vincenzo Gallo?' Harry said.

Dyan looked down at his paper again. 'No, that wasn't the name.'

Harry looked at Charlie and raised his eyebrows. 'Do you have a name for the banker she worked for?' Charlie asked

'Alberto Gallo' Dyan said, smiling at Harry.

Harry smiled back. 'You wouldn't happen to know if he is in anyway related to Vincenzo Gallo?'

'I believe he is the father,' Dyan said.

Charlie looked at his watch, one thirty. 'You have been very helpful,' he said, 'even if it took us a little time to work out the rules.'

Crick looked at Charlie and then at Dyan, not understanding what Charlie meant. 'Have you not tried to get her back to Israel to speak to her yourselves?'

'We would like to have, how would you say, a chat,' Dyan said. 'Some departments believe she should answer for interfering in an operation, they are very annoyed and now you have told us she is involved in criminal behaviour, it could bring embarrassment and press investigations, which they would not take too kindly to.'

'Hopefully if we get our hands on her you can have her after, but again thanks for your time,' Charlie said.

'I'm glad I could be of help,' Dyan replied, 'and I know I can rely on you not to allow any of this to get out.'

'You can,' Charlie said, standing up. 'We will be getting back to the investigation now sir,' he said, turning to Crick. He and Harry shook hands with Dyan and left the office.

Once outside Harry said 'Don't you just love those loose-tongued spooks?'

'They have their own way of not saying anything unless you ask the right question, Harry,' Charlie said. 'Now Rebecca Rosen is on the move, the team are tracking her phone so let's get the car.'

Jordan was still relaying the information to the inspector on the route they should follow. Manjitt was in the car behind which had caught up with them. Both cars were travelling along the A12, just coming up to Gants Hill roundabout.

'They say she can't be that far away from us now,' Jordan said.

Rebecca Rosen got out of the taxi that had taken her to London City Airport, paying the driver. She walked through the main doors and made her way to the Air France desk. She asked if her ticket was there, showing her passport. The ticket was passed over and she was told there were no delays, her flight would take off at three as scheduled. Looking at her watch the time was one forty five. Picking up a free newspaper from the display by check-in she walked over to the coffee bar. Taking a seat she put her briefcase down beside the chair, opening the paper to have a read. A waiter approached and she ordered a coffee.

Archie Salmon had been wandering around Woolwich seeing if there were any easy pickings to be had. He had bumped into a few mates who were on the look out for the same thing, he wanted to get enough money together to see his dealer later and get a couple of wraps of heroin. He went in the opposite direction from his mates, he didn't want any competition or to share any of the spoils he might get. He stood outside Prince Regent train station on the Docklands Light Railway, watching passengers coming and going, but none looked worth the trouble of robbing. He decided to head towards Beckton Retail Park, he could wander around the car parks and shops, there was bound to be something he could steal. He could go by the big Excel centre, but he knew there were no conferences on today so it would be empty, nothing to rob there. He decided to wander past the airport. It was dangerous there as security was always tight. You usually only got one look around before they spotted you and threw you out, but it was on the way to the retail park so he would give it a look.

He had been standing opposite the taxi drop off point outside the airport. He hadn't seen any security on the main doors, he knew they would spot him as he only had on a dirty hooded top, scruffy jeans and trainers, not something someone who was waiting to board a plane would be wearing. But he had nothing to lose, they could only throw him out. As he crossed the road his eye caught a woman paying a taxi off. She was dressed in a smart business suit that shouted to him money. In her hand she had a large briefcase. He stopped when he reached the same side of the road as her, and watched as she entered the airport. Moving to the doors but not going in, he saw her walk over to an airline desk. She was there for a minute or so, then picking up a paper she walked over to the coffee bar, sitting down at a table. He watched as she placed the briefcase on the floor beside her, she started to read the paper. He waited as he saw a waiter bring her a coffee. He had a look around the concourse, he didn't see any security but knew he would get one chance at the briefcase. Walking through the doors making directly for the coffee bar, he came up behind the woman who was drinking her coffee and reading the paper. He didn't look left or right but his eyes stayed on her. As he got closer he held his breath. Kneeling down slightly behind her chair, his hand snaked out grasping the briefcase. He slowly slid it backwards. Once it was clear of the chair he stood up with it, turned and made for the doors, still holding his breath. He expected the woman to shout or security to stop him any second. Getting to the doors and passing through, he turned right, heading back towards Canning Town. The briefcase felt heavy; hopefully it had a mobile phone or lap top inside. He would make for home and get it open. As long as he got enough money from the fence he would sell them to, he would be happy. The briefcase might be worth a few pounds on its own.

They had been told by the mobile phone company to turn right

374

at Gants Hil.l 'They say she's heading towards Ilford,' Jordan said. The inspector drove the car down Cranbrook Road.

'Where is she off to?' Cramer said. He had a map out on his lap.

'The boss and Harry are on their way,' Danny told Jordan, who nodded.

'Pull over, inspector, they say she has come to a stop,' Jordan said. 'They are just trying to narrow the spot down.'

The inspector pulled over. The car Manjitt was in stopped behind them. Everyone sat quietly, waiting for Jordan to get instructions.

Rebecca Rosen heard the call for the boarding of the Air France flight to Luxembourg. She folded the paper and reached out her hand to pick up the briefcase. Not feeling it, she looked down, checked the other side of the chair; it was gone. She looked all around her. Seeing no one carrying it, she sat back in the chair shaking her head. Some secret agent you are, she thought, laughing to herself she stood up. Someone will have a nice surprise when they open the case. She walked across the concourse to the passport control.

Harry was on the phone to Danny. 'They've stopped in Cranbrook Road,' he said to Charlie, who had just turned the Bentley onto the start of the A12 by the Blackwall tunnel. The emergency lights were on the top of the car, he still had to press the horn to move cars out of the way, who didn't seem to see the blue lights coming up behind them.

Archie Salmon had retraced his steps back towards his flat, just passing Prince Regent station. He was excited that he would score later; the day might just turn out to be a good one.

'Have a look at him.' PC Morris turned his head to look where his partner was pointing. I don't think he looks the city type, do you?' The two police officers were sitting in their patrol car in a side turning. 'I think I know him,' PC Morris said. 'I have pulled him a couple of times for street robberies.' As he said it, his partner started the patrol car. Pulling out onto the main road they came up slowly behind Archie Salmon. As they got alongside him, PC Morris opened his door and jumped out. He had hold of Archie before he even realised the police were there. 'You off to work?' Morris said.

'I've done nothing wrong,' Archie protested.

Morris took the briefcase from Archie's hand. 'Is this your briefcase?' he asked.

'I just found it,' Archie said.

'Oh really, and where were you going with it?' Morris asked.

'I was going to hand it in,' Archie said.

'Get in the back of the car, we can chat,' Morris said, taking Archie by the arm and guiding him to the rear door of the patrol car. Once he had Archie in the back, he climbed into the front beside his partner. Half turning in the seat to look at Archie he said, 'I know you, don't I?'

Archie looked at him. He couldn't remember this copper, 'I don't think so.'

'Yes I do,' Morris said. 'I nicked you a few months back for robbery.'

'I think you got me mixed up with someone else,' Archie said.

'What's your name?' Morris said.

'Archie Salmon,' he replied.

'So where did you find this briefcase?' Morris's partner asked.

'It was up there.' Archie pointed in the direction of the station.

'I think you've nicked it,' Morris said.

'I found it,' Archie replied.

'Okay, we'll go to the police station to sort things out,' Morris said. Archie slumped back in the seat; maybe the day wasn't going to be good.

Manjitt had walked up to the first car and was standing next to it talking to Cramer. Jordan still had the phone to his ear. He had his window down. Looking at Cramer and Manjitt he said 'You two, we don't have time for a cosy chat about what you will be doing later.'

'Harry says he and the boss are about fifteen minutes from us,' Danny said from the back seat of the car.

'Okay everyone, we're moving,' Jordan called out. Cramer climbed in the back with Danny. Manjitt ran back and got in the car behind. 'Keep following the road down,' Jordan said to the inspector. 'We should come up to Ilford train station. They say it has stopped round the back of that.' The inspector drove down Cranbrook Road.

'There's the station,' Danny said, pointing from the back seat.

'Pull over by the station,' Jordan said to the inspector. 'Danny, call Harry, ask him what he wants us to do.'

Danny got on the phone to Harry.

Rebecca Rosen looked at her watch. Two thirty. She was queuing up to board the plane, she was annoyed with herself that she had lost the briefcase, a silly thing to do. It wasn't the money so much as her own passport which was inside. Still, she would sort that out when she was home. She found her seat and sat down. She looked out of the window at the old docks which had been converted into the airport and upmarket flats. She had enjoyed her time in Britain. Maybe I will come back again sometime and do some proper sightseeing, she thought, settling back into her seat. Doing her safety belt up, she closed her eyes.

Harry had taken the call from Danny. 'They're sitting outside Ilford station, he says that she has stopped round the back of it,' he said to Charlie.

'I think we should get the locals in to block all the roads that lead away from the station, tell Jordan to get the inside of the station covered so she doesn't get on a train, then get round the back see if they can spot her,' Charlie said.

Harry spoke to Danny. He then put a call through to Ilford police station, requesting all available officers to Ilford station.

'There's one thing that worries me, Harry,' Charlie said.

'What's that, boss?' Harry asked.

'Well, we know what a smart woman she is. She's has been one step ahead of us all the way, and after meeting our friend from the Israeli embassy this seems a bit to simple. Do we think she would really make such a simple mistake as turning her phone on, she would know we would be monitoring it.' Charlie said.

'You think she has given it to someone else?' Harry said.

'I don't know Harry, but I have a bad feeling,' Charlie said.

CHAPTER TWENTY

PC Morris was standing in the custody suite of Canning Town police station. He had placed the briefcase on the duty sergeant's desk. Archie Salmon stood beside him, he was looking down. 'We picked him up with this briefcase sarge, he said he found it,' Morris said.

The sergeant looked up at Archie. 'Come on, you might as well tell us where you got it,' he said.

Archie looked at the sergeant. 'I found it, I told him that.' He pointed at Morris.

'Okay, if you want to stick to that I will write it up. Put him in number two cell, we will get you out in a while for questioning,' the sergeant said.

Morris took Archie away to the cells. When he got back the sergeant had finished the paperwork. 'Have you checked on the system to see if there are any reports of bag snatches?' the sergeant said to Morris.

'No not yet sarge, I will do now, there's no way he found that bag,' Morris said.

'Have you tried to open it, to see if there's an address inside?' the sergeant asked.

'I did in the car, but it's locked,' Morris replied.

'Okay, check if anyone has reported a theft, if not we will have to break the lock,' the sergeant said.

Ilford station and the surrounding area was swamped with police officers, the traffic had become gridlocked. It took Charlie longer than he thought it would to get there because of the traffic. When he finally arrived, he found the inspector outside the station organising the local officers. He told Charlie the rest of the team were around the back of the station. Charlie and Harry made their way around the station to the back. Finding the rest of the squad checking all the parked cars, Jordan said that the phone company had told him she had to be within a hundred radius, and she had not moved since stopping. There were no houses, so she was either in the station or hiding in a car. No-one was being allowed into the area, and everyone leaving the station was being checked.

Charlie stood with Harry watching the squad and local police going over the cars. 'What do you reckon, Harry,' he said.

'The area's sealed off, but we know she can become invisible when she wants,' Harry said. 'I'm starting to think you might be right boss, it might be another wild goose chase.'

Morris came back to his sergeant, he hadn't found any report on the theft of a briefcase. 'He might have nicked it from a car and no-one has found out yet,' the sergeant said. 'Oh well, you'd better break it open, see if there's something in it with an address on.'

Morris took his keys out, he had a pen knife on the key ring. He proceeded to try and prise the case open. It didn't budge. 'This lock is solid,' he said to the sergeant, who was sitting behind his desk.

'You'd better get a big screwdriver or something,' the sergeant replied. Morris went away, coming back a minute later with a large screwdriver. He proceeded to work on the briefcase lock.

'I can feel it starting to give,' he said. There was a snap and the lock broke. Morris opened the case. 'Jesus,' he said.

'What you got?' the sergeant asked. Morris turned the case to show him. The sergeant stood up when he saw what was in the case.

'There's a passport tucked in the side,' Morris said. Pulling it out, he had a quick look and passed it to the sergeant. 'How much do you think is here?' he asked.

'I have no idea,' the sergeant said. Opening the passport he glanced at it. 'You'd better get in touch with this woman. She might need to tell us where she got this money from.' He went to hand the passport back, suddenly stopped, and had another look at the passport and the picture. 'Don't touch anything else in the case,' he said, showing Morris the passport. 'This is the woman they have been looking for in connection with the three murders. I'll ring Scotland Yard, you get the prisoner into an interview room.'

She felt that moment when the wheels left the ground and the plane began to soar into the air. At London City Airport it was even more pronounced as the planes went into a steep climb straight after take off, Rebecca Rosen opened her eyes and watched London getting smaller below, her watch said one minute past three, she would be landing in Luxembourg in about forty five minutes.

They had looked in most of the cars in the car park. The inspector had informed Charlie that everyone had been evacuated from the station and checked the suspect wasn't amongst them. Manjitt and Danny were over in the far corner where some building work was being done. 'Looks like she has slipped through our fingers again,' Harry said.

'She's a bit of a ghost, Harry,' Charlie replied.

Jordan came over to them. 'We've checked nearly every car, nothing boss.'

'Hippie is waving his arms,' Harry said. Charlie and Jordan both turned to see Danny standing on the back of a lorry. They walked over to him. Manjitt was standing beside the lorry looking up at Danny as the rest arrived at the lorry.

'Well Hippie, what's got you excited?' Harry said.

Danny lent down at the at the back of the lorry. 'I think we have the phone,' he said, bringing a mobile into view.

'How did you spot that, Hippie?' Jordan asked.

'I've been ringing her number as we've been searching, and I suddenly heard it,' Danny said.

'Well done, Danny,' Charlie said.

'She could be anywhere now,' Harry said.

'Does this mean we have been following the phone and not the woman?' Danny asked, as he jumped down from the lorry.

'You have it in one,' Charlie said. 'Come on, let's get back to the cars and head for the office, see if we can work out how she has pulled this off. Jordan, let the inspector know to call off the search and unblock the roads.'

As they got back to the Bentley Harry said 'She's made right mugs out of us again.'

'It's getting a habit,' Jordan said.

As they stood beside the Bentley, Charlie's phone went off. He listened for a minute, spoke and then rang off. 'That was Canning Town police. They have just picked a up a known street robber with a briefcase full of money and Rebecca Rosen's passport. Jordan you come with me to Canning town, Harry you take the rest of the squad back to the Yard, catch up on everything that needs tiding up and say thanks to the inspector who helped us out.' Charlie looked at his watch, it read three fifteen. 'As soon as we have anything I will call you.'

When they had arrived at Canning Town police station, Charlie and Jordan were met by a detective inspector. He told them what they knew about the man they were holding, where he had been stopped and what he had told them. He said his officers had counted the money; there was £150,000. Holding open the case so they could see the money, he handed Charlie the passport and a file on Archie Salmon. Charlie looked through it. Passing it to Jordan he said to the detective inspector 'Okay, I think we should have a word with this character'.

He and Jordan followed the detective inspector to an interview room. When they entered, Archie Salmon was seated at a table. He was leaning back talking to a constable. The constable stood up, he was told to leave by the detective inspector. Charlie sat down. Jordan leaned on the wall to the side, the DI sat down next to Charlie.

'Now Archie, I want you to tell us where you got the briefcase,' the DI said.

Archie looked at Charlie and Jordan. 'Who are these two?' he said. 'I've never seen them around here before.'

'Are you deaf?' Jordan shouted. It made Archie jump, even the DI was a bit shocked.

'I think what my colleague is saying in his own way is can you answer the detective's question,' Charlie said.

Archie looked back and forth between the two. 'I told you, I found it.' He lent back in the chair smiling.

'We don't believe you,' the DI said.

'I really don't care what you believe, that's my story,' Archie said. He knew they didn't have any idea where he had got the bag or they would have charged him already.

Charlie opened the file he had been given on Archie Salmon. 'From your file I see you're a petty robber and a drug user,' he said.

Archie looked at the big bald man sitting in front of him, 'I don't have to answer your questions,' he said to Charlie. He looked at Jordan. 'What are you staring at, bro?'

Jordan laughed. 'Did he just call me bro?' he said to no-one in particular, walking around the back of Archie Salmon, who was still leaning back in the chair smiling and feeling clever. Jordan kicked the back leg of the chair. Archie hit the ground hard. Before he had time to say or do anything, he felt the big black policeman grab him by the collar and lift him so he was suspended in the air facing him. 'Do I look like your bro?' Jordan snarled into Archie's face. He didn't wait for an answer, he shook Archie like a rag doll. 'I am not your bro, you understand?' Archie nodded. This copper is mad, he thought. Jordan let go of him, stood the chair up straight then grabbed Archie and shoved him down into the chair.

'Now before we carry on, do you want to change your story?' Charlie asked.

'No, I found it,' Archie said defiantly.

'Oh dearm' Charlie said, 'Can you put the case on the table please?' The DI picked it up and put in on the table. 'Now Mr Salmon, is this the case you say you found?'

Archie looked at it. 'It might be'

'I'm sure it will have your fingerprints on it.' Charlie opened the briefcase. Archie Salmon's eyes widened when he saw all the money.

'A lot of money isn't it. Do you want to tell us where you got it from?' Charlie asked.

'What do you mean?' Archie said, dragging his eyes from the money and looking at Charlie.

'I think you should come clean,' Charlie said. 'We know this money is mixed up with three murders, what we don't know is your part in them. If you tell us, maybe we can put a word in for you but I can't guarantee you won't get twenty years.'

It took a little time for the phrase twenty years to register with Archie, he was still thinking of the bag full of all that money. 'Twenty years, what you talking about?' Archie said.

'I am going to have to charge you with conspiracy to murder,' Charlie said. 'It would seem to me that you're moving this money about for the person we suspect was involved with the killings.' Charlie put Rebecca Rosen's passport on the table. 'Now I am going to give you one chance to tell the truth. You see I have not had a good day, so it's up to you.'

Archie looked at the policeman who had spoken to him. He had never seen him before. He turned to the detective inspector who he knew. 'I don't know anything about a murder and I didn't know the bag had all that money in. You know me, I'm not someone who would be mixed up in murder.' The DI said nothing; he knew it was the call of the Chief Superintendent.

Charlie pushed his chair back and sighed. 'Where did you get the bag, it's your last chance.'

Archie wasn't sure how to play this copper, but he wasn't going to let himself be pushed around. 'I found it,' he said.

Charlie shook his head and stood up. Turning to Jordan he said 'Charge him with conspiracy to murder.' Charlie picked up the bag and passport, turned and left the interview room.

Jordan grabbed Archie by the hoodie he had on, lifting him from the chair. 'Come on bro,' Jordan said. 'We're going to charge you.'

'Wait a minute,' Archie cried. He was on tip-toe, being half-dragged by Jordan to the door.

'Too late, my friend,' Jordan said. 'We only give one chance.' He shoved Archie into the arms of the D.I. 'If you can take him down to the custody suite, I will see my boss and get any other charges he wants to put on him.' Jordan walked off down the corridor.

The DI turned to Archie. 'You got yourself in big trouble now.'

Archie pulled himself up straight. 'Who do they think they are?' he said. 'I'm not going to be pushed around.'

'You're an idiot,' the DI said. He pushed Archie up against the wall. 'Do you realise what's going on, these coppers are not messing about and they don't like people messing them about. Get it into your brain, you could get a life sentence for what they are going to charge you with. Am I making myself clear?'

Archie looked at the DI. He had met him a few times when he had been nicked before. He had always been fair. Maybe he should see if he can swing a deal. 'Okay,' he said. 'I will tell you everything I know but I want a deal.'

The DI shook his head. 'I don't think you realise you had the deal in there, but you turned it down. I think that superintendent wants to put you away for twenty years. I don't think there's anything I can do for you now. You won't get bail, you will be locked up till it goes to trial.'

Archie was now beginning to panic a little. The thought of twenty years in prison was getting through to him. 'Okay no deal, I will tell you everything straight,' he said.

The DI took him back into the interview room. Sitting him down, he told Archie he would go and see if he could persuade the other officers to give him one last chance.

The DI walked into the office along from the interview room. Charlie and Jordan were sitting drinking tea. Jordan stood up. 'Do you want a cup, sir?' he said to the DI, who declined the offer. Turning to Charlie he said 'He's ready to spill all he knows.'

'That's good, thanks for the heads up on him,' Charlie said to the DI. 'You're right about him, he does seem a cocky sod. Jordan, you go back in and take the statement with the DI.'

About forty-five minutes later Charlie was parking the Bentley outside London City Airport. He had called Harry to keep him up to date on what they were doing. Archie Salmon had told them all he did to get the briefcase. He had given them a full description of the woman who was carrying the bag and how he stole it. Charlie and Jordan made their way into the airport, going to the security office.

Harry was sitting in the office alone. He had sent the rest of the team home, except Manjitt, who had gone off to the hospital to take a statement from Tim Green. It had been a long day. The report of the day's events was written up in front of him. He sat back and stretched. Charlie and Jordan walked into the office. 'Not keeping you up, Harry?' Charlie said walking towards him.

'I can see by your faces that it was like the rest of this investigation, chasing a ghost.' Harry said.

Charlie flopped into his chair. Jordan waved a DVD. 'We have something for you to watch, Harry,' Jordan said. He went to the television and pulled it across to the desk. He put the DVD in and pressed play. 'It's edited down, so you just get the good bits.' The three of them watched the television for ten minutes. When it had finished, Jordan switched the TV off.

Harry turned to Charlie. 'The blonde woman, that's her is it?' he said.

'Yes, if it hadn't been for the lowlife stealing her bag, we would have no idea where she had gone or what she looked like,' Charlie said.

'But we have her passport,' Harry said.

'She was using an American passport in the name of Liza Clinton,' Jordan said.

'Where did she fly off to?' Harry asked.

Charlie smiled at Harry. 'Luxembourg.'

Harry laughed. 'Now that doesn't surprise me.'

'Jordan, take the DVD down to Danny's mates and get some stills from it,' Charlie said. 'Then send them off with a full report on her to Interpol and the police in Luxembourg. Make sure they know she is on our most wanted list.' Jordan took the DVD from the television and left.

'So boss what do we do now,' Harry said.

'We need to speak to Amanda Moore,' Charlie said, 'but I don't see us getting hold of Rebecca Rosen any time soon.'

'You think Vincenzo Gallo was involved?' Harry asked.

'I think there are still questions a few people need to answer, Harry. I'm not sure if we will get to ask them though' Charlie said. He picked up the phone on his desk. 'I am going to get hold of Crick to let him know what's happened. I dare say he will call a press conference.'

CHAPTER TWENTY ONE

The two men entered the office. They stood in front of the desk of the old grey-haired man who was reading a file he had been given. Looking up he said 'I have received a flash report from London. It's about time this problem was sorted out.' He passed the file over to one of the men. 'It could get very embarrassing for us, I don't think we should take the risk of anything getting into the papers, or one of our ex-employees finding themselves in a British court.'

'How would you like it dealt with?' the man who took the file asked.

The old man looked at him. 'I don't want this problem to come up again.' The two men left the office.

The old man turned his chair to look out of his office window, looking down on Charles Clore garden. It was in full bloom. He would have a walk through it before he went home.

Jordan had come back to the office with news that he had sent the new pictures of Rebecca Rosen off to Interpol and the Luxembourg police. Harry had told him to get off home. Charlie had finished talking to Crick about the case, he had placed a call to Amanda Moore, she had told him it would be fine for him to call in at the bank that evening as she was staying late.

'I don't think you will get too much out of her, boss,' Harry said, talking about Amanda Moore. 'I think it was long in planning and Gerald Parkin was something that got in the way and had to be dealt with.'

'I think you're right, Harry, and I don't think there's any way she is going to give us anything if she is involved. But just for peace of mind, if nothing else,' Charlie said.

'Has to be done, boss,' Harry said. 'You want me to come along with you?'

'No Harry, I will see her alone,' Charlie said. 'You start getting the files in order, so I can write up the final report on the case for Crick and the top brass.' Charlie stood. 'I will let you know how I got on later.'

'Have fun,' Harry said.

Rebecca Rosen was sitting back, a glass of brandy in her hand, the meal had been as good as she expected, the Mosconi never failed to deliver the perfect meal. 'What do you intend to do?' her dinner companion asked.

Rebecca took a small drink of brandy. 'I will go to Italy for a few days, then I feel like a long holiday in the Far East.'

Vincenzo Gallo leaned forward. 'My father is very happy with the way things have worked out,' he said. 'I will let him know you will be calling in, and when you travel east you can use my house in Singapore if you want.'

'Thank you Vincenzo, will you be coming out to Singapore soon?' she asked.

He smiled. 'As soon as I've tied things up, I reckon in a couple of weeks, I will fly out.' He took hold of Rebecca's hand. 'We can spend some good time together.' He leaned forward. 'What about the police, do you think they will be after you?'

She shook her head. 'I think they will be chasing their tails. I need to get a new passport, I can't use the one I have.'

'I'll arrange that for you,' he said. 'I will get a new Italian one delivered tomorrow morning.' He smiled. 'Shall we go?'

Charlie had arrived at the bank's offices and been shown to

Amanda Moore's office. She was seated behind the desk when Charlie entered. She stood and came round to meet him, he kissed her cheek. 'Would you like a drink, Charlie?' she asked.

'Why not?' Charlie said. 'It's been one of those days.' She went to a cabinet in the corner.

'What would you like, Charlie,' she said.

Charlie looked over. 'I will have whatever you're having'

Looking over her shoulder, 'I have some white wine open.'

'That's fine with me,' Charlie said. He watched as she poured the wine. She turned and walked towards him, handing him the glass. 'I understand congratulations are in order,' he said.

'I don't understand,' Amanda replied.

'I thought there was a successful takeover of Sir Mark Coale's company,' Charlie said.

Amanda Moore walked back round to her side of the desk. She sat down. 'But we were on the losing side of that deal.'

Charlie held up his glass, smiling. 'The way I hear things, your husband was.'

She smiled back at him. 'I keep forgetting you are a very well-informed policeman, Charlie. You will have to tell me where you get your information.'

'It's just things you pick up,' he said.

'I had warned my husband away from the deal, but he wouldn't listen,' she said.

'But you have not been too badly affected by the way things have turned out,' Charlie said.

She took a drink from her glass. 'How do you mean, Charlie, my husband has put the bank in a bad position.'

'Is it true you have filed for divorce?' Charlie asked.

She looked a little surprised. 'You really do have very good informants, Charlie.' She held up her glass in salute. 'Yes I have, but it has been something that would have happened sooner or later. This deal just brought things to a head.' Smiling, she said 'It does mean I will be available to have dinner or anything you fancy doing, Charlie.'

Smiling back, Charlie said 'That's a very tempting offer, is it true your father was one of the big backers in the takeover?'

'I can see there's not a lot you don't know about the deal, but why does it concern you,' she asked.

'I think the deal was the reason for the murders,' Charlie said.

She took another drink from her glass. Standing up, she came round to Charlie's side of the desk. 'I thought it was Gerald Parkin's blackmail that was the reason,' she said as she perched on the desk, crossing her legs.

Charlie watched her. 'We thought it was, but lots of things have happened to change our minds. Does the name Rebecca Rosen mean anything to you?' He watched her closely.

She turned away and reached for her wine glass, turning back and shaking her head. 'I don't think so, why should it?' Charlie didn't notice any change in her.

'We believe that's the real name of the killer,' Charlie said.

'I', sure you will catch her, Charlie, after all you seem to have all the information,' Amanda said.

'I only wish that were true,' Charlie said. 'We think someone was tipping her off about our progress in the case.'

'Can I get you a refill?' Amanda Moore asked, easing her way off the table. Charlie shook his head, she walked back to the drinks cabinet. 'So do you have any idea who it might have been?'

Charlie watched her back as she leant over to pour another wine for herself. 'We have our suspicions,' he said.

She turned, taking a drink from the glass and walked back towards him. 'Only suspicions Charlie, you do surprise me.' She sat again on the corner of the table.

'There's some times in an investigation when you know something to be true, but you don't have the evidence to prove it,' Charlie said.

She smiled at him. 'That must be frustrating for you, but I'm sure when you have captured that girl, she will give you all the information she has.'

Charlie drank the last of the wine from his glass. 'If only it were that easy,' he said. 'We believe she has left the country.'

'That's a shame,' Amanda said. 'So what do you do now?'

'We try to tie up all the loose ends,' Charlie said, 'so if a time comes when we do finally catch her, we have a cast iron case to take to court.'

Amanda stood up from the table. 'I'm free tomorrow for dinner, Charlie.'

Charlie was slightly taken aback. 'That is a very tempting offer, Amanda,' he said.

'I will be dining alone at home,' she said, 'you could come over.' She moved closer. 'You wouldn't have to rush off.' She placed her hand on his shoulder.

'Now that sounds like it would be a very nice evening,' Charlie said. He stood up.

'So would you like to come over?' She slid her hand down Charlie's arm.

'I would, but I just need you to answer one question for me,' Charlie said.

'Go ahead, Charlie, ask away,' she said.

'Was it you who was passing on information you heard or found out to Rebecca Rosen?' Charlie asked, looking at her.

She looked up into Charlie's eyes, he saw the smile in them. 'Charlie, I have never heard of that woman.'

'I so want to believe you,' Charlie said.

Harry had been sitting quietly in the office since Charlie had left to go and visit Amanda Moore. It had been annoying how they had been run around by Rebecca Rosen, but Harry felt he understood her a lot more now he knew her background. Going over the day's events, there were a few loose ends he wanted to tie up Where had she been hiding? It must have been in the Bow, the car had been left there and her phone switched on in the area. She liked to plan ahead, so any house or flat she had used must have been rented or bought months ago. He picked up his phone, one by one he called the team, telling them to come back to the Yard as he had a couple of jobs that needed clearing up. After a few moans of 'you only just said we could go home,' they all said they would be in asap.

Harry started writing up a list of things he wanted answers to. The car needed tracing, where had it been boought, the house or flat needed to be found, when had the airline ticket been bought, the taxi that had dropped her at the airport, the driver needs to be spoken to, forensics needed to be chased up about anything that had been found at Tim Green's house. He would give Manjitt a call soon to ask her if she had got anything from talking to him at the hospital. He picked up a file from his desk and started to scan through it. Stopping, he added another couple of things he thought needed checking out to his list.

Charlie sat in his Bentley outside Amanda Moore's offices. She had looked very upset when he had asked if she knew Rebecca Rosen. She said she had answered his questions and if he didn't believe her, she would not expect to see him at her house for dinner tomorrow evening. She had not said anything else, just went and sat at her desk reading some papers. Charlie had left the office without asking another question. He was still unsure about her. He thought she was being truthful, he had interviewed enough suspects to get an idea when someone was lying. But that meant someone else was tipping off Rebecca Rosen. Who could it be? They had been through all the suspects, for one reason or another it would appear that they were in the clear. He didn't believe there was anyone on his team who was leaking information. He started the car. But how did she manage to seem to be one step ahead of them?

Vincenzo Gallo was seated in his town house in the Belair district of Luxembourg city. After finishing the meal, Rebecca hadsaid she was going straight to the flat she was using and rest. The light breeze had the curtains fluttering. He sat with a glass of wine and a cigar looking out towards the river. He had enjoyed the evening, Rebecca was such an engaging woman, dangerous, but fun.

She had told him a certain amount of what she had been doing in England. He knew a little, as he had been slightly involved passing messages and keeping her up to date with any changes to the plans that had been made. He knew his father and his friend in London had made a fortune out of the takeover of Sir Mark Coale's oil company. He had not thought it would be possible when his father had told him of the plans he and the friend in London had laid out well over two years ago. But he should have known not to doubt them, as they had been in business for a long time and he had not known them make a wrong move.

It had all gone like clockwork until his father had told him about a man who was messing things up with threats of blackmail. He had spoken to the friend in London, and a plan was put together to actually use the man to their advantage. The friend in London had persuaded the man, Gerald Parkin, that far greater money could be made from buying shares in different companies with some inside knowledge. They had used him to set up a number of front companies. Parkin had been persuaded to use the bank in Luxembourg, so they always knew about any movement of money he made. But when he started to get greedy and began to talk to other people about what was going on, he had to be dealt with. His father had sent Rebecca up to him, a false employment history had been created, she had travelled to London, met with his father's friend. Apparently, according to Rebecca, they had got on very well, got very close and were going to meet up again when things had quietened down.

Rebecca had been given all the information that was known about Gerald Parkin. It was decided whilst she was there to see if she could get close to Sir Mark to double-check that he had no other plans to safeguard his company when they made their move. It was left to Rebecca to decide how she would do things. It had taken her a little time to gain the trust of people, but once she had, everything had gone to plan, except Sir Mark getting suspicious, and employing a private detective that had to be dealt with, and that policeman who was so tenacious with his investigating. Still, all was well now.

He knew his father had spoken to the American lawyers who were holding the shares bought over in the States. It had been planned so it did not seem that only one group was involved. It had all gone through. The money, minus the lawyers' not inconsiderable costs, had been transferred back to Italy. His bank had sold all the shares it held and transferred all the money.

His father was planning a dinner in a couple of days to celebrate. His friend from London was coming over. He would travel down to Rome to join them. His phone rang disturbing his thoughts. He listened for a few moments, then said he would call back in five minutes.

Harry had given out the jobs to the squad as they had wandered in. He had told them he wanted all the answers to his questions by the morning. Charlie had come back. 'I thought you sent everyone off home Harry but I just saw Danny and Jordan going out of the building,' he said.

Harry was at his desk, papers and files still spread over it. The white board was to one side, covered in pictures and drawn lines, but in the centre linking all of them up was a picture of Rebecca Rosen. 'I had, boss, but the more I thought about things, I just knew we had to have some answers, so I got them back. I gave each of them a list of things I want answers to.'

'Have you spoken to Manjitt?' Charlie asked.

'She's on her way back from the hospital,' Harry said. 'How did you go with Amanda Moore?'

Charlie sat down at his desk, lent back and put his feet up, his hand-made shoes resting on the desk. He explained to Harry what had happened.

'So you're not sure if she's the one passing on any tips she might know,' Harry said.

Charlie shook his head. 'I don't know Harry, I really don't.'

'You're not letting any feelings get in the way, boss?' Harry said.

Charlie looked at Harry. 'No-one else could ask me that Harry, but coming from you I understand it. No Harry, I genuinely don't know if it was her. She's either a very skilled liar or she doesn't know. I think you should have a crack at her Harry, just to make sure my judgement's not clouded.'

'I had to ask, boss,' Harry said.

Charlie nodded. 'I wouldn't expect anything else, Harry.'

'I will have a chat with her, though,' Harry said. 'We really do need to clear things up, and if we get close to the person who was tipping her off, we may be able to link them into the murders and charge them too. I will call in tomorrow and see her. You fancy a cup of tea, boss?' Charlie nodded.

Manjitt arrived as Harry got up. 'You want some tea, Manjitt?' Harry asked.

'Yes please, Harry,' she said, as she pulled a chair across to Charlie's desk. He still had his feet up and was leaning back in his chair. 'You look like you had a good day, boss.'

'Thank you Manjitt, it's nice to know you have my welfare at heart,' Charlie said. 'Now did you find out anything from Tim Green that might help us?'

'I feel quite sorry for him, boss,' Manjitt said, 'he really did think he had found the love of his life, but she was just using him all along.'

Harry came back with the tea. Passing the cups to the others, he sat down. 'Manjitt is just telling me how Tim Green was used,' Charlie said.

Manjitt continued. 'She had things well worked out, he never asked her too many questions and it appears whenever she needed time away, she spun him the work story, which he believed.'

'Didn't he have any suspicions?' Harry asked.

'I think he couldn't believe his luck that he had this good looking woman living with him who had excepted his marriage proposal,' she said.

'So she kept her two lives completely separate?' Charlie asked.

'Yes, he never met anyone, it was a hideaway for her,' Manjitt said.

'So it must have been a shock when the private detective turned up,' Harry said.

'It's strange, but Tim Green said he thought she didn't seem surprised,' Manjitt replied.

'Why, what did he say?' Charlie asked.

'He said when he answered the door and the man asked for

her, she came out and told him she would deal with it. He said she seemed to know the man, or had expected him,' Manjitt said.

Harry looked at Charlie. 'Do you think she knew him, boss?'

'I don't think so, Harry,' Charlie said. 'Nothing we have found points in that direction. But remember what our friend from the embassy told us, she was trained in surveillance and counter-surveillance, so maybe she had spotted him and knew she was being followed.'

'If she had, it didn't seem to bother her,' Harry said, 'and she took the time to go round to his house and blow it up, so she must have known where he lived.'

'She could have worried that he might have some information on her at his house,' Manjitt said.

'You think she blew it up hoping anything that was in there got destroyed?' Charlie said.

'Manjitt could be right, boss. She may have been worried, she probably didn't have time to search the place. I'll put a call through to the fire brigade, see if anything turned up.' Harry picked up his phone.

'Did Tim Green mention anything else? What about the solicitor he had?' Charlie said.

'I asked him about that, he said Rebecca sorted it out for him. She told him her work had recommended them to her,' Manjitt said. 'I think when she thought we were getting close, she nudged Tim Green our way to buy herself a bit more time.'

'It looks like it,' Charlie said. 'Still, he's got himself a nice car as a consolation prize.'

Harry put his phone down. He was smiling when he turned to Charlie. 'The fire brigade just told me they found a safe in one of the walls. They can't get it out yet as it's under a part of the house that can come down at any moment, so they're taking their time.'

Charlie sat up. 'Harry I don't care about the house. You call them back, tell them I want that safe out now. If the rest of the place falls down, who cares. Get a bulldozer if you have to, but get that safe, it might have something she was hoping we wouldn't see in it.' Harry picked up his phone again.

Vincenzo Gallo had called Rebecca Rosen. He had spent a couple of minutes talking to her, she said she would come over to his house and discuss things with him. When he got off the phone, he placed a call back to London, saying he would have an answer in an hour to the question. He would get Rebecca to call herself with it.

After getting off the phone to London, he put a call through to his father in Rome. He explained what he had just been told. His father said to let him know what was decided later. Vincenzo also asked his father to send a new passport by overnight courier as Rebecca needed a new one. He put down the phone. Picking his drink up, he thought about what he had been asked. It worried him, but on the other hand he understood a vast amount of money was to be had. He would wait and see what Rebecca thought about it.

Harry put the phone down. 'They will have it out within the next hour,' he said.

Charlie stood up. 'Come on then let's go over there. Who do we know can open a safe up quickly, no questions asked?' he said.

Harry stood. 'Now that's not a question a policeman is usually asked. Any thoughts, Manjitt?'

'Safe crackers I don't have numbers for Harry, sorry.' she said.

'Come on you two, let's go. Harry, you can get someone on the way,' Charlie said.

Harry opened his desk drawer taking his black book out. He followed Charlie towards the office door. Manjitt was beside him. 'Harry, do you want me to hold onto that little book for you while we're out and about?' she said.

'Very nice of you to offer Manjitt, but I will keep hold of it,' Harry said, opening it up as he walked and turning the pages.

It took them about twenty minutes to reach what was left of John Russell's house. The light was starting to go as the evening drew in. They had to park the Bentley around the corner, as the road the house was on was cordoned off. Showing their identification to the policeman on duty at the police tape barrier, they were allowed through. Harry found the chief fire officer and introduced him to Charlie, who explained why they needed to get their hands on the safe quickly. The fire chief said he would get things moving. 'Any luck with someone to open the safe, Harry?' Charlie asked.

'I have someone coming over, boss,' Harry said.

'Dare I ask who they are?' Manjitt said.

'You can ask, but you won't get an answer,' Harry replied, smiling.

The three of them watched as firemen dragged some large metal cable across the road and into the house. The front of it was half missing, one floor from upstairs was all. Across the road in front of the house, two cars could just be made out under the rubble.

'Looking at that lot, it's a miracle no one was killed when it went up,' Manjitt said.

'I don't think she cared who got in the way,' Harry said. 'The chief fire officer said it was only because most people were at work and the children at school that no one else was hurt.'

The firemen brought the metal cable out of the house and attached it to the back of one of the fire engines. The chief fire officer came over and told them they had looped the cables around the wall inside. They were going to try and pull the cable so it dragged the wall down. He hoped the safe would come free and not get buried under the floor from above. Then that would come crashing down. He told them to move back, and he signalled to his officers to get on with things.

The three of them walked back to the barrier and watched. As the fire engine began to move away from the house, the cables became taut. The engine noise grew louder as it seemed to come to a halt for a moment, then there was a loud crash. The road behind the engine filled with dust. The fire engine motor was turned off and there was silence again. They stood watching as two firemen accompanied the chief fire officer back through the dust into what was left of the house. A couple of minutes later they saw them carrying the safe out from the house. It was brought over to the barrier and placed in the road. Charlie thanked the chief fire officer and his men for their help. Turning to Harry, Charlie asked 'Has you man arrived yet?'

Harry turned and scanned the road. A number of people stood around watching what was going on. 'Not yet boss, but he will be here soon.'

'Do you reckon our luck will change, and inside we'll find all the evidence we need to clear this case up,' Manjitt said, looking at the safe. Harry and Charlie both laughed. Manjitt looked from one to the other. 'I take it you don't hold out much hope.'

'If we get something that gives us some information we don't have, it would be nice,' Charlie said.

A transit van came to a halt the other side of the barrier. The police officer approached it, spoke to the driver then walked over and spoke to Harry. 'It's our man,' Harry said. 'I will have a quick word.' He ducked under the tape and went to the van.

'Boss, do you think he makes notes on everyone in that black book of his?' Manjitt said.

'I dare say he does, and one day when you are chief constable somewhere, you will get a call from Harry reminding you of something you did and asking for a favour,' Charlie said.

'Me, chief constable?' Manjitt said, laughing. 'Harry could have his favour if I were chief constable!'

Harry came back. The van reversed up to the tape and stopped. A small man who was no taller than five feet, dressed in a blue boiler suit, got out and came to the back of the van and opened the doors. Charlie saw the inside was like a small workshop. Harry told the police officer who was guarding the tape barrier to help the small man lift the safe into the back of the van. Once it was in, the small man got into the back. Before he could close the doors, Harry climbed in with him. Charlie and Manjitt both heard Harry say 'Nice try, but you're not opening it without me.' The little man pulled the van doors closed.

After five minutes the van doors opened and Harry climbed out. He had a number of files in his arms. Turning to the little man he said 'You get rid of the safe, I will make a few calls and see what I can do for you.' Harry walked over to Charlie and Manjitt. 'I've only had a quick scan through these, but some look interesting.'

'Let's take them back to the Yard and have a good read,' Charlie said. The three of them made their way back to the Bentley.

Rebecca Rosen had taken a taxi from the flat she was using to Vincenzo's house. She was intrigued at what he had told her. On arrival, Vincenzo opened a bottle of wine, poured them both a glass and sat down in a chair opposite Rebecca, who sat on the sofa. Taking a small drink of wine, she asked 'What do you think, Vincenzo, should I do it?'

'I'm not the one to tell you what you should do, Rebecca, you know that. As far as I and my father are concerned you have done all that was asked of you.' He took a drink from his wine and continued. 'This is something different; it's a lot of money that is being offered, but it would mean going straight back to England. With the police on alert for you it could be dangerous.'

'That's part of the fun, Vincenzo,' she said. 'I know you won't understand that, but it's like a drug for me.' She took another drink from her glass. 'Have you arranged a new passport for me yet?'

'I spoke to my father a while ago, he will send one overnight by courier, it should be here first thing in the morning,' he replied.

'I suppose it will have one of my old pictures in it,' she said. He nodded. 'I will need to dye my hair dark. It's a shame, I was just beginning to enjoy being blonde.' She smiled 'I will call London now and discuss things.'

Vincenzo lent forward and pushed the phone that was in the middle of the table in front of him towards her. She placed her glass on the table. 'The number is on speed dial,' Vincenzo said, 'Press seven.' She followed his instructions. It started to ring. She picked her glass of wine back up and leaned back into the sofa.

Vincenzo watched her. He was both in love yet very frightened of her. He had no idea just how far she wouldn't go to do whatever she wanted. He knew she would never settle down with him, although they spent a lot of time on holidays together and meeting up. He had never told her how he felt. He did get jealous when he knew she was sleeping with other men and woman to get what she wanted, but to her it was part of the job she did, it meant nothing. He wondered if she would ever be able to have a real relationship. She was still talking on the phone. He stood up and pickedhis glass up. 'Do you want more wine?' he asked. She looked up at him and nodded yes, passing him her glass while she continued to talk on the phone. Vincenzo walked over to get the wine, refilled their glasses and brought the drinks back. Rebecca put the phone down and he passed her glass to her. She took a small drink. 'That is a very interesting proposition,' she said.

Vincenzo took his seat opposite her again. 'Will you do it?' he asked.

'It's a lot of money on offer, you could say I would never have to work again,' she replied.

'But will you take the risk? The police must be looking for you,' Vincenzo said

'Ah, but they're looking for Rebecca,' she replied. 'The passport you have coming up, what name will it be in?'

'I don't know, I can ring and find out,' he said.

'It doesn't matter, my point is I will be someone different. They won't even know I'm back in the country,' she said.

'So you are going to do it?' he asked.

'Of course, I will be in and out before they know anything,' she said.

'I still think it,s risky,' Vincenzo said.

She stood up and walked to the window. 'That's the whole point Vincenzo, the risk is the drug and for the money I am being offered, I think it's worth the chance. With twenty million pounds I can do anything.' She turned back to look at him. 'I've been offered half the money up front. When I ring back and confirm, they will transfer the money to a new account at your bank. Can you arrange things with them for me?' He nodded, she walked back and picked up the phone.

There were five files in the middle of the desk. 'Let's hope our Mr Russell was a good private detective, and found out a few things about Rebecca Rosen that we didn't know,' Charlie said. 'Okay,dip in.' He picked up a file. Harry and Manjitt followed suit, and they all began to read.

It was Harry that spoke first. 'From what I'm reading here, he seemed pretty methodical in his reports.'

'Mine too,' Manjitt said. 'It's all day and time noted.'

'I have an idea,' Charlie said. 'Manjitt, you take them all home with you. Start from the first entry then work your way through. You can give us a full report in the morning when all the team are in. Otherwise we'll be going over the same thing.'

'I like that thought, boss,' Harry said, tossing his file to Manjitt.

'When I become a detective sergeant, will I still be treated this way?' Manjitt said.

Charlie looked at Harry, and in unison they both said 'Yes.'

Manjitt scooped up all the files. 'I love this job. What more could a girl want than to go home with a good book?'

'Just think yourself lucky you have such an understanding boss who knows how to keep you happy,' Harry said.

'Harry, you always have my welfare in your heart,' she said, standing up.

'See you about 9.30, Manjitt, you can have a lie in,' Charlie said.

'You're too kind, boss,' Manjitt said. 'See you in the morning.' She left Harry and Charlie sitting at the desk.

'You know, the more I think about it, Harry, the more I think we have missed something,' Charlie said.

'How do you mean, boss?' Harry asked.

'Well let's look, we thought firstly Gerald Parkin was murdered because of the blackmail,' Charlie said. 'Then we discovered he was making money buying and selling shares. What we don't know is how he made the jump from the blackmail to the shares, who was it that put him onto it.'

'I thought we had Amanda Moore in the frame, boss,' Harry said.

'Yes we do, but I have my doubts.' Charlie held up his hand as Harry looked at him. 'No, it's not that I fancy her,' he said.

Harry smiled. 'Well that's an admission, anyway.'

Charlie carried on. 'No what I'm saying, Harry, is he wasn't blackmailing her, so apart from at the parties, he never came into contact with her. And if she had no idea in the beginning of what he was doing, she couldn't have been the one setting up the share buying.'

'Boss, we don't know if he was meeting her outside the dinner parties,' Harry said

'That's true, but what it gets back to is, if she didn't know he was blackmailing anyone, why would she approach him? We know he wasn't well liked amongst the group, surely she could have arranged things without involving him,' Charlie said.

'That's true boss, but we have been through everyone else. I thought we had ruled them all out,' Harry said.

'Manjitt might find something in the files from Russell's house, but I'm just not sure we are right to put Amanda in the frame as an accomplice,' Charlie said.

'Boss, I will go over to her office first thing tomorrow, ask her a few questions. I know she won't be trying to undress me as I do.' Harry smiled. 'Unless my animal magnetism gets to her.'

'Harry. I will go along with whatever you say after.' Charlie said as he stood up. 'Come on, let's call it a day. You can write Crick's report up in the morning. I have to go up and see him, I think Macready has been onto him again.'

CHAPTER TWENTY TWO

Charlie was sitting in his front room. He had some music on in the background, but was running the case through his mind. There must be something they had missed, he thought. His three dogs were lying on the floor in front of him, tired out after he had played with them for half an hour in the garden when he had got home. The fire was burning nicely, he had a glass of wine on the table next to him. His phone rang, disturbing his thoughts. He picked it up and found it was Harry calling.

'Sorry to call you, boss,' Harry said, 'but I have been thinking about what we said in the office about Amanda Moore.'

'That's okay Harry, I've been going over the same thing,' Charlie said. 'Have you thought of anything?'

'Well I've been thinking. When me and Jordan went to interview her husband during the takeover,' Harry said, 'we got confused because he was with Sir Mark Coale working on a plan to save his oil company.'

'Yes that's right,' Charlie said, 'that's why we ruled those two out.'

'I know boss, but if Stanley Moore knew Amanda's father was involved with the takeover and all the money he had backing him,' Harry said, 'and after all, she had warned him not to back Sir Mark. Why did he still go ahead with what he must have known was a lost cause?'

'Sir Mark was a very good friend of his, Harry,' Charlie said.

'Come on boss, these people are driven by money. No, he must have had another reason,' Harry said.

'So what are you saying, Harry, is that Stanley Moore was playing both sides?' Charlie asked.

'No boss, I don't think he was. I think he was playing for Stanley Moore,' Harry replied. 'Think about it, he knew what Sir Mark's strategy was, after all he was helping to plan it. He knew who was likely to be involved in the takeover, his wife had warned him. Now if he also had knowledge of who controlled those shares that had been bought over the last couple of years, he was in the very place to make sure they got the best price to profit from the takeover.'

'That's an interesting idea Harry, he would be at the centre of everything if what you say is true,' Charlie said.

'We know he had Rebecca Rosen at his house on a number of occasions,' Harry said. 'Supposedly for some slap and tickle, but they could have been working things out together.'

'Go on Harry, you're starting to make sense,' Charlie said.

'He was also in touch with Gerald Parkin on a regular basis. The blackmail thing would have been a great cover for him. He would know what Gerald Parkin was up to. He could have tipped Rebecca Rosen off about him,' Harry said.

'But why kill Parkin or Angela Cook?' Charlie asked.

'Maybe Gerald Parkin got greedy or discovered he was being used. I don't know about Angela Cook, she may have worked something out. I'm only surmising, boss,' Harry said.

'So do we get Stanley Moore in for questioning,' Charlie said?

'I think we should speak to Sir Mark Coale first, ask him how much Stanley Moore told him, did Sir Mark know that Stanley Moore's father-in-law was heading the take over from the beginning,' Harry said. 'Then we might have a better picture of who was doing what.'

'Okay Harry, we will run with that,' Charlie said, 'I will get on to Julian, try and find out if he has heard anymore. We need to know where we can find Sir Mark Coale. You see if you can track him down, try and get to see him as soon as you can, Harry. And Harry, I still want you to question Amanda. We have to be sure about her too.'

'I will try and track down Sir Mark and let you know as soon as I have an address for him. I can call in on Amanda on the way to the Yard first thing in the morning,' Harry said.

Charlie put down the phone, picked up his wine and took a drink. Harry had come up with a good theory. Putting his wine down, he put a call through to Julian.

Rebecca Rosen, her hair now short and dark, boarded the Eurostar train in Brussels. It was seven forty. Vincenzo had driven her from Luxembourg. He had not spoken much to her on the journey, but had made his feelings clear that she should not have agreed to go back. It was nice that he cared but Rebecca knew that the money she made from this last job would leave her free to do whatever she wanted for the rest of her life. Vincenzo had checked with his bank that morning. The first ten million pounds had been deposited in her account; the next ten would go there when the job was done.

The new Italian passport was in her bag. Also she had a small change of clothes, tracksuit, sweatshirt and trainers. She had dressed in business attire, and looked the part of a business woman travelling to London. She planned to book in to a nice hotel, go and carry out the job she had been paid to do, spend one night, then be back on the train to Brussels the next morning.

She knew she would have to check out the area around the house where her target would be, but she had been promised some drawings of the layout. They would be sent over once she had booked into the hotel. All she needed to do was phone her contact and say where they should be sent to.

Taking her seat, she opened the magazine she had bought. It would only be two hours before she was in London and with the time difference, it would be just before nine. Plenty of time to get organised and ready, she thought. She felt the train jolt, then begin to move.

A man stood on the platform and watched the train pull out. He and a colleague had been watching Vincenzo Gallo for a few days. They had seen Rebecca come to his house. Staying well hidden, as they knew Rebecca's skills at counter-surveillance, they had placed a tracking device on Vincenzo's car. It had not been possible to get close to Rebecca to carry out the instructions they had been given if she should turn up in Luxembourg. He made his way back to the car in which his colleague was waiting. He told him she had got on the train to London. He took his phone out and called the embassy, they would have to get a team ready in London. From what he knew of the operation, that was the last place they wanted her to be caught.

It was only eight thirty when Harry pulled up outside Amanda Moore's offices. The London traffic was as heavy as ever and a light drizzle was falling as he got out of the car. It was a red route so no parking at all was allowed. He took the emergency light from under the seat, stuck it on the roof and turned it on. That would keep the parking wardens away. He went up the few steps and into the bank. After introducing himself at the reception, a phone call was made and he was shown up to Amanda's office.

When he entered Amanda, stood up and came round from behind her desk. 'Hello Harry, have you come to arrest me?' she said.

'Not unless you have a confession to make,' Harry replied. Smiling she said 'I never make confessions, Harry.' She gave him a kiss on the cheek, catching him off guard. 'Harry, is that a blush I see?'

'Just keep it a secret,' Harry said. She went back round her desk and sat down. Harry took the chair opposite her.

'So Harry, to what do I owe this early morning call?' she said.

'We are just trying to tie up some loose ends in the case, and for my own peace of mind I wanted just to clear a few things up with you,' Harry said.

'I thought that was what Charlie did when he came by yesterday,' Amanda replied.

'Sometimes he forgets things,' Harry said.

'Come on, Harry,' she said. 'Charlie is a smart cookie, you need something better than that as a reason for coming here.'

Harry smiled. 'The boss said you were sharp.'

Smiling back, she said 'Is that how he sees me?'

'The boss never gives much away about his private life,' Harry said, 'but I think, and don't ever tell him I said this, he quite fancies you.'

'Harry you're not trying to soften me up before questioning me, are you?' Amanda said.

'Cross my heart,' Harry said.

Smiling, Amanda Moore said 'Okay Harry ask away, what is it you want to know?'

Harry sat back in his chair. 'Do you think I can have a cup of tea? It was a rush to get here this early, so I didn't have time to make one this morning, and I can't function properly till I've had one.'

Amanda Moore picked up her phone and asked for a tea and a coffee to be brought into the office.

Charlie had arrived at the squad's office and found all the team already there. 'What's got into everyone?' he said, looking round. A chorus of 'morning boss' came from different desks. Charlie walked to his, calling Manjitt over to join him as he went. Sitting down, he checked for any messages that had been left. Manjitt took a chair in front of him Looking up he said 'Come on, give me some good news from those files we got from Russell's safe.'

'Well boss, he was a meticulous man. Every day is written up, he had been trailing her for a couple of months. He even notes at one point he thinks she knows he is following her.'

'I think he was right about that,' Charlie said, 'but does he give us anyone else?'

'He ran checks on the people she was meeting. He has a file on Tim Green, Angela Cook and Gerald Parkin. He seemed to do good background work on them. I suspect he had someone in the police passing him information.'

'I will let police records know, they can run a check on who has been accessing information on them apart from us. They can deal with that,' Charlie said. 'Carry on.'

'He has her going to Stanley Moore's house, but he also has her meeting him for dinner on a couple of occasions too.'

'I don't remember Stanley Moore telling us he had dinner with her,' Charlie said.

'But Stanley Moore thought her name was Jayne Cavill,' Manjitt said, 'so he wouldn't know who he was dealing with.'

'Well we will find out if that's true later. Did Russell have her down as Jayne Cavill for long before he gets her real name?' Charlie asked.

'From the beginning of his surveillance, it took him about two weeks before he changed her name to Rebecca Rosen,' Manjitt said.

'So why didn't she do anything about him sooner if she knew he was following her?' Charlie said.

'Perhaps she didn't see him as a problem, or she just wanted to finish the job she was doing. After all, she did kill him in the end,' Manjitt said.

'Yes, but I don't think she knew he would turn up on her door step,' Charlie said. 'Tim Green said she didn't seem to be expecting anyone on the morning he knocked on the door.'

'Perhaps she was going to kill him anyway, and him turning up saved her going to Russell's house. After all, she seemed to know where he lived,' Manjitt said.

'So Russell doesn't have her meeting anyone else,' Charlie asked.

'No, only the people we already know about. But then again, we know she was good at losing tails when she wanted to, so there's nothing to say she didn't meet someone without Russell knowing,' Manjitt said.

'Okay Manjitt, well done. Now if you want to make detective sergeant go to the canteen and get me a bacon roll' Charlie said,

'Walking all that way gives a girl an appetite, boss,' Manjitt said.

Charlie took five pounds from his pocket. 'Okay get yourself one too,' Charlie said.

Manjitt took the money and went off towards the door. As she got there she stopped and said 'Hippie, the boss wants a tea and you can do me one as well. I will be back in five minutes.'

Danny looked up, but before he could answer Manjitt was out the door. He stood up and went to make some tea. Jordan spotted him and said 'Good idea, Hippie, do me one too.'

Danny shrugged his shoulders. 'I think we should get a machine put in here.'

'You know Harry won't have that,' Jordan said. 'He likes the personal touch.'

Charlie had watched the goings on and called out 'Anyone else have any information they want to give me?'

It was Cramer who came over first. 'I traced the car. It was bought with cash seven days ago. I spoke to the dealer. All he remembers is a woman, he couldn't remember what she looked like. Bit of a dead end, but at least we know she was planning ahead.'

'She's good at that,' Charlie said. Danny came over with Charlie's tea. 'I have to compliment you on the jumper you're wearing, Danny.'

'Not bad, is it boss?' Danny said. 'I got it from a charity shop not far from where I live.'

From across the other side of the office Jordan called out 'You should have left it there.'

'My only problem with it, Danny,' Charlie said, 'is it's not Christmas yet, and having a big red jumper with Santa Claus and his reindeer across the front looks a little premature.'

'I just thought it would cheer people up when they saw it, boss,' Danny said.

'Well it does that, Danny,' Charlie said, taking a drink of tea. Manjitt came back into the office and passed Charlie his bacon roll. She sat down and started to eat hers.

'Didn't you get me one,' Danny asked.

'The boss treated me for all my good work on the case,' Manjitt said. 'Where's my tea, Hippie?'

Charlie looked over at Jordan. 'What you got for me, Jordan?'

Jordan stood up and walked over to join the others. 'I have been ringing round all the estate agents and property companies in the area but haven't had a bite yet. Mind you, there are hundreds of them so it might take a bit more time yet.'

Charlie nodded. 'Manjitt, you give Jordan a hand with that. Who was chasing up the taxi driver?'

'I was, boss,' Danny said. 'I am waiting for a few taxi firms to get back to me.'

'Get back onto them Danny, tell them we consider this very important. If they can't give us an answer in the next hour, tell them we will have traffic police stopping all cabs to give them vehicle checks for the next two weeks. That will get them moving,' Charlie said. Danny laughed and went off to his desk.

The announcement said that the train would soon be pulling into St Pancras station. Rebecca put the magazine down. Although she had read it from cover to cover, she couldn't remember any of the articles, as she felt that nervous excitement that she got whenever she had a job to do. Standing up, she made her way along the corridor to stand by the door. She easily blended in with all the other travellers. Glancing at her passport which was in her hand, she checked the name, Maria Soldati, and slipped it back into her bag. The train came to a halt; she was the third person out of the carriage door. She walked with the crowd along the platform. She looked around her, checking from memory if any faces came to mind that she had seen before. Stopping without warning occasionally and turning to look behind her to see if anyone else had stopped, moving from one side of the platform to the other checking to see if someone was doing the same, she didn't see anyone.

She made her way to the taxi rank, where there was a small queue but lots of taxis to go round, so it didn't take her long before she was in the back of one and being driven along in the London traffic.

The man had been standing on the overhead walkway as he saw the train come in. He had watched carefully as the passengers had got off. Her description had been passed from Luxembourg, but he had a picture of the woman in his hand to help him spot her. He picked her out as his eye caught someone with dark hair stop in the crowd suddenly. He moved along the walkway to get a better look Happy it was her, he spoke into a microphone that was on his lapel, informing other members of the team outside the station that the target had arrived and was heading for the taxi rank.

Rebecca was in the back of the taxi that was taking her to the Dorchester hotel. She had rung and booked a room last night, she had decided to get used to how she was going to live in the future. Everything would be first class, and the Dorchester was a nice place to start. Two cars back was another black cab, the man driving it was relaying the route Rebecca's cab was talking into a radio while another man was seated in the back. He was dressed in a dark business suit. He occasionally whispered instructions to the driver. They must not lose sight of the woman. Their instructions were clear: she had to be neutralised. Nothing else was acceptable, all the people working on this job knew that their careers could be affected by failure.

Harry had finished talking with Amanda Moore. He said 'Thanks for taking the time this morning to answer my questions, Amanda. I hope you understand that we have to cover every possibility.'

'Harry, you don't have to worry. I know I don't have anything to hide, so I'm not worried in the slightest. I don't know why Charlie didn't just come out and say what you have,' Amanda said.

'The boss is the shy type,' Harry said.

Amanda smiled at Harry. 'I will bear that in mind, Harry.'

'There's one more thing you could help me with,' Harry said. 'I need to track down your husband and Sir Mark Coale, just to ask them a few questions. You wouldn't happen to know where they are living or working?'

'Well, my husband is staying at a house in Notting Hill that belongs to a friend of his. As for Sir Mark, I think he's in

London. I understand he has been meeting his lawyers about getting compensation for losing his job. I can give you the number of his lawyers, they can put you in touch with him.' She took a book and opened it, looked through a few pages then wrote down a number. 'Do you want me to write the address and phone number of the house my husband is at?' Harry nodded. 'He's also talking to his lawyers about the divorce, he's after a lot from me but he won't get it,' she said with a determined voice. She passed the paper over to Harry.

'Thanks for your help, Amanda,' Harry said as he stood up. Amanda stood and came round the desk.

'That's okay Harry, I hope to see you again' She planted a kiss on his cheek. 'Ah you're blushing again, Harry,' she said.

'Amanda, will you promise you never do that when any of my squad are around?' he said.

The black cab pulled up in front of the Dorchester and the uniformed concierge stepped forward and opened the door. Rebecca stepped out and paid the driver. The concierge signalled a well-dressed man in the uniform of the Dorchester staff to come and take Rebecca's bag. She slipped a five pound note into the concierge's hand and followed the man into the Dorchester. She glanced around the vast, well-lit and beautifully decorated entrance. At the reception desk she gave the name Maria Soldati. The register was checked and the young woman behind the desk passed her a form. Rebecca started to fill it in.

They had followed the cab that was carrying Rebecca to the Dorchester. When they saw it stop, they pulled off Park Lane and into the street that ran alongside the hotel. The man in the back got out and walked towards the front doors of the hotel. The concierge opened them for him and said good morning sir. He saw Rebecca standing at the front desk signing papers.

A man stood beside her holding her bag. He walked up so he was standing a few steps behind her, then he leaned forward, trying to hear her room number or the name she was using.

Rebecca finished filling in the check-in forms and pushed them over to the young woman behind the reception desk. She turned slowly to look round the hotel while she waited for her key. It was a lovely hotel. I can get used to this she thought. She noticed the well-dressed man standing a little way behind her waiting to book in. Turning back to the woman, she asked about having some sandwiches and coffee sent up to her room. The woman said she would arrange that. Rebecca glanced to her left and saw two other hotel staff standing behind the reception desk. The woman at check-in handed her key over and said the man who had her bag would show her to her room.

She followed the man towards the lifts, stopping by a table where some magazines were spread across it. She asked the man if she could take one to her room, he told her of course. Sorting through them to find one she liked, she looked back at the reception desk. The man was talking to the woman behind the desk. Rebecca saw him turn and walk back out of the hotel. She picked a magazine up and carried on following the man with her bag to the lifts. She knew the man at reception was there because she was. He could have gone to any of the other staff behind the desk, but stayed behind her, he purposely made no eye contact with her and never once looked in her direction. Who was he, police? No, they would have been all over her. Was he another private detective?

She hadn't been followed onto the train in Luxembourg, she was sure of that, so someone must have picked her up at St Pancras. The lift took her up to the fourth floor and she followed the man to her room. He opened the door and she went in. He put her bag down and she passed him a tip and he closed the door behind him as he left. She walked across the room and looked out of the big window. She had a great view of Hyde Park stretching out on the other side of Park Lane from the hotel. She took out a new mobile phone that Vincenzo had given her and dialled a number. When it was answered she only spoke for a minute, giving the hotel she was staying in and the room number, and ended the call without saying anything else. She continued to gaze across at the park, smiling to herself. I will be doing a lot of this good living, she thought. There was a knock at the door and she heard a voice call room service.

Harry arrived back at the office. Looking round, he saw all the team on the phone or going through files. He walked over to Charlie, 'See you got them all hard at it, boss.'

'Still trying to tie up those loose ends, Harry,' Charlie said.

'Talking of loose ends, I think you can put your mind at rest over Amanda,' Harry said.

Charlie smiled. 'That's nice to know, Harry.'

'She was also helpful.' Harry passed over a sheet of paper as he sat down. 'That's the address of the house Stanley Moore is staying at.'

Charlie glanced at it. 'I think we should do a check on the address.'

Harry turned looked around the office. 'Cramer, come over here,' he called. Cramer got up from his desk and walked over too them. 'I want you to check an address out for me.' Charlie held out the sheet of paper, Cramer took it, looking at the address. 'I want to know who owns it, and get onto the phone company. I want a list of any calls coming and going from it. You can also get Stanley Moore's mobile phone records.'

'Okay, Harry,' Cramer said.

'Asap,' Harry replied. Cramer walked off. Harry turned

back to Charlie. 'I also got hold of Sir Mark Coale's solicitor. I've arranged for us to meet him at their offices at twelve.'

'Well done Harry, you have been a busy bee,' Charlie said.

Harry sat down. 'I also sent Crick's report up to him as I came in.'

'That reminds me,' Charlie said. 'I have to pop up and see him, anything I should know about in the report?'

'Only the usual,' Harry said.

Charlie stood up. 'I will go up now, it will leave the rest of the day free.' He walked round the desk, he put a hand on Harry's shoulder.

'Thanks, Harry,' he said.

Harry looked up. 'Only doing my job, boss.' Charlie walked off. 'Hippie,' Harry called out.

'Yes Harry,' Danny said.

'Tea,' Harry shouted.

Charlie got to Crick's office and found him on the phone. Crick signalled Charlie to sit down. Crick was looking very tanned, must have spent the last couple of days under the sunbed Charlie thought. Putting down the phone he said 'Morning Charlie, I read your report, so what are the chances we catch this woman Rebecca Rosen?'

'Well we have alerted Interpol, the police in Luxembourg and the Belgium police as we know the diamonds ended up there,' Charlie said.

'So we can put her name out to the press now?' Crick asked.

'I don't see why not,' Charlie replied.

'That's good, I have had Deputy Commissioner Macready on about things,' Crick said, sitting back in his chair, 'so the case is all tied up now.'

'Not quite sir, we still have a few loose ends to close down,' Charlie said.

Crick sat forward again. 'There's nothing that is going to cause a problem, is there?' he asked?

'I hope not, it's just we need to question a couple more people to clear up something that has been bothering us,' Charlie said.

Crick sat further forward, a worried look on his face. 'She is the killer, you don't think it's someone else.'

'No sir, but we think someone was helping her,' Charlie said.

'Please tell me he's not a Lord,' Crick said.

'No, he's not a Lord, and we don't really have any hard evidence yet, but we are hoping to get some answers later today,' Charlie said.

'Okay Charlie,' Crick said, sitting back. 'Keep me up to date. I will organise a press conference to make the announcement about Rebecca Rosen.' He saw Charlie frown, 'and no, you don't have to be present.'

Charlie smiled. 'Thank you sir,' he said, standing up. 'If anything turns up I will let you know.'

Rebecca Rosen sat eating a sandwich which had been brought to her room along with a pot of coffee by room service. A little while later a package had been delivered; inside she found the plans to the house and the grounds, also there was a map of the local area and one photograph. She had laid them out on the table, studying them as she drank her coffee. She noted all the security cameras that were marked in the garden and around the house. There was a number written on the plans that was the security alarm code, so she could turn it off when she entered. She took another drink from the coffee. It didn't look too difficult a place to get in. Now who was it who had followed her to the hotel, she thought, not the police, and doubtful it was anyone associated with the private detective. Whoever it was must have known she was arriving on the train, so they must have seen her board it in Luxembourg, but she knew no-one had followed her off the train. She had to assume whoever they were would be staked out watching the hotel waiting for her to leave. She would have to lose them, which she thought might not be that easy if they had managed to track her this far. She smiled, but I know they're here now, and London is a big place. She checked the time. Eleven forty five, no hurry she would go and use the hotel gym and get a massage. This is the life, she thought.

Harry and Charlie were seated in the office of Sir Mark Coale's solicitors. Sir Mark was behind the desk flanked by two men, he introduced them as his lawyers.

'Thank you for taking the time to see us,' Charlie said.

'That's okay, its a nice distraction,' Sir Mark said. 'But I thought I had cleared everything up the last time I spoke to your officers.'

'Since you did, a couple of other things have come up which we think you could help us with,' Charlie said.

'Let's get one thing straight,' Sir Mark replied. 'You don't think I was involved with the murders, do you?'

It was Harry who spoke. 'No sir, we don't think you were, but we think something you might be able to tell us might help with the case.'

'That's good, then ask away,' Sir Mark said, smiling. 'Do you want a drink or anything?'

'No thank you,' Charlie said. 'Now as we understand things, Stanley Moore had been organising your defence against the company takeover.'

'That's right, a lot of good it did though,' Sir Mark replied.

'You had a meeting with Vincenzo Gallo at Amanda

Moore's dinner party. Was that just you and Stanley Moore, or was his wife in on the meeting too?' Charlie asked.

'No, just the three of us,' Sir Mark said.

'I understand Mr Gallo does not speak English too well, do you speak Italian?' Charlie asked.

'No, Stanley translated for me,' Sir Mark replied.

'Did you find out much from your meeting?' Harry asked.

'Mr Gallo wasn't very helpful. He said his bank was not in a position to speak for the people who owned the shares, so it was a bit of a dead end,' Sir Mark said.

'So when the takeover came it was unexpected?' Charlie asked.

'Well not totally. As you know, we had heard rumours, but the timing came as a surprise. We didn't think it would happen so soon. It didn't give us much chance to form a defence,' Sir Mark said.

'What was Stanley Moore's reaction to it?' Harry asked.

'Stanley was as surprised as anyone,' Sir Mark replied.

'When did you know Stanley Moore's father-in-law was backing the American oil company?' Charlie said.

'I didn't know that until after it had all happened,' Sir Mark said.

'He didn't tell you,' Harry said.

'No, I don't think he had any idea till the last minute,' Sir Mark said, looking at Harry.

'That's a bit strange,' Charlie said, 'as we know his wife had told him a good while before that her father was backing the American bid.'

Sir Mark turned and whispered something to the lawyer on his right that neither Charlie or Harry heard. Turning back he said 'That is news to me.'

'Why do you think he never told you?' Harry asked.

'Maybe he was being a loyal friend,' Sir Mark said. 'As I

understand from rumours he and his wife are divorcing, so maybe he wanted to get back at her.'

'But from what his wife has told us he knew well in advance. He knew the powerful backing that was behind the bid,' Harry said.

'But it was the two stakes that had been built quietly by Mr Gallo's bank and those in America that swung it,' Sir Mark said.

'Did you discuss that much with Stanley Moore before the takeover was launched?' Charlie asked.

'We did, you know we had the meeting with Vincenzo Gallo that Stanley arranged,' Sir Mark said, 'but we couldn't find anything out about the Americans, so Stanley said we should wait until the bid, then they would break cover and we could approach them. Unfortunately they had already done a deal to sell to the American oil company.'

'Didn't that seem strange to you?' Charlie asked.

'What's strange? We had tried to find out, but the shares were held by some New York lawyers as nominees,' Sir Mark replied.

'What I mean is, Stanley Moore knew his father-in-law was behind the group underwriting the American bid. A New York law firm is holding a lot of shares as nominee. It might have been assumed that an agreement had been made to sell to the Americans already, or at least the Americans had spoken to them,' Charlie said. 'After all, as I understand it, when the takeover started, all the shares that were held by Mr Gallo and the Americans were already promised.'

Sir Mark sat quietly for a moment. 'Are you saying that Stanley was in cahoots with his father-in-law all along?'

'No, I think he may have had an idea who the mysterious buyers were,' Charlie said.

'But if that's the case he would have known that they were going to back the takeover all along' Sir Mark said,

Harry and Charlie sat quietly, letting Sir Mark's statement hang in the air. They watched one of the lawyers lean over and whisper in Sir Mark's ear. He nodded and the lawyer got up and left.

'Why would he not tell you if he knew?' Harry asked, breaking the silence.

'There's only one answer to that,' Sir Mark said. 'I don't want to think he may have been playing both sides, but if he was, as I understand it from the city, he has put his bank in a perilous situation.'

'I spoke to Amanda Moore this morning,' Harry said, 'and what you've heard is right. Stanley Moore has put the bank in a bad way. He underwrote all the costs of the defence himself on behalf of the bank.'

'Well, at least I won't be the only one unemployed,' Sir Mark said, smiling.

'Now if I can just ask you about Jayne Cavill, who we now know is really called Rebecca Rosen,' Charlie said.

Sir Mark looked a little surprised at the question. 'I thought we had been through that already,' he said.

'Just a couple of questions to clear up. You told us she was seeing Stanley Moore outside the parties. Is there anything else you could tell us about that?' Charlie asked.

'Well, I only know what Angela told me,' Sir Mark said. 'Jayne, or whatever name you called her, went to Stanley's house a few times and he took her to dinner on a number of occasions.'

'Did Angela tell you how many times, or where they went?' Harry asked.

'No, it only came up in light conversation, when we were just chatting about Jayne,' Sir Mark said.

'Did Angela tell you anything else about her that you can recall?' Charlie asked.

'Not a lot, as I said it was only in passing really,' Sir Mark replied.

'Now you told us when we spoke to you last time, that Rebecca, sorry I will call her Jayne so you don't get confused,' Charlie said, 'you told us she talked to you about business. I know you said it sounded like she was after a job, but thinking back, did she ask any questions that you now think may have been to do with the takeover?'

Sir Mark thought for a moment before answering. 'I told you it was after we had all been drinking and having fun, so I'm not too certain. But now you ask, there was one time she asked about buying other companies. I explained how you went about it. When I finished, she did ask what if someone tried to buy my business, what would I do.'

'So you may have given her some idea of the strategy you would use,' Harry said.

'I may have, but as I said we had all been drinking,' Sir Mark said.

'But she may not have been drinking as much as you,' Harry replied.

'Now, you said she broke into your office and got into the drawers of your desk. Did you have anything in there that may have been useful to people involved in the takeover?' Charlie asked.

'All my papers were in there, a list of shareholders who I had spoken to about staying loyal and who could be relied on, those who were likely to sell their shareholding. I suppose if you sat down and read all the papers, you could have worked out what the proposed strategy would be,' Sir Mark said.

'But you would have to sit down and read every paper to find that all out,' Harry asked.

'Yes, there was a lot there to go through,' Sir Mark said.

'Did you see if she had a camera?' Charlie asked.

Sir Mark sat quietly for a moment. 'When I viewed the CCTV from the office, I can't say if I saw her with one. But now I recall, she didn't put the papers on the desk, she put them on the floor behind it. So if she had a camera you couldn't see if she was taking photographs.'

'When you sat down with Stanley Moore to defend your company against the takeover, you must have shown him all the details you had anyway. So what use would they be to him, if he was going to see them anyway?' Harry asked.

Sir Mark turned and spoke quietly to the lawyer who was still in the room. Turning back he said 'This was a long time before there was any thought of a takeover, and knowing who had what amount of shares and who would back the board one hundred per cent and who would likely sell, would have put a potential bidder in a strong position. It would also allow people to approach those they knew would sell well in advance.'

'Well, I don't think there's any more we need to ask you, Sir Mark,' Charlie said. 'You have been very helpful, but if I could just give you one piece of advice?'

'Go ahead, Charlie,' Sir Mark said.

'Next time a policeman asks you a question, give him an honest answer first time. Don't have brain failure, you might not get into the position you find yourself in now,' Charlie said.

When they got back to the Bentley, Harry asked 'What do you reckon, boss?'

'I think he has been well and truly played. From what he told us about Rebecca Rosen in his office, we can assume she took pictures of the papers in his desk. There's no other reason for staying out of sight,' Charlie said.

They both got in the car. 'You think Stanley Moore is the one who she was working with?' Harry asked.

'I think she was working with him,' Charlie said, 'but getting the evidence is the problem' Charlie started the car.

'Give Cramer a ring and ask him what he has got on the Notting Hill house where Stanley Moore is staying, and did he get anything from his phone records. We will go and drop in on Stanley Moore now.'

As they drove away, Harry got on the phone to Cramer. He spoke to him for five minutes as Charlie headed west towards Notting Hill. Harry got off the phone just as Charlie was driving along Euston Road, passing Kings Cross and Saint Pancras railway stations. 'The house is owned by a Swiss company, Cramer said he could try and trace it but it would take some time, but he thinks it's probably a tax dodge,' Harry said.

'I can ask Amanda who owns it,' Charlie said.

'He has got Stanley Moore's mobile phone records being sent over to him, but he got the house phone records,' Harry continued. 'He said the phone wasn't used much over the last few months, but strangely, last night a call was placed to Luxembourg.'

Charlie looked over and smiled. 'I like the sound of that,' he said.

'Well, it gets a little better,' Harry said. 'The house received three phone calls back from the same number in Luxembourg it had called.'

'Well, I suppose he could have been speaking to his friend Vincenzo Gallo. I think he's up to his neck in this case,' Charlie said.

'Cramer is going to see if he can get the police over there to find out who the phone belongs to,' Harry said.

Charlie nodded. 'Cramer's done well since he's been with us' he said. Charlie started to accelerate as he joined the start of the West Way flyover.

'I think it's been a bit of a win win for him too,' Harry said.

'Why's that, Harry?' Charlie asked.

'He and Manjitt have got very close,' Harry said.

Charlie turned his head to Harry, smiling. 'Harry, do you ever not know what people are up to?'

'I have no idea about you, boss,' Harry said, looking straight ahead.

It was Charlie who laughed out loud this time. 'Yeah right Harry, I believe you. Well that's nice for the two of them, but when the case finishes we won't be able to keep Cramer on. I got a whisper that Manjitt has passed her detective sergeant's exam. We can't have three detective sergeants on the team, so Cramer will have to return back to the fraud squad. That reminds me, Harry, we will need a new detective constable to take Manjitt's place when she steps up.'

Harry was smiling. 'She will make Jordan's life a misery once she's on the same rank, and poor old Hippie,' Harry laughed.

'I wouldn't worry about Danny, he just ignores most of what people say to him anyway,' Charlie said. He turned the car off the West Way and headed down the West Cross route towards Shepherds Bush.

'I will have a look around for a new detective constable who will fit into the team,' Harry said.

Once Charlie had reached the roundabout at Shepherds Bush, he turned left along Holland Park Avenue. 'I haven't been around this area for years,' Harry said.

'Did you work over this way?' Charlie asked.

'I worked out of Hammersmith and Shepherds Bush nicks for a few years,' Harry said. 'It looks a lot nicer now than it did then, we were raiding a different brothel every week around here and still couldn't close them all down.'

Charlie turned left off Holland Park Avenue and made his way through a maze of roads till he came to Saint Johns Garden. Charlie parked up was on a slight hill with the church of Saint John at the top dominating the view.

'This is all very nice,' Harry said, looking around at the houses. They both got out of the car. 'How shall we play it when we question him?'

'Let's see where he takes us, but if he gets stroppy let's just take him in and see how that shakes him up,' Charlie said as they walked up the hill. Stopping at a house on their left, they walked up the few stairs and rang the bell. After a minute a woman came to the door. She asked them what they wanted. Harry showed his warrant card and told her they were there to see Mr Moore. She let them come into the entrance, asking them to wait as she disappeared towards the back of the house.

'Cramer says he thinks this is a tax dodge,' Harry said. 'If it is, it's certainly working. I reckon this place is worth a couple of million easy.'

Charlie looked around. 'Give me the countryside any day Harry. I don't think I could move back into London,' he said. The woman reappeared and asked them to follow her. She led them down the hall and through a door. It opened up into a large sitting room were they found Stanley Moore sitting at a table on which a number of newspapers were open. Through the windows they saw a garden which from the outside of the house you wouldn't have imagined would be as big as it was. Stanley Moore stood up.

'I didn't think I would be seeing any more of the police,' he said.

'We are just tying up loose ends,' Charlie said.

Stanley Moore sat back down at the table. He didn't ask Charlie or Harry to sit. Charlie pulled out a chair opposite him at the table and sat down anyway. Harry walked across the room and looked at some of the paintings hanging there.

'I would ask you if you wanted a drink,' Stanley Moore said, 'but I am going out somewhere soon, so can you ask your questions and be gone.'

Harry turned around from looking at the pictures hanging on the wall. 'Going anywhere nice?' he said.

Stanley Moore turned in his chair. 'I have to meet with my lawyers.' Turning back to Charlie, he said 'What is it you want?'

'We wanted to ask you a few questions about the takeover?' Charlie said.

'The takeover? I thought I had sorted that out with him,.' He pointed over at Harry, who strolled back to where they were sitting.

'Ah, but I don't think you told us everything' Harry said.

'What do you mean?' Stanley Moore asked.

'You didn't say that you knew your wife's father was backing the takeover bid,' Charlie said.

'And don't forget boss, he forgot to tell Sir Mark,' Harry said.

'I don't know what that has got to do with your investigation,' he said. 'And I believe my knowledge of takeovers and what needs to be done in them is greater than yours.'

'That's probably true,' Harry said, 'but it didn't do you much good, you lost.' Stanley Moore glared at Harry.

'Why didn't you tell Sir Mark that your wife's father was involved?' Charlie said.

He turned back to look at Charlie 'I didn't know for certain, she only told me at the last moment.'

'Are you sure?' Harry said.

'Are you calling me a liar?' he said.

'In this case we have met a lot of people with forgetful memories, but if you want to use the term liar that's fine with me,' Harry said.

Stanley Moore said nothing for a moment. Charlie sat watching him. He knew Harry had got to him already.

'I'm not saying anymore about the takeover.' Stanley

Moore broke the silence. 'That has nothing to do with your investigation.' Charlie sat back, he knew Harry would like that.

'Oh so you're an expert on our investigation,' Harry said. 'Well, let's put the takeover to one side for a moment and talk about your girlfriend, Rebecca Rosen.' Charlie saw a recognition at the name in Stanley Moore's face.

'I have never heard of her,' he said.

'Oh yes, I forgot' Harry said. 'You prefer to use the name Jayne Cavill.' Stanley Moore didn't answer.

'You told us you entertained her at your house on a number of occasions,' Charlie said. 'How many times was it?'

Stanley Moore was looking a little worried. He said 'I don't know what you're trying to do, but I think I should have my lawyer with me if you want to ask any more questions.'

'Is that why your wife's divorcing you, because you were sleeping with Jayne Cavill at your house?' Harry said, ignoring Stanley Moore's words.

'Who do you think you are?' he said, standing up. 'You can leave the house now.'

'What I want to know,' Harry said, again ignoring what Stanley Moore said, 'is what your relationship with Rebecca Rosen was.'

'I don't know anyone by that name. Now you can leave please,' he said.

Charlie stood up. 'I think we should start again Mr Moore. Let me have a word with my officer.' Charlie walked over and whispered to Harry, who walked to the door and left the room. 'Now, if you would like to sit down please, and let's try and get the questions answered, then we can be out of your hair.'

Stanley Moore sat back down. 'I'm glad you're seeing some sense,' he said, 'but your officer was way out of line.'

'Now Jayne Cavill, you spent time with her at your house, is that right?' Charlie asked.

'Is that against the law?' Stanley Moore asked.

'No it's not. Did you ever meet her away from the house?' Charlie asked.

'You know I did, at the parties,' he said.

'Apart from the parties,' Charlie said.

'No, never,' Stanley Moore said.

'Are you sure. We have been told you took her to dinner on a number of occasions,' Charlie said.

Stanley Moore looked a little worried. 'You have been misinformed,' he said.

Harry came back into the room. He nodded to Charlie. 'Mr Moore has just told me he never met Jayne Cavill for dinner,' Charlie said.

Harry walked over to the table. 'Is that right?' he said, looking at Stanley Moore. 'I know you have been very busy, you don't think your mind is playing tricks on you?'

'I never met her for dinner or anything else,' he said.

'What is your relationship with Vincenzo Gallo?' Charlie asked.

Stanley Moore looked a little taken aback by the question. 'What has that got to do with you?'

'I think that's for us to decide,' Harry said.

Stanley Moore sat back in his chair. 'I think I've had enough of these questions, you can both leave now, and if you want to speak to me again you can contact my lawyers.' Before Harry or Charlie could say anything, they heard the front doorbell sound.

'Is there something you don't want to tell us?' Harry asked.

Stanley Moore stood up. 'Enough questions, please leave the house.'

The door to the room opened and the woman came into the room. 'There are two more police officers here,' she said. Behind her standing in the doorway were two uniformed police constables.

'What in heaven's name do they want?' Stanley Moore said.

'Don't worry yourself, sir, they're with us,' Harry said. 'They're your transport to the police station.'

Stanley Moore looked confused. 'What are you talking about?'

Harry signalled the officers to come over to them. 'Now sir, these nice policemen are going to take you for a ride to the station and we can continue our chat there, seeing as you're not prepared to answer any here.'

'This is ridiculous,' Stanley Moore said. 'I want to phone my lawyer.'

'You can do that when you get to the station,' Harry said, turning to the uniformed officers. 'Okay, take him away.'

One of the officers took hold of Stanley Moore's arm, who seemed to be in a state of shock and said nothing as he was led from the room. Harry pulled the other officer aside and spoke to him for a second. The officer nodded and left.

'What did you say to him?' Charlie asked Harry.

'I told him to make sure he gets stuck in lots of traffic on his way to the Yard, and to take at least two hours to get there,' Harry said.

Charlie stood up smiling. 'You have a devious mind, Harry.'

'Thank you, boss,' Harry said as he followed Charlie out of the room.

Rebecca Rosen sat on the bed with the map of the house and the area around it. She felt nicely relaxed after a light workout in the hotel gym, followed by a massage. She had changed into a dark tracksuit and trainers. She glanced at her watch, just coming up to three. She stood up, went to her bag on the dressing table and took five hundred pounds out and her passport, slipping them into her pocket. She walked back to the bed, picking up the map which she folded and put it in the other pocket. She had decided not to return to the Dorchester when the job was over, as whoever was watching her would be plotted up waiting for her to come back. She would just book into a small hotel somewhere till morning. Now, the first thing she would have to do is identify anyone who was following her. The second thing was to lose whoever it was.

Leaving the room she took the stairs down. When she reached the ground floor she walked over towards the front desk, looking in the mirror behind it to see if anyone was watching her. She saw no one. Giving the man behind the desk her room key, she turned and walked towards the main doors. As she passed through them the uniformed concierge asked if she needed a taxi. She said no.

Rebecca stood on the steps for a moment scanning the area. Seeing no-one obvious, she turned to her right, making for Park Lane. Turning right again and breaking into a trot, she went along the side of the hotel and up Park Lane towards Marble Arch. The traffic was all coming towards her, so if her followers had been in a car they would have had to drive down to Hyde Park corner roundabout, which was always heavy with traffic, go round that and come up the other side of Park Lane to catch up with her.

After trotting for a couple of hundred yards she suddenly darted to her left and ran across the road, weaving between the traffic, some of which got very close to knocking her down. Reaching the centre of the road, she vaulted the first crash barrier, but before jumping the next and continuing across the road she turned and looked back down the road. About a hundred yards away a man in jeans and a sweat shirt was halfway across the road, running in-between the traffic. She saw another man in a suit still on the pavement looking in her direction. Smiling she turned, vaulted the next barrier and again took her life in her hands as she weaved between the fast moving traffic. As she reached the other side, she went through a gate into Hyde Park, breaking into a sprint to try and put some space between her and her followers. She made her way towards Speaker's Corner. When she reached it she passed through a gate and found herself opposite Marble Arch. Looking over her shoulder, she still saw the man in jeans trotting towards her, but at least two hundred yards away. She couldn't see the man in the suit, but if they also had a car she would have to get into Oxford Street and lose herself amongst the shoppers.

Looking to her right, she saw the traffic had stopped at a set of lights. She sprinted across the road running beside Marble Arch itself. She did not wait as she reached the junction of Edgware Road and Oxford Street, but ran across the road, darting in between the traffic, a bus nearly knocking her over.

On reaching the other side she turned to her right making her away along Oxford Street. She stopped running and began to walk. There were plenty of shoppers going about their business and she felt comfortable now the odds were in her favour. Glancing over her shoulder she didn't see the man in jeans. She had a quick look for the man in the suit but couldn't see him either. She wanted to get to Selfridges department store. Once inside, she would use one of the back exits to disappear.

CHAPTER TWENTY THREE

Charlie and Harry had got back to the Yard and had called all the team together, told them what had happened that morning. They asked for any thoughts.

Manjitt said 'It might be an idea to revisit Sir Martin Oliver, he knew a lot about Stanley Moore. He might be able to tell us a few things that he forgot to mention when we spoke to him before.'

'That's an idea, you and Danny go and see him, and remember we don't have much time to pin Stanley Moore down. His lawyers will be screaming blue murder as soon as he rings them, so make sure Sir Martin understands we will take a dim view of any more lies or evasions,' Harry said. Manjitt nodded to Danny and they both got up and left the office.

'Cramer, any more on the phone calls?' Charlie asked.

'I was a bit lucky there, I managed to speak to an officer in Luxembourg who we had spoken to before about the case. He ran a quick check, the house is owned by an Italian company, the only registered person living there is a Mr Vincenzo Gallo,' Cramer said.

'Well done, now it would be interesting to know why the flurry of phone calls last night,' Harry said. 'What about the mobile records?'

'Not arrived yet, I will go and see if I can chase them up,' Cramer said, He left and went to his desk.

'What have you got, Jordan?' Charlie asked.

'I've been trying to chase down the house or flat she used as a hideout, but so far I've drawn a blank,' he said, 'although Hippie got hold of the taxi driver who dropped her at the airport. He told him he picked her up from Bow Road, so I have been concentrating in that area for now.'

'Alright, you carry on with that for now,' Charlie said. Jordan got up and left them.

'What now, boss?' Harry said.

'Well Harry, before we go and chat to Stanley Moore, I want you to get someone up from the fraud squad and you take them through what we know about the takeover,' Charlie said. He looked at his watch. 'How long do you think we have before he's dropped off here?'

'I think we have another hour, although I could always make a phone call and get it delayed a bit more,' Harry said.

'Let's play it by ear. When you talk to the fraud squad, see if they think there's anything in the evidence that we maybe able to hold him on,' Charlie said. 'I know his high-powered lawyer will be demanding we let him go, so if we can keep our hands on him, it might give us a chance to put a case together.'

'I will get on it straight away,' Harry said.

The man in the taxi was driving up Park Lane. It had taken him some time to get through the traffic, he heard on the radio that the two men following the woman had lost her at the beginning of Oxford Street. Luckily the second car that was on watch with them had been parked at the back of the Dorchester and when it heard she was going up Park Lane towards Marble Arch, the driver had gone through some back turnings and was now in Duke Street, about to turn onto Oxford Street. He continued to listen as he spotted one of his operatives on the corner of Marble Arch. He slowed and gave a blast on his horn. The other man turned saw the taxi, came over and got in. 'How did you lose her?' the driver said. The other man shrugged. The driver moved off, trying to manoeuvre through the traffic and get onto Oxford Street.

The other car that was looking for Rebecca was now moving up Oxford Street from the other direction. The driver and his passenger were scanning the street for the woman wearing a tracksuit with dark hair. They were just coming up to Selfridges when the passenger saw her on the other side of the road waiting to cross. He pointed her out to the driver, the passenger quickly got out, crossed the road and stood looking into the window of the department store, keeping one eye on the woman as she started to cross the road. The car driver got on the radio, letting the driver of the taxi know they had picked her up again.

Rebecca Rosen walked past the man looking in the window, taking no notice. She turned left and walked into Selfridges; the first thing to hit her was the strong sweet smell of perfume. She moved between the different counters selling all the big name perfume brands. Seeing the floor guide for departments, she quickly scanned it, taking in the signs for stairs. The second floor would flush out any followers who she hadn't spotted but were still on her tail. She carried on walking, not looking back, and boarded the escalator to take her up. She stood sideways, seeing if anyone else got on who stood out from the other shoppers around her. She saw no one. Getting to the first floor, she stepped off the escalator, walked a few paces, stopped, turned and watched the people coming up behind her. It was the menswear department, so she carefully scanned the faces of all the men coming up. She stayed there for a minute but none of them looked like the two men she had seen on Park Lane. She walked over and took the escalator up to the next floor.

Getting off, she found herself exactly where she wanted to be, in the ladies department. Looking around she saw the sign for lingerie, any man coming over to this department would stand out like a sore thumb. Walking quickly, she slipped through the aisles towards the back, stopping by a high rack of nightdresses which hid her from view, but by pulling them to one side afforded her a clear sight of the escalators. She stood there for two minutes, not moving. when a man appeared at the top of the escalator. Getting off, she saw him look around. He went to his left, looked over into the dress department then came back looking in the lingerie area, then walked back to the escalator and stopped. A minute later another man came up and joined him. Rebecca watched them talk, then the second man got on the escalator and went up to the next floor. That's good, Rebecca thought, I have you two now. She would wait a while, then move along the back wall around the shop towards the stairway and get out of the shop that way.

The security guard in the operations room of Selfridges was watching the security cameras. 'Bob, what do you make of this woman?' he said to the guard next to him. He pointed to a woman in the ladies' lingerie department who appeared to be hiding and sorting through nightdresses.

'Looks suspicious, you'd better alert floor security about her, they can have a word,' the other guard said. He got on the radio to floor security, giving the woman's description and where she was. He carried on watching her, in case she stole anything or moved somewhere else.

Rebecca was waiting for her chance to move, now she had seen her followers. But the man by the escalator was a good watcher. His head was constantly on the move scanning all around him. She was going to have to be careful if she was not to be spotted. She saw a man and woman get off the escalator behind the man and come into the lingerie department. There was no recognition between them and the man. She would give it another couple of minutes to make sure there wasn't anyone else before she made her move.

The security guard was still watching the woman, who had not moved since they had spotted her. He saw the two store detectives come into view and watched as they approached her.

Rebecca saw the couple who had got off the escalator make their way into the lingerie department and head towards her. The man who was following her was still standing looking around. She would make her move in a minute. The couple came right up to where she was hiding. 'Excuse me,' the man said, 'we are store security. Do you mind telling us what you're doing?'

Rebecca was slightly taken aback. 'Just looking for a present for my sister,' she said.

'You have been observed acting suspiciously, we must ask you to leave the store,' the man said.

Rebecca was looking past the couple at the man who was now looking in their direction. 'You must be mistaken,' Rebecca said. 'I'm just doing a little shopping.'

' I'm sorry madam, but I must ask you to leave,' the woman said.

Rebecca now saw the man who had been following her start to move in their direction. He could clearly see her, now she had been forced to move from behind the rack of nightdresses. He was within ten feet of her now. Rebecca suddenly threw her arms forward catching the male store detective in the chest. He went flying backwards, crashing into the man following Rebecca. Before the female store detective could react, Rebecca had kicked her in the side and she went down screaming in pain. Rebecca ran towards the two men who were trying to regain their feet. Ignoring the store detective, she lashed out with her fist, striking the follower in the temple. He fell backwards. Rebecca didn't wait to see what her handywork had done, but carried on running towards the stairs at the back of the department The security guard who was watching the camera had seen all that had happened, pushed the emergency alarm and got on the radio to tell all security staff to make their way to the second floor.

As Rebecca ran through the department, out of the corner of her eye she saw the second man who had followed her appear from the escalator, coming down from the third floor. She knew he had spotted her as she saw him start to run in her direction. She reached the stairway and pushed open the doors, turning to the right and running down them.

The security man had relayed all that was going on. The woman had attacked the store detectives and a shopper, so he warned everybody they were dealing with a violent person. As Rebecca turned the corner of the stairway coming to the first floor, two men were coming up. They stopped when they saw her. 'Now miss, take it easy and relax,' one of them said. Rebecca halted for a moment. She heard the clang of the door above. It must be the other man, she thought. Taking a couple more steps down, she suddenly jumped forward, crashing into the two men below her. As they all fell backwards, she grabbed the man closest to her so she landed on top of him. He gasped as he hit the floor. all the wind knocked out of him. The other store detective was scrabbling to regain his feet as Rebecca rolled off the other one, twisted and was on her feet faster. Her right leg snapped out, catching the man flush in the face. Out of the corner of her eye she saw a shadow, felt a pain in her side and was thrown back against the wall. Regaining her senses, she turned and saw the other follower. She smiled inwardly. This is fun, she thought. Sliding along the wall, putting the two prone store detectives between her and the man, Rebecca sized him up. Fit and strong, just how I like them. He noticed

Rebecca's move and he moved to cut off her escape down the stairs. This is what Rebecca wanted. She leapt forward, crashing into the man. He toppled backwards and with nothing behind him but the down staircase he lost his balance, his arms windmilling, trying to regain his footing but failing. He started to fall down them. Rebecca was still holding him, with one hand gripping his jacket. Her other hand went to his face, her sharp nails finding one of his eyes. The scream he let out must have been heard through most of the shop. As they hit the floor below, Rebecca rolled away from him and crashed into the wall. As she stood up, the man was on his hands and knees, his head turned in her direction. His right eye was a bloody mess, with blood pouring from the socket. Rebecca saw him twist his body and his right hand went into his jacket. Two more store detectives had come through the doors above. They started to shout down at Rebecca and the man, but Rebecca hardly heard. She knew what the man was after. Pushing away from the wall she leapt at him, just as his hand came from under his jacket holding a pistol. As he brought his hand up to aim, Rebecca was on him. It was unfortunate for the man that all his weight was now on his left arm. Rebecca's foot connected with his elbow, snapping it instantly. Another scream left the man's mouth, but he still brought the pistol up towards Rebecca. Rolling to one side, she grabbed his right arm just as the pistol went off, the bullet striking the wall and ricocheting off the concrete. The two store detectives dived for cover above, getting on the radio to ask for armed police as a gun had been fired. Rebecca now had the man where she wanted him. His only good arm she had tightly in her grip, twisting it till the gun fell from the man's hand. As she saw it drop, she let go of his arm with one hand and used it to chop down on his neck. The man immediately went limp. As she let go of him he fell to the ground. She had one glance at the pistol lying on the floor, smiled, jumped up and continued down the stairs not looking back. Coming to the ground floor, she went through the doors leading to the street. Glancing to her left, she saw Oxford Street. Don't want to go there, she thought, so turning right and crossing to the other side of the road she walked quickly till she reached a road junction. Looking up at the road signs, she saw she was at the junction of Orchard Street and Portman Square. She didn't want to stay on the street any longer, as she could hear the noise of police sirens coming from all directions. Looking up and down the street, a taxi was coming towards her with its for hire sign on. Holding her hand up she hailed it. As it stopped she was in the back in an instant. Hearing the driver ask where she wanted to go, she said the first thing that came to mind, Harrods. She saw the driver switch the for hire sign off and the taxi moved back into the traffic.

Rebecca leaned back into the seat, her side stung from where she had received the blow in the fight. She would check it out later, but she had that feeling of elation that she always got after a fight or an operation. Rebecca rested her head on the back of the seat. There is one thing, she thought. The pistol had been a .22 Beretta, a gun she had been issued with herself when she was on an assassination mission. So her old employers wanted her dead. I will have to be on my guard all the time now, she thought.

The two store detectives had waited till the woman had disappeared down the stairs before they moved. They had told security to call a couple of ambulances as both the store detectives upstairs and the shopper were injured, and the two others who had fought the woman on the stairs were in a bad way, along with another man who was also down on the ground. One of them stayed with their injured work colleagues, whilst the other one went down the stairs to check

on the man who they saw draw a gun. When he reached him
he saw a lot of blood coming from the man's face, he picked
up his arm looking for a pulse. Turning his head to the store
detective above, he said 'I think he's dead.' Suddenly the doors
behind them opened, and two policemen appeared with guns.

Manjitt and Danny walked into Sir Martin Oliver's gallery.
There were a number of people standing round looking at
pictures. Manjitt couldn't see Sir Martin, so she walked over
to the desk where a young woman was seated. 'We would like
to see Sir Martin,' she said as the woman looked up at them.

'Can I have your names?' the woman asked.

'Lord and Lady Truscott,' Manjitt replied. The woman
looked at her in a disbelieving manner, but picked up the
phone and called up to Sir Martin's office. She repeated the
names given her by Manjitt. Replacing the phone, she told
Manjitt Sir Martin would be down in a minute. Manjitt and
Danny walked away from the desk to look at some of the
pictures hanging on the wall. 'How much do you think they
would charge for this picture?' Danny said, looking at a
number of diagonal broad stripes painted across the canvas.

Manjitt looked at the picture. 'I reckon its more than your
yearly salary,' she said.

Danny nodded. 'That's not bad, I can appreciate that,'
Danny said.

'You're not serious,' Manjitt looked at Danny.

'Can't you see the pattern and movement in the painting?'
Danny said.

Manjitt shook her head in wonderment. A voice behind
them said 'The young man is right, the painting is full of life.'
They turned and found Sir Martin Oliver standing there. His
face registered recognition when he saw Manjitt.

'Hello Sir Martin, I hope you remember me, Detective

Constable Virdee,' she said, 'and this is Detective Constable Kane.'

'Yes, I remember you but what is it you want? I thought I had answered all your questions,' Sir Martin said.

'If we could talk in your office? I'm sure you don't want our conversation overheard,' Manjitt replied.

'Yes alright, follow me,' he said. They followed him across the gallery and up to his office. He walked around his desk and sat down. Manjitt and Danny took seats opposite him.

'Now, what is it you want?' he said.

'My boss sends his regards and says he knows you will answer our questions without any problems. He told us to tell you he hopes he doesn't have to come down here and ask you himself,' Manjitt said.

Sir Martin sat back in his chair, a resigned look on his face. 'Okay, ask away.'

'Now you identified the woman in this picture with Angela Cook as Jayne Cavill,' Manjitt pushed the picture of the two women across the table.

Sir Martin picked up the picture and looked at it. 'Yes, that's her,' he said, passing the picture back.

'Now, you told us that Angela was seeing Sir Martin Coale away from the parties,' Manjitt said.

Sir Martin nodded. 'Yes, that's right.'

'We want you to tell us all you know about the other girl,' Danny said.

'What's to tell? Angela brought her along,' Sir Martin said.

'But you had dinner with the two of them, was that on more than one occasion?' Manjitt said.

Sir Martin took his time answering. 'Just the one occasion, yes.'

'You sound like you're not sure,' Danny said.

'No, no it was only the one time,' he said.

'Did you have dinner alone with Jayne Cavill, or meet her besides at the parties?' Manjitt asked. Again Sir Martin hesitated. 'Now, if you are going to think about everything you are prepared to tell us, we will get up and leave and you can deal with my boss.'

Sir Martin took a deep breath. 'Okay, I'm sorry, yes I did meet her separately for dinner.'

'Why?' Danny said.

'It was nothing sinister, I knew she spoke Italian and I had some rich Italians who were interested in some expensive paintings. I asked her if she would go out to dinner with them.' He stopped then began again, 'And make sure they had a good time, to help make sure they bought the pictures.'

'You mean sleep with them?' Danny said.

'Yes, but you have to do everything to get a sale,' Sir Martin said.

'And did she go to dinner with them?' Manjitt asked.

'Yes, she did,' he said.

'Do you remember the name of the Italians?' Manjitt asked.

'No, I can't recall their names,' Sir Martin said.

Manjitt and Danny sat quietly, not saying anything but just staring at Sir Martin, who started to fidget in his chair.

'What I meant to say is I will have to look through my files,' he finally said.

'Well done, good of you,' Danny said. The sarcasm not lost on Sir Martin.

'Did you meet her any other times?' Manjitt asked.

'No,' Sir Martin said.

'Do you know if she was meeting anyone else away from the parties?' Danny asked.

Again Sir Martin hesitated. 'Come on, Sir Martin, we don't have all day,' Manjitt said, raising her voice.

'Well it was just the once. I had been to see some friends in

Chelsea and we went out to dinner. When I got to the restaurant and we were being shown to our table, I noticed Jayne sitting with Stanley Moore in the corner.'

'Did he see you?' Danny asked.

Sir Martin smiled. 'No, he was too busy talking to Jayne.'

'Did you tell him you had seen him?' Manjitt said.

'No, I never mentioned it,' Sir Martin said.

'Did you tell anyone else?' Danny asked.

'No, I never told anyone,' Sir Martin replied.

'What was the name of the restaurant? And can you remember the date?' Manjitt asked.

'The restaurant is Italian, beautiful food, it's called La Famiglia. I can't really remember the date,' Sir Martin said.

'And you never saw her with anyone else, or were told she was meeting other people,' Manjitt asked.

'No, that's the only time,' he said.

'Well, thank you for being so helpful,' Manjitt said, standing. 'Now before we leave, do you want to have a look in your files for the names of the Italians?'

Rebecca had been dropped off at Harrods by the taxi. When she entered she looked for the toilet signs and made her way there. Once inside, she entered a cubicle, undid her track suit top and pulled up her sweat shirt. She saw the beginnings of a large bruise starting to show on her side. Running her hands across it, she winced. She might have a cracked rib, she would go to a chemist and buy some strong painkillers. When she had done the job and left the country she would find a doctor to check it out. Tidying herself up, she left the cubicle, went and washed her face and ran her wet hands through her hair. She felt hungry after the fight. I will get something to eat before I do anything else, can't go to work on an empty stomach.

The man was seated behind the desk at the Israeli embassy in London. He had the telephone in his hand, but was holding it slightly away from his ear. The two men standing in front of him could clearly hear a voice screaming down it from the other end. At the end of the conversation, he said 'I will do all I can to clear things up, sir.' He put the phone down and turned in his chair to face the two men standing. He said nothing for a minute.

'Now as head of operations in London and the whole of the United Kingdom, I could start by asking why I wasn't informed you would be carrying out a job here. But putting that to one side till later, what about your injured operatives?' Mr Dyan said.

The taller of the two men in front of him said 'We have one man killed and another in hospital.'

'God what a mess, could you not recover your men before the police arrived?' Dyan asked.

'No sir, we had no time,' the man said.

'And you have lost the person you were attempting to eliminate or capture?' Dyan said.

'Yes sir, she has disappeared again,' the man replied.

'So, do you have any good news about this sorry episode?' Dyan said.

Both men in front of him remained quiet. The silence was broken by the phone on the desk ringing. Dyan picked it up, listened for a second then said 'Okay put her through.' After a short conversation he replaced the phone. Looking back at the two men in front of him, he said 'That was an assistant director of MI5 asking me to come over for a chat. It was put politely, but it ended with the words in the next fifteen minutes. Could either of you hazard a guess what she wants to talk about?' Both men shuffled their feet looking down at the floor. Dyan stood up. 'You will not leave the embassy. I will see you both again when I get back from my chat with British intelligence. I want some ideas on how you are going to put this mess right.'

Harry put the phone down. 'That was the boys in the van,' he said to Charlie. 'They will be here in half an hour.'

Charlie looked up from the file he was reading. 'Okay Harry. I'd better pop up and have five minutes with Crick and put him in the picture. If things go wrong with Stanley Moore, there's bound to be a row about it.'

'Okay boss, I will keep going through everything Stanley Moore has told us, so if he starts to change his story we will have him,' Harry said.

Charlie got up and left. He met Manjitt and Danny coming back to the office and told them to sit down with Harry and tell him everything they had learnt from Sir Martin Oliver. When he got up to Crick's office Charlie found him with his secretary, a stack of files on his desk, looking a little harassed. Crick looked up at Charlie. 'I have to start the budget review,' he said.

'A worthy job,' Charlie said, the irony lost on Crick. 'I just wanted to bring you up to speed with the case.'

'Take a seat, Charlie,' Crick said. He told his secretary to take fifteen minutes for a break and she left the office. 'So Charlie, any news about the woman you're after?'

'Not yet sir, but we're getting Stanley Moore in for questioning, as we believe he was working with her,' Charlie said.

'He's not involved in the murders, is he?' Crick asked.

'I'm not sure yet, but I believe he has some connection to what's been going on,' Charlie said.

The phone on Crick's desk rang. Picking it up, he listened then said 'I have the officer in charge of the investigation with me now.' He carried on talking for a minute then put the phone down. 'That was interesting, the call was from a commander at West End central. There's been a shooting at Selfridges department store. One man is dead and a number of other people are injured, but he wanted me to get hold of you. Apparently the suspect is a woman. He thinks the woman involved is the one you're after. One of his officers told him it looked like her. He's viewed the CCTV and compared it to the pictures your team sent out, he's of the same opinion.'

Charlie sat forward. 'But why would she come back?' He took out his mobile and called Harry, repeated to him what Crick had said. He told Harry to send Jordan down to Selfridges and talk to the commander and view the CCTV for himself. As Charlie got off the phone and before he could speak to Crick, the phone on the desk rang again. Charlie watched as Crick talked for a minute. When he put the phone down he looked at Charlie.

'That was our friends from Thames House. The dead man is an Israeli national. He wasn't shot, he fired the gun but he was killed by a woman he was fighting. Also another Israeli national was knocked out in one of the stores' departments, along with a number of injured store detectives.'

'So why are the spooks from Thames house phoning you?' Charlie said.

'They've had our friend Mr Dyan in for a chat,' Crick said. 'They didn't go into everything. But we can assume they were Israeli agents trying to capture her for some reason. And as we had inquired about her before they thought it best to let us know.'

'Could you try and get another meeting with Dyan?' Charlie said. 'It would be handy if we could speak to him, seeing as it would appear he knew she was in the country and never told us.'

'I will try, Charlie, but it sounds like Thames House are fuming at what's happened,' Crick said.

Charlie stood up. 'I'd better get back,' he said, 'I want to bring everyone up to speed that she's back in the country.'

'Okay Charlie, I'll see what I can do about meeting Mr Dyan,' he said.

When Charlie got back to the office, he found the entire team sitting round Harry's desk except Jordan. Harry filled Charlie in on what Manjitt and Danny had found out from questioning Sir Martin Oliver. He said Jordan would call in as soon as he got something definite on what had happened down at Selfridges.

Charlie pulled a chair over and sat down with the rest of them. 'So if we assume it's Rebecca Rosen,' he said. 'Why has she come back, she was away scot free? What is so important that she has risked a chance of getting caught?' He looked around the faces of his team, waiting for an answer.

It was Danny who spoke first. 'We never found the pictures from the parties. Maybe she was after them, or she has some money stashed away.'

'I don't think it's pictures,' Harry said. 'What good would they do her, she's not going to blackmail anyone, we know all about what went on.'

'What about coming back for money?' Charlie said.

'I don't buy that.' Manjitt said. 'We know her bank account was pretty healthy. She bought those diamonds, and for all we know she has money somewhere else, she was getting money sent from Israel, remember.'

'But she did lose hundred and fifty thousand when the druggie stole her bag,' Danny said.

'No, I don't think it's either of those,' Charlie said. 'To take the risk she's taking, it must be to clear up something.'

'You think she's come back to kill someone else?' Harry said.

'I do, Harry,' Charlie replied. 'But who is it?'

'Well, if she thought Stanley Moore could be a weak link to her, it could be him,' Manjitt said.

'Okay, anyone else we can think of?' Charlie said.

'Sir Martin Oliver.' Danny said. 'He knows a lot that went on.'

'But couldn't she have killed those two anytime she wanted before we got onto her?' Cramer said.

'What about Lord and Lady Dorres?' Danny said.

'Blimey, I would happily bump those two off,' Harry said, 'but it's the same, she could have got to them when she was here.'

'So why come back?' Charlie said.

Harry said 'You know boss it's strange. She gets out of the country untouched, we have no idea where she had gone, except she took a plane to Luxembourg, but she could have gone anywhere in Europe from there. Is it me who finds it strange that there are a number of phone calls to and from Vincenzo Gallo yesterday and she reappears? And as I recall, she worked for his father in Italy. She could have been hiding at his house all along.'

'That's a good point Harry, let's stick with that' Charlie said. 'So what do we think the phone calls could have been about?'

'They must have been about the takeover,' Danny said.

'Yes, what other reason would Stanley Moore ring Gallo for?' Manjitt said.

'Are they planning an attempt to bump off Sir Mark Coale?' Cramer said.

'That could be a reason, but they've already taken him to the cleaners, why stir things up for themselves?' Harry said. 'No, there's something else going on we can't see yet.'

'Cramer, have you got Stanley Moore's mobile records yet?' Charlie asked.

'No not yet, I will call them and say we need them now,' he said.

'Tell them if we don't have them in the next hour, someone will be arrested for obstructing the police. But make sure you get them and when you do, check first if there are any phone calls to the number Rebecca Rosen was using.'

'Manjitt, you get Stanley Moore's bank details, you might get a bit of trouble trying to get access. If you do, see Harry, he will help you. When you get them, first thing you do is check if he paid for a dinner at that restaurant Sir Martin said he saw him at. Then check if he paid any money into the account that was in the name of Jayne Cavill, and any other large payments going to our friend Vincenzo Gallo.'

Cramer and Manjitt got up from the desk and went off. 'Now you two,' Charlie said to Harry and Danny, 'I have a little job for you, but I have to make a phone call first.' Charlie put a call through to Amanda Moore, he spoke to her for a few minutes. When he got off the phone, he said to the two of them. 'Now listen, this is going to be a bit naughty. According to Amanda Moore, the house Stanley Moore has been staying at is owned by a friend of his who lives in the Middle East and they won't be home anytime soon. There is a house keeper there at all times. Harry and I met her when we nicked Stanley Moore earlier. Now what I need you to do is get into the house to have a look around.' Charlie turned to Harry. 'Any ideas, Harry? Stanley Moore must have some things in the house that he would rather us not know about.'

'Boss, surely you don't want us to do something underhand,' Harry said.

'No not us, just Danny and you,' Charlie said, turning to look at Danny.

'Boss, I want to know if this will help with my police career,' Danny said.

'Without a doubt, as long as no one knows what we have done,' Charlie said. He turned to Harry. 'So any thoughts, Harry?'

'Well, with the housekeeper being there all the time, we need her to invite us in to look around. If the alarms were to go off, she would call the police,' Harry said.

'I like your thinking Harry, I will leave it with you and Danny,' Charlie said, 'while I sort out Stanley Moore when he arrives.'

Charlie got up and left the two of them and made his way down to custody to speak to the officer in charge about the suspect that was coming in.

Harry stood up. 'Come on, Hippie, let's go and get an invitation to tour Stanley Moore's hideaway.'

Rebecca was just finishing a nice meal in Harrods restaurant, she sat back and took a drink from the glass of wine she had brought with the meal. She knew from the trouble at Selfridges that the police were not stupid enough not to view the CCTV. Someone would recognise her and realise that she was back in the country, but they would have no idea why she was here. She had her new passport and enough cash to slip back out of the country when the job was done without any problems from them. One thing that did bother her though, she must have been followed when she was with Vincenzo in Luxembourg, she would try and ring him, to warn him to be on the lookout. It also meant she couldn't go back to Luxembourg, but she would work out later which country she would fly to. Finishing off her wine, it was time to make her way to the house. She would take the underground as far as she could and walk the rest of the way. She wanted to walk around the area to get a feel of the place before breaking in.

Mr Dyan had returned to the embassy. He was annoyed, he wasn't used to being torn off a strip and embarrassed like he had been by the director of MI5. He was determined to get this sorted out, he picked up the phone and told his secretary he wanted the two operatives in his office. He then put a direct call through to the foreign ministers office in Tel Aviv. He had the idea of a plan in his head, but would need the highest backing to salvage something from the disaster.

The two men entered the office whilst he was still on the phone. He pointed to the front of his desk. The two men came over and stood there waiting. After he put down the phone he looked at them, said nothing, letting them sweat. He could see they were worried about their futures. Then he told them of the plan he had got the green light from Israel to run with. They left the office to organise what he had told them. He picked up the phone and called the Israeli embassy in Belgium.

Harry parked the car, they were in the road that ran parallel to St Johns Garden. 'What have you got in mind, Harry,' Danny said.

'Well first things first,' Harry replied. He took out his phone and placed a call to an inspector in the local nick. When he got off the phone, he got out of the car and went to the boot. When he came back Danny saw he was holding a large catapult.

'I know it's a silly question, Harry, but what's that for?' Danny asked.

'Hippie, don't tell me you don't keep a catapult in the boot of your car for emergencies,' Harry said.

Danny looked at him lost for words, so he stayed silent. Harry wound down the window, took a ball bearing from his pocket and put it in the catapult. 'Let's hope I haven't lost my touch' he said, as he pulled the thick elastic back. He was aiming at the first floor window at the back of the house

Stanley Moore had been living in. He let the shot go, but hit the wall below the window.

Danny, who had been craning his neck to see were Harry was shooting at,said 'looks like you've lost your touch, Harry.'

Harry took another ball bearing from his pocket and fired again. This time the breaking of glass could clearly be heard, followed by a high pitched alarm going off. Harry sat back. 'Ah can't you hear the house calling to you Hippie, come and save me.'

Danny smiled, looked at Harry and said 'I worry about you sometimes, Harry.'

Harry's phone went off. He answered and said 'Don't worry, we will take it.Call all the local cars off. Turning to Danny, he said 'We have to investigate a report of a break-in at a house near us.' He started the car, drove round the corner to St Johns Garden and parked outside the house. The alarm was still sounding. 'Come on then, Hippie, let's put the housekeeper's mind at rest, show her how efficient the police are.'

They both got out of the car and walked up to the door and Harry rang the bell. The door was opened nearly immediately by the woman Harry recognised as the house keeper. It was Danny who spoke. 'Hello madam, we have a report of a break-in.' He showed her his police warrant card. 'We were just passing when we heard the emergency call.'

'Yes, I heard some glass breaking in one of the upstairs rooms and the alarm went off,' she said.

'Okay, can you turn off the alarm, and we will search the house to check no-one is inside. Are there any other people at home?' Danny asked.

'No, there's no one else in,' the woman said. She turned and pressed some buttons on the alarm box on the wall beside the door. The alarm stopped.

Harry and Danny went into the house. Danny said 'We will go upstairs and check things out. Why don't you go and sit in the kitchen till we have made sure everything is okay and there are no burglars in the house.'

Charlie was standing in the custody suite when two constables walked in with Stanley Moore between them. Seeing Charlie, Stanley Moore said 'I suppose you're feeling good with yourself, I have been stuck in that van for over an hour.'

'I am sorry about that, sir,' Charlie said. He turned to the two constables. 'Why has it taken you so long to get here?'

'Sorry sir, but the traffic was very bad. I think there was a accident and some road closures so it's at a standstill in places,' one of the constables said.

'There you go sir,' Charlie said, looking at Stanley Moore. 'Even you can appreciate the state of the London traffic.'

'I want to ring my solicitor now,' Stanley Moore said.

'Well, the custody officer will look after you,' Charlie said, pointing to the officer behind the desk, 'As soon as his paperwork is done, he will let you make your call.'

Stanley Moore walked up to the desk. 'Come on, get on with it,' he said, 'and I want to make my phone call,' turning his head to look at Charlie. 'I want to make it clear in front of everyone here, I will not be answering any questions till he arrives.'

'I will leave him with you,' Charlie said to the custody officer. 'Ring me when his solicitor arrives.' Turning to the two constables he said 'Well done boys, if you need anything just ring the squad room and ask for me.'

'Yes sir,' they said in unison, smiling.

Harry found the room on the first floor were the window had been broken. He said to Danny, 'Before we start having a look around for anything interesting, find the ball bearing I used.' The two of them started to search the floor. After a couple of minutes Danny discovered it beside a pillow on the bed. He tossed it to Harry. 'Well done, Hippie,' he said. 'We don't want forensics finding it and asking questions. Open the lock and slide the window up so it looks like someone has been in here searching.' Danny walked over to the window, twisted the lock and pushed the window up far enough so anyone outside could climb in. 'Now let's see if Stanley Moore or our burglar has left anything lying about,' Harry said, rubbing his hands together.

Danny shook his head. 'Harry, it's always an education working with you.'

As Charlie got back to the team's office his mobile rang. It was Jordan. He confirmed the woman on the CCTV was Rebecca Rosen. Charlie told him to get back to the Yard straight away. As he walked to his desk, he saw Cramer talking to another man. Cramer saw him and came over with the man beside him. 'Sir, this is Inspector Grainger from the fraud squad, he had a call from Harry about some information.'

'Yes, sit down, Grainger,' Charlie said. 'How are you doing with those phone records?' he asked Cramer.

'Got them all through now, I am just checking them for any numbers that would interest us,' he said.

'Okay, get on with it. We need to tie him into this case,' Charlie said. He sat down in his chair. 'Take a seat, inspector. I don't know how much Chief Inspector Davis told you.'

'He said you suspected fraud, insider dealing, money laundering,' Grainger replied.

'Yes, that about covers it,' Charlie said. He stood up. 'Now I know he had a file he put together for you with all the relevant information and names in.' Charlie walked over to

Harry's desk. Papers and files were all over it. He picked a few up, glanced at them and put them down again, moved some more papers to check some more files but they weren't the one he wanted. 'One moment,' he said to Grainger. Taking out his phone he called Harry. After a chat lasting thirty seconds, he lifted up a bunch of files and extracted the bottom one. Walking back to Grainger, he passed it over. 'He has his own particular filing system,' Charlie said.

'I have heard of Chief Inspector Davis, sir,' Grainger said. 'I don't think there are many people who would tell him how he should keep his files.'

'You're right there,' Charlie said.

'How is Cramer getting on with you?' Grainger asked.

'He's a good officer, I think he will do well in the future,' Charlie said.

'I look forward to having him back and bringing some of what he's learned from your team with him,' Grainger said.

Charlie sat back, smiling. 'Not all he's learned, I'm sure,' Charlie said.

'Well, all the good bits,' Grainger said.

'Inspector, surely you're not saying he may have picked up some bad habits?' Charlie said, still smiling.

'Perish the thought, sir,' Grainger said, smiling back.

'One thing,' Charlie said. 'I have Stanley Moore in a cell downstairs. We believe he is at the centre of everything that will interest you. I will be questioning him a bit later, when I've finished with him, if you want to have a chat I will call you.'

'That might be a good idea,' Grainger said. 'I will have a quick read through this file, make a few phone calls to city regulators, find out if they have heard anything.' He stood up. 'Thanks for the heads up, sir.'

'That's okay, one last thing,' Charlie said. 'You might

want to speak to Sir Mark Coale. We think he is the one who's been turned over. I think you might find him more than helpful.'

'I will do, sir,' Grainger said. He turned and left the office.

Charlie's phone rang. It was Crick. He told Charlie he had been onto Thames House about another meeting with Dyan. He was assured Mr Dyan would be in touch. Crick said he had given them Charlie's number so Dyan would ring him direct. Charlie thanked Crick, said he would keep him up to speed when he had got the call. Putting the phone down, he saw Jordan come back into the office and walk towards him. 'Well, what did you get?' Charlie asked.

'Got a copy of the CCTV.' Jordan held up a CD. 'She really made a mess over there, boss.' He pulled the television over, slipped the CD in and sat on the edge of Charlie's desk as the picture came on. 'It's only about five minutes long, I only wanted the bits that she was in.' As they were watching Manjitt came over and stood and watched. When it was finished, Jordan said 'That's definitely her.'

'Yes, that's her,' Charlie said. 'I see her hair's gone dark again.'

'According to the security they picked her out because she was acting suspiciously,' Jordan said.' They thought she was hiding to do some shop-lifting, but it would seem she was trying to avoid our two Israeli friends.'

'Well, you'd better get that picture out to all forces, and make sure they know she should only be approached with extreme caution,' Charlie said.

Jordan got the CD from the television and went off to get some still photographs from it to send out. Charlie turned to Manjitt. 'Did you find anything?' he asked.

She laid a sheet of paper in front of him. 'I highlighted his dinner date,' she said.

'Well done, are there any other strange ones?' Charlie asked.

'Well, there are quite a few restaurant dinners and stays in hotels, but as we have no idea whether it was with her, it could just be work,' Manjitt said.

'Okay, what about payments to her?' Charlie asked.

'There are a couple, when she was using the name Jayne Cavill, not large amounts. I suspect he has accounts abroad that he could use to move any big payments about,' Manjitt said.

'I bet I know whose bank that would be,' Charlie said.

Vincenzo Gallo had spoken to his father about his thoughts on Rebecca going back to England. His father had told him not to worry and he would see him in a couple of days when Vincenzo came to Rome. He left the office and walked towards a local delicatessen he used. He felt a bit peckish. He would have a stroll and clear his head as he ate, then go back to the office and finish off the work he had to do.

He crossed the road and turned the corner into a narrow street. The deli was about fifty yards further along. A white van went past him and stopped. The passenger got out and opened the sliding side door to do a delivery. Vincenzo was going to cross over to the other side when the man stepped back and said 'Go on sir, you pass.' Vincenzo thanked him and went to go by. As he got level with the door he felt a shove in his back. He fell into the van where hands grabbed him, pinning him down. The door slammed shut and he was in darkness. He heard a voice say 'Stay still and you won't be harmed.' A hood was pulled over his head and he felt his arms pulled behind him and felt his hands being roughly tied together. He lay still. God, I'm being kidnapped, he thought. The van's engine started and he felt it move off.

Harry and Danny had been through all the rooms on the first floor and found nothing. Danny went down and spoke to the housekeeper to let her know to stay where she was. As they had found a smashed window that had been forced open, they would check all the rooms to make sure no one was hiding in the house. When he rejoined Harry, they went up to the second floor. 'This is a really nice place,' Danny said.

'We are not looking for a place to live, Hippie,' Harry said. He opened a door and went in. Danny followed him. 'This looks like the room he's been sleeping in.' They saw men's clothes laying on the bed and the back of a chair.

'Very nice,' Danny said, looking round.

'Less of the estate agent, and look in those drawers over there,' Harry said pointing to his left. Harry opened up some wardrobes. They were filled with suits. He heard Danny going through the bedside cabinet.

'Harry, bingo,' Danny said.

Harry turned to see Danny holding up a large brown envelope. He was pulling some pictures out. 'I think the vice squad would like these,' Danny said.

Harry walked round the bed. Taking the envelope from Danny, he glanced at the pictures. 'I recognise a few of the faces, these must be the ones Gerald Parkin was using to blackmail them. But how did they come into Stanley Moore's hands?' He looked at the address. 'It was sent to him at his bank's office. I can't quite make out the postmark on it, but when we get back to the Yard you can take it down to forensics, see if they can work it out. Right, Hippie boy, throw a few things onto the floor and mess the room up a bit. I will go and see the housekeeper'.

Harry left and went downstairs. He told the housekeeper that someone had been in the house, but it looked as if they had disturbed them and it was all clear now. They would arrange for forensics to come round and check for fingerprints. Danny came into the kitchen. Harry told the housekeeper they were off, there was nothing to worry about, but don't touch anything upstairs till the other police had been. As they walked back to the car, Harry called the local inspector and arranged for a forensics team to be sent over to check the house for prints, and if the inspector needed a favour to call him any time.

CHAPTER TWENTY FOUR

Charlie was sitting with Manjitt, talking over the possibilities of what Rebecca Rosen could be up to. Jordan came over to join them. 'I had a bit of luck,' he said, pulling a seat up and sitting down. 'I just got a call from a letting agent, a flat they had rented out on a short term lease was up for renewal, but when they tried to contact the person they got no response, so one of their agents went there to check things out. They found a pile of money and some clothes. I phoned that inspector we met at Bow police station. I can't pronounce his name but Harry calls him Lenin. Anyway, he said he would take a team down there and check things out. He will give Harry a ring when he's got something.'

'Well done, Jordan,' Charlie said. 'I was going to ask you to get me some tea, but I can still taste the last one you made.'

'I will get the teas,' Manjitt said.

'Ho ho, after promotion,' Jordan said as she got up.

'No, I don't want stomach cramps from the dishwater you call tea,' she replied.

'In that case, I will have one too,' Jordan said, smiling and leaning back so he was out of range of Manjitt's legs. Manjitt walked off, then stopped and spoke to Cramer who was walking towards Charlie.

'What do you reckon on those two, boss?' Jordan asked, pointing at Manjitt and Cramer.

'I reckon you should mind your own business,' Charlie said.

Jordan chuckled as Cramer got to them. 'What's the joke?' he said.

'It's nothing, what have you found out?' Charlie asked.

'I got his mobile records, he never called the phone Rebecca Rosen was using,' Cramer said.

'Oh well, it was worth a try,' Charlie said.

'But she called him twice,' Cramer said, 'and I checked the dates. One of the calls was the day before we found Angela Cook's body.'

'That's interesting,' Charlie said, 'it all adds to the list of things Stanley Moore needs to tell us about.'

Manjitt came over with the teas and put the cups down on the table. 'Did you get the new pictures we have of Rebecca Rosen out, Jordan?' Charlie said.

'Yes boss, and I made sure they know how dangerous she is,' Jordan replied.

'Here's Harry,' Manjitt said. The rest of the team looked up as Harry and Danny walked into the office and came and joined them.

'How was the trip?' Charlie asked.

Harry passed over the envelope. 'It was most enlightening, especially for Hippie here,' Harry said.

Charlie pulled the pictures from the envelope and looked at them. 'You didn't let the young lad see these,' Charlie said to Harry.

'I couldn't stop him, boss.' Harry said.

'Do you mind?' Danny said. 'I have just taken part in a very important undercover operation, and this is the thanks I get.'

'These need a bit of explaining,' Charlie said, ignoring Danny.

'Hippie is going to take the envelope down to forensics, see if we can get the postmark and date of off it,' Harry said. Charlie passed it back to Harry, who handed it over to Danny.

'Also tell them to see if they can get any DNA off the seal. Someone must have licked it to stick it down, and there might be some prints on the photographs.'

'Before you do that Danny, just wait a minute,' Charlie said as he opened his desk drawer and took another envelope out and passed it to Manjitt. 'You can open it now.' All the rest of the team were looking at Manjitt, wondering what the boss had given her. She tore it open and pulled out a sheet of paper. She read it and looked at Charlie, smiling.

'Well, what is it?' Jordan said.

'You're looking at Detective Sergeant Virdee,' Charlie said. A cheer went round all the team, and Manjitt thanked everyone.

'It's well deserved,' Harry said, 'and we can have a drink to celebrate when we get this investigation over.' He turned to look at Danny. 'What you standing about for Hippie, get that envelope down to forensics.'

'I'm going, Harry,' Danny said.

'So Stanley Moore had the pictures all the time,' Charlie said.

'He has some explaining to do,' Harry said. 'And it gives us a reason to hold him in custody. We can have him on a blackmail charge with Gerald Parkin.'

'I like it,' Charlie said. 'Buys us some time and will shake him up.'

'Where did you find the pictures?' Cramer asked.

'Hippie and I were driving in the area were he was living,' Harry said 'when we heard of an attempted break-in at his house, and knowing Rebecca Rosen was back in the country we went over to investigate. But it was just a normal burglary, we checked the house out and found these lying around in his bedroom.'

'That was a lucky break for us,' Jordan said, smiling.

Cramer looked back and forth between the team members, not realising what the knowing smiles meant. 'And Harry,' Jordan continued, 'the inspector from Bow will be calling you. We think we've found the flat Rebecca Rosen was using to hide out at.'

Vincenzo Gallo felt the van come to a stop and the engine was turned off. He had no idea how long he had been driven for, as he had lost all sense of time. It wasn't long, but he couldn't be sure. He heard two men talking, then the door was opened and he was picked up and pushed out. He nearly fell but was caught by the man outside. He heard the van door close behind him as he was pulled along. He was helped up some steps and they walked another twenty yards or so before they stopped. A voice said 'Here, sit down,' as he was pushed into a chair. He heard the two men talking but did not understand what they were saying, it sounded Arabic.

'Mr Gallo,' a voice said from his right. Vincenzo twisted his head in that direction. 'We do not wish you any harm.'

'If you ring my father, I am sure he will arrange any money you are demanding for my release,' Vincenzo said.

'We do not want any money, and I have no wish to speak to your father,' the voice said. Vincenzo was confused now. 'I am going to ask you some questions, you will answer my questions without hesitation, or I will kill you.' Vincenzo heard the sound of a gun being cocked and felt the cold steel of a gun being pressed into his forehead. 'Do I make myself clear, Mr Gallo,' the voice said.

'Yes, yes,' Vincenzo said. 'Anything, I will tell you anything.'

'Now we would like to find an old friend of ours who we believe you know,' the voice said. 'Rebecca Rosen.'

'Yes, I know her,' Vincenzo said. 'But she's not here, she has gone abroad.'

'I know that,' the voice said 'she went back to England.'

Vincenzo was trying to think. If they knew she'd gone to England, why were they asking him? 'What you are going to tell me is why. You see, she has killed a colleague of ours over there today, and we are very annoyed. If we think you are not telling us everything you know, we will kill you.',Vincenzo could feel the sweat running down his back and felt himself shaking. 'Do I make my self clear?'

'Yes,' Vincenzo said, his voice catching.

Charlie got a call from the custody officer letting him know Stanley Moore's solicitor had arrived. He told the rest of the team to get on with tying up the loose ends and trying to track down Rebecca Rosen. Turning to Harry, he said 'The lawyer's arrived, shall we go down and start?' They left the office and as they made their way to the custody suite Charlie told Harry about expecting to get a call from Mr Dyan. As they got to the custody suite, the officer told them they were in interview room two. Harry pulled over the custody log and looked down the page. 'Boss, there's a surprise.' Harry pointed to the solicitor's company name. Charlie had a look and saw it was the same group who represented Tim Green when he was brought in for questioning.

When they entered the interview room they found Stanley Moore and his lawyer sitting at the table. Harry asked the constable who was standing inside the door to leave. Charlie sat down and Harry went through the procedure of turning on the tape recorder and saying who was present, then he sat down. It was Stanley Moore's lawyer who spoke first. 'My client would like to make a formal complaint about his treatment, there are no grounds on which you have brought him here, so we would like to ask for his immediate release.'

'Now we have got your speech over,' Harry said, looking at the lawyer, 'we will start the questioning. We feel your client has not been full and frank with his answers to questions he has been asked.'

'He's the trouble maker I told you about,' Stanley Moore said to his lawyer.

'It's nice of you to remember me,' Harry said. 'Now, do you know Rebecca Rosen?'

Stanley Moore sighed. 'I have already told you I have not met anyone by that name.'

'Do you know Jayne Cavill?' Charlie asked.

'You know I do, I have told you that, and have been completely honest about my involvement with her,' Stanley Moore said.

'Now you told us you met Jayne Cavill at the parties you attended,' Harry said.

'Yes I've admitted that,' he replied.

'And you said she came to your house,' Harry said.

'Yes, I have told you that too,' Stanley Moore said in exasperation.

'If my client has already answered these questions, what are we doing here?' the lawyer said.

'Well, we just want to be sure we have got nothing wrong,' Charlie said.

'And you never met her anywhere else,' Harry asked.

'Yes, I never met her anywhere else,' Stanley Moore repeated.

'Now, if I can ask you about your relationship with Vincenzo Gallo?' Charlie said.

Stanley Moore looked a little thrown by the question. 'What has that got to do with your enquiry?'

'Well, if you answer the question we might know,' Harry said.

Stanley Moore looked to his lawyer, who nodded. 'He is a banker, I know him professionally.'

'And the last time you met him was at the dinner party at your house?' Charlie asked.

'Yes that's right, you were both there, or have you forgotten?' Stanley Moore said.

'No, I haven't, and thank you for a lovely evening,' Harry said. 'But you don't socialise or speak to him regularly.'

'No, I don't,' he said.

'So, since the takeover of Sir Mark Coale's company, you've had no contact with him,' Charlie asked.

'No none, and I still don't know what this has to do with your enquiry,' Stanley Moore said.

'I will let you into a secret,' Harry said. 'We don't either, but we think you do.'

It was the lawyer who spoke. 'My client has explained his dealings with Mr Gallo, which are few and not on a regular basis, and unless you're accusing him of some financial irregularity, I see no reason to continue with this line of questioning.'

'Thank you for your thoughts on the matter,' Charlie said, 'but we will decide what questions to ask.

'Have you or anyone representing you had any dealing with Mr Gallo or any banks he is connected to in the last two years?' Harry said.

Stanley Moore looked at his lawyer, who answered. 'My client is the chairman of a large bank. He would not know all transactions that may have taken place between his bank and any associated with Mr Gallo.'

'But as an individual, for yourself, you have had no dealings with him?' Charlie asked.

'I think I have answered that question for my client,' the lawyer said.

'Well, you haven't, but we can come back to that at a later date,' Charlie said.

'Would you like to tell us about your relationship with Gerald Parkin?' Harry asked.

Stanley Moore had confusion on his face for a moment, then said 'You know about that, I have been over it with the police on a number of occasions.'

'If you could just humour us and go over it again,' Charlie said.

Stanley Moore looked at his lawyer, who told him to answer. 'I knew him from dinner parties and meeting him at gallery openings and other places, but he turned out to be a blackmailer, as you well know.'

'Can you just tell us about the blackmail?' Harry said.

'You really want me to go over it again?' Stanley Moore asked.

'It would help us,' Charlie replied.

'Well, he approached me and said he would expose me in the media about my attendance at sex parties,' Stanley Moore said.

'And you paid him off so he didn't,' Harry said.

'Yes that's right,' Stanley Moore replied

'But wouldn't it be just his word against yours. No paper would print anything if there was no proof,' Charlie said.

'Have you forgotten, I told you he had pictures,' Stanley Moore said.

'Oh yes, sorry,' Harry said, 'and when you paid him you got the pictures from him.'

'No, I didn't want them. hHe promised he would destroy them,' Stanley Moore said.

'You don't expect us to believe that, do you?' Harry said, 'Surely getting the pictures off him was the point?'

' No, I just wanted him to stop the blackmail,' Stanley Moore said.

'And you believed him? What was to stop him coming back and demanding more money at a later date,' Charlie asked.

'I made it clear to him that he would not get any more money out of me,' Stanley Moore said.

'And of course he was murdered, so he couldn't come back for more,' Harry said.

'Are you implying my client had something to do with the murder?' the lawyer asked.

'Just making an observation,' Harry said, 'but it was a lucky break for Mr Moore.'

'We have already made it clear he had nothing to do with the murder of Gerald Parkin,' the lawyer said.

'Yes, you keep saying that,' Charlie said.

'So why did you trust him not to come back for more money?' Harry said.

'I just did,' Stanley Moore said.

'Well, we can come back to that as well. It doesn't look like we are doing very well with your answers, Mr Moore,' Harry said.

'Now let me ask you about Angela Cook,' Charlie said. 'She also attended the parties you were at, is that right?'

'Ye,s but she was involved with Sir Mark not me. You should ask him about her,' Stanley Moore said.

'Thank you for the advice,' Harry said. 'Did you know she was passing information to Gerald Parkin?'

Stanley Moore looked to his lawyer. Before he could answer, Harry said 'What's so hard about that question you either did or didn't know?'

Stanley Moore turned back to face Charlie and Harry. 'I didn't know.'

'That was easy, wasn't it?' Harry said.

'So where did you think Gerald Parkin was getting his

information and the pictures about the parties from?' Charlie asked.

'I have no idea,' Stanley Moore said.

'But he had pictures, who do you think was taking them?' Harry asked.

'Well, from what you say, it was Angela,' Stanley Moore said.

'Good guess but wrong, it wasn't her,' Harry said.

'So if it wasn't her, who do you think it could be?' Charlie said.

'As I said, I have no idea,' Stanley Moore replied.

'And it never crossed your mind to wonder how Gerald Parkin got the pictures?' Harry asked.

'No, it didn't.' Stanley Moore said.

'That sounds a bit strange to me, but let's move on,' Harry said. 'Now, did you discuss Gerald Parkin with Jayne Cavill?'

Stanley Moore's lawyer spoke. 'I thought my client had answered all the questions about that woman.'

'Oh, so you know all the questions I need to ask,' Harry said. 'You sit back and listen, if you want to interrupt go ahead, but don't tell me what questions I should ask.' The lawyer sat back. Harry turned back to Stanley Moore. 'Well, did you speak to Jayne Cavill about Gerald Parkin?'

'No, he never came up when I talked to her,' Stanley Moore said.

'What about Rebecca Rosen?' Charlie said.

Stanley Moore was about to say something and stopped himself, then said 'I don't know anyone called Rebecca Rosen.'

'Now, if I can talk to you about your dealings with Mr Gallo,' Charlie said. 'As I understand it, you were working with Sir Mark Coale to try to stop his company being taken over, and Mr Gallo was involved through his bank. Would you like to tell us how?'

'I don't see what this has to do with anything,' Stanley Moore said, turning to his lawyer.

'I agree,' the lawyer said, 'this seems like a fishing expedition to me. You have no real evidence and are trying to trap my client into making an incriminating statement.'

'Oh well, if that's what you believe,' Charlie said. 'I think it's time for a break now, but Mr Moore, I know you're not being honest with us and you know it too. So we'll take an hour break. Think very carefully about what you tell us, because when we come back. I will want some truthful answers.'

'You have no right to say that to my client,' the lawyer said.

Harry ignored the lawyer and said 'We know you're lying Stanley, the more you do the deeper the hole, and the longer the prison sentence you will get, so take my boss's advice, think carefully while we are gone.' Harry said the interview was suspended, Charlie said he would arrange for some tea and sandwiches to be brought down to them and he and Harry left the interview room.

'I think that went very well,' Charlie said.

'Yes boss, he's up a creek without a paddle, and he doesn't even know it,' Harry said.

Charlie arranged for tea and sandwiches to be taken into the interview room with the custody officer. He and Harry went back upstairs. When they got back to the office all the team were at their desks. 'Gather round, children,' Harry shouted out as he and Charlie sat down.

When everyone came over, Charlie said 'Now, the questioning of Stanley Moore is going well, we expect to start to turn the screws when we go back for the next session. But how are we doing with Rebecca Rosen?'

'That commander who got in touch from West End Central has been on,' Jordan said. 'They checked CCTV around Selfridges and saw her get in a taxi. They traced the driver and he took her to Harrods. The commander said he has a team checking the CCTV in and around the store to try and pick her up again.'

'So we still don't have a clue what she's up to,' Harry said.

'I have something,' Danny said.

'Well, don't sit there Hippie, speak up,' Harry said.

'She got a bit sloppy, her DNA is on the flap of the envelope,' Danny said,'and a couple of the photographs have her prints on them, along with Gerald Parkin's and surprise, Stanley Moore's.'

'That's good,' Charlie said. 'What about the postmark?'

'That's a bit of good news too, boss,' Danny said. 'The postmark is from the City of London and the date is the same day she went and cleared out her safe deposit box.'

'So we can assume she had the pictures in the safe deposit box since killing Gerald Parkin,' Harry said. 'She takes them out along with her money but she posts the pictures to Stanley Moore. Why?'

'Maybe he wanted to use them later on,' Jordan said.

'What would be the point?' Charlie asked

'He could be just a bit of a pervert and likes looking at them,' Manjitt said.

'I go along with that,' Harry said.

'Whatever the reason, it ties Stanley Moore in with her now,' Charlie said.

'I don't know boss, he could say she was blackmailing him and he bought the pictures off her,' Danny said.

'Hippie's right, it does give him an out on that part,' Harry said.

'But he has not said anything about being blackmailed a second time, and what about the phone calls to and from Luxembourg,' Charlie said.

'He has some explaining to do there, but he might just say it was business,' Manjitt said.

'So we are really no nearer nailing him,' Charlie said.

'He might make a slip, boss,' Harry said.

'Not with that lawyer he has,' Charlie said. 'We need something that ties him in with Rebecca Rosen that he can't get away from.'

'You heard the boss,' Harry said to the rest of the team. 'Keep looking.' They all got up and went away to their desks.

'Well Harry, when we go back in, unless he and his lawyer are stupid, the team have just shown us the excuses he can use to worm his way out of things,' Charlie said.

'We will keep pushing, he might make a slip,' Harry said.

The phone on Mr Dyan's desk rang. He picked it up and listened. Asking them to stay on the line, he put a call through to his secretary, telling her to get the two operatives who were working on the assignment in to see him. He resumed his conversation, asking the odd question. When he had everything he put down the phone just as a knock came on his office door and the two men entered.

Telling them to take a seat, he asked them what arrangements they had made. They informed him they had a team and cars on standby to move as soon as they were needed. After listening to them, Dyan picked up his phone, punched a number in and spoke for a few seconds, then turned to the two men. He told them that after speaking to Tel Aviv he did not want any more chances taken. This problem had to be resolved.

A man came into the room without knocking. He was small in a crumpled suit wearing round rim metal glasses. Mr Dyan did not introduce him by name, but told the two men that he would be in charge of the whole operation, and they should follow any instructions he gave them without question.

The man in glasses told the two men to wait outside. When they had left the office he turned to Dyan, and asked what Belgium had told him. Dyan told him about the abduction of Vincenzo Gallo and related his conversation to the man, who listened carefully. When Dyan was finished, the man asked, 'I just want to be clear, termination of the problem comes before everything else.'

'Yes,' Dyan said. The small man nodded. 'We will be on our way to the house,' he said, and without saying anything else he turned and left. Dyan picked up the phone; they would need a clear run at things, so he would buy them some time.

Charlie's mobile rang just as he was standing up to go back to the interview room with Harry. He held his hand up and Harry stopped. The conversation lasted about two minutes, when he had finished he turned to Harry. 'That was our friend from the Israeli embassy, he apologised about Rebecca Rosen, he said he had no idea she had come back to the country. The man killed was from a different agency which he had not been informed about, but he assures me now that he has a full team trying to track her down, and as soon as he gets any news on her whereabouts he will call.'

'You believe him, boss?' Harry asked.

'He's a spook Harry, when do we ever believe anything they say?' Charlie said. 'Come on, let's go and see if we can trip Stanley Moore up.'

Rebecca walked out of the underground station, had a quick glance at the AtoZ road map she had bought and turned left. She knew it was about a thirty to forty minute walk to the house. She was not going to take the main roads; having looked at the road map, she had seen there was a way of getting to the house by using the back turnings and country lanes. It was just beginning to get dark, and she wanted to reach the house and check the plans she had been sent matched the layout, then find a good place to watch it from before she broke in. Her side still stung even after taking the pain killers, but putting that from her mind she walked past the shops, whose lights were starting to light up the pavement in the growing gloom of the evening, and carried on her way.

Charlie and Harry re-entered the interview room. Harry told the constable to take the tea cups and plates that had the leftover sandwiches on them out, when they were both seated, Harry repeated the usual speech for the tape. It was Charlie who spoke. 'Mr Moore,I hope we will get some truthful answers from you this time.'

'My client has answered all your questions truthfully,' the lawyer said.

'Glad you think so,' Harry replied.

'If I can just ask you,' Charlie said. 'Do you have any connection with bank accounts held in the British Virgin Islands or the Cayman Islands?'

Stanley Moore looked at his lawyer, it was he who answered 'I can't see any reason for those questions, and as a banker my client would have connections all over the world.'

'What about on a personal level? Does Mr Moore have any private holdings in those places?' Harry said.

Again it was the lawyer who answered. 'Mr Moore has investments through many different companies who may have connections in those places, or anywhere else in the world.'

Harry shook his head. 'I can see you're not going to give us a clear answer to that,' he said. 'What about the blackmail by Gerald Parkin. You told us you paid him a total of £350,000, is that correct?'

'That's right,' Stanley Moore said.

'Nice of you to say something,' Harry said, 'I thought we were only going to talk to your lawyer. But having paid the money, I find it hard to understand that you didn't demand the pictures you said he had.'

'I told you I didn't,' Stanley Moore said.

'I am finding it hard to believe that you trusted him to get rid of the pictures,' Charlie said. 'Why would you?'

'My client has answered these questions already,' the lawyer said.

'Now, when you were questioned about this before', Harry said, ignoring the lawyer, 'you said you gave him two banker's drafts for the money, is that right?'

'Yes, I have told you that already,' Stanley Moore replied.

'Did you speak to your wife about it?' Charlie asked.

'No, I didn't,' he replied.

'Why didn't you?' Harry said.

'It's not something you would discuss with your wife,' Stanley Moore replied.

'But wouldn't she find out about it? She works at the bank?' Charlie asked.

'If she saw that drafts had been raised, she would have no idea what they were for,' Stanley Moore said.

'Now you told us you only met Jayne Cavill at the parties and your house,' Harry said.

'Yes,' Stanley Moore said, sighing, looking at Harry. 'We have been over this a number of times already.' He looked to his lawyer.

The lawyer sat forward and said 'My client is right, he has answered every question about that woman you have asked. What's the point of going over it again?'

Charlie ignored the lawyer and said 'After Gerald Parkin was murdered, did you see her again?'

Stanley Moore sat back and raised his eyebrows. 'No, I did not.'

'So she never approached you or phoned you for money after Gerald Parkin's murder?' Harry asked.

'No, she didn't, 'Stanley Moore said.

'So she didn't get in touch with you and try and blackmail you,' Harry said.

'How many more times do I have to repeat myself?' Stanley Moore said, he looked to his lawyer again.

'It doesn't matter how many different ways you ask the question,' the lawyer said. 'The answer will be the same.'

'So she never threatened you that she had the photographs and would expose you unless she was paid money?' Harry said.

'For the umpteenth time, no,' Stanley Moore said.

Charlie pushed the file he had on the table forward. The lawyer and Stanley Moore glanced down at it. 'Earlier today, the housekeeper at the house you have been staying at reported an attempted burglary,' Charlie said. 'When the police attended, they found a window had been broken and forced open. Some items in some of the rooms were disturbed, drawers and cupboards opened, but the police who attended believe they disturbed the burglar.'

'And you think that has something to do with my client?' the lawyer asked.

'No, not at all,' Charlie said. 'But the police who attended did find one particular item that is of interest to us.' Harry noticed a change come to Stanley Moore's face, and he sat up straighter. Charlie still did not open the file, but left it sitting in the middle of the table.

It was the lawyer who spoke. 'Was there much damage, and did the housekeeper say what had been stolen?'

'We understand forensics are going to check things out, she

will then be asked to make a check to see if anything has been stolen,' Harry said.

Charlie reached up and pulled the file back across the table towards him and said 'Now, you told us you had not spoken to Mr Gallo since the dinner party. Is that correct?'

'We are going back to the same thing, and my answers will be the same,' Stanley Moore said. He leaned in and whispered to his lawyer for a moment.

The lawyer spoke. 'I have to say on my client's behalf, and I repeat, that this line of questioning is a fishing expedition. Unless you stop repeating yourself, I will advise my client to not answer any more questions.'

'Thank you for your observation,' Harry said. 'Now yesterday, did you stay at the house all day, or did you go out anywhere?'

Stanley Moore looked at his lawyer, who shrugged. 'I was at the house all day,' Stanley Moore said.

'Did you have any visitors?' Harry asked.

Stanley Moore sat back and sighed. 'No, I had no visitors. What are you asking me about yesterday for?' He looked at his lawyer.

'I have to agree with my client this line of questioning does seem pointless,' the lawyer said.

Harry carried on. 'So apart from you and the housekeeper, no-one else was in the house at all.'

'The answer's the same,' Stanley Moore said.

'So can you explain a phone call made from the house to Mr Gallo's house in Luxembourg,' Harry said.

Stanley Moore sat forward. His lawyer leaned in and whispered to him. It was the lawyer who spoke. 'My client can't explain that.'

'Let's look at the possibilities, then,' Harry said. 'Maybe the housekeeper knows Mr Gallo and phoned him up for a chat.

Or she might know the housekeeper who works for him and wanted to swap recipes.What would be your guess, Mr Moore?'

'My client has nothing to say on that,' the lawyer said.

'So putting aside the call made from the house to Luxembourg and the reason behind it,' Harry said, 'could Mr Moore tell us about the three calls made from Luxembourg to the house?'

'My client has said he has no recollection of phone calls,' the lawyer said.

Harry sat back. 'I have no doubt that when we question the housekeeper she will tell us that the phone calls were made and received by Mr Moore,' Charlie said, 'now if he wants to tell us about them, it might help him and us to understand what's going on.'

Stanley Moore sat forward, but his lawyer put his hand out to stop him saying anything. Harry spoke. 'So now we have proved that you have not been 100% honest about your dealings with Mr Gallo.'

'You have not proved anything,' the lawyer said.

'My apologies,' Harry said. ' Is there anything else you think you might have been forgetful about?'

Stanley Moore said nothing. Charlie pushed the folder back into the middle of the table. Stanley Moore and his lawyer both looked at it. Charlie spoke. 'Jayne Cavill, you said she never tried to blackmail you.'

Stanley Moore looked at his lawyer, who nodded. 'Yes, I had no contact with her,' he said.

'And you told us you have never heard of Rebecca Rosen,' Charlie said.

'Never heard the name,' Stanley Moore replied.

'Well, we know Jayne and Rebecca are one and the same person,' Charlie said. 'And I think Mr Moore knows too.'

'I think my client has made it clear he had no knowledge of that,' the lawyer said.

'Mr Moore, you said that you had no contact with Jayne.Rebecca after Gerald Parkin was murdered,' Charlie said.

Stanley Moore looked at his lawyer, who nodded. 'Yes, that's right,' Stanley Moore said.

'But that's not true, is it?' Harry said.

'Do we have to keep on with this?' Stanley Moore said.

'You got a phone call from her the day before Angela Cook was murdered,' Harry said, ignoring Stanley Moore's question.

Before Stanley Moore could answer, his lawyer spoke up. 'My client has no recall of getting a phone call or speaking to anyone claiming to be Jayne Cavill.'

'But it wasn't just one phone call, was it, Mr Moore,' Charlie said.

Stanley Moore said nothing. 'You seem to have a hard time remembering phone calls,' Harry said. 'It's not some kind of hearing problem, is it?'

'Now if I can take you back to Gerald Parkin,' Charlie said.

'What else can my client tell you that he hasn't already?' the lawyer said.

'I'm sure we will find something that has slipped Mr Moore's mind,' Harry said.

Charlie pulled the file he had placed in the centre of the table back towards him. The lawyer and Stanley Moore's eyes were both drawn to it. 'Now, what I don't understand,' Charlie said, 'is you pay three hundred and fifty thousand pounds to Gerald Parkin, but you don't want the pictures he has. And you want us to believe that he wouldn't have tried to use them again, yet you can't give us a reason why he wouldn't have come back for more money.'

'Well, someone murdered him, boss,' Harry said, 'so

whoever did that would know he wouldn't be coming back for more money.'

'My client has already told you he did not kill Gerald Parkin, and you have no evidence to show he was in anyway mixed up in it,' the lawyer said. Stanley Moore crossed his arms and sat back in his chair.

'So what did he expect Gerald Parkin to do with the photographs?' Charlie said. Stanley Moore said nothing. 'Did you speak to anyone else about the photographs Gerald Parkin had?'

'My client has answered all these questions,' the lawyer said.

'I just want to clarify in my own mind,' Charlie said, 'that after paying Gerald Parkin the second lot of money, Mr Moore was not approached again about the pictures, and he didn't tell anyone else what was happening.'

Stanley Moore looked at the lawyer, who lent in and spoke quietly to him. Stanley Moore then sat up and said 'For the last time, I did not take the photographs from Gerald Parkin, I didn't tell anyone else about them. Why would I? They are something I didn't want anyone else knowing about.'

'And that's the strange thing,' Charlie said. 'You don't want anyone else knowing about them, but you don't take them from Gerald Parkin, who could at any time have come back and demanded more money or even pass them to someone else.'

'My client has said all he is going to say on that subject,' the lawyer said.

'I would like to disagree with you on that point,' Charlie said.

'Earlier we told you about the break-in at the house you are staying at,' Harry said. 'Well, something interesting was found by the police investigating the break-in.'

Charlie pushed the file back into the centre of the table, opened it and turned it around. 'As you can see these pictures are of people, yourself included Mr Moore, at the parties you attended.' Charlie pulled one out and placed it separately on the table. 'This is you, Mr Moore.' Charlie pointed at the picture. 'You don't have to name the two ladies in the picture, or tell us what you are doing. We can work that out for ourselves.'

Stanley Moore had sat forward. His eyes were glued to the pictures, but he said nothing. His lawyer whispered into his ear. Stanley Moore looked away from the pictures and spoke quietly to his lawyer. 'My client has not seen those photographs before, they must have been placed in the house by the burglar to implicate my client.'

'That is a very good excuse,' Harry said, 'but...' Harry put a file on the table he had with him, he slowly opened it, '...this is an envelope the photographs were found in, as you can see by the address, it was posted to Mr Moore's office.'

'There is nothing to say that envelope wasn't planted along with the pictures at the house,' the lawyer said, smiling at Harry.

Harry smiled back at the lawyer and said 'Now, we know Mr Moore has not been telling us the truth, but I think he's not been totally honest with you.' Harry turned to Charlie. 'That's bad, isn't it boss, not being truthful with your lawyer.'

'It would seem to be a bit naughty, Harry,' Charlie said.

'There is nothing to prove those items were not planted at the house during the break-in to implicate my client for some reason,' the lawyer said, ignoring Charlie and Harry's attempt to get under his skin. Stanley Moore was sitting back, he had a bit more of a worried look on his face.

'That would be a plausible excuse,' Charlie said, 'if the photographs and the envelope didn't have Mr Moore's fingerprints on.'

The lawyer looked at Stanley Moore. He moved his seat closer and spoke quietly to him. Stanley Moore answered him in a hushed voice.

'And we found Rebecca Rosen's DNA and fingerprints on the envelope and pictures,' Charlie said.

'I would like to take some time to speak to my client privately,' the lawyer said.

Charlie looked at his watch. 'We're going to keep your client in overnight, because it's quite clear he has not been truthful, and has a lot of questions to answer. He really needs to think carefully about what he tells us next time he speaks to us. He is in possession of pictures he denied having, which we know Gerald Parkin had before he was murdered. You must understand it's not looking good for Mr Moore, he really does need to come clean and tell us all he knows.'

Harry ended the interview and switched off the tape.

CHAPTER TWENTY FIVE

Rebecca had been walking for twenty minutes. She had finished the bar of chocolate that she had bought along the way, and was now on one of the main roads that ran in and out of North London. The traffic on the A41 was quite heavy coming from the direction of central London. All the workers were making their way home from a hard day's work, she thought. She glanced at the AtoZ map. She knew she wanted to cross the road. Waiting for a small gap in the traffic, she darted to the small island in the middle. The traffic coming from the other direction wasn't as heavy, so she was able to get to the other side quickly. Making her way to the hedge that ran alongside the road, she found a small gap, climbed on to the fence that was half hidden by the greenery, and vaulted over, finding herself in a large field.

Looking to her right she saw the trackway she was seeking. The hard concrete stuck out from the grass fields around it. Crossing the field quickly till she was on the trackway, she turned away from the traffic that was now hidden behind the hedge and started to walk. She knew following this track would take onto a walkway that crossed above the M1 motorway, which in turn would take her all the way to the road that ran in front of the house. But she would leave the trackway before that, and cross some fields so she could go round the back and have a look at the house from there. From looking at the layout on the plans she had, there was lots of cover to find a vantage point to watch the house for a little while without being seen.

The two Israeli agents were parked in their car about fifty yards off Barnet Lane on the road that ran up to the house, which was another five hundred yards further along. Any traffic approaching the house would have to pass them, as there was no other way to get to it. The rest of the team were in two cars parked about half a mile in either direction on Barnet Lane itself, but could be at the house in a minute when called for. The small man had travelled with them to the house, not saying a word throughout the journey. He just sat in the back sucking strong mints, none of which he offered them, but when they parked he had told them to stay in the car and keep watch, he would scout the area. They should only move if he gave instructions over the radio. Otherwise there should be no talking. They did not know his name and he hadn't told them, they just called him sir. He had disappeared up the road towards the house ten minutes ago.

Charlie and Harry came back into the office and found Manjitt and Cramer going through some files. 'What are you two doing?' Harry said.

'We are just going through Stanley Moore's phone records,' Manjitt said. 'We have Rebecca Rosen's and when she was Jayne Cavill, and are trying to match up the phone calls made between them.'

'Well done,' Harry said, 'keep at it, the more we can tie him in to her the better.'

'Where are Jordan and Danny?' Charlie asked.

'They've gone down to West End Central to see the commander there,' Cramer said. 'He's done quite a good job of tracking her, he traced a taxi that picked her up a couple of minutes after the trouble at Selfridges. It took her to Harrods.'

'Blimey, was she doing her shopping or something?' Harry said.

'Not really, Harry,' Manjitt said. 'But she's a cool one. Jordan called in, said they have her on CCTV in Harrod,s sitting down and having a meal.'

'I don't suppose they have her trapped in Harrods, do they?' Charlie said.

'No, but they know when she left Harrods she went to the Knightsbridge underground station. Jordan says the commander has British Transport Police trying to track her movements on the CCTV from the train she got on, and at all the stations the underground runs through from Knightsbridge.'

'I will give Jordan a ring, boss,' Harry said 'see if there's any more news'

'Who wants a cuppa?' Charlie said. Manjitt and Cramer put up their hands. Harry nodded as he picked up his phone.

Charlie made the tea, dropping two cups off to Manjitt and Cramer. He put Harry's down on his desk, he was still talking on the phone. Charlie looked at his watch, went over to his desk and made a phone call himself. He spoke for only a couple of minutes, and when he finished he looked over at Harry, who was sitting back with his feet up and drinking his tea. 'What did Jordan say, Harry?'

'He and Hippie are at Green Park station with a couple of West End Central armed officers. British Transport Police have tracked her to there, she got off the Piccadilly Line train, they know that, but two other underground lines run through the station, the Jubilee and Victoria. They are just trying to track what one she got on, or did she leave the station and go out onto the street? But it's quite hard, as it's the rush hour, so there's lots of people about, and we know how good she is at hiding.'

'At least we have half a chance,' Charlie said. 'I will give Crick a ring, let him know how things are going, I will tell him to give that commander at West End Central a call and thank him for his help.'

Charlie got on the phone and spoke to Crick for five minutes. When he put it down he said 'He's getting excited again.'

'Ah that's good for him,' Harry said, 'his tan will be shining tomorrow.'

'Harry, I am going to go over and have dinner with Amanda,' Charlie said. 'So you can call me straight away if you get a definite of where she has gone to ground.'

Harry looked over the top of his tea cup. 'I hope my phone call doesn't come when you're in the middle of anything, boss.'

Charlie stood up. 'It's just dinner, Harry.'

'Of course it is, boss, that's what I meant,' Harry said. He leaned to one side as the pen Charlie threw at him went by his head.

'Ring me straight away, Harry,' Charlie said.

'I will boss, have a nice time,' Harry said. hHe watched Charlie leave the office and picked up the phone and called Jordan again.

Rebecca was sitting hidden amongst some trees at the back of the house, which was well lit up. The gardens closest to the house were also lit by floodlights. She had checked the position of the cameras against the plans and spotted all of them. She had been told that they would only be on record and that no one would be monitoring them, but she would stay out of their view as much as she could, just in case. There would be two servants in the house, so she would do her best to avoid them. She had already spotted a window on the first floor which was open. She knew she would be able to climb up and get into the house easily enough using that, then go and disconnect the alarms and do what she was being paid to do. It was dark now, she looked at her watch, give it another hour then she would move in and do the job.

The small man from the embassy had checked out the front of the house. If he was her, he would not try and enter this way, so he had made his way along the fence that ran around the house to the back, found an overhanging tree and used it to get over the barbed wire that topped the fence. He had found some large bushes that were just in the darkness of the garden and sat down. The grass was damp, but he didn't care, he had sat for days in worse places waiting for a target to appear. He took out an extra strong mint and popped it in his mouth and sat silently watching, not the house but the grounds around it.

Harry was talking to Jordan, who told him that she was spotted boarding a Jubilee Line train going north. They had the time that the train left Green Park, so were now checking all the CCTV at all the stations ahead that the train would have passed through. He and Hippie, along with the two armed officers, were going to get on the Jubilee line train, and follow her path. Harry said to keep him up to date with any more news. After he put down the phone, Harry called Manjitt and Cramer over. He told them to leave the phone records for now, and get a London underground map and a large map of London and put them out on the table. He wanted to try and get an idea whether she was heading back towards Bow, where she had hidden before, or had another bolt hole she was going to hide at.

Manjitt and Cramer went off to get the maps. Harry sat back. What is she up to, he thought, why come back? Maybe she had meant to meet Stanley Moore, but she wouldn't know he had been arrested unless she had called the house he was staying at. He rooted around on his desk till he came to the address of the house which had the number on and picked up the phone and called it. The phone was answered by the housekeeper. Harry introduced himself and asked if there had been any calls to the house after Mr Moore was taken away by the police. The housekeeper told him no. Harry thanked her and rang off. Manjitt and Cramer returned with the maps. Harry stood up, he told them to open them up and lay them out on the boss's desk. once they were open Harry said 'Right, she got on a train here...' He took a pen and circled Knightsbridge station. 'She took the train and changed at Green Park...' he circled that. 'She then boarded a Jubilee Line train going north. Now what is she up to?'

'She's heading back towards the West End,' Cramer said.

'She could change trains again and go back towards Bow,' Manjitt added.

Harry's phone went, it was Jordan. The conversation lasted a minute. 'Okay, that was Jordan' Harry said. 'He and Hippie and two armed officers are on the Jubilee Line tracing her path. British Transport Police have a dozen men checking all the stations that the train she got on would pass through. So far they have got up to Swiss Cottage...' Harry circled that,'...and she hasn't got off yet.'

'Well, it doesn't look like she is going to Bow, she's heading in the wrong direction,' Manjitt said.

'She could have got off and doubled back,' Cramer said.

'But she doesn't know we are on to her, so she could have taken the underground in that direction straight away,' Manjitt said.

'So where is she going?' Harry said. He pulled the large map of London over. He marked where they knew she had been and drew a line connecting them, till he got to Swiss Cottage. 'So we know she never got off the train here, so she's still heading north.'

Cramer pulled the underground map back over. 'She has two more opportunities to change onto another underground line.' He pointed at the two stations she would pass through where she could change lines.

'She could get off anywhere along the way,' Manjitt said.

Harry's phone went again, it was Jordan. Harry listened, told Jordan to keep ringing in every few minutes.

'Jordan said the CCTV has been checked up to Kilburn, and she never got off.' Harry circled Kilburn.

'Well, that only leaves one more chance for her to change lines,' Cramer said, pointing at Wembley park station.

Harry pulled the London map back over, drew the line of her progress as far as Kilburn. 'So what do we see, looking at her journey?' Harry looked at them.

'Nothing, Harry,' Manjitt said. Cramer shook his head

'Me too,' Harry said, 'but she is on her way somewhere. This woman doesn't do anything that's not planned.'

Rebecca saw a man come out of some French windows at the back of the house. He looked up at two of the security lights that were above the windows, one of which was flickering. He went back inside leaving the door open. I could get in the house now, she thought, but she stayed still, watching. The man reappeared carrying a ladder. He was followed by a small woman. Rebecca watched as the man placed the ladder up against the wall and climbed up. The woman stood at the bottom of the ladder and passed him something. Rebecca saw that he was fixing the light, so they must be the two servants who are in the house. Nothing to worry me there, she thought.

The small man had seen the same scene play out in front of him as well, but he only glanced at it for a second. His eyes were mainly on the surrounding grounds. He had seen no movement, but he knew that if she was going to fulfil the job she had been given, like him she would be here watching and waiting.

Charlie had arrived at the front gates of the house. He waited a few seconds after pressing the entrance buzzer and the gates began to swing open. As he pulled in, he thought about the car with two men in it he had seen parked in the road further down. He had made a note of the registration number and would ring Harry to get it checked out. As he got to the front of the house, he parked the car facing the lake and got out. Turning, he walked towards the house. The front door opened before he got to it, and he saw Amanda standing in the doorway. She was wearing a long red dress, her blonde hair hanging loose around her shoulders. As he reached her, she smiled and said 'Hello Charlie, I'm glad you came.'

Charlie smiled back. 'So am I, you look stunning,' he said.

She kissed him lightly on the cheek and took his arm, closing the door behind them. 'I haven't had anything cooked, I thought we could sit and drink some wine, eat some nibbles and get to know each other, now you're not going to lock me up,' she said.

'That sounds good to me,' Charlie replied.

'I told the staff they won't be needed tonight, so they will be off to their rooms on the second floor. We have the place to ourselves.' She led him past the dining room and into the library. 'I remember you said you liked this room, so I had the fire lit.'

Charlie saw the fireplace was blazing away, giving off that comforting and warming glow. The main lights were off and just a few lamps were on. A sofa was in front of the fire with a small table in front of it. 'You sit down, Charlie, I will get some wine.'

Charlie went and sat on the sofa, Amanda joined him, she

had an ice bucket with two bottles of champagne in them 'I thought we could share these' she expertly twisted one of the bottles while holding the cork, there was a light pop 'can you hold the glasses Charlie'.

Charlie picked up the two glasses from the table and Amanda poured the champagne into them. She put the bottle into the ice bucket and took one of the glasses from Charlie. 'Here's to a lovely evening,' she said.

'I hope so,' Charlie said. They both took a drink. 'I'very nice, but do you expect me to help you finish both bottles off? I do have to drive home later.'

'You don't have to drive home, Charlie,' Amanda said.

Charlie looked up at her standing in front of him, never said anything for a while, then said 'I guess I don't need to.' Amanda leaned down and kissed him.

Harry took a call from Jordan. All stations had been checked up to Wembley Park and she hadn't got off, and there were only four more stations on the line before it terminated. Harry told him to keep in touch. He related to Cramer and Manjitt what Jordan had said. 'So let's look at the big map, there are only four stations left, so where is she going?' All three glanced down at the map on the table.

'Amanda,' Charlie said. 'I just need to call Harry for a second.' she was lying with her back against him, her glass in her hand.

'Charlie, I thought I was a workaholic, but you beat me.' She looked back over her shoulder. 'Don't worry, I understand, but I expect you to make it up to me later,' she said.

Charlie took his phone from his jacket that was lying on the floor beside the sofa. 'You will have to think of something I can do,' he said as he dialled Harry's number.

'I may be able to think of something,' Amanda said as she ran her hand up Charlie's leg.

He didn't try to stop her this time. 'I can't get a signal,' he said.

'Yes it can come and go for some reason, the best place to get a good signal is out by the lake, but you can use the phone in the hall if you want,' she said.

Charlie felt her hand slowly running up and down his leg. 'I will give it awhile and try again later.' He put his phone down.

'So are you going to tell me about yourself, Charlie?' she said, turning her body so she was lying alongside him.

He picked up the champagne bottle. 'Do you want a refill?' he said. She held out her glass and he poured some for her, refilled his own glass and put the bottle back in the ice bucket, then picked his glass up and took a drink. He started to tell her about himself.

Rebecca had waited a good forty-five minutes since the two servants had gone back into the house. It was time to move, she said to herself. She stayed in the darkness of the trees for as long as she could, till she darted to the corner of the house, staying close to the wall and edging along. She came to a stop underneath the open first floor window. She climbed onto the windowsill of the one below, reached up and used the decorative stone around the top of it to pull herself up. Wedging her feet in between the brickwork as foot holds, stretching she was able to grasp the bottom of the first floor windowsill. Using her legs to push, she heaved herself up and was in the room. It had taken no more than fifteen seconds. She stayed still by the window and listened.

The small man had seen the figure sprint from the trees and move along the back of the house. It was her, he knew that.

He watched as she expertly climbed up to the first floor window and entered. He stood up, and walked in the darkness of the trees till he was opposite the open window. He stared at it, waiting to see if a shadow moved inside.

Harry took a call from Jordan, he told him that she had got off the train at the last station Stanmore. A British Transport Police car was waiting for them outside the station, and as soon as they got there they would have a drive around, but Jordan didn't hold out much hope ,as she had a couple of hours' head start on them and may even have had a car parked there to use. Harry told him to stay in touch.

'Right, she got off the train here.' Harry circled Stanmore station on the big map of London. 'Go and have a look in the files see if it crops up in any of the statements, it must mean something.' Manjitt and Cramer went over to the files and began to have a quick look through them. Harry sat down and began to go over her journey again, she must have gone there for a reason, but why?

Charlie had told Amanda about his early life, and how he ended up in the police force and that he had a hundred and fifty million in the bank.

'Well, no-one could say you're after my money,' Amanda said.

She had told him about her early life. Being an only child of one of America's richest men, she could do whatever she wanted. She told him after university, where to her surprise she had done extremely well, she had gone off the rails and spent two years partying all round the world, and could not remember some of it. But her father had indulged her. That stopped when she got news of her mother's death. She had flown home, and ever since had worked, first in her father's bank learning the business and being highly successful to the point where she was respected as a banker and not because she was her father's daughter, and then joining the Moores' family bank when she had married Stanley, helping to build that up to be one of the most respected investment banks, not just in Europe, but the world.

'I really do have to make that call to Harry,' Charlie said.

'There is one thing,' Amanda said. 'Well two things actually, before you do.'

'What's that?' Charlie said.

'Well, after your phone call' Amanda said, 'Why don't we take the champagne upstairs. You're not driving home now, so I might as well show you my bedroom.'

Charlie could not stop himself laughing. 'You have a way of making an invitation sound so innocent,' he said.

Amanda joined in the laughter, then put her arms round Charlie's neck, pulling him in to kiss.

Rebecca had moved away from the window and was standing with her ear to the door listening for any movement outside. After a minute she turned the handle and opened the door. All the lights were on in the corridor. Putting her head out, she looked both ways, saw no-one, so went out closing the door quietly behind her. She wanted to get to the alarm system, turn it off and cut the phone lines, which were all in a small room just before the kitchen on the left. She edged along the wall with her back to it, till she came to the top of the stairs. Looking down, all the doors off the hallway were closed. She glanced upstairs, saw nothing. Everything was still and quiet, so she started to slowly make her way down the winding staircase. Reaching the bottom, she went round to her left. She knew from the plans that the kitchen was along this corridor, and the little room should be just before it. She stopped for a moment and thought she heard laughter, but there was just silence, so she quietly carried on towards the kitchen.

The small man had seen light for a second flood into the first floor room where Rebecca Rosen had climbed into the house, and then it went dark again. She must be moving about the main house now. He knew she would try to get to the alarms and switch them off, it would make it easier when she wanted to get out of the house. He had hoped to spot her before she was able to get into the house, but there was no way he could prevent her from carrying out what she had been hired to do now. He would wait till she came back out. She would not come out the same window, that's why she would turn the alarms off. She would use the back door, but he knew all about her training, she would try and use the same way out of the grounds as she had used to enter, she knew the layout and probably felt comfortable moving about this way. He sat back down, took out a mint and popped it in his mouth. He took a pistol out of his inside pocket, quickly checked it was ready for use, then put his hand into his side pocket and retrieved the silencer, slowly screwing it onto the front of the pistol.

Harry was sitting looking at the large map of London. He was looking at the area around Stanmore. What was she up to, he thought. If she didn't have a car when she got off the train, does she have a flat or house she's using, and how far is it from the station? Manjitt and Cramer came back. Harry looked up at them. 'Nothing, Harry,' Manjitt said. 'Stanmore doesn't appear anywhere.'

'Well, she's somewhere here,' Harry said. He took his pen and drew a circle around the Stanmore area. His hand suddenly stopped at roughly two o'clock on the circle. 'Oh god,' he said.

'What is it, Harry?' Manjitt said.

'Amanda Moore, she lives here.' Harry pointed to the map. 'Get hold of Jordan, give him her address, tell him I think she's going there to kill Amanda Moore. Tell him the boss is at the house too.' Manjitt took her phone out as she went to get the address. Harry took his phone out and called Charlie, he got a message that the user wasn't available at the moment. 'Cramer, get her home number and ring it.' Cramer went and joined Manjitt, who had Amanda Moore's file open.

Rebecca had found the small room with the alarm system in. She closed the door behind her and switched on the light. She walked to the alarm cabinet that was on the wall and tapped in the alarm code she had been given. The alarm sign went to off. She grabbed the wires that came out the bottom off it and tugged. She knew from the details she had thatthe phone lines ran from it too. A few small sparks appeared and she dropped the wires. That's the phones out as well, she thought, now to do the job and be gone. She had to find her target, she knew where the bedroom was and would make her way back upstairs.

'I really have to call Harry,' Charlie said as he lay facing Amanda on the sofa.

'Okay,' she said, 'I will get some more ice from the kitchen, we can take the other bottle upstairs with us.'

Charlie swung his legs off the sofa and stood up. He put his hand out and Amanda grasped it. Charlie pulled her up to him, she lightly kissed him. 'Go on and make your phone call.'

She picked up the ice bucket with the full bottle of champagne still in it, grabbed their glasses and put them in with the bottle, taking Charlie's hand. They walked towards the door.

'You said you wanted to tell me two things before we went upstairs,' Charlie said.

'Oh yes,' she said, 'but don't worry, I will tell you when I have you in bed.'

'What a nice thought,' Charlie said.

'Don't let Harry know, he might get jealous,' Amanda said and laughed. Charlie laughed with her. She opened the door and they stepped out into the hallway.

Manjitt had got Jordan on the phone, and as soon as she told him what they thought she heard the sound of the emergency siren go on in the background and the noise of a car engine being driven quickly. Cramer was on the phone next to her. Harry had joined them. 'Jordan is on his way to the house,' Manjitt said.

Cramer spoke. 'The phone line's dead.'

'Come on you two, let's go,' Harry said, and all three ran out the office.

Rebecca stood by the door, listened for a moment, heard nothing and switched the light off, turned the door handle and came back into the corridor, closing the door quietly behind her. She suddenly heard laughter again, then saw a door opening further back along the corridor towards the front of the house. She quickly ducked into the kitchen and stood out of view. She heard voices.

Amanda and Charlie came into the hallway and walked towards the front door. 'If you walk to the right of where you parked your car, Charlie, you should get a signal,' Amanda said. 'I can't guarantee it, it's pretty hit and miss.'

Charlie pulled open the door just as Amanda said 'Hold on' Charlie turned. 'I thought the alarm was on,' she said, 'but I guess that it hadn't been turned on by the servants, as they knew I had company and probably thought you might not be staying.' She kissed Charlie, 'but you are. I will turn it on before we go up.'

Charlie stepped out in to the cool night air. 'If you can't get a signal,' Amanda said, 'there's a phone in the drawing room, or you can use the one in the kitchen.'

Charlie turned. 'I will be quick,' he said. Amanda waved and went back into the house, leaving the door open.

Rebecca had heard the voices going away from where she stood. She put her head round the doorway and saw a woman and a man walking towards the front door talking. The woman had an ice bucket in her hand, she was holding the man's hand with the other. She watched as the man opened the door and went out. The woman stood by the door for a second, waved, then turned around without closing it. Rebecca ducked back into the kitchen. It was her target. She didn't get a good look at the man, he was big, but so what? She heard footsteps coming towards the kitchen. Looking round in the darkness, the only light came from the security lights outside throwing a small amount of light into the room. She walked quickly away from the door and ducked down behind the island in the centre.

Charlie walked past his car and dialled Harry's number, but got no signal. He walked a little further and tried again. Still nothing. He would use one of the house phones. He turned and walked back towards the house.

Jordan was on the phone to Harry. The police driver had told him they were about five minutes away from the house. Harry let Jordan know they were on their way and that the house phone lines were dead. Cramer was driving, emergency lights flashing as they weaved through the London traffic. 'It will take us about half an hour to get there, Harry,' he said.

'Just keep your foot down,' Harry said. He put a call through to AS Crick and told him what was happening, and asked him to get the local force to the house too and get the area sealed off.

Rebecca heard the woman come into the kitchen. She was quietly singing to herself, and the lights had come on. Rebecca put her head around the corner of the island and saw the woman, who had her back to her at the large fridge. One of the doors was open and she had the ice bucket placed on a ledge inside. The sound of ice cubes being dispensed into it echoed around the kitchen. Rebecca stood up quietly, looked around and saw a set of knives on the kitchen top by the window. Moving as quietly as she could, she got to them, pulled one out and moved towards the woman.

Amanda walked towards the kitchen. She hadn't felt this happy in a long time and the chat she had with Charlie when they were lying on the sofa was just so natural, she had told him things that she had never discussed with anybody else, and hearing Charlie tell her his story of how he came to be a policeman, about his family, had been so honest that she actually felt this man might be the one she had been searching for all those years.

She switched the light on in the kitchen. She was singing to herself, a song that she listened to a lot. Adele's make you feel my love, she was glad Charlie couldn't hear her, as even she would admit she had a terrible singing voice. She went to the big American style fridge, opened one of the doors, put the ice bucket on the small ledge inside, took the two glasses out and pressed the ice dispenser. The clink clink of the ice filling the bucket seemed to rhyme with her singing.

Charlie got back to the house. He closed the door behind him and walked towards the drawing room where he and Harry had stood drinking and watching everyone when they had come to the dinner party. He opened the door. The light was on. He looked around the room and spotted the phone on a table. It was just to the left of the painting of Amanda that hung above the fireplace. I must ask her about that, he thought.

Rebecca was about six foot away from the woman, the knife in her hand, two more steps and the job would be done. The woman suddenly turned. Rebecca saw a shocked look on her face. Without hesitation, Rebecca moved quickly. The knife came up and struck the woman in the centre of the chest.

Amanda thought she would change the dirty glasses for clean ones. She made sure the bucket would not fall out, and turned to put the dirty ones in the sink. As she turned round there was a woman coming towards her. She froze in shock, her mind at a loss, who was she? The woman was suddenly close and she felt a sharp agonising pain in the centre of her chest and fell backwards.

Rebecca pulled the knife out as the woman fell back against the fridge. The ice bucket and the champagne bottle were knocked out and crashed to the ground, the bottle exploding. Rebecca didn't hear it, but stepped in closer to the woman and drove the knife into her chest a second time. The woman hadn't uttered a sound, except for a gurgling noise, which Rebecca knew meant the wounds were fatal.

Amanda felt the pain. Her mind was screaming, but she could not seem to make her voice work. The pain was unbearable. Charlie where are you, she thought. She saw the woman come at her again and felt another sharp pain in her chest. Charlie, help me!

He felt her punch him a couple of times, which to his surprise hurt him. He felt a sharp pain in his arm, but continued to try and hold her. He was losing his temper, he twisted her hair so her face came round. He was looking at her no more than five inches away. He could swear she was smiling. He felt another punch just at the top of his leg. I've had enough of this, he thought, and tilted his head back and threw it forward. The head-butt caught her right in the face. Charlie heard a crack, good he thought, that's your nose gone.

God, this man is strong, Rebecca thought, as she struck him again with the knife. The man twisted her head and she saw him look at her. He did something she hadn't expected and head-butted her in the face. She felt her nose break and tasted blood in her mouth. Her eyes watered, but again her instincts kicked in and she struck out with the knife again, catching the man in the hand which was holding her hair. She felt him release his grip and she rolled away and got to her knees to look at the man.

Charlie got a look at her face. It was blood spattered, and her nose was pouring blood. He felt a sharp pain in his hand, which forced him to let go of her hair, and she rolled away from him. He went to get to his knees, but felt weaker than he had ever felt before in his life. He struggled, putting a hand onto the ground to steady himself. His sight was becoming hazy, he saw her kneel up about five feet away from him.

Rebecca saw that he was badly injured. He was struggling to regain his feet, he would not be able to follow her, and she needed to get away and sort her injuries out and find somewhere to stay. She stood up, turned and stopped. Standing there looking at her was a small man in glasses.

The man had watched the fight becoming more and more vicious, a fight for survival, he had no idea who the man was but he was giving a good account of himself. But he knew Rebecca's training would overcome him. As he got close, he saw Rebecca roll away from the man who was struggling to get up. He saw she was holding a knife in her hand, he halted and watched as she stood and turned.

I know you, Rebecca thought, you were my sergeant at combat school, what was your name, ah yes!!,

He raised the gun. He saw some recognition come across Rebecca's face for a moment. He fired at her head. The gun hardly made a sound, she dropped backwards and fell to the ground. The small man stepped forwards, aimed the gun at her head and fired two more shots. He turned without a backward glance and walked back towards the trees, unscrewing the silencer as he went, being careful not to burn his fingers as he didso.

Charlie raised his head to look at Rebecca who was standing now. He thought he saw a small man in front of her, then everything went black.

Jordan had reached the front door and was banging on it. Danny and the two officers reached him and joined in the banging and shouting to open up. The door opened and a man stood there. 'Who are you?' Jordan asked, grabbing the man.

The man answered that he worked for Mrs Moore. He had heard crashing coming from the kitchen. Jordan let go of him and told one of the officers to stay with the man. He asked where the kitchen was and the man pointed. He, Danny and the other officer ran towards the kitchen. Jordan reached it first, he saw a woman in a red dress lying with her head slumped back against the fridge, the floor looked to be covered in blood.

'That's Amanda Moore,' Danny said looking down at her, but before he could say anything else, Jordan pointed at the back door, which was hanging off its hinges.

'Call an ambulance,' Jordan said to the armed officer as he led Danny to the back door. As they stepped through it, they saw the boss on the ground,lying still on his side. About ten feet away they saw Rebecca Rosen on her back, her arms outstretched. Danny went and knelt down next to Charlie. Taking his hand he felt for a pulse. 'I can just about feel one,' he said.

Jordan ran back into the house, told the officer to get the gates open and get the car up to the house and bring the first aid kit through to the back garden. They had an officer down, hurry that ambulance up. Jordan went over to Amanda Moore, who was lying against the fridge. He leant down and looked for signs of life, but she was dead. He walked back across the kitchen and went outside, where he saw Danny holding the boss's head and talking to him. 'How is he, Danny?' he asked.

Danny looked up. 'He's in a bad way, I can't get him to answer.'

'Keep talking to him,' Jordan said. He walked over to Rebecca Rosen. He was surprised to see that it looked like she had been shot. He took out his phone, but couldn't get a signal.

Harry and the rest of the team were still about fifteen minutes from the house when they heard a call of 'officer down' come over radio.

The two agents in the car had ducked out of sight when the police car with lights flashing had turned into the road. They had discussed whether they should get on the radio to the small man and tell him, but he had said no radio unless he called. They were just thinking they had better do something when the back door opened and the small man got in. 'Back to the embassy,' he had said, 'and tell the other teams to stand down.' He made no mention of what had happened, but sat back and took an extra strong mint from a packet and put it in his mouth. He didn't offer one to them.

When Harry arrived at the house there were police all over the place. Three ambulances were parked near to the open front door. Leaving the car, he walked into the house, followed my Manjitt and Cramer. He asked a constable were the officer in charge was, he told them at the back of the house. They walked through to the kitchen. Harry immediately saw the body of Amanda Moore. The three of them skirted around her body and went through the broken back door. Jordan and Danny were standing just outside. Harry saw three paramedics around Charlie, who was lying on his back. Jordan saw Harry. 'It's bad,' he said. 'He's been stabbed a number of times.'

Harry looked at Danny, who he saw had blood all over his clothes. 'Are you alright, Hippie?'

Danny turned. 'Yes, Harry.'

'Do we have any idea what has happened here?' Harry said.

'Rebecca Rosen is over there,' Jordan said pointing. Harry and the rest of the team looked to where he was indicating. 'She's been shot.'

'Shot?' Harry said. 'Do we have a gun anywhere?'

'We had a quick look around, but didn't find one,' Jordan said. 'But we need to have a better search later.'

They moved aside as another two paramedics came out the kitchen door with a stretcher and laid it beside Charlie, who was carefully moved onto it. They watched as he was carried into the house. 'Hippie, you and Cramer go to the hospital with the , Harry said. Cramer and Danny followed the paramedics into the house. 'Right, let's see if we can get a handle on what's gone on here.'

It was two o'clock in the morning when Harry, Jordan and Manjitt got back to the Yard. They had left a forensics team at the house going over the scene. Not much had been said on the journey. Manjitt had called Cramer, who told them the boss was still in surgery. Harry had called Crick to let him know what had happened. Crick said he would be in early and come and see Harry in the squad's office. 'You two sit down,' Harry said. 'I will get us some tea.'

While Harry made the tea he called Danny, who told him there was no change. Harry told him he should go home and get changed, but Danny refused and said he would stay at the hospital. Harry walked over to his desk and put the tea down. He told the others he had spoken to Danny who said there was no change. As he sat down, he asked Jordan to run through what happened from the minute he got to the house again for him.

He and Manjitt listened to Jordan go over everything he remembered. When he finished, Harry said 'Well, we know the boss didn't have a gun. So did Amanda Moore own one, or did Rebecca Rosen have it with her? Or was there someone else in the garden?' Harry took a drink of tea. 'And until we've had a good search of the place, we won't know if the gun's there or not. Jordan, you can go back to the house in the morning and take charge of the search. And they have security cameras, so see if they have any of what happened on camera.' Jordan nodded. 'Manjitt, you will come in with me in the morning to carry on the questioning of Stanley Moore. He knows something about what's gone on tonight.'

'Harry, the boss looked in a terrible state,' Manjitt said.

Harry sat forward. 'Listen, you two,' he said. 'I understand,

and no one is feeling it more than me, but if we let things slip the boss wouldn't forgive us, so whatever happens, we do our best to sort this out.' They both nodded. 'But keep an eye on Hippie, he looked really shocked.'

'He sat talking to the boss till the paramedics arrived,' Jordan said, 'although the boss wasn't conscious.'

'Well, keep an eye on him,' Harry said.

They had finished their tea and sat quietly when Harry picked up his phone. 'I'd better ring Mike and Maggie at Charlie's house, to let them know what's happened,' he said. 'Manjitt, you'd better try and get hold of Amanda Moore's father in America and break the news to him. Jordan, do me a favour, there's a red book in the boss's desk, look up Julian Squires' number. Tell him what's happened, and the hospital the boss has been taken to. Let him know I will call him tomorrow.' Manjitt and Jordan got up and left Harry.

When Harry got off the phone from speaking to Mike, he left the office and made his way down to the custody suite. It was quiet when he got there. Two officers were behind the desk. He asked what cell Stanley Moore was in. The officers asked if he wanted him out for questioning, but Harry told them no. He just wanted to tell him some bad news. One of the officers came from behind the desk and unlocked the door that led to the cells. He switched on the corridorlights. Harry told him he would speak to the prisoner alone. Harry walked along the corridor, his shoes echoing off the concrete. Funny, he thought, you never heard that during the day. He came to the cell occupied by Stanley Moore, whose name was chalked up on a small blackboard outside. He pulled the small flap on the door open, but the inside was in darkness. Harry looked to his left, saw the light switch and flicked it on. Looking back through the hatch, he saw a sleeping figure under a red blanket. Harry called out. The figure moved but didn't respond. Harry called again louder. He saw Stanley Moore turn and look towards the door, his hands shielding his eyes from the glare of the light. 'Mr Moore, can I have a word with you please,' Harry said as he saw Stanley Moore sit up.

Stanley Moore recognised the voice. 'I have nothing to say to you. How dare you wake me up in the middle of the night? I will speak to my solicitor about this in the morning.'

'Mr Moore, I have some bad news for you, if you could just come to the door.' Harry said.

Stanley Moore swung his feet off the bed, throwing the blanket aside. His suit was all dishevelled and creased. He stood up and came to the door. 'What is it, and if this is some kind of trick to deny me sleep, I will have your job.'

Harry waited till he was standing at the door. 'Your wife has been killed,' Harry said.

Stanley Moore made no reply for a few seconds then said 'Killed? How, when?'

'Earlier this evening, at your house in Elstree,' Harry said.

'What happened, was it an accident or something?' Stanley Moore asked.

'We're not sure yet, police are there trying to find out what happened,' Harry said.

Stanley Moore stepped back from the door. 'Thank you for letting me know,' he said.

'Ithere anyone you want to contact and speak to?' Harry asked

Stanley Moore looked back at Harry through the hatch. 'No thank you I'm fine. I will sort things out with my solicitor in the morning.' He turned away and went and sat on the bed. Harry watched him for a moment.

'Do you want me to leave the light on?' Harry asked.

'No, turn it off,' Stanley Moore said.

Harry switched the light off. As he went to close the hatch, he heard Stanley Moore whistling. He recognised the tune as happy days are here again.

It was eight o'clock in the morning. Harry, Manjitt and Jordan had stayed in the office all night sleeping fitfully in their chairs. Harry told the two of them to go home, have a quick shower and change of clothes. Manjitt should come straight back, but Jordan was to go to the house, get the search started for the gun and find out if forensics had found anything that might help them.

He had taken a call from Bernie Thompson, who had heard the news about the boss and wanted to know if there was anything he could do. Harry asked him to go to the hospital and make sure Hippie and Cramer went home to get some sleep and a change of clothes. He told Bernie to carry Hippie home if he had to. At a quarter past eight AS Crick came into the office. Harry ran through all the events of yesterday for him, and what they knew so far had happened at the house, which Harry admitted wasn't a lot.

Crick said he would sort out any dealings with the press, and Harry should concentrate on the investigation, but keep him informed of any developments at all times and to let him known as soon as there was any news on Charlie. When he was gone, Harry decided he would go down to the police gym and grab a shower.

The office phone had been going all morning, with fellow officers ringing up to ask after the boss. Manjitt had come back to the office looking a little refreshed but still tired. Harry explained how they had conducted the interview yesterday and what he wanted to get out of the one with Stanley Moore today. He had got a call from the custody suite that Stanley Moore's solicitor had turned up at nine thirty to have a meeting with Stanley Moore. Harry had sent a message down to tell them questioning would start again at ten thirty.

Jordan phoned in and told Harry that a search of the garden had begun, but no gun had been found so far. He said that he was getting some divers in to check the lake as well. Forensics said Rebecca Rosen was shot three times in the head. Harry passed the news on to Manjitt, and told her to ring the hospital to get any news before they went down to start the questioning. He called Crick to let him know what was happening.

Stanley Moore sat upright next to his solicitor. He had a more confident look on his face, Harry thought, as he went through the process of turning the tape recorder on and saying who was present.

'Now Mr Moore, there are a number of things we would still like answers to,' Harry said.

But it was Mr Moore's solicitor who answered. 'My client is totally innocent of any crime, except maybe naivety in believing he was doing the best at the time for his family. I would like to make a statement on my client's behalf, to help clear up any confusion around this affair.'

Harry looked sideways at Manjitt and sat back. 'Please continue,' he said.

'My client was approached by Gerald Parkin, who threatened him with exposure over his attendance at the adult parties. At first he refused his demands, but on being shown pictures, he gave in and paid. Stupidly he did not ask for the pictures, as he did not want to risk his wife seeing them. After Gerald Parkin was killed, Mr Moore was phoned by a second party, who said ownership of the pictures had come into their hands, and they demanded even more money than Gerald Parkin. My client recognised this person from their voice as Jayne Cavill, and that is the only name he has ever known her by. This time my client paid, but demanded the pictures, which were sent to his office. Those were the ones you found at the address he was staying at. He was going to destroy all of them, he didn't want to take them to the main family home as he was worried his wife would see them. They had been going through a few personal difficulties lately, due to the pressure of this investigation. But my client had every hope that things would be sorted out and they would have gone back to being a happy couple they were before all this started. Now my client has been informed of his wife's death, and he is very upset at the news. All his answers throughout this investigation have been to try and keep the truth of his involvement in those parties away from his wife, who he loved dearly and did not want to hurt or embarrass. All his dealings with Sir Mark Coale and the takeover of Sir Marks company have been above board, his financial records will bear that out. My client will not be answering any more questions, and unless you are going to charge him with a crime, there is no reason for him to be held any longer.'

Harry sat quietly for a moment. 'Thank you for that statement, I will have to confer with colleagues and get back to you shortly.' Harry stood up. Manjitt looked over at Harry surprised and stood too. She followed him out of the room. Harry didn't say anything till he got back to the office.

'He knows,' Harry said as they walked towards his desk.

'He knows what?' Manjitt asked

'He knows that not only his wife has been killed, but that Rebecca Rosen is dead too, his solicitor must have brought the news to him,' Harry said.

'But how would he know?' Manjitt asked.

'I dare say his solicitor has friends in the press, or even on the force,' Harry said, 'who have let slip the second person killed at the house was our suspect.' Harry sat down. 'He knows if she can't talk, we have no case against him. Everything we have is circumstantial, and his wife being killed is a bonus, although I believe he had her killed, but it will be nearly impossible for us to prove it.' Harry sat down. Manjitt took the chair opposite.

'So what do we do now, Harry?' Manjitt asked.

'I hate to admit it, but there is not a lot we can do,' Harry said. 'He has thought up a plausible defence for all his actions, the loving husband trying to protect his wife from his stupidity, now distraught at his wife's death. A load of cobblers, but we can't prove any different without proof, and everyone who might help us is dead.'

'You mean he is going to walk away from this?' Manjitt said.

Harry nodded. 'The events last night have got him out of trouble. He knows if we have no Rebecca Rosen, we have no case.'

'You reckon he organised for her to be killed?' Manjitt asked.

'He was somehow involved, for sure,' Harry said. 'She was working with him, but he didn't know we were on to her, so her being killed has done him a favour. We have seen no evidence that he was speaking or paying anyone else, that just left her. What we need to do is try and trace Rebecca Rosen's movements before she got to Selfridges. She must have come from somewhere. We know she left the country, so why go to Selfridges?' Harry looked up at Manjitt. 'Get onto the boys at West End Central, see how they are doing with their investigation, they might have traced her movements.' Manjitt got up and walked to her desk, but diverted when Jordan's desk phone rang. She picked it up and listened, made a few notes then came back over to Harry.

'That was the police officer in Luxembourg Jordan has been speaking to,' Manjitt said. 'He asked me to pass on a message to Jordan that the body of Vincenzo Gallo was found shot dead in a disused warehouse this morning, after an anonymous tip off. He wants Jordan to ring him and pass on anything he knows about Gallo's dealings with anyone we suspect might be mixed up in his death.'

Harry sat back and stretched. 'Someone is covering their tracks. Let Jordan know when he gets back in to give him a ring and pass on all we have,' Harry said. Manjitt nodded and went away to call West End Central for any news.

Harry picked up his phone and called Inspector Grainger from the fraud squad, who the boss had told him about. He explained what was happening with Stanley Moore, and if he wanted to question him before they let him go he could. Grainger told him they weren't in a position at the moment, but there was a lot of information that they were getting in, and they might be able to put a case of insider dealing and some other chargers together later. But it looked very well planned, with lots of hidden assets to try and trace, and who owned what, it might take years. Harry said to let him know if they did manage to put anything together. Harry then phoned AS Crick and talked to him for a few minutes to put him in the picture.

Harry left Manjitt in the office and went back down to the custody suite. Entering the interview room where Stanley Moore and his solicitor were still sitting in their chairs, he said 'It has been decided at this moment that you are free to go, although we might need to speak to you again at a later date.'

Stanley Moore and his solicitor both stood. 'If you need to speak to my client again,I would ask that you contact us first to arrange any meeting,' the solicitor said.

Harry watched them leave the room. Stanley Moore looked over his shoulder as he went out the door and winked at Harry.

EPILOGUE

It had been two months since Charlie was badly injured on the night when Amanda had been murdered. He hadn't been able to attend her funeral, which had taken place in America, but he had got a nice letter from her father, thanking him for trying to save his daughter's life. The person who had shot Rebecca Rosen hadn't been found, and no clues to their identity had been uncovered. Harry had told Charlie that the fraud squad were working with the City of London police to try and put a case together against Stanley Moore.

It was Charlie's first day back at work. The team had all visited him at the hospital and his home at one time or another, but this was his first day back in the office. He walked in at just after nine, it was like he hadn't missed a day. Harry's desk still looked like someone had tipped a filing cabinet on it. Danny was standing making tea, dressed in a kaftan and sandals, Jordan had his feet up on his desk reading a newspaper and Manjitt was sitting at her desk looking at the computer. The only difference was she had a young man with her that Charlie didn't recognise.

'Good morning, everyone,' Charlie said.

'Morning, boss,' came from all around the office. Charlie walked over to his desk and sat down. Harry walked over to join him. 'Morning Harry, anything important on the list today?'

'Morning boss, good to have you back,' Harry said. 'No, nothing major. I was waiting for you to come in before I set them to work. There are a number of cases that need tying up with paperwork, and some outstanding statements to chase up.'

'I notice a new face sitting with Manjitt,' Charlie said.

Harry looked over, then back at Charlie. 'Oh yes, I was going to tell you about him when I came down to dinner last Sunday afternoon, but I thought I would wait till you got back to work.' Harry said, smiling.

'Is he the new detective constable you said you would get for the team, now Manjitt's been promoted to detective sergeant?' Charlie asked.

'Yes and no,' Harry said.

Charlie looked at him.' Do you want to expand on that answer, Harry?'

'Well,I did put some feelers out to find us a new detective constable, and I went up to see AS Crick to make the arrangements,' Harry said. 'But he told me not to bother as he had someone in mind.'

'Are you telling me that Crick has sent him to work with us?' Charlie asked.

Harry was smiling. 'Crick said he came with impeccable recommendations from all the police teams he has worked in.'

'He's not on one of those fast track to the top programmes, is he?' Charlie said. looking at Harry.

'He could well be,' Harry said. 'Do you want him over for a chat?' Charlie nodded.

'Manjitt, bring Jumbo over to meet the boss,' Harry shouted across the office. Charlie looked up at Harry. 'Jumbo, he doesn't look big?' he said.

Harry smiled but said nothing and went and stood behind Charlie. Charlie noticed that Jordan and Danny had come over to stand by his desk as Manjitt arrived with the new man.

Danny put a cup of tea down in front of Charlie. 'Nice to have you back, boss,' he said.

'Thank you, Danny.' Charlie looked him up and down. 'I'm

glad you haven't lost your sense of fashion while I've been away.'

'Not a chance, boss,' Danny said. He didn't leave Charlie's desk, but stayed standing next to Jordan, who had joined him and was smiling at Charlie.

'You look happy, Jordan, did you get lucky last night or something?' Charlie said.

'I get lucky every night, boss, you know that,' Jordan said.

'In your dreams, you do,' Manjitt said as she stood in front of Charlie with the new man.

'Hello Manjitt,' Charlie said. 'It was nice to come into the office and see one of my team working.'

'Thank you boss,' Manjitt said 'and this is detective constable Cecil Merrick.'

'It's a honour to meet you, sir,' Merrick said holding out his hand, which Charlie shook. 'I have heard so much about you' It was all said in an accent that was heard on the playing fields of Eton, or at a Buckingham palace dinner.

Charlie heard Harry giggle behind him. All the others had broad smiles on their faces, looking at Charlie.

'Well, I am sure ' an honour to meet you too,' Charlie said. 'How have you settled in?'

'Everyone has been so kind to me, they have been taking me through what we will be doing,' Merrick said.

'That's good. Well, I will have a longer chat with you once I've had a catchup with Harry here,' Charlie said. 'Now you lot get off and do some work.' The team walked away from the desk. Harry came out from behind Charlie. 'Harry, where did Crick find him?'

'I checked his background out when Crick brought him down,' Harry said, 'his dad was in the army, a brigadier, and his mother, who's retired now, was the Chief Constable of Yorkshire. I think that's why Crick wants to talk to you about him.'

'You don't think Crick has planted him with us to get some inside info on what we are up to during an investigation?' Charlie said.

'No. For one thing, Crick's not that sharp, and I don't think Jumbo could lie to us if we asked him if that's what he was sent here to do. He seems that honest, he would tell us,' Harry said.

Charlie stood up. 'Okay Harry, I will go and see Crick and see what he's got to say. And Harry, why do you call him jumbo?'

'Boss you can't see me shouting 'come here, Cecil' can you? And his name is Merrick,' Harry said. Charlie looked at him blankly. 'Remember John Merrick, the elephant man?'

Charlie shook his head. 'Harry, even after all these years I still don't know how your mind works.'

Charlie had just reached the phone when he heard a loud crash echo through the house. He turned and called out to Amanda but got no reply. He forgot the phone and walked to the door and called out again. Still hearing nothing, he walked quickly in the direction of the kitchen.

Rebecca stepped back from the woman and watched as she slid down onto the floor, the blood flowing into the champagne making a large bubbling red pool. She heard a man's voice call out twice. Turning, she went to the kitchen door to leave the house. She would be in the darkness of the trees in a few seconds, and across the fields and away.

Charlie got to the kitchen and was greeted by the sight of Amanda slumped on the floor in front of the fridge which was open. The ice bucket and a broken champagne bottle were lying around her. What caught in his mind was that the champagne appeared to be red. Out of the corner of his eye he caught a movement. He looked up and saw Rebecca Rosen at the kitchen door that led to the garden.

Rebecca turned the key in the door and pushed it to get out, but it wouldn't open. She pushed again, it still wouldn't open. She looked over her shoulder and saw the large man who had gone out the front door appear in the kitchen. Turning back to the door, she looked up and saw a bolt, reached up and slid it across. She pushed at the door again, it still wouldn't open, she looked down and saw another bolt.

The appearance of Rebecca Rosen had shocked Charlie for a moment. He glanced back at Amanda and saw she was badly hurt. The front of her red dress had a large damp patch that Charlie could see was blood. Amanda's eyes were closed. Charlie looked up and saw Rebecca Rosen reaching up for the bolt at the top of the door. He moved quickly, nearly slipping in the champagne, went around the island and threw himself at Rebecca.

She was just going to reach for the bolt at the bottom of the door. Turning her head slightly to see what the man was doing, Rebecca was surprised to see him nearly on top of her. Before she could react he had leapt onto her. The backdoor flew open, glass smashing, as they crashed through it.

The small man in the trees saw the two bodies come crashing through the back door. They hit the ground and fought each other. He got up from where he had been sitting and walked quickly but calmly towards them.

Jordan and Danny leaped out of the car as it came to a halt in front of the gates of the Moores' house, the two firearms officers just behind them. Danny pushed at the gates but they were locked. 'Over the wall' Jordan said. One of the officers leant against the wall and cupped his hands, Jordan went first, placing his foot in the cupped hands. The officer pushed him up. Jordan reached for the top of the wall, pulling himself up and over. Danny quickly followed; as he landed he saw Jordan was already twenty-five yards up the driveway, sprinting towards the house.

Rebecca felt the air knocked out of her body as the man landed on top of her. As they hit the floor, he had hold of her hair. Even winded her natural reaction was to strike out; she still had the knife in her hand and punched the big man with it, twice in the side and twice in the arm.

Charlie had grabbed her hair as he crashed into her by the door, and was pleased to hear her gasp as they hit the floor outside.